COWBOY
IN SEARCH OF GRACE
And The Little White Lies

By

Cam Locke

DEDICATION

I dedicate this book to my husband and sons, Charlie, Gray, and Riley K. Charlie made it possible for me to travel to many rodeos and jackpots throughout the South, driving long hours at the time without complaint.

My friends, Nancy McEnaney, former trick rider and rodeo performer, and MaryAnn Self, barrel racer, are still with me though I spend many hours writing and miss the riding camaraderie we've enjoyed through the years.

ACKNOWLEDGMENT

I would like to thank Steinbeck Publishing & Writing Solutions for all they have done to make traveling through the ups and downs of getting your book "out there," something I could never have done and spend time writing, too. It's a massive effort to market a book, and they offered every opportunity for me to highlight my writing.

A big thank you to those who bought these books. I hope you enjoyed the first two along with *Cowboy in Search of Grace*. I love sharing the history of the Old West, as well as the modern West that still represents much of the way it was one hundred years ago.

ABOUT THE AUTHOR

I was born loving horses, cowboys, and rodeo. Born in Tennessee, as a teenager I eventually found my way to the Fairground stables in East Memphis. They were a remnant from the past Thoroughbred race track, long gone, where six stables survived as boarding facilities for those who lived in the city. With no ability to buy a horse, I hung out there as much as a fourteen year old could just to be around the horses.

As an adult, I raced in shows and rodeos throughout the southern states for many years, sometimes on someone else's horse. But my heart belongs to Texas where my family lived for several years. Our time there was the best. In Texas, we bred quite a few AQHA race horses and sold the colts at The Heritage Sale in Oklahoma City. While in the Texas-Oklahoma neighborhood, I entered barrel races, too, at shows and rodeos.

Remembering those days, I love writing historical and contemporary novels about Texas, where my western romances blend history, fact, and fiction and focus on ranching, rodeo, cowboys, and cowgirls. I want to thank you so much for reading my historical and contemporary books about the grandeur of the Old West, Rodeo and Ranching. I hope you enjoy them as much as I do writing them.

Cam Locke

Also by Cam Locke

First Book: Dear Darling Lilli

Second Book: The Four Steps

Third Book: Cowboy in Search of Grace

And the little white lies

Table of Contents

CHAPTER ONE

Life is a river. You can row your boat gently, and slowly,

or you can catch the ripples, the runs, and then a waterfall.

Whatever your speed, stay in the moment and enjoy the trip.

All streams end somewhere.

1906 *Randall & Grace*

Phoebe lost consciousness and her vision blurred. She did not recognize the man who stood there for a moment, wearing galluses and a worn hat, before he mounted his horse and rode away at a fast gallop. When she woke, hurting and exhausted from her deep dive into the world of black, the atmosphere was heavy with the scent of earth. Her breath hitched, as the sounds of her sobs echoed across an expanse of big bluestem grass, dotted with basket flowers.

The chorus of howling coyotes and a relentless assault of biting insects was terrifying and stressful. The night was cool as early spring had arrived throughout eastern Texas, and as the sun rose, its rays painted the edges of the clouds with beautiful and breathtaking shades of violet and red.

Confused and hurting, she quieted down and her breathing evened out. Stillness and silence replaced life's sounds around her once more. Somehow, she had to make it home before the scorching day took her last drop of strength. So, she stumbled onto her feet with everything that she had in her and took a step forward.

* * *

Randall Jackson was tall and slim with bulging muscles on his arms, and he was a well-known blacksmith in the town of Annona, Texas. He was easygoing and a friendly person, and his boss, a cowman ranch owner, often allowed him time away to work for others in the surrounding vicinity as a smithy. Despite his key role as a cowhand at the Red River Ranch where he spent most of his days, he enjoyed the work that involved engaging his hands.

1

He squeezed the heavy nippers, his tall frame holding onto a horse's hoof between his knees. When working alone, he often talked to the horses he was shoeing. His voice resounded near the horse lean-to as he explained to the big, brown bay. "Apologies for the crooked nail. Don't worry about it. I'm sure I didn't quick you. Now, this nail is a winner, Coyote." The horse shot Randy a stony stare.

"I never intended to offend you, you chucklehead. You're going to be fine, I swear." Randy groaned with the effort, his voice light, as he took a straight nail out of his toolbox and put it through the horseshoe he held against the sole of Coyote's left hoof. He breathed in and carefully pounded it all the way into the hardened outer shell with three taps of the hammer. He didn't want any mistakes. A misplaced nail could ruin his reputation as a skilled farrier if it caused an abscess. Shy of being a perfectionist, he made it a point to do nothing half-ass. That, and he didn't want to hurt the horses that he catered to.

Randy stood and stretched. He watched several turkey buzzards gliding in large circles high in the blue sky. Although the morning air was bearable, soon the heat would start rising. In another hour or more, it would become stifling.

Luckily, the two-stall barn had an overhang that offered shade on sunny and warm days like these and made it easier to work. Still, his undershirt was damp under the arms. But Randall enjoyed working on Coyote because he was well-behaved even when standing on three legs. Randy never realized how fast the time flew by when he was working on him. The gradual rise in heat took him by surprise as by mid-morning, the temperature was ninety degrees.

Once he was done, Randy lowered his hammer to rummage through his supply box. A pair of black scuffed boots laced to mid-calf caught his attention. Still bent over, he craned his neck to look upward.

An angel stood in front of him wearing a full-length pair of jodhpurs and a loose white blouse. The girl looked familiar. She wore her long hair in a roll at the back of her neck, framing a perfect unblemished face, and she had the bluest of eyes that watched him through narrowed lids. Her lips were perfect wearing a slight smile.

He stood, captivated by her presence until he realized that he was staring. As he glanced at his undershirt, stained with sweat and dirt, his expression turned into one of embarrassment—a sheepish smile brought out a dimple. The cotton shirt looked like someone had dipped it in horse manure. Coyote had done that, using Randy as a rubbing post to remove mud from his head that he'd rolled in earlier.

As he regained his composure, he breathed in and said, "I apologize, ma'am, for my unkempt appearance. Somethin' I can do for you?" In his adult life, he'd been awkward around women. He hesitated, searching for other words to say to fill the silence that had enveloped them. When nothing came to mind, he smiled again but felt he must resemble a cow chip. And smell bad, too.

"Yes, actually. I hate to interrupt you, but I haven't had the pleasure of meeting you yet. Just thought you should know that I'm moving into my sister Corrine's house, or I should say my house now. I wanted to thank you for taking care of Coyote."

When Randy said nothing, she shifted her weight to her left leg, uneasy under his stare. His hazel eyes with specks of amber and green never left her blue ones. His sun-bleached hair dripped sweat down his neck, and it looked disheveled as if he'd raked his hand through the long strands several times. Smile lines along his cheeks creased his smooth, tanned face. He was tall and fit, too. His sweat-glistened forehead or stained shirt was not a problem for her, as she was more interested in the broad shoulders beneath the clinging material. Besides, she had spent similar days working on her farm covered in hay, grass stains, and mud from head to toe.

Standing before him, he could tell that she was a Texan. Her gaze was devoid of the awe that typically met cowboys from Easterners, misled by romanticized notions. He wiped his palms along his trouser legs before answering.

3

"No, it's okay. I'm not that busy."

With fingers shoved into her front pockets, she looked at him and around the barn. Her pause before she spoke reflected the careful thought behind her words, which were as sweet as pouring honey over biscuits. He now recognized the similarity in features between the sisters, except for this sister's modest demeanor and tone. "I came to the funeral. I'm sorry we didn't meet. And I'm very sorry for your loss."

One side of her mouth lifted as though he'd said something funny. He kept looking at her as he said, "I'm happy to help if you need anything. The horse needed a re-set, so I shod him one last time for Corrine." With the way she looked at the ground and seemed reluctant to talk, Randy thought that she looked like the kind of girl who took a while to warm up to males, especially cowboys.

However, for her, this cowboy had a civility about him that was laid-back, making studious eye contact that held your attention. The rest of him held her attention, too. "Alright." She glanced at Coyote's hooves. "His hooves look good." No cracks, or unevenness in his stance. She spoke quietly, "Coyote belongs to me, not my sister. I would appreciate it if you continued to shoe him. I don't get many opportunities to use him, but I want to be prepared if I do."

"I didn't realize. I mean I thought he belonged to your—Corrine." Randy broke his stare and reached for another nail. Her blue eyes were near turquoise. She bore little resemblance to Corrine. She was soft and inviting in the little interaction that they had today, while Corrine had many hard edges.

"My name is Grace Madden." She held out her hand, and he reached to grasp it, first taking the nail from between his lips that he'd forgotten.

"Glad to meet you, Grace. I don't run into attractive women while shoein' horses every day. I'm Randall Jackson. Please call me Randy. Everybody else does." Had he been too forward by complementing a female he'd just met? Maybe so, but damn, she was pretty.

Their hand grasp lingered longer than seemed normal as they stared at each other for the umpteenth time, lost in thoughts that were likely too forward for a first meeting.

Grace nodded her head—eyes meeting his and averting once more. Randy caught her looking at him from top to bottom at times, interrupted by glances to the ground, all in a vain attempt to not show her interest.

Despite her polite and composed demeanor, Randy could tell, even after hearing her first words, that her mind was racing, much like his own. Was she thinking about him as they stood holding hands trying to figure out the attraction that had sparked between them?

As Randy analyzed their meeting in his mind, Grace did the same. She had hoped that she hadn't come off as someone who didn't trust easily. Because her head was full of thoughts like, *What did he mean by attractive? Was he being fresh?*

She wondered if Corrine captivated this cowboy as much as she did other men. Handsome, with a genuine smile, broad shoulders, and well-developed arms, hardened from demanding work, he was a man who made a woman feel protected. She liked that. He was a better match for her in comparison to the men Corrine favored. But, he'd learn fast, she was not prone to imitate her sister's behavior. Finally, they both let go of the other's hand, hiding a laugh under their breath. As Randy went back to his search for a different nail, Grace spoke up once more, picking up the conversation.

"Are you from Red River?"

Randy put his hammer in his smithy bag and shifted his weight to one leg. "Yes, ma'am. I've been with Mr. Sullivant for ten years now."

"Nice family, everyone says."

"That's true. Mr. Sullivant came up an orphan, it's said, and had the smarts to keep his ranch afloat during drought and cheap beef prices."

"That's what I was told. About Mrs. Sullivant, too."

Randy studied his anvil, giving himself a chance to get his words in order. Criticized in her youth, Lilli Sullivant was truly a decent woman. "She's a mighty fine lady. Makes sure we got the latest new fandangle in the bunkhouse." Randy ended on that as he turned back to his work.

Grace nodded behind his back. "I saw Mrs. Sullivant once in a new Buick going through Annona. Driving to Clarksville to visit her mother, I heard."

Randy grinned. Secrets in a small town didn't exist. "Mrs. Sullivant loves that automobile. Not every day someone receives such a thing for their birthday."

Grace looked at the ground to disguise her scan of every inch of the blacksmith once more. The man stirring through a container of horseshoes seemed too tall for someone who stooped over to shoe horses daily. The day was starting to become unbearably hot, so he was only wearing a t-shirt with loose buttons on the chest and short sleeves that clung to his biceps. Arms that could snap a bone without straining. Grace found herself more comforted than afraid by the fact.

"No, they don't." Grace thought she'd be lucky to receive any birthday acknowledgment. "I should go. I won't hold you from going about your business."

The girl was looking to bolt, but he wasn't ready for her to leave. His was a lonely occupation, as working ranchers and farmers weren't always home when he dropped by to trim, re-set, or shoe their horses or mules. The four-legged regulars weren't conversational partners. No matter how much he talked to them, the conversation was always one-sided. He thought it a blessing to be

6

interrupted by someone, especially a pretty woman. He longed to say something impressive to entice her to stay longer, even if to just admire her. He struggled not to let his gaze fall lower than her chin.

"Are you coming to the contest that Mr. Sullivant is sponsoring?"

Yes, anything to be free of the farm for a while, she thought sullenly. "I am. There's been no time for me to ride. So, I have to practice my roping for the next few days. Coyote won't be at his best, but he'll do okay. I just hope to draw a good calf."

She waved him off as she turned away. "I've got a load to carry into the house. I've been hauling belongings over every day, but everything's here now."

He watched her hips sway as she walked away. "Do you need any help?"

"Oh, no. No. I guess I'll see you in six or eight weeks?" Thinking of seeing him for any other reason than putting shoes on her horse was nonsense. But why did he tell her she was pretty if he wasn't interested? Perhaps he was a wordsmith wanting to get into her back door.

"Sure. If you're not here, I'll catch Coyote and leave you a bill inside your screen door."

"Thanks, Randy. I'm glad we finally met, and that I caught you here."

"Me, too, Grace. And if you decide to accept my offer of help, let me know."

With a fluttering wave, she walked back to her wagon to fetch more items that belonged in the home that was taken from her, as well as the horse. When wanting something, Corrine concocted sad stories to put herself in the middle of your life, taking advantage of everything you owned.

Randy watched her walk away until she disappeared behind a large red cedar. He sighed heavily, dissatisfied with their conversation that didn't go the way he wanted. Then, he went back to hammering the last nail into Coyote's shoe. Not fully focused on his work, he caught a movement out of the corner of his eye. Boxes and bags filled Grace's arms as she climbed the steps to the house's back entrance and went inside the small white clapboard. She was a shapely woman with an appealing personality. Someone her size carrying a load and not dropping half of it seemed impossible. Grace, however, handled the task well with little jostling of the irregular-sized bundles in her arms. Randy could easily tell that she was a woman used to hard work.

As he saw her make what was seemingly the last trip, he decided she was through toting her goods from the cart to the small, but sturdy residence. With nothing more captivating to see than her stellar figure climbing the porch stairs, he clinched the last of the nails in Coyote's right rear foot and gathered up his tools.

He took care when packing them away in the wagon that Mr. Sullivant allowed him to use for his off-the-ranch work. As he was climbing onto the seat, he heard the screen door slam. Grace was trotting toward him. Her unbound hair bounced over her shoulders. Long, beautiful, and not as light as his, the honey color streaks brought out the strong blue of her eyes.

"Everything okay?"

"Yes." *And it was another reason to talk to the blacksmith again.* "I wish to pay you today. I dislike being beholding."

"Thank you, but it wasn't necessary. I trust you'll pay me when you're ready."

Grace blushed. Although not as forward as her wild sister, she was curious about the tall farrier and his daily activities, even though it was none of her concern. "What jobs do you perform for Mr. Sullivant? I mean other than a blacksmith."

Randy was flattered she asked. "I started out as a cowpuncher, but I've always had a knack with machinery. Now, I repair Mr. Sullivant's manufactured and horse-drawn equipment. Even work on his automobiles. Then, there's the plows, hay mowers, and many other tools that need sharpening or mending every day. Keeps me busy, but I still work cattle, too."

Grace nodded. "That's swell, Randy. I'm sure you stay mighty busy."

She smiled at him with perfect white teeth. He noticed, too, that there were no rings on her left hand. "And you, Grace? I'm not being nosy—only interested. What do you do?"

"I have my business. At my momma's place." She pointed northwest, "I raise and sell poultry and eggs. Then, there's twenty-five dairy cows, too, and I sell milk and butter along with the other. It's good to know a mechanic in case my old cart over there goes to pieces. I often stay here," she swung her arm toward the house, "to enjoy time away from the farm."

He looked at the worn two-wheeled cart and an old horse tied next to his. She shaded her deep blue eyes while looking up at him. Taken by their depth of color, he struggled to pay her a compliment without sounding half-witted. "I don't mean to be fresh, but you don't look the part of a milkmaid. It's surprising to see a young lady such as you working in such a demanding field—I mean, dairying is hairy work." He had no idea what he was saying. Once more, he found himself struggling to keep his focus on her face and not scanning the curves exposed through the thin fabric. As his gaze meandered, he barely held himself back from licking his lips.

Grace blushed, with no idea how to handle such a compliment. "Well, thank you. But I'm tough despite what you think." She knew he was thinking about things no one discussed in public. She wasn't totally naïve and innocent. Corrine had a lot to do with her education.

"I have no doubts about that."

Grace couldn't help smiling again. "Randy, best to get started on the road. I'm sure you have other chores to do."

She sounded sincere, but he figured that she just wanted to stop entertaining his random thoughts of lust. He reached for the box seat to step on board.

"Oh, when will you be back? I need to be sure I'm here."

"I guess that depends on Coyote and you. If he doesn't throw a shoe and depending on how you use him, I'd say between five and seven weeks."

She managed a smile while thinking, *that's too long*. "Alright. How may I reach you? If something unexpected occurs to my horse, such as a hoof injury or . . . something? He has to be sound for the roping at the contest. It's the only thing I've done for myself in a long time. You have taken such good care of him." Her voice dropped an octave. She had no good reason to ask him to come back earlier to reset Coyote's shoes.

"The big house has a telephone. They'll get a message to me." His grin was one-sided. He liked her. She got straight to work. Ace-high. No running around the bush. He gave her a one-sided grin. "Guess I better git." He released the brake, told the horse to 'walk on,' and drove away with a back-handed wave. He wondered how the two sisters were so different. Corrine liked a fun time, with a drink or two involved. Randy was never told what she did with Coyote other than use him as an extra expense and a yard ornament. He'd think of a way to meet up with Grace sooner than when Coyote would need a shoe reset.

Well, that was that. She sighed as she waved goodbye and ambled across the grass, dreading the unpacking and storing away the items she'd brought from her mother's to Corrine's. *My house,* she corrected herself. Her sister wasn't the only one allowed to enjoy herself or have a boyfriend. Corrine was no longer there to strong-arm everything that Grace had ever wanted. Though she had no other family members, she didn't wish to be compared to Corrine. After four or five beers, her sister had no qualms about going home with any cowboy and also exploiting their mother as a reliable source of income when she ran out of money.

10

The tall, handsome farrier crossed her mind. She thought she'd swoon when he looked up at her, his extended arm bulging with muscle. That's what women did in the novels she occasionally read. The thought made her laugh, and she felt like one of those female protagonists in those romance novels. He had a youthful face, but everything else said he was a mature man; a shadow of a beard, and unkept hair, lighter than any she'd seen. His body was powerful, with blond hair dusting his forearms that bulged into corded biceps.

He seemed a decent guy, but, another cowboy in the past had treated her badly. She knew that not every cowboy that she came across was similar to the one in the past, but it still made her steer away from men in tall Stetsons. She preferred relationships where both partners gave unconditional love, but wondered if that was even possible. She got nothing in return from Skip.

She liked Randy's composed and calm way of dealing with Coyote, even when Coyote was difficult. But Coyote's roping instincts and skills made him worth the aggravation. Her vision for the gelding's future included a plan to build up his strength after lazing around the pasture and to find her seat in the saddle. It had been a lengthy period since she had ridden a horse or roped a cow. All of Annona was abuzz about Red River Ranch's flyer. The coming show offered the only recreation she'd had for quite some time. Women took part in the shows, more popular than ever, alongside cowboys in roping and bronc riding. Grace had a robust appetite for competition. In past shows, whether roping against a male or female roper, it was always exciting.

Before getting undressed for a bath, she put away her underclothes in drawers and a small closet. Now wearing her robe, a sense of relaxation and freedom slowly began to overcome her as she started a coal fire in the stove in the kitchen to heat the water for the tub.

After the bath, she grabbed a knife and sliced a loaf of bread into small pieces, then loaded them with roast beef she'd cooked earlier in the day. Tomorrow she'd have to do a thorough cleaning. While

Grace lived at the dairy taking care of their sick mother. Corrine never cared for cleaning floors, and it showed.

As she sat to eat, three urgent raps sounded on the kitchen door. She put her meal on the table, pulled her robe closer, and opened the door. Randy stood there gazing across the pasture.

As the door opened fully and Randy turned to her to speak, he briefly stopped breathing. He gave himself a mental kick. "Sorry to bother you. I started home and realized I forgot something."

He noticed she wasn't dressed for visitors and forced himself to shift his gaze towards the barn, controlling himself. Then he looked back at her. "I reckoned you needed to know, as I didn't want you to think someone was stealing out of your barn." Long strands of her hair had fallen across her cheek, and she pulled it behind her ear. Shit. Her fine silk robe was sticking to her curvy breasts and hips. *Look the other way, idiot!*

Despite their earlier spark, the way he swept his eyes over her made Grace hot and cold. She tightened the belt around her waist. "That's fine. Help yourself."

"Okay. I'll leave you to whatever you were doing." He stared a minute longer. She bore a striking resemblance to a girl he'd dreamt of with seductive, unkept hair. Unsettled by the way she met his gaze, he backed down the stairs.

The image of her—barefooted and gripping her thin cover outlining the shape of her breasts and a waist he could embrace with one arm—stayed with him, even as she slowly closed the door.

As Randy left, Grace leaned against the doorframe, embarrassed that her hair was damp and out of sorts. She experienced an emotion and could not attach it to a recognizable category like love, hate, friend, or adversary. His thick, straight hair which he swept back and held in place with hair tonic heightened his air of male confidence. Her thoughts were carnal, but she didn't feel like a sinner or regret he'd seen her at her worst. Should they cross paths later under different circumstances, she'd know if she made a mistake in evaluating him when he showed he was less dependable than the men who were beating the road for work. Not expecting a different outcome after her experiences with other men, she sat at the table again and picked up her meal, only to be interrupted by a faint knock at the door.

"For Pete's sake." Then she recognized Alice Ann looking in through the glass. "Oh. Come in, friend! Have a bite to eat." She opened the door and a stout woman in a pinafore over her dress and men's lace-up boots entered the room.

"No, no. I don't want to interrupt your day. I wanted to see how your move was coming along and if you needed any help." She thumbed over her shoulder. "After leaving the farm, I passed Randall Jackson up the road."

"Take a chair. You're not interrupting. I need company right now. Mr. Jackson left here a while ago. Corrine kept Coyote here, and he'd been shoeing him. I came up before he left." Grace gave thanks Alice had not arrived ten minutes sooner seeing her dressed as she was, with a man staring at her through the open door. Her cheerful employee and friend's arrival significantly improved her mood, especially after Randy Jackson disappeared from her sight.

"Are you and Garrett doing well?" She changed the subject before Alice said anything else about Randy. Alice had a habit of exaggerating events, and by the time the third person heard it, it did not resemble the whole truth.

Sitting opposite Grace at the kitchen table, Alice Ann shifted her ample butt in the chair, accepting the glass of tea Grace set on the table. "We're doing fine. The doctor thinks he's getting stronger. As Garrett's walking around the house now getting his stamina back, he still needs his rest periods during the day. The pneumonia took him down, and Ethan's worried about his big brother. I thought to stop by to see if you need any help with the milk or egg deliveries."

"I sure do. The funeral is over and I've moved my things back here. I will be at the farm tomorrow. I appreciate Ethan doing my part of the milking, but unless I get those cans of milk into bottles and deliver them to the general store, it's for nothing. My regular customers likely need more, too. And eggs. Lordy, I don't need my clientele to buy their dairy elsewhere."

Notwithstanding her worry over lost business, as Grace pushed her hair still damp from washing behind her shoulders, she lost all thought of business. The simple movement made a shiver run down her spine as it reminded her of Randy looking straight at her. She must have looked affright, but that's not what his hazel eyes conveyed. It was more hunger and yearning. She pushed him out of her thoughts barely catching Alice's words.

Alice Ann gestured toward the filled boxes and the household goods scattered on the floor to make her point. "Don't rush yourself. Unless Garrett has a relapse, I'll return to work at the farm tomorrow if you're tied up here. Now that Garrett is moving around, he's eager to return to his job. And Ethan. That young'un is exhausted. He's a child trying to keep up with grown men. But he's a right smart boy who wants to make sure the farm runs to plan. Working as hard as he is, he struggles to wake up in the morning. But, he ain't missed a day of milking. I was in Annona today visiting Aunt Martha. Poor soul's gettin' feeble. Thought I better check up on you." She glanced at the window. "Goodness, it's going to get dark on me if I don't get moving."

Grace squeezed Alice Ann's hand across the table before she got up and followed her outside. Alice's mule was eating the leaves from a tree where she had tied him. Grace didn't envy her the long drive in the dusk of the evening to the south side of Clarksville in the rickety cart that she came in. Alice and her family lived a short distance away from the Madden's dairy. Since Alice's mother passed, she, Garrett, and Ethan, Garrett's younger brother, lived in Alice's family home.

Soon after Grace's mother had passed, she wasn't sure what to do with the house at the dairy, as she had lived there most of her life. Perhaps she'd sell it and use the money to move the dairy closer to her own home in Annona. The only thing she knew now was to return to the farm in a couple of days to help with the chores and pay Alice Ann, Garrett, and young Ethan. The vagrant hands will skip to town if she doesn't pay them on time. And sometimes, the worst of the homeless men stole things they pawned in a far away place when they left.

When Alice disappeared down the drive, Grace walked back to the small house before anyone traveling the road noticed her wearing nothing but a robe. She felt excited to be settled back in her own home at last. She lived at the dairy, in her mother's house to take care of her when she was sick. Then her excitement ran a close race with guilt for a moment and came in second to a bout of sadness. She was alone.

Corrine was gone, and her mother was gone. Although her sister was distant and uncaring, Grace was grateful to have a blood relative nearby, though she never understood Corrine's immoral character and wild nature. They'd been complete opposites their entire lives. Everyone who had met them apart or together always described them with the most differing vocabulary possible. And yet. And yet now, when she had lost even Corrine, with all her differing nature and opposing personality, she missed her. Because now, she had no one. No one to come home, to fight with, or on occasion share things. Grace thought how difficult and complicated a thing grief was and how it twisted all that remained behind.

Her mind strayed to the blacksmith. Before now, even though she had seen Randall around in Annona several times, they had never spoken. He'd be driving one way with his blacksmithing equipment in the back of a wagon. She'd be in town delivering milk and cheese from house to house. And they'd go about their own paths without interacting with each other.

However, when she met Randall Jackson that morning, she recognized him at once. From the moment he threw compliments her way, she wondered if he was another bum cowhand who drank his money away. He was nice, but, ten-to-one, he was flirting, not meaning it. At least that's the way she interpreted it when he called her *pretty*. She was mature enough to admit that she felt an intensity between them as they stood there holding an overly long handshake, but other than that momentary attraction, she did not feel any genuine interest from him towards her. However, there was that unspoken draw for her that kept him on her mind.

With impressive height, stunning eyes, and a kind demeanor, his muscular strength was enough to make any woman want Randall Jackson to take a liking to her. But she was stupid enough to fall for it and snake bit because of it in the past, and handsome faces didn't guarantee *happily ever after's*.

Back in the house, the soft glow of the setting sun came through a window. Grace poked a fork at her food. She'd been unable to think of anyone else since meeting the cowboy farrier and how brazen she'd been in the doorway when he knocked at the door.

The scent of wild honeysuckle wafted through the open window as a bluejay fussed in a tree. A bittersweet atmosphere filled her senses because she realized that the most sensible course of action was to accept the undeniable truth: there could never be a connection between her and him. She must stay composed and keep the livelihood of herself and her employees at the forefront to keep the dairy solvent.

Dejected, she felt that her moodiness would diminish once she adjusted to her decision that she'd stay single. Putting her personal life on hold to avoid getting hurt, she planned to stay away from the blacksmith. Besides, their paths would never meet often. Too, preparing Coyote for the Red River roping and traveling between Annona and Clarksville to fulfill customers' orders, she would not have the energy to think about a man's interest in her.

Exhausted, she picked at her cold food for a minute, then covered it with a cloth for breakfast. She promptly ignored the treacherous part of her brain that whispered loudly to her, *but he could make you happy*.

* * *

Randy

After stopping by the side of the road and changing from his dirty undershirt into his clean outer shirt, Randy turned the horse toward Annona. He replenished his supply of horseshoes and nails at the mercantile, gave the clerk a list of the ingredients the ranch cook needed, and then went shopping himself. He added a second bag of flour, bacon, and butter to his haul before paying the clerk and loading it in the wagon.

Randy drove to the town's outskirts. With a pull on the reins, the horse slowed to a stop, and he tethered it to a large block in front of a two-story house. After knocking on the door of the white Victorian dwelling, he entered, carrying one of the food bags, and closed the door behind him.

Headed toward Annona, Alice Ann tapped her ancient mule with the buggy whip, urging the fragile animal into a rapid walk as they wove through freight wagons, wagons piled high with cotton, and automobiles that crowded the narrow road in Annona. After making it through the traffic, and then driving by the homes dotting the outskirts of town, she saw a parked horse and vehicle in front of Mrs. Goss' boarding house. She recognized the red painted wheels and saw Randy on the porch before he disappeared into the house.

Alice was curious why he was at Mrs. Goss' place. No one had boarded there for years. In the small town, privacy was unknown, secrets wormed their way from the woodwork, and Alice was always available when they appeared. But with the sun shining in her face, and the early evening horseflies agitating Jasper, Alice Ann forgot about Randy and the boarding house. Shading her eyes with the brim of her bonnet, she slapped a large horsefly that had bitten her arm and continued on about her day.

CHAPTER TWO

Enough Problems

Grace & Randy

Two days later, Randy tied his horse in front of the mercantile. Once he was done, he noticed that at the next hitch, a tethered horse pulling an old wagon resembled Grace's. The surprise made his mouth dry and his pulse quicken.

The unexpected image of her in her silken, rose-colored bathrobe—the fabric shimmering faintly—suddenly popped into his head. His cheeks burned, flushed with the bold, uninhibited thoughts, a warmth spreading through him like a sunbeam. He felt far from shy or awkward.

He attributed the heat rising in his groin to his imagination instead of the Texas broiler where he lived. But if he couldn't manage himself, he'd have to miss seeing her. He couldn't go around and picture her in that fine attire every time he saw her. As much as he had tried to be smooth-talking with her, she was sure to catch him in the middle of his vision.

He sighed heavily, if he had the makings he'd roll a cigarette to lower the extent of his want for her. That would help distract him from what was going on in his nether regions. He walked up two steps to stand in the shade beneath the overhang with no notice of a reprieve from the temperature. At the door, he swiped the sweat on his face with his neckerchief and saw Grace through the window. His eyes followed her every action, as mundane as they were, Grace had something about her that captured Randy's attention like no one else did, not even her sister Corrine.

As Grace handed money for her purchases to the clerk, she was aware that Randy just came in and stood at the end of the counter watching her. Suddenly, self-conscious in her split skirt that stopped at her ankles, she had a thought that she was not dressed in her best, but she didn't expect to see Randy at the general store. Overcome with the urge to do something about her appearance, she smoothed her hair and rolled it into a coil at the back of her neck. Even tied as messily as it was, the long tresses ended above her waistline, and the simple style kept it presentable when bound with a ribbon. It was the most convenient way to style her hair, while she ran errands and other tasks that needed to get done in the sweltering summer heat.

Randy watched her fluster about her appearance, as he had seen countless women do around other men, and nodded. They smiled at one another, and Randy wondered if it was him specifically who was making her nervous, or if she would've done the same with anyone else around. Somehow, he wanted to be the one to make her feel and act differently, but in the most pleasant way possible, unlike when he had knocked on her door that one evening, days ago when she appeared uncomfortable and on edge. *But, damn, he couldn't forget it.*

Without talking, he stepped to the counter and gathered her bags in one arm, and led the way outside with her trailing him. It was impossible for Grace to stop looking at the muscles flexing across his broad back. Even with all her reservations, she couldn't deny the fever she felt when he picked up her supplies, a simple thing that her ex-cowboy had never considered.

She liked to act independent, but that didn't mean that it wasn't nice to be shown consideration and care every once in a while, not because she couldn't do something, but because she didn't have to. Randy might not know this yet, but his little act did something to her lonely heart. As he carried her things, Grace couldn't help the small smile that adorned her face.

After loading her supplies onto her worn wagon, he turned around. Within an inch of bumping into Grace, his breath mingled with hers, with just a step forward.

In effect, her body responded with an intense need to touch him, contrary to anything she'd ever experienced before. She took a step back instead, with an irresistible whimsy to remove his Stetson hat and give him a hard kiss. The thought tinted her cheeks a bright pink, and she took a couple of breaths to make it a little less obvious. Despite that, she stammered when she spoke. "Randy, you are such a g-gentleman. Thank you."

He propped an elbow against the wagon, and Grace concealed her heated impulses with a shy and polite smile. She wondered if her face were tinged bright pink, so she did the one thing she knew would work best—began to make conversation.

"How long have you been shoeing horses, Randy?" Grace acknowledged that the question held little importance. But given their proximity, she struggled to think what to ask. Her past experience in talking to people just to make the situation less awkward had been made useless with Randy standing in front of her.

"A couple of years. Most days are full of customers needing help with smithing or shoeing, but it's been more interesting since I ran into you. I guess you figured I liked you from the first day. I was happy to help you, Grace. It wasn't no trouble a'tall to give a pretty woman such as you a hand." He gestured at the goods in the wagon.

It was the least he could do right now. Randy knew dairying was hell. Chasing Longhorns and other breeds of cattle was five times better than milking cows twice a day.

He said I'm pretty, again. Blushing, she looked away unable to meet his unwavering gaze. "And I've really enjoyed talking with you. The honors should go to Coyote for bringing us together." Her voice was soft and tired. For now, she would conceal the turbulence in her heart.

From the way she sounded, he'd bet his hat that she hadn't had a day off in months. Taking in her appearance, and with his mind made up, Randy gathered whatever confidence he had in him and spoke. "Are you busy this Saturday, Grace?"

What came out was definitely not what he had intended to say. *Of course she'd be busy seven days a week. The best you have is to ask*

21

a thoughtless question? So, he cleared his throat and rephrased the question with a half-smile playing on his lips. "I mean are you interested in having dinner with me? Thought we'd go up to Clarksville, insofar there's not a proper restaurant in Annona. Really, what I'm saying is, I'd like to know you more."

Her heart pounded and she became emotional at his little ramble. The way he stumbled over his words, trying to put effort into his question, for her—*for Grace*. She couldn't help but hold her bottom lip between her teeth, in order to stop it from trembling. "Thank you. That's kind of you, but I don't want to interrupt your work. Though, it depends on everyone who shows up that day. My transients don't hang around long."

Grace's concern touched his heartstrings, but he wasn't deterred from his goal. "I can sit with that. The ranch has the same problem sometimes with chuck-line riders. Tell you what. I'll show up early in case you're short of hands and help you wrap up the day so we'll have time for a splendid dinner."

Grace turned to climb aboard the wagon, his hand at her elbow with a firm grip. Settling on the bench, she leaned over to speak over the street noise. Her fingers entwined in her lap. "That's why Alice Ann, Garrett, and I are so close. They're there seven days a week if not sick. Now Garrett's little brother helps, too. Other than that, I don't count on anyone else. I appreciate your kind offer."

Her mouth was close to his when she spoke. Grace was the girl of his dreams. But here she was in the flesh, and her smooth firm skin made his blood run hot. He reached up and palmed her elbow, kneading the soft underpart of her arm. "You got me, Grace. I'd be happy to help."

And just like that, in another two minutes, they set a time for him to arrive before their date. Randy handed her the reins laying across the wagon seat. "See you Saturday."

Grace nodded feeling ambushed by loneliness. Coerced by lust. And all reasoning gone. She was in a miserable state torn between newfound happiness and fear of the unknown. For some reason, she said "yes." The likelihood of a poor cowboy trading cattle ranching for a dairy farm lifestyle was zero. She knew she was thinking too far into the future. Still, she felt justified in her feelings and her reasons to put distance between them. A girl who took care of herself had to be careful with her reputation. Single or married—she could be ruined if she had to seek a divorce.

The horse moved forward with a lurch when the whip brushed his rump. Grace looked back to see Randy standing in the same spot, and before she looked forward, a terrific jolt threw her backward. The wagon tilted at a strange angle as she watched the left rear wheel roll away on its own. Several startled passers-by stopped long enough to gawk.

"Oh, hell." Still watching her, Randy cursed as the wheel broke loose. He trotted to the wagon to make sure Grace was unharmed by the impact and inspected any further damage from the wheel's loss. He saw she was fine and ran to fetch the runaway wheel where it had keeled over in the middle of the street.

Grace jumped to the ground, breathing through clamped lips. The suddenness of the whole incident left her edgy inside. *Thank the Lord* the horse didn't bolt into the street when the wagon became wobbly and wreck it around a post. But then, she began to worry about the mishaps that happened too often, and her anticipation of Saturday night with Randy fell with a dull thud—a knot tightened painfully in her stomach.

His offer to help at the dairy had been her downfall. Her wish to not further entangle herself with him was impossible to carry out now. There was no way to deny him.

After jumping to the ground, frustration oozed from her every pore. She kicked the remaining wheel and wrapped both arms around her middle with hands locked on her elbows. Unable to fix or mend something of this size on her own, and having to ask for help, was a sign of failure or weakness. And neither was acceptable.

Stupid wagon. Wait till Randall Jackson found out she had enough problems to give half to the citizens of Annona and enough left to send him running. She sighed showing her frustration and had to calm herself. She took a deep breath in and let it out, unmoving as she repeated the act a couple of times. Her arms dropped to her side as she waited for Randy's view on the chances of the wagon being repaired. Grace watched as he rolled the run-away wheel back to the wrecked wagon and crouched to inspect the axle to find the reason to why the wheel came loose.

There weren't any tools on his wagon to repair it. But, it turned out to be his lucky day because he'd get to drive Grace home. She didn't have a choice. Standing up, he noticed her expression, the pinch between her brows and her clenched lips, displaying her disgust for the wagon breaking down in the middle of the road.

"Well, nature played an inconvenient trick on your vehicle. Happens with old wagons. Let's load your supplies onto my wagon and I'll take you home. We'll tie your horse to the back. And once back at Red River, I'll return with the proper tools to fix this thing. The spokes were loose and unstable before they broke and too weak to travel these rutted roads from earlier rain. So, no surprise, something broke over the rough terrain. I'm not sure when I'll have it fixed, but the plan is to have the wheel repaired by Saturday."

The shopkeeper and two farmers joined forces to push the broken rig to the side of Main Street and tossed the wheel into the wagon.

Randy stood by as she climbed into his vehicle first. She was staring off to the side but turned to face him when he joined her.

"Please pardon my hissy-fit," she said in the most off guard way he had heard her speak until now.

Randy sniffed in acknowledgment. Damn. She needed a break.

"Although I try to oversee the condition of the farm's equipment, everything goes wrong one day after the other. Please don't think I'm not appreciative of this. I'm just not used to having someone around so helpful. Thank you."

24

The horse walked several yards before Randy looked her way. She was practical, wearing a long skirt with a tucked shirtwaist, her going-to-town attire. Not fancy, yet not something to wear while washing up the milk cows waiting to be emptied. But, damn, that clinging silk robe was his brain's first and last thought daily. *Open your mouth, nitwit, and talk.*

"Grace, you have me whenever you need help. I had a hankering to see you. I'd find it delightful to call on you now and again." She turned to look at him. He looked overlong into her beautiful blue eyes. "Lots of times, not only this Saturday."

Lord, the man was a bold one. And she had no reason to refuse.

"Yes, you may." Her heart pounded, and she spread her fingers across her chest, praying he couldn't hear it.

His brain shouted with happiness, do something! Out of the view of the gossips, Randy placed a hand over hers. Her hand twitched in surprise, then she flashed him a shy smile. They talked little for the rest of the ride. He saw the roof over the second floor hay loft of the milking barn in the distance. Water dripped from the wet trees from a recent shower leaving water marks over Grace's purchases from the store.

"Turn here, Randy. It's the least muddy this way, and then, make a turn when leaving the barnyard."

He followed her directions, and after pulling the horse to a halt, he crossed to her side of the wagon to give her a hand climbing from the seat. He set her purchases on the ground unsure what to do with them.

The long porch that ran the length of the back of the house in the early days had been closed in long ago making the kitchen larger. They hesitated at the steps to the door where she turned to thank him for his help, prompting him to lean over her, one arm around her shoulders. When he placed a soft kiss on her cheek, he worried he had gone too far when she drew back. But then, she wrapped her arms around his neck and gave him a kiss on his lips.

"I shouldn't say this, but just to be plain, I'm nothing like Corrine."

"No, you're not." His arms made quick work of pulling her into him until they both broke away from the next kiss to take a breath and damn if she didn't stand on her toes and pull his face to hers, this time with a shy kiss that said goodbye *but come again, please.* And who was Randy to reject such a heartfelt request?

She waved to him as he settled on the wagon seat, picked up the reins, and drove out of the yard. Craving a final glance, he looked back only to find her gone.

Grace walked to a kitchen chair to sit and lay her head on the table. She shut her eyes, afraid of making too much of the past hour. Before today, there had been only herself. But after feeling the strength in his arms, the gentleness in his caresses; then the way he'd taken over to smooth things out when the wagon broke down, she knew she needed him. She wasn't a soft woman. The push, pull, and lifting of farm work, combined with hours of sterilizing equipment and milk deliveries had kept her in as good a shape as any cowboy. Considering the difference in size she conceded.

Then, she chastised herself for behaving like Corrine. But she thought, too, they had committed no sins, nothing had happened that she should feel ashamed of. The desire that made her heart beat faster after kissing and being held by Randy Jackson was strong. If he proposed, it might change her life. Her reservations at getting to know him and being close to him were waning fast, with each gesture he made and with every soft smile and sweet way of his, he was quickly disarming all her walls to her heart.

Grace shook her head a little too much and a little too fast, trying to dispel the thoughts of one Randy Jackson. But, she couldn't hide the warm feeling in her heart and the smile that followed from herself. *Saturday, huh? For once, I can't wait to see how it goes.*

* * *

Saturday came bringing a gusty wind to rattle the gates and the tin roofs over the dairy barns. Steady sheets of rain didn't matter, as nothing interfered with relieving the ladies of their load. Hurrying past the thirty-foot silo in the wet air, Grace was in the milking parlor, even before dawn, spreading feed in the stanchions. Throughout the night, she hardly slept as she imagined how things would unfold when Randy Jackson arrived.

She prayed the storm was short-lived, or they'd have to settle for cornpone and beans in Annona. She laughed as she had picked out the perfect outfit and didn't want to waste it sitting at her kitchen table. She expected Alice and her family to enter the big sliding doors anytime to get the cattle in place and their teats cleaned for milking. She planned to do her part, and then get cleaned up before Randy arrived early in case she needed an extra worker, as he promised. But her scraggly crew of helpers showed up on time to join them, leaving time to visit with Randy before they went on their outing.

Grace followed Alice into the cooling room and helped her upend a forty pound can of milk into a hand cranked cream separator.

"Alice, Randy Jackson is coming over today to return the wagon wheel he took to repair. And even if he hasn't finished with it, he's dropping by." For now, Grace knew not to mention more about Randy or Alice Ann will talk her to death wanting to know everything. She busied herself cleaning empty milk cans, instead of making eye contact with Alice. Through that chore, she brushed her palms together and sat down on a bucket.

"He asked me to dinner this evening. Think we're about done here, so I'm going to the house. If you need my help, come get me."

"Well, Jiminy Christmas! When did this happen? Where y'all going?" Alice wiped her face with the end of her apron. She turned around to see Grace clear the door, and Alice giggled. "Yep, he's gonna fix your wagon wheel alright."

* * *

Randy pulled up in a wagon with Grace's repaired wagon attached to the back of the box by the wagon shafts. He backed it into a lean-to and undid the ties lashing the shafts to his wagon. On his way back to the house, a young boy walked by swinging a milk pail and stopped by the wagon side before Randy stood from his seat.

"Hi, Mister. You here to see Miss Grace?"

Randy formed an opinion of the tall young man by scanning him from top to bottom. His overalls hung by one strap from his narrow shoulders, and the pant legs were wet to the knees from the downpour. "I am."

"My name's Ethan, Mr. Jackson. I'd shake your hand, but it's covered in cow snot. Can I take your horse around to the hitching rail for you? Alice Ann says that you and Miss Grace are courtin'. I guess they call it datin' now. She said y'all have a date for dinner in Clarksville." Ethan swatted away the gnats and mosquitos buzzing around his ears, scanned the skies, and looked at the tall man. "Guess the rain has moved on, lucky for you and Miss Grace."

Awed by Mr. Jackson in his black cowboy hat and boots, he had watched the road for an hour waiting for his arrival to talk to the well-known cowboy. Tired of the chores and cleaning cow paddies from the milking parlor floor, he aspired to be a cowboy driving cattle, not milking them, when he was older. The Red River and Eberly ranches weren't too far away, and he reckoned they'd be 'round long enough for him to walk up to the head honcho and get a cowhand's job in a few years. Right now, his brother was stepping in the way of his leaving the farm, saying he was still a child.

"Miss Grace is in the house getting pretty. Best knock on the door."

After Randy stepped off the wagon, Ethan took the horse by the bridle. "Your cart is right here when y'all are ready to leave. Your horse will struggle a mite if the Stagecoach Inn Road is sloppy." But Mr. Jackson looked able enough to handle a mere muddy road. "Uh, can I ask you something, Mr. Jackson?"

"Sure."

"It'll be four years 'fore I'm a man, Mr. Jackson, but I'd shore 'preciate your speakin' for me so I'm able to land a ranch job someday."

"I guess you'd be right about the road. And I'll surely put in some good words for you. Thanks, Ethan." The boy had manners, but it annoyed him that everyone in Annona was talking about him and Grace by now. Randy watched the young man tether his horse, then headed for the back door. He waited a minute for someone to answer his knock.

Randy removed his hat when the door opened. "Ma'am, I'm here for Miss Grace Madden." His smile said he didn't mistake the girl at the door for a stranger. He'd have known Grace anywhere, dressed as he had never seen. Her lacy white top was tucked into a wide, black belt fastened with a turquoise stone buckle. A gray skirt fit tightly around her hips and fell below to her heeled boots of shiny black-patent leather. The grin on his face grew into a full smile as she invited him in.

Grace curtsied in answer to his funning around. "Come in, Sir."

"The wagon's parked in a shed. Ethan helped. Nice kid. And the wheel is fixed. Should last a lot longer now."

"He is a good young man. He's the little brother I never had, and I'm very fond of him. He's never lazy or whiny. He'll make a girl happy one day."

Randy smiled. Right now, all Ethan wanted was to be a cowboy.

They spent another ten minutes catching up on their week but eventually ran out of things to say while standing in the kitchen. He brought extra clothes to lend a hand in the barn as he promised, but Grace said the entire crew showed up and finished early. With that, Randy opened the door and had the good fortune of helping Grace, as she hiked her skirt to the wagon seat. Close enough to smell her scent, he wondered why such a woman paid him any mind after seeing him at his worst shoeing Coyote.

Not as shy when at the mercantile and she was angry, Grace moved closer to him. When she slipped her arm through his, he thought something between them might bloom after all. After guiding the horse to the road, they started off in a trot toward Clarksville. Her closeness assured Randy of her approval.

She was beautiful to him from the first day. Everything about her was flawless tonight.

They talked about the gossip going around Annona, the saloon owner throwing out a drunken cowboy, and the Red River cowboy event coming up in three weeks. He'd never been so at ease talking about trifles with other women. He liked that they shared many of the same ideas from breaking horses to appreciating a good cow and even their differences about other things.

After an hour's ride, Randy drove into a quiet, grassy spot near what was once a stagecoach stop, now a restaurant, and tethered his horse to a rail, away from other traffic.

He opened the wide double front doors flanked by two gas lanterns and held Grace's arm as they entered a large room with cozy gas lights flickering against ax hewn log walls. Pristine white tablecloths covered the tables, while the massive fireplace remained undisturbed since the previous winter.

A woman showed them to a table, and the waiter took their order and left with a promise to return with their steaks in short time.

Grace scanned the room amazed at the beautiful renovation of the log structure. The banister on the steps was new, while the original steps squeaked as patrons of the inn came and went from the diner to the second floor of rooms. *How did she never hear of this lovely place?*

Feeling shy, Grace rested her hands in her lap. "I'm having a wonderful time, Randy. Thank you for inviting me out. Isn't it wonderful this beautiful place wasn't destroyed, but has a new purpose?" It was her first time there, and she loved the rustic feeling of the building.

Grace spit out words that never hit where she aimed. She wasn't funny or coy. And she wouldn't allow her conduct to sink to Corrine's level. Her confidence fell a notch sitting across the table from a man she never thought would ask her out. And she never thought she would accept. Randy was clean-shaven and smelled of freshly mowed hay and new leather boots. His high crown cowboy hat lay in the extra chair, and the paisley scarf around his neck matched the color of his eyes. Sometimes she wondered why any man would find her interesting. She was plain and recognized the back end of her cows and their tag numbers better than most faces.

Again, across from one another, Randy watched Grace who was looking everywhere except at him as though she were anxious. But, it was difficult to believe this was her first outing with a man. The wholehearted kiss in her yard, unseen by anyone, didn't appear to bother her. So, why so skittish now? A one-sided grin covered his face. "It's you who needs to be thanked, Grace. I'm honored you'd even consider going out with me. Pretty women don't choose men who have little to offer them. But if you agree, I would like to know you better."

She never thought she would be left speechless, but his compliment left her with mixed emotions. She reached across to put her hand over his. "I can hardly wait to meet again."

He smiled at her sudden change in mood.

Unable to look into his hazel-green eyes with brown and gold flecks, she soaked up the connection in the grip of his fingers. "What manner of man are you, Randy Jackson? The only side I've seen of you is you're good with horses and filled with thoughtfulness." She drawled the last three words and swung her gaze at him waiting for his answer.

Randy leaned closer across the table. "I don't know, Grace. When you find out, let me know." Something about her made him sense more confidence in himself and concern for her safety. "Till then, I'm a jack of all trades, not rich, and if I'm not in the pasture roping a cow, I'm under the hay baler 'cause it's broken." He took her hand in both of his and disregarding anyone near them, he kissed her palm. "Other than that, I'm liking you more each time we meet. Can't tell if you feel the same, but if you do, I'd be a happy cowboy."

Grace sat back as the waiter set their plates down before them and asked if they needed something more from the menu. Randy told him, "No, thank you." She put a smile on her face as any normal woman would do, and was thankful for the interruption that saved her from having to respond to his comment.

He was touched by her smile and watched Grace eat. How she carved her steak, stirred her potatoes and gravy, and the way the fork traveled to her lips with the elegance of a duchess, defied her upbringing on a farm in a small Texas town. He wanted his children to be taught such manners, however she learned them. He wanted beautiful little girls like her, and God help his sons if they took after him. Grace finished dinner first, but he wasn't ready for the night to end.

Randy downed the last of his Pearl Beer. "You remind me of Miz Sullivant, Grace."

Grace raised her eyebrows. "How? I've never met her. All I know is what I've heard. Her mother is married to the mayor of Clarksville. I think after Mr. Eberly passed away."

"You two are independent. She's a business woman. She runs her own ranch and helps Red River, too. You're running a dairy operation. You're not afraid of hard work or getting your hands dirty. Women of character who take on endeavors for the long haul rarely quit when things go crazy."

Randy swore her eyes turned from turquoise to a deeper blue.

"Randy Jackson, you are going to make me cry. I've never received such praise. You asked me earlier about us seeing more of each other. That's how I understood it when you mentioned wanting to know me better. Yes, I'm interested in discovering more about you, too. I'm flattered."

* * *

Once again on the wagon, he glanced at her often, proving that he wasn't dreaming. However, as he was wide awake, he thought it best to not think further into the future. Unsure exactly what he was feeling while with her, he wanted to give it a chance to define itself.

While the trees cast shadows on the road, the sun was still too high to see the fireflies. He reached beneath the bench to find his gun hidden in a feed bag, a habit he'd developed, though this area of Texas was pretty tame now. The law had taken care of the worst of the outlaws by locking them up and hanging or shooting them. But not everywhere. When he was younger, someone shot him in the arm, and he took care to prevent it from ever happening again. Back at the farm, he pulled the horse to a stop. Grace's face appeared pale in the twilight, but her blue eyes were dark pools. "Tell me about your family, Grace."

"It is boring, but I was born here." Grace nodded toward the clapboard house. "Daddy left when I was three. Corrine was two. When momma and daddy first married, they bought this property with the big barn on it, with four or five sheds, and fencing in place. I think it was a noted cattle ranch long ago that was sold in parcels. Anyway, momma was a worker. She bought five cows that had recently calved from Alice Ann's mother, and the herd grew. And as I grew, I became the hired hand. Corrine was never helpful and detested the barn, cows, and anything work-related. As sisters, we had our moments. Did she ever tell you how she ran away when she was eighteen?"

Randy heard a wistful note in her tone. He smoothed her hair and drew in the scent of roses.

"Grace, I never was well enough acquainted with Corrine to hear of her history."

Grace was glad to hear her sister had no connection to Randy Jackson. "No one heard if she was dead or alive. Then she showed up two years later and tricked our mother out of her last dime. When

Momma became ill, Corrine left again and mom passed away. I sent her money for transportation, but she never came to the funeral." She looked at Randy, still listening and staring at her with a somber face. "Appendicitis had put me in the hospital when she showed up for more money. She stole my horse, and I didn't find her for a long time. Next time she was home, she had enough money to buy the Annona house. I don't want to know how she came by it. I didn't have time to ride, so that's how Coyote came to be there when you started shoeing him. I inherited the house being Corrine's sole relation." Grace gazed at Randy, worried her story disgusted him. "I loved my sister. I missed the companionship, the confiding, the trust sisters have in one another. But rumors kept floating to me. If it wasn't about Corrine, it was about me. Things she told to others that weren't true."

Randy pulled her close and planted a tender kiss on her forehead. "I'm sorry, Grace. Growing up wasn't a cinch for either of us. If God sees fit to grant me children, I will protect them from inner conflicts such as yours and mine, if possible."

"What is your story, Randy?"

He laughed, but there was nothing humorous in the sound that echoed. "Too long to tell before nightfall. We'll get an earlier start next time, and you will know about me. Plus, you're the only person who gets up earlier than I do." He released her from his hold and helped her step from the wagon.

The moon was a sliver of silver in the darkening sky. The porch steps still held the sun's warmth where they sat in the dusky surroundings as the sun set. No one was on the road this time of day disturbing their privacy, and Alice's family had walked home earlier.

Grace's hair had escaped its pins and fell across her back. She snuggled as close as possible with her head against his shoulder. He placed a finger beneath her chin, lifting her mouth to his. She was willing, and he felt warmth radiating from every part of her. Randy grasped her jaw in the palm of his hand and with the other, pulled her into the kiss. He caressed her neck with his fingertip, sending pleasurable shivers through her arms and legs.

"Randy."

"What?"

"I want to stay here with you forever, but we will pay for it in the morning if we do."

He noticed once her attention was on the dairy, her shyness disappeared, and her tone was insistent. She had transformed into a confident businesswoman. Not wanting to keep her from much needed sleep, Randy kissed her again and took her hands, pulling her to her feet. The sun had disappeared, and dark clouds raced across the moon. "I'll ride over in a day or two. Meanwhile, we'll have time to decide about us. Or rather your deciding. I already have."

"Oh." *So soon? He had made up his mind just like that.* "Okay."

Randy turned to open the door and walked her through it. They kissed again before he turned to leave, taking a last look as she waved goodbye, and he walked the steps unrushed to help slow his racing thoughts. A cowpuncher didn't make enough money to take care of a wife. His black smithing efforts brought in extra pay, and more as a mechanic for Mr. Sullivant. But, he knew he'd never be a dairyman tied down to a farm day and night. Milking cows was less challenging than working cattle on a ranch, but hard work. The open range offered freedom, with varied tasks. The only life he wanted was one of beeves, horses, dust, and trailing herds, not sitting on a stool and milking.

His feelings were strong for Grace, and she gave the impression she was interested in him. But useful answers for plans involving the two of them weren't likely to show themselves until they spent more time together, as their present desires and realistic outcomes were as distant as the Milky Way. He blew out an anxious breath, relaxing his tight shoulders, as he reasoned a future together. He held onto the belief that if they endured and survived, things ought to fall into place.

CHAPTER THREE

"Success is not a destination, it's a journey." — Anonymous.

1906 Andelacio Slade

Andelacio Slade had worked for several ranches west of Texas for the past four years as an experienced cowhand.

He was an uneducated cowboy other than his mother teaching him how to read. His father was un gringo loco who beat him and his mother for sport. Before he could kill the bastard, he disappeared one day, with Andelacio's blessing, leaving him and his mother penniless. His troubled childhood had molded him into a man with a fistful of words as he avoided conversation.

His adult life included escaping the law for robbery and breaking into houses. No one paid attention to a lowly half-white cowboy, prompting him to keep a low-keyed and unassuming demeanor. All he wanted was to be left alone, follow orders, and when he had enough money, to ride away as he had neither family nor friends. He left his past behind in Mexico as he worked his way to north Texas, doing odd jobs at various ranches. Working cattle or riding fences in remote areas wasn't as risky as living near a populated area.

When he rode up to the Eberly Ranch compound, Art McCarthy, the Eberly jefe, wasn't interested in his prior ranch experience. "The Eberly Ranch ain't hiring. The Red River Ranch next to ours is looking for help. Wait here and I'll write a recommendation to give to Rupert Rutherford, the Red River Ranch manager."

Andelacio nodded but thought he could speak for himself without a note. "Si. Mucho gracious," he mumbled as he mounted his horse. He was dark as his mother, but his facial features were Anglo-Saxon. Many assumed he got his tan from the sun, but were amazed when he spoke with a Mexican accent. People's reactions to him were always unpredictable; sometimes he was treated kindly, while other times, people never knew how to react to him. Though

37

Andelacio didn't fret over their remarks, for him with the way he had grown up, other people's opinions didn't matter much, if any.

When the cowboy returned, he handed the note to the half-breed without speaking a word.

Andelacio folded it into his vest pocket. "At least it ain't rainin'," he muttered in perfect English. His belly grumbled with acid. It hadn't had a full meal except for a pheasant and small wildlife that he'd killed after leaving the last outfit two weeks ago. He never stayed in one place for an extended period. Hiding behind a meek persona, he made everyone think that he wasn't capable of more than chasing cows. His life was largely a lie.

Two miles down the road, he turned at a sign hung on a fence saying, "Red River Ranch." He had to endure another lengthy ride to reach the main compound. Several corrals came into view, and a cowhand leading a fine-looking horse pointed him toward a small dwelling close by. He knocked on the ranch foreman's cabin door, removed his hat, and waited. A wiry, long-haired cowboy stepped from the door. At first glance, Andelacio mistook him for an Indian by his long hair in thick braids.

Rupert Rutherford squinted one eye as he sized up the man standing in front of him. He was young and of average height, his shoulders were broad, and his chest matched them on the nail. Brawn wasn't the crucial factor needed to chase cows. Brains were beneficial, which was lacking in many cowboys. A decent judge of character, he didn't bother reading Art's note.

"I 'spose the King and the Waggoner was too big for your liking."

"Si. Andelacio Slade, here. All ranches have fencing, herding, and corral work done. The smaller the spread, the shorter the ride back to the bunkhouse. I'd rather not ride from sunrise to sunset to get from one end to the other."

Rupert held out his hand to Andelacio. He liked the mild-mannered man. After reading him the ranch rules and they agreed on his pay, Rupert said, "Go on to the bunkhouse. It's that-away.

It'll be quiet in there tonight 'cause some of 'em have gone to bed or bedded down outside for the night. After you meet 'em, they'll educate you further. You got questions, ask me. They're liable to send you out where you can't find your way back."

Though Rupert made his last remark with a smile, Andelacio understood every word. He fed his horse in a barn, then released it in a corral with the others, following the boss's directions. Now at the bunkhouse door, he knocked the road dust from his pant legs, stomped his boots, and entered the kitchen door. A Chinese cook looked at him surprised, fussing about something in a foreign language that sounded near to *Who the hell are you*?

Andelacio didn't understand a word, but he recognized the tone. He outstared the funny looking man in strange clothes wearing a strange hat. His jet hair was as long as a woman's hanging in a single braid. Chattering to himself, the small man pointed to the eating utensils on the shelf motioning the cowboy who smelled of days without a bath, to grab a knife and fork. The cook turned away to grab a nearby plate. After filling it from cooking pots still on the stove, he motioned for the new cowboy to sit at the table. He'd already emptied the coffeepot and shoved a cup of water toward the new hand who ate the food in less than five minutes. The little man stayed, holding his nose. Andelacio didn't blame him. He could hardly stand smelling himself. The satisfied cowboy shoved the empty plate back at the cook, grinning with approval.

As soon as the cook saw him put down his fork, he shooed him toward another door with a wave of his hand. Exhausted, Andelacio opened the door at the other end of the kitchen-dining area looking for a bed, but walked into a lounge such as he'd never seen to house cowhands. He joined two more cowboys in the furnished room.

A wiry cowboy strumming a guitar looked up from a plush couch. "Howdy. I'm Jimmy. Where you from?" asked Jimmy Waldron sitting on a leather Davenport.

The new hire found a chair and sat before answering.

"Many places."

Jimmy removed a straw from his mouth. "Interestin.' Do you have a name?"

Another cowboy sat silent on an upholstered bench. He lay down his newspaper and crossed his arms across his chest.

Andelacio remained rock-steady, though he was still wary of being questioned. He ignored Jimmy, instead focusing on the man sitting on the bench. "My name is Andelacio Slade."

"Good to have you join Red River. I'm Randall Jackson." He stood to shake the cowboy's hand, thinking Jimmy had begged for a brawl, nosing into a stranger's business. A man only told you his history after he learned to trust you. He had a firm grip. Jimmy was no match for the new cowhand in a fistfight.

"So, you won't say where you're from, Lasso?"

Andelacio controlled the sneer he wanted to flash at the loose-lipped cowboy named Jimmy. He was skinny and Lasso, twice his size, had no desire to talk further. Others had baited him into fights before, part of the reason he wanted to start his life over. These were the consequences of being a new hire, and he ignored Jimmy's insult when he miscalled his name.

Where Jimmy talked Texan with a loud, drawn-out Southern drawl, Andelacio was soft-spoken. "I grew up in Mexico, amigo, near the ocean," he lied.

Jimmy struggled to make out the soft-spoken flawless English of the Mexican man, even though his dark hair and skin spoke of his Spanish background.

Lasso waved his arm at the well-furnished room. "The bunkhouses I've slept in looked nothing like this bunkhouse." Neither did the shack he was born in. He wanted to stroke the fine fabric and remove the skinny ones in dirty dungarees from the leather cushions lest he soil them. Pictures of Red River's prized bulls and race horses decorated the walls, a fancy box held magazines, and one of the chairs was covered in spotted cowhide. His gut reaction was a sense of safety and value. He wouldn't say anything more and let the others think he was half-witted and soft.

Randy laughed. "Mrs. Sullivant donated the leather furniture from the big house after she replaced it. Not ready for the rubbish heap, it's quite luxurious for dirty cowhands to romp on."

"Ol' Randy over there, he's been in every part of Mexico once. Ain't ya Randy?" In fun, Jimmy pushed Randy's boot that was resting on his knee, with his own.

Ignoring Jimmy's redneck behavior, he corrected Jimmy's assertion. "Not exactly. When I was young and foolish, I crossed the border once, but on the spur of the moment, I returned to Texas and haven't left since. Nice people, but I missed ranching and there wasn't any work. I didn't speak the Spanish either. Now you, Andelacio, have a perfect American accent."

Andelacio leaned forward, putting the two chair legs on the floor. His shaggy black hair fell around his ears disguising his age as he gave a youthful toss of his thick mane. His answer came with a Mexican accent. "What do you mean, Señor?"

"Damn. You sound fancy as a real Mexican!"

"He is a Mexican, Jimmy. Or at least part. Why not sound that way?"

"Randy, I ain't saying he doesn't. But that takes a smart fella to talk in two languages!"

"And that's why you scarcely speak English, Jimmy!" Randy laughed after punching Jimmy's shoulder. "I'm gonna call it a night, boys. Five o'clock comes early and quitting time is fourteen hours from that, so g'night."

Randy left the sitting room and took a swift shower at the end of the bunkhouse row modeled after the one at Eberly Ranch. He rinsed his socks and underwear in the galvanized tubs mounted on a stand and rung them out to dry. Putting on fresh long johns, he draped the wet ones over a clothesline before returning to settle into his bunk where he lay wide awake. "Nice guy," he said to no one. *Jimmy ought to watch his mouth.*

Grace was on his mind most nights. His thoughts heated his body along with the sticky humidity coming through the window. Three days remained before returning to her house to re-shoe Coyote. It had been a while, but he remembered distinctly their date. He wanted to speak with her again for more answers about her sister. Too, why hadn't they met before the burial? His heart thumped as he imagined her in her robe with her hair hanging damp and mussy.

For now, he was caught in a tight spot caring for another, while he longed to be free to pursue Grace. The complication wasn't going away for a while, but when it played out, he'd carry on with his own life. A slight breeze brought relief through the window. He turned his back to the opening, letting the air soothe his burning skin.

Andelacio noted Randy's departure. So, before anyone asked more questions, he decided to bed down, too. He rose from his chair and turned to follow Randy.

Curious, Jimmy leaned back on the Davenport. The hat he slapped on the cushion sent out a dust cloud. "I heard of someone like you, Lasso. Spoke two languages, English and Spanish. I got a cousin living near the coast. When he wrote to tell me his ma died, he mentioned that there was a man who should have landed in the calaboose 'cause he was doing a heap of unlawful things close to his town, Los Mochis, then he disappeared." He raised his eyebrows and the corners of his thin lipped mouth. "*G-T-T!* You know, *gone to Texas*—'cause of outlawry? Was that perchance you? Guess Mr. Sullivant would appreciate knowing about that."

Andelacio turned in his own well-mannered time, a slight smile on his face contradicting the hate in his eyes. "Now I know why the other men call you a *bastardo mentiroso*. That's up to you, amigo."

He walked in Randy's path through a door, chasing the dangerous thoughts in his head about slugging Jimmy. A concrete floor was on the other side. Looking further, he saw a wooden walled cubicle that held a shower, stopping him short. His last bath was a week ago in a creek. Surprised to see it, he stripped, leaving his clothes on the floor, and turned the single knob. The water was cool. Leaving it on to stream across his tired body, it helped wash away the trouble in his head after sparring with Jimmy. The one named Randy talked with sense.

Grace

Grace rode Coyote when staying in the Annona house to the farm to build his stamina. The exercise, too, lowered his sour mood during the lengthy jog. The early breeze made a swishing sound as it passed through the tree branches and leaves.

During the fall, farmers' wagons loaded with long stable cotton going to market congested the road. Now, it had a light flow of residents, businessmen, and tinkers coming in and out of Annona. She avoided the ruts as she rode the dirt road, and arriving at the farm, she traveled around the house with its tall roof and two chimneys. The old place brought back memories of her mother and, by chance, images of her sister. She scowled. The morning had already turned sour. She pushed away her sadness and rode Coyote towards the cowshed.

She expected Alice Ann, Garrett, and Ethan to have the cows up this morning. She stepped from Coyote, unsaddled him, and turned him into a small wooden pen. Lowing cattle, heavy with milk, greeted her behind the barn, waiting their time to enter the milking parlor. In the dairy barn, they locked the bossiest cows into the stanchions to keep them from taking over a section from the temperate cattle. She stopped a moment observing the hired help cleaning the cows' udders. She'd fire them if they cut corners, not keeping the sanitary practices she demanded.

She sighed in relief knowing that the grain bins were full, and they had baled the hay for the coming winter. The spring bull calves were old enough to be sold at the next auction. To be sure of that, she would have to check her calendar.

She found Alice Ann in the horse barn where they stalled the draft horses. "Ga' morning. Something wrong with the horses? You're usually somewhere else this time of morning."

"Not sure, Grace. They were hanging around the barn and I saw one limping. I felt 'em out, but he appears to be fine."

Grace stooped to examine the leg of the Percheron. "His cannon area is warm to the touch, but I see no visible reason for it.

"We'll rub liniment on that part and put 'em back out to pasture. We'll check him again tonight. If I see Randy, I'll ask him to examine his legs. I'm going to the chicken house later to see how the egg laying is progressing. Will y'all join me for breakfast?"

"Sure will. We're starving."

Grace patted Alice Ann's shoulder and headed for the house. Electricity had made it as far as Clarksville. Beyond there, candles still burned on tabletops and in candle holders on the wall. Oil lamps sat in various places. Within the hour, pancakes, bacon, eggs, and hot coffee sat on the wood stovetop to stay hot. Grace rang the dinner bell, and Alice, Garrett, and twelve year old Ethan Turnbow came through the barnyard gate and into the kitchen.

Grace started filling plates. "Come in before it curdles!"

Garrett's body was tough as a rawhide string, while his little brother's face was still showing baby fat. The kitchen was heated from the stove as they sat to have breakfast.

"Have a seat. I thought we better discuss business after breakfast."

The others pulled their chairs and sat.

Garrett replied with his mouth full, taking care not to spit out a mouthful of eggs onto the table, "This is real nice, Miss Grace. Are we celebrating something?"

"I hope you enjoy it, Garrett." He took a biscuit to clean up his plate, then popped it into his mouth. "No celebration. Just want to say I'm grateful y'all are my employees. I have a plan I want to share about you and the dairy."

"A plan involving all of us?" asked Alice. "Oh, 'fore I forget it, I meant to mention something I saw in Annona."

Grace looked at Alice waiting for her to continue. "Mention what?"

"Remember when Randall Jackson left your house the day I came over to visit?"

Grace answered with eyebrows raised. "Yes." *He said I was pretty.*

She appreciated everything Alice and Garrett did for her. They helped run the dairy to perfection, to looking out for her. But she did not want rumors spread about her and Randall Jackson just because he shod her horse or they had dinner together. At first, she rejected the notion that it meant anything other than his attempt to be kind.

Managing a dairy, she didn't believe she was a normal woman who could ever give a man her full attention. Love? Truthfully, it was nothing more than a simple infatuation. But even she did not consider it simple. Particularly the day the wagon lost a wheel, and he came to the rescue. His attention made her feel safe and cared for, feelings she'd never experienced before. After they went on a date, even thinking about him made her wonder what he was doing. Shoeing someone's horse? Working on Mrs. Sullivant's Buick? Anyway, her personal life was her own business.

She arched her eyebrows looking interested in Alice's story. But Alice Ann would never hear about Randy and her fooling around, especially, the kisses they shared.

Alice Ann placed her fork on the China plate. "On my way to the dairy, I passed his cart and horse tethered at Mrs. Goss' place. I didn't see if he went in. The horseflies was so thick I was busy shooing 'em away from Gus. The door opened a crack, though, so I presume he did."

Grace kept eating, stalling to look uninterested. "I cannot understand why I ought to be concerned that Randall Jackson was at Mrs. Goss' front door. I imagine he was tending to her aged mule."

Grace no longer wanted to mull over business with Alice Ann's family. She did her best to separate her employees from being her friends, too, and failed at it. If not for the three's full devotion to the dairy's day-to-day operation, she'd never be able to manage with the random help from the transients. She had nothing much she wanted to say other than to ask how younger heifers were working out and to remind them of the government's new rules on sanitation. But she did tell them her new idea.

"I wanted to say that I think Ethan is at an age where he can handle taking the full cans to Murdoch's and bringing them back empty."

Although it amounted to a simple duty, Ethan's eyes brightened over the added responsibility. He nodded his head in accord. "That will give you, Garrett, more time to plow or mow and take care of other management-related tasks that Ethan is too young to perform. Of course, you just recently recovered from pneumonia, and I want you to be sure you are healthy and able to take up your usual tasks."

"How do you feel about that, Ethan?" asked Alice.

He grinned. "That's swell with me. Won't be any problem." The wagon trip was an easygoing chore and would take him away from the milking parlor for a while. And he could dawdle on Mainstreet, if he had time after dropping off the cans at the cheese processor. He might get to see Fanny Newsom while he was passing through town, too.

His goal was getting to an older age, and to set out on his own to become a cowhand. When the weather was good, he slept out under the stars like the cowhands dreaming of breaking wild horses and herding cattle over the open land.

Though it would be a chore to acquaint pesky milk cows with horses, he would be happy because then he'd be a genuine cowboy.

However, the easily frightened things were bound to stampede and harm themselves. Although the mild cows were docile, Ethan believed that changes in temperature and in the herd hierarchy led to difficulty handling them once in a while. And that wouldn't do, if he was sitting on a horse.

At the sound of Miss Grace's voice, he brought himself back to the present.

"I am happy you joined me for breakfast. If you have nothing to add, we'll get to work again. Leave the dishes. Pearl is working today to clean up. I made these biscuits and eggs for the other men if you don't mind taking it to them, Alice."

"Of course." Alice Ann and Garrett left with plates of food and were back in the milking parlor at five-thirty, and Grace began making her rounds in the chicken coop. The air outside was clear and fresh compared to the warm kitchen.

The cattle were waiting in the open-sided barn where they ate and drank. To start the process of emptying their bags of gallons of raw milk, the ladies gathered at the milk parlor door. The relentless routine exhausted Grace every day.

She returned to the house at nine in the evening, at the earliest, coated in hay sprigs, grain dust, cow excrement she had stepped in, and smelling a foul sweat on herself when finishing the day.

With no other way to warm water besides the wood stove, Grace-filled a large, galvanized tub with water every morning at Annona, or the dairy if staying there for the night, and allowed it to absorb the sun's heat for her evening bath. She brought the lukewarm water back into the house by bucket and filled the clawfoot tub in a small closet. After easing into the placid water, she almost fell asleep before grabbing a bar of soap to scrub the day's sweat off, too exhausted to care.

The next morning, Grace joined Ethan to deliver the dairy orders. They loaded five-gallon cans of milk onto the wagon for transport to the Murdoch-Ballard Cheese Plant. The glass bottles of milk sold to residential customers in Clarksville rode behind the bench seat.

Ethan deftly handled the delivery of the sizeable cheese orders to the mercantile. Then, they stopped at other businesses on the way to the cheese processing plant. The four saloons in Annona were on the delivery list using gallons of milk a day to sell to their customers. It soothed their stomachs and headaches from hangovers. Grace found Ethan was smarter than she realized as he handled everything without a hitch. On the way back to the farm, the horse moved in a fast trot past Mrs. Goss' home.

A saddle horse tied to the hitching post drew Grace's attention. While the brown horse wasn't familiar to Grace, a movement at the door caught her eye. A woman in a tall man's embrace stood in the doorway. They disappeared together, shutting the door. Though the house was yards away, Grace recognized the tall man's back. She looked straight ahead fighting her imagination and the trouble it stirred in her heart. Her eyes burned with tears as she fought looking back. She pretended to have something in her eye wiping away the moisture with her sleeve, too embarrassed to let Ethan see her crying.

She had no right to check any of his doings. But, saying he was just a friend would be lying to herself. How did she fall in love with him so quickly?

Angry, she clamped her teeth, replacing her tears with disgust for herself. A man had taken her pride and trust. Humiliation turned her face red. Sadly, it wasn't the first time. She'd promised herself never to be fooled by a man a second time. And yet, here she was, at the same place once more.

The sun was setting as she returned home. She often stayed at the farm for a couple of nights before returning to Annona and her home, to avoid having to make the return trip.

Shunning a bath and after graining Coyote, chickens, and the goat, she collapsed onto the bed. But only to toss and turn atop the thin

48

quilt. Heat and humidity filled the room that lasted until early morning even with the windows wide open. When she closed her eyes for the last time, she could feel a tall man's fingertips gliding over her arms, giving her a delightful shiver in the steamy night. His muscled arms held her as she stood on tiptoe to caress the hair at the back of his neck. While it was a breath-taking memory, she must stop imagining it over and over because it couldn't happen again.

She sat on the bed before the sun rose the next morning. From sunrise to sunset, the farm required crushing work. She never knew the reason her mother chose such a grueling occupation as a dairy farmer. There had never been enough money to buy gasoline equipment to make it easier because of the dairy's low profit margin.

Since seeing Randy in the arms of another woman, she felt that her entire existence was pointless. She had no relatives still alive, and few friends other than the Turnbow's. Despite their bond, they could not fill the emptiness in her heart. The burden of the farm and the enormous responsibility she carried were becoming too much for her to bear. She was aware of a potential buyer for the property, but she refused to deal with them. If she did, her mother would haunt her forever. After seeing Randy's familiarity with a woman at the boarding house, she decided not to wait around for his attention. The love she'd yearned for her entire life was a lie. She decided that she must take strong measures to escape the terrible despair that had haunted her since losing her last relative, Corrine.

A rooster's crow announced the rising sun. A rough, incomplete thought crossed her mind how to escape her miseries.

CHAPTER FOUR

*"True cowboys are the ones who aren't afraid to get dirty." —
Lane Frost*

Randy

Randy shifted in the saddle on the ride to Annona. His back was hurting like hell. He gave a swift jerk to the lagging pack-mule, bringing him beside the horse.

The day before, he had limped out of the corral, a victim of the other men's laughter when a young bronc had tossed him on his tailbone. Injured or not, his blacksmithing, which brought in more income, was second only to his work as a hired cowboy caring for the Red River and Eberly ranch's livestock and equipment.

He packed his blacksmith tools in a canvas backpack, everything but an anvil and forge that he couldn't haul on the back of a four-legged animal. In his blacksmith shop, he had forged a number of horseshoe sizes that fit an array of hooves and packed them with his medicines and poultices for sore knees, ankles, and cannon bones. Occasionally, he used his home-made remedies to treat hoof abscesses and other ailments that could affect horses, even humans. Shopkeepers, liveries, ranchers, or those who farmed or traveled by horseback between Clarksville and Annona were his regular customers. He liked it that way. It brought in extra money to add to his wages.

Two weeks after their date and burning to see Grace, Randy rode straight to her house in Annona. Stepping from the saddle, he tied the horse and mule to a low branched tree. The eerie quiet stopped him as he scanned his surroundings. When no one answered his knock at the door, he decided that she must be at the dairy.

On the outskirts of Annona, Randy tied the animals outside the Goss house and searched his pack to pull out a wrapped package. The same woman, who had opened the door before, greeted him, and they entered the house. He was there for an hour, and then he came out and remounted his horse and headed toward Clarksville.

He had made a promise to Grace to shoe Coyote, but his real motivation was to see her once more. He came days earlier than the scheduled time, hoping to kiss and hold her again. He couldn't wait and used Coyote as his excuse.

He slapped a latigo saddle string against his thigh in unison with the rocking motion of the horse. Occasional horseflies buzzed the sweating animals searching for the best place to bite. Riding up the drive, he'd passed countless times, the two-story house came into view. Four large red barns were impossible to miss and rose a short distance behind the house. He saw their red boards through the towering tree limbs and leaves. The cows dotted a distant hill, with the morning milking finished. After tying his horse to a post, he covered the ground with a quick walk to the house.

Surprised at the back door, Alice invited him, and she wasted no time sitting him at the kitchen table. She glanced at him. The sheen of sweat on his face showed he'd been shoeing earlier.

"Mornin,' Randy." She directed her ample cheeks toward the center of the kitchen chair and eased herself onto the seat. A blue bandana was wrapped around her head to protect her hair from the assaulting dust and sweat during the hot day. The tall cowboy at the table was clean-shaven and looked younger than his years. Knowing why he was there, Alice didn't expect more than a *howdy* from him as he looked to be on pins and needles to join Grace.

He took a short sip from the glass she handed to him. "Is Grace in the barn?" Impatient, Randy looked at Alice expecting a simple reply to his question. When Alice didn't answer, he wondered if she was hiding something. He hoped there hadn't been any accidents or illnesses on the farm.

"Not exactly." Flummoxed, Alice postponed her reply further with a long swig of tea. She braced herself for his reaction.

"Randy, there's something I need to say. You may not like it, but it's the bald-faced truth. Two days ago, Grace had me and Garrett sit right here and made us a proposal. According to her, she was exhausted. She said she'd had enough of the long days and heavy work that this farm demands. We nearly fell out when she suggested that Garrett and I buy this place, as she aspired to be free of it to travel."

"What?" The sharpness in his voice resonated through the air as if a bull had gored him. He stared at her. After a moment, he cleared his throat and started again. "What? What made her do something so irrational? Where is she now?" He gritted his teeth, holding back a barrage of profanities.

She was sorry for them both because anyone with a brain saw that they were in love. His eyes bore into hers. "To answer your question, I don't know where she is except by the postmark on the letter that she sent me, Randy. I'm completely honest when I say that her sudden departure also broke my heart."

Sadness filled her voice as she spoke with resignation about the loss of a friend.

Randy shook his head as Alice continued. Grace was gone.

"It was nothing like we'd had a barn fire or she was getting sick. Well, the last one's probably true. Grace said having nothing but cows to tend had worn her to the ground. Seems she wanted something else to tend." She rolled her eyes towards Randy.

"There're cows in the morning, cows 'fore you go to bed. She told us she decided one day that she wanted to be free of the dairy and we made a deal that suited us both.

"Grace didn't mention where she planned to go." Alice shook her head. "I don't believe she had any idea. It was as though the farm finally broke her, and she didn't want nothin' to do with it anymore. A dairy ain't easy to manage. It seemed to me other reasons, too, were driving her away, but she wasn't saying, what. It's just herself, she has no family here now.

"Anyway, here's the letter I received yesterday. She promised she will stay in touch." Alice Ann handed him a letter postmarked Dallas. "Grace has been gone since Thursday a week and a half ago. In the letter, she wrote that she was doing fine and may take a train to Sacramento. Whether or not she did, she hasn't written us about it. She said she'd tell us when her plans were complete, so we shouldn't worry. But we're *still* in the dark."

Randy looked out a window. His jaw clenched. A deafening pause told Alice what she needed to see; this cowboy was hurting and confused. Alice pitied them both.

She placed a hand on his arm. "Randy, this farm wore her out. This place is a coal mine of work. No off days. Cows got to have daily attention. You're an experienced cowboy. You've worked cattle herds a long time. These dairy cattle are worse than trying to drive them fire ants back into the mound. Grace will be back and it won't be long. She was raised here. Everyone Grace knows is here. And you."

Alice's brows furrowed in concern as she wrapped her fingers around his forearm and squeezed tightly. "Grace said nothing, but I could see it plain. If you had been there, you'd a seen it, too. I know she loves you, Randy."

"Me?"

The corners of his mouth turned into a frown. "Well, too late, now. She never gave us a chance. The dairy and the ranch both kept us too busy to spend much time together, but we were just getting to know one another. She didn't even have the courtesy of telling me she was leaving here." Randy paused to stare out the window again.

"Where is her horse?" His words were blunt as he noticeably excluded Grace from further discussion.

Alice was confused as his narrowed eyes locked onto her. "Coyote? He's out back."

He squared his shoulders and set his mouth in a firm line. "I guess the least that I should do is check on him though it's not been five weeks since I shod 'em. Are your cows having hoof issues? Any equipment need repairing?"

"No. All is fine." His voice and the abrupt transition from talking about Grace's disappearance to her horse became a blur to Alice.

She evaded eye contact, unsure of Randy's state of mind, and headed toward the back door, and gestured for him to follow. "He's kept in the largest pen. But I've been turning him out on pasture every day, too."

"Okay." At the corral, Randy picked up his feet. Coyote stood without a halter, well acquainted with the ritual. "Hooves and shoes seem fit." Randy stared down the four legs with his hands on his hips. "Alice Ann?"

She looked at him waiting for his question.

"What if I took Coyote home with me? If the horse handles cattle as well as Corrine told her cowboy friends, he's an ace cow horse. I've never seen what he can actually do, but he needs using now and then."

"I don't think Grace would mind, Randy. What you plannin' to do with 'em?"

"There's a competition coming up at the ranch soon. I'd be much obliged if you'd allow me to use him. I plan to get him in shape and rope on him. I assure you I'll take care of him. The show had Grace worked up, saying she wanted to enter the roping, and now…"

Alice looked at the ornery horse. Every morning at feeding time, he'd back his ears and make a run toward her. He always stopped before he got too close, shaking his head side to side and threatening her. She couldn't understand what Grace saw in the ornery jackass. "I know you will treat him good, Randy. I don't see a reason not, seeing it's you. It's best if you keep the cussed thing so he'll have something to do other than stand here all day. Good luck at the cowboy competition."

He nodded a thanks and fastened a halter on Coyote's head. "Alice, please call the house if you don't mind when you find she's coming back and tell the Sullivants or the housekeeper to give me the message." Randy pulled a stubby pencil from a hip pocket and wrote the number on a feed bag tag. He ripped it off and handed it to Alice.

Alice glanced at it before nodding her head. "It's obvious to me, she loves you, Randy," she repeated.

"Thank you, Alice, for telling me. The feeling's been mutual, but now, I don't know."

His voice took on a deeper and sharper tone. Up until now, he hadn't fully understood just how strongly he felt drawn to Grace. But, he'd be damned if he'd let himself appear to be defeated in front of Alice.

Without another word, he mounted the horse and gathered the lead ropes of the other two in his hand.

After seeing Randy off, Alice was shaken by his abrupt departure and turned to go about her business. "My, that was surprising."

* * *

His horse's hooves softly beat against the dirt road, a rhythm matching the rider's troubled thoughts. He thought he understood his and Grace's connection. He'd been dead wrong.

"I'll get through this." The horse shook its head shaking off the relentless flies. "How would you know?" Randy reached low to maim a biting insect before it bit the tormented horse—talking to no one special. Just a horse.

I'm such a gunsel. I felt the callouses on her palms when we held hands. Such a small thing, but it said a lot. He was completely unaware of her difficulties running the dairy farm and how tedious the work had become.

He knew all her curves by heart and how her reluctance turned to desire whenever they kissed. Her lips started the fire that burned in his heart. Now his heart was scorched with guilt with thoughts of him being the cause of her disappearance.

Randy looked down the road as his imagination followed its own road. One he had not traveled until he'd met Grace. He dreamed of her nightly wanting to hold her, to slowly remove the robe, and to brush her hair behind her shoulders. To kiss her everywhere. But that only caused him to become hard, and with no gratifying release. He was oblivious to the sun high in the sky casting its hot rays on the newly cut grass wafting its scent through the air. Sweat trickled down his face and soaked the back of his shirt as Grace consumed his thoughts. Would she return?

Coyote and the pack mule dragged back on their lead lines bringing him back from his skepticism. He gave them a tug to catch them up beside his horse. All day, while visiting farms to fix equipment and shoe horses around Annona, he kept replaying Alice's portrayal of Grace's undoing in his mind. On the three stops that he made, the harder he worked at his job, the more she occupied his mind.

By dusk, he'd traveled south through Annona. In thirty minutes more, he turned up the long Red River Ranch road. The cook was ringing the dinner bell. Before answering its ring, Randy unpacked the mule at the horse barn, unsaddled his horse, and put Coyote in a stall with the other two to feed later.

When he entered the kitchen, he was the sole man eating at that hour. The other men within hearing distance would be coming in soon. After poking at his food, he shoved the plate away. Leaving the table, he returned to the barn to take care of the horses and mule. Back at the bunkhouse, Randy fell into a chair in the sitting room. Staring at the wall, and chewing on a toothpick, visions of Grace in her bathrobe with her hair still damp galloped around behind his closed eyelids. Beneath sweeping dark brows—his gaze met her blue eyes. *Damn her*. He flung the sliver of wood across the room.

The relentless day had left no room for respite. Fatigue settled heavily upon his weary frame, and each passing moment seemed to stretch on endlessly. The dim light of evening cast long shadows across the room.

He opened his eyes when he heard Andelacio come in and sit down in a chair near the old metal barrel stove.

"Hola mi bue n amigo. You look like hell. You have a bad day today?" Randy looked like he'd walked from Annona on foot.

"I'm just fine," he droned sarcastically. "You ever have one of them days?"

"Hmmm? What do you mean?" Andelacio untied the bandana around his neck and wiped his face. Lasso had never heard Randy sound so down. He should take himself to get a shower before the other chuckleheads got in the way. Maybe he'd feel better.

"Women. What's it mean, when the one you thought might favor you disappears without a word?"

Andelacio chuckled. "Maybe she doesn't like you."

Randy hated confiding in anyone, but if he didn't talk about it, he'd be a worthless shit for days. "No, I think she did. I think she knew for sure, I liked her."

"Where is the woman now?"

"Hell if I know. Grace sold her farm. I found out today when I rode out there to take care of her horses. The help said she left a week ago and read me a letter that she received saying she was in Dallas and might go to California." Randy watched Lasso light up a stubby cigar and blow the smoke into the air.

"Will you go after her?"

Randy cocked his head. The thought of chasing a woman across the country never entered his mind. "For what? It'd be a big waste of time and money." Besides, he had to know first if he was plain angry or if Grace held a deeper significance in his life than he knew. Despite that he'd told Lasso that it would be useless, his strong attraction to her was goading him—to *go find her and bring her back.*

"I was kind'a looking forward to seeing how we'd get along. Would we grow together or die alone? Looks like I got an early notice." Frustrated, he raised his hand. "Is that what you'd do? I mean, if you cared enough, you'd just take off and find her? Damn, Lasso, what if she tells me to quit bothering her? What then?"

"You tell me, Randy. Is she worth the effort? Are you not man enough to follow her wishes? Otherwise, you'll be one miserable bastard not knowing where she is or why she even ran away. Amigo, you must think about it. Then decide."

Andelacio put out his cigar, stood, and stretched. "I'm going to bed. I'm very interested in the outcome, but now if we don't get to sleep, we won't be fit to get up to work in the morning." He slapped Randy on the shoulder and exited into the next room for a quick shower and then to his cot.

Randy studied the wall, trying to put two and two together. Ten minutes later he quietly followed Lasso to the bunk room, and silent as possible, left his clothes in a heap on the floor and rolled into bed. It was too warm to start a proper fire in the stove, so he lay on top of the cover in his long johns, thinking over Lasso's words. He was a man all right, but still a miserable bastard. Mr. Sullivant might not think highly of him up and leaving his job going after a woman. Every man Mr. Sullivant hired, no matter the age, looked up to the boss. Anyway, what would he use for money? Train fare would cost more than setting out on a horse, but the train was faster. Then he might not find her in Dallas, costing him even more.

He ran it over his mind so many times, he'd gotten over the shock that she had left abruptly, but that didn't stop him from feeling angry as doubts entered his mind. Perhaps she wanted a man with greater potential. He had thought about it before. As a boy, his father, Burnett, had him convinced that he wasn't worth a Barber half dollar. As a man, he came to realize his father was a damn fool.

If William Sullivant hadn't taken him on as a sixteen year old cowhand, he would have never matured to be the man that he was.

He'd wait a while to see if Alice Ann received another letter telling Grace's whereabouts. His eyelids grew heavy when a half-baked plan crossed his mind. Everything depended on the cowboy contest.

CHAPTER FIVE

The Cowboy Competition

Randy & Lasso

The ranch hands tacked flyers on every building in Annona, Clarksville, and the surrounding area announcing the contest.

For the past two weeks, Randy used Coyote to enhance both of their roping abilities by working Red River's cattle as often as possible. Swinging the large loop around his head with his index finger pointed down the coil of rope in his palm, he stood in the stirrups and leaned forward to throw the loop. It sailed through the air with a whir to settle over the steer's horns. Coyote slid to a stop, halting the heifer's flight, and he backed up to take the slack out of the rope, something he was taught several years in his past. Randy knew there weren't many more of his caliber that held a natural fascination for tracking cattle. He was a fast and fearless horse; a natural at handling grown bovines at the end of a rope. The gelding never panicked if charged by a momma cow or had a problem in the ravines or through the wooded terrain.

As soon as Randy's loop wrapped both horns, Lasso threw his rope and caught the back legs to lay it down for branding. Lasso seldom missed catching both legs making it easier to throw the cattle down for branding.

Branding, managing cattle in general, the mechanical work at Red River or Eberly Ranch, and his blacksmith jobs filled Randy's days, making most of his working hours too busy to dwell on Grace's whereabouts. Whenever there was idle time, impassioned memories of their kiss and the closeness of her body in his embrace did haunt him.

She said the competition was her chance to have fun and to escape from the dairy. He had wanted that for her. He understood the farm had tied her there for years without a break, and he felt guilty roping on her horse. They only met weeks ago, but according to Alice Ann,

Grace was suffering from boredom from sitting under a cow's belly for hours a day and lacked outside interests to bolster her spirit. It hurt that she didn't confide in him as though he wasn't trustworthy. But what did he expect her to say when they had only just met? He racked his brain. He was jeopardizing everything that he owned to find her and beginning to wonder why. *He felt utterly mad to yearn so intensely, yet his guilt was even more unbearable.*

* * *

It was one of those weeks when Red River was short of hands, making it difficult for Randy to be gone for a lengthy time. The dodgy cowhands had spent their money Saturday night drinking and partying. Until they sobered up again, they would be useless for days. The more reasonably sane ones would ask their friends to cover for them.

Several had gotten into trouble in Clarksville, and Mr. Sullivant wouldn't go all the way there to post bail, but he didn't fire the derelicts knowing that they couldn't work elsewhere.

He muttered curses over their going off guzzling Bluestone and keeping him from going after her. After several long days of punching cattle, Randy hitched a horse to a wagon where he stored his shoeing tools. That afternoon, after finishing his work for customers in Annona, the next stop was the Madden Dairy. Aside from a garden of weeds surrounding the house, the old place remained unchanged. He walked to the big milking parlor behind the residence and found Alice cleaning milking equipment in a foul smelling vat of chemical-based sanitizer.

Alice Ann looked up with a pleased expression on her face. "Howdy, Randy. We ain't got no hoof or leg problems on any of our livestock." She washed her hands in a big steel sink and dried them with a towel, which was hanging around her shoulders. The men were cutting hay, and she was beat and glad for the company.

His response was a quiet "Oh," accompanied by a subtle nod, his mind preoccupied with the possibility of a new letter from Grace.

His search for her relied on her latest letters to Alice revealing her location.

Alice Ann studied his face. He was leaner and suntanned, and his dark mustache was sun bleached to sand-colored brown turning downward at the corners of his mouth. His hat flattened his hair, but it stayed in place when he raked his fingers through it. She knew the real reason for his visit and why he had suffered the bumpy ride on the rut filled road.

"Glad you showed up, though. Let's step in." She led Randy to the door. "Got a recent note from Grace. Come on in and read it." Inside the door, she pulled a sheet of paper from an envelope. "Here, you take it. I've already seen it." She passed the handwritten note to Randy and took a seat in a rocking chair.

He sat at the kitchen table, bare of the wildflowers Grace kept in a vase. He unfolded it, taking his time. He swore under his breath when his shaking hands caused the sheet to rattle.

September 22nd, 1906.

Dear Alice: I am yet in the Dallas locality, but have traveled to Red Oak and may be here a couple more weeks. To my surprise, I found employment at a cattle ranch outside of there. I wanted to fill my purse with money before striking out too far on my own. The ranch owners are nice and have extended an offer of room and board that I'd be foolish to decline. The work is less demanding and the hours are shorter compared to the dairy. I took the time on my lunch break to let you know you're not to worry. If or when I leave here to go wherever the tracks take the train, I promise to send you a letter.

Till then, I am yours, Grace.

He noticed the postmark. Grace had mailed the letter from Red Oak, a small community near his childhood home. As he came to the end of the short missive, she hadn't mentioned his name. But he didn't expect she would. His good sense asked *why bother with her.* His heart answered *because Lasso claimed you'll regret it your whole life if you do nothing.* At least, he would live to know that he had done his best.

Randy handed the letter back to Alice Ann. He didn't mention that he was going to look for Grace. He'd decided that he was daft, and there was no point in advertising it. "Miz Alice, I 'preciate you letting me read your mail. At least I know Grace is safe and sounds well. I guess I need to be going. Still have errands to run, but if you receive any more updates, please let me know using the telephone. The Sullivants will give me the message."

Alice pushed her ample self from the chair and held out her hand. "You're welcome, Randy. I'm fine with it. I miss her myself. It worries me she's near Cowtown. Some parts of Dallas and Fort Worth ain't full of nothing but rough cowboys and outlaws. But," she sighed, "it appears that she's working for some nice folks."

"True, it's no place for a single woman. Part of Fort Worth is called Hell's Half Acre." His parents' ranch near Red Oak was thirty-four miles from the notorious town's red-light district, and full of criminals and brawlers. Randy nodded as he put his hat back on. "Thanks, again, Miz Alice. Tell Mr. Turnbow I'm sorry I missed him."

Alice saw him out the door. "I will, Randy." She sailed through the house to find Garrett, her cheeks puffed with a wide grin. *He's going after her!*

* * *

It wasn't the Sullivant's ranch's first competition show, and it had become a late summer tradition. On the day before the show, nineteen cowboys set up camp close to the bunkhouse in Red River's pasture. They rode in on horseback for miles, others came by train if they had saved enough in their pouch. Some came in wagons from other ranches in the east Texas area, eager to prove themselves as the champions of their chosen occupation, roping or riding broncs.

Campfires flickered over their bed rolls, and lanterns lit up the faces of their cards as they played poker. Young and old, fit or frail alike, gambled on their prospects of being crowned *the champion cowboy.*

The morning broke without a cloud. The stringed flags overhead made popping sounds when the breeze stirred them. Imitating Bill Cody's Wild West show, Red River's cash incentives attracted the best competitors to earn the title of champion in their respective events. The best attracted a bigger audience.

Spectators began arriving as early as nine in the morning. Their wagons, saddle horses, and two Ford Model Ns were parked on the grounds. The crowd spread quilts under shade trees or claimed a seat by leaving a hat or handkerchief in a preferred spot on the bleachers that William had built. Cowboys and spectators were placing bets at the far side of the corral separating the bawdy men from the ladies and children milling around.

William Sullivant strode through the crowd carrying his son in his arms. He was pleased to see the number of ticket payers waiting for the show to start.

After putting Cody on his feet, the three year old ran to the pen holding the calves used for roping. A bronc rider in Angora chaps and a bright red shirt handed the toddler a rope. Cody ran swinging the heavy hemp and fell on his knees from the weight of it. William encouraged his son to get up and showed him how to spin the tail of the heavy lasso.

"Mr. Sullivant!"

William turned around. Two women wearing wide-brimmed cowboy hats and high-top boots walking toward him looked too young to be experienced cowgirls. "Hello, ladies." He tipped his hat.

The one sporting spurs and an embroidered vest said, "We came from south Oklahoma, Mr. Sullivant."

"That's a long way."

"Yes, it is. A friend from Clarksville wrote to say you were having a show. Camille and I hopped on the first train and arrived here this morning. We want to enter the Bronc riding, please."

"As you already know, ladies, these competitions have no regulations. But, I've got a few of my own rules. I've allowed cowgirls to bust out a bronc, but just experienced cowgirls. If you've previously ridden broncs and are aware of the potential consequences of injury, I will give you the go-ahead…"

Within earshot, Randy closed his eyes ignoring the women and the rules Mr. Sullivant was explaining. To cover his travel expenses for a few weeks, he had to win the $25 prize money. Only God knew when he'd have a regular paycheck again. There were still some loose ends that needed to be tied before he embarked on his search for Grace. However, he found himself lost in thought, weighing his choices before settling on one.

Coyote brought him back to the bustling around him. Randy pulled the horse's head away from a nearby cow pony's tail before he got kicked in the teeth.

"Lasso!" He grabbed Andelacio's arm as he passed by on foot.

"Hey, compadre. What is your draw?"

"Not long from now. Bronc riding is almost over, and Mr. Sullivant included an insane new spectacle where you ride a steer with nothing to hang onto. Why'd anyone want to do that?"

Andelacio spit a stream of tobacco over his shoulder. "Have no idea. He'll introduce bucking bulls next. Sounds like suicide."

"Don't know about riding bulls, but he believes the crowd will like bucking steers. At least they did at the Lazy T Ranch near Dallas. A kid jumped on the back of a steer when they were herding them out of the pen after steer roping. It caused a big laugh from the crowd. So, Mr. Sullivant's going to put that in the show, too."

Randy stepped from Coyote and motioned for Lasso to follow him.

Away from everyone, they turned the corner of Randy's blacksmith shop, near the big corral. Randy took a deep breath to calm his trembling insides. "Uh, Lasso, you remember our conversation a couple of nights ago about my lady friend?"

Lasso saw that Randy was tense. He'd have to steady himself if he expected to win any money. "Yes. You were very troubled."

Randy sniffed and took a deep breath to calm his uneasiness. If Lasso agreed to help, suddenly everything that he had been considering might actually work out. The possibility of winning the money gave him hope, too, that he could finally carry out his plan. He smiled to himself thinking if it didn't work, he could blame Lasso for suggesting he was not a man if he didn't go after his woman.

"I have a favor to ask if you don't mind. I'm gonna do it, Lasso. I've decided to find Grace. That's my friend—uh, my girl's name."

A warning flashed through Andelacio's head that it was close to time to move on to a place far away. He'd let down his guard with Randy, who had become a close friend when he intended to keep his distance from everyone to protect himself. Despite this, he trusted Randy's sincerity and was open to helping him as long as he didn't probe into his past life.

"Shoot, my friend. What do you need me to do while you are gone?"

Still second guessing himself, Randy said, "You were right. She's all I think about, Lasso. Guess I'll put myself out of my misery and get on with it. But there's someone who depends on me in Annona. While I'm gone, I need you to check on her twice a week."

"Amigo, why not ask your friend Jimmy? Why me?"

"Because Jimmy ain't as smart as you, Lasso. And you know it. The biggest thing is, I trust you to keep your mouth shut."

Randy heard Mr. Sullivant on the megaphone. He had to get ready to catch a calf. "Look, I gotta go. Can we talk about it later after all this hoop-la is over? If I'm not the winner, I can't go, and you won't have to worry about doing me a favor. Think about it in case I do win. I sure plan to."

"Go on," Lasso nodded. "And . . . Mr. Sullivant?"

"I haven't talked to him about it yet, I mean my taking off to see my folks."

"Oh, to see your folks." The quirk on his mouth made clear that he knew Randy was lying.

"Well, you don't expect me to . . ."

"We do what we have to do."

Randy already felt it was wrong to lie to his boss. But he couldn't tell him the reason he must leave for a while. He hated lying. Especially to Sullivant. Chagrined at himself, he looked away, aware of the fact that he was becoming a low life.

"All I'm sure of right now is, if I don't win this roping, I can't make it out of Annona." He mounted Coyote and left Andelacio to think about his request.

The audience was raucous, making it difficult to hear. Mr. Sullivant's voice echoed across the bleachers and drifted over to the cowboys awaiting their event. "Let's give a big hand to Wild Willy Perrigan who rode the bronc, Little Annie, to a standstill." He waited a minute to speak again as the noise lowered. "As soon as this ol' bangtail is escorted outta here, our next event in this show today is calf roping. The cowboy who lassos his calf and ties it the fastest will win this contest. First up is Artie McCarthy. I know you remember this cowboy! He's already won the first bronc riding event! Don't leave too early folks. Another round of bronc busting is coming up."

Rupert, no friend of Artie's, spit tobacco juice that landed down the calf's leg that he and another cowboy were holding to keep it steady until Artie gave a nod. It was necessary for roping that Art catches the calf, runs to it, and grabs the front leg to tie up with the other two legs. Amusingly, to Rupert, Art's hand would land in the tobacco as he legged down the calf.

Artie swung his rope twice and steered his horse to the starting line. The flagger waited for the rider's nod to drop his flag, and the timer's thumb hovered over the stopwatch. The flag dropped, the calf released, the clock punched, and the roper kicked his horse to start the chase.

Two seconds earlier, Artie's horse sensed his rider's adrenalin rush. Expecting the running start, it became keyed-up and reared on his hind legs, adding a few seconds to their total time with a delayed start. He caught the bawling calf, and Ann, his wife, waved her hanky and clapped for him as he re-mounted to exit the grounds. Time: twenty-one seconds flat. Seven more ropers were called before Randy heard his name announced.

The milling cowboys and townsfolk became lively again whistling and clapping. Dust covered boots, pants, and anything of a dark color as hooves churned the loose dirt.

"Now, for Randy Jackson!"

The butterflies in Randy's stomach had died of old age while they waited for his turn. With a calm touch, he rode Coyote to the start line to wait for the flags to drop and the calf to move. With his future life depending on a successful catch, he refused to allow doubts and blunders to exist in his plan to win. It went this way when the pressure to do everything correctly and fast became a reality. He relaxed. His eyes stayed focused on the calf. Coyote quivered, his dancing hooves stirred the dirt. He nodded. The handlers released the calf. When it crossed the line, and the bay horse felt Randy lift his weight from the saddle, he bolted into a run and stayed close to the calf's flying tail.

When the Hereford swerved to the left, Randy pitched his slack to the right and the loop settled, throwing the calf flat. Feeling the familiar jerk on the slack rope, Coyote buried his back hooves into the ground, squatted low, and backed up.

Before the horse came to a full stop, Randy had dismounted, grabbed the rope, and followed it with both hands down to the calf. He picked up its left front leg and threw the bawling animal to its side. Swiftly, he positioned himself astride the calf and extended his long legs to the maximum. He lowered his butt to the calf and rotated his hips to bring his knee forward to gather three legs.

His hand flew wrapping the rope around them in a blur. He tightened the hooey, and stood, throwing his arms into the air.

He had drawn a staid four-hundred pound calf that lay still and took the tie without a twitch. The crowd was clapping. So great was his concentration on stringing the legs, he didn't hear the noise.

He watched the official timer pass the results to Mr. Sullivant who, filled with pride, shifted his gaze from the winner's name on the paper to Randy.

"Ladies and gentlemen. Randy Jackson is our champion calf roper who has broken the record here at the Red River Cowboy Competition. He roped and tied his calf in fourteen seconds flat! What an incredible time. Our top hand is Randy Jackson!"

A smile broke across Randy's face, and his body sagged with relief. After hearing his time, he slapped the dust from his pants, pushed his hat to the back of his head, and mounted Coyote. Trotting through the gate, he navigated through the bystanders to reach the barn and attend to Coyote as the Texas sun had lathered his neck. Randy patted him, proud of how well he performed as a cow horse. As he celebrated his win in the roping event, a tinge of disappointment washed over him because it wasn't Grace on Coyote, the horse she had yearned to ride in this event.

The ranch competition ended as the sun settled low in the west. The local cowboys returned to the bunkhouse except those still caring for the livestock used in the events.

Randy joined the other hands in the bunkhouse kitchen and devoured a steak. Heading to the sitting room to find Lasso, he found him puffing on a cigar. His black eyes turned into slits as the smoke levitated through the air. He watched Randy wipe his hands on his handkerchief.

"You roped well today."

"That catch couldn't have been better, Lasso. Still, you can never be sure that all will fall in the right place. The calf might'a fought me or I could've missed. And, it wouldn't have been that fast without Coyote holding 'em tight."

"Some things are better left unseen if they interfere with moving forward. What is it you need me to do to help you find your woman?"

"Your words got me thinking, and you convinced me to find her. I'm still uncertain of the outcome, and unsure of the duration of my absence. So, while I'm away, Lasso, I need someone to take care of an important chore. And be able to trust them to keep it quiet. Any gossip may hurt someone else who I love."

Lasso was aware of Randy's dark mood, and his sober expression wasn't taken lightly. Curious about his request, Lasso leaned forward. "Life lacks meaning without trust, my friend."

Randy gave a slight nod. Two problems weighed on his mind now. After a deep breath, he still felt unsure how to disclose his secret. "This regards a relative, my sister. When we were younger, our parents were strict, too much so. I ran away from home when I was sixteen. I've been here ever since I happened upon this ranch and was penniless and hungry. My parents guarded my sister like a criminal and prevented Phoebe from having friends, even school friends. And absolutely, not boys. The weight of those rules still haunts me."

Lasso flicked his ashes into a tin can. "Hmm." His puzzled expression conveyed his interest and a multitude of unanswered questions.

"After I left home, an older man came to Red Oak. The bastard pretended he loved her. From what she told me, he was old enough to be her daddy. He tricked her into slipping away one evening and assaulted her. My parents shamed her and made her leave home with little money to care for herself."

Randy scanned the room and its three doors for eavesdroppers. "She contacted me 'cause she didn't know what to do. I sent her money for the train trip here. A family not too far from our farm helped her until she bought a ticket to Clarksville. She's in Annona now. At Miz Goss' place. Only we three know this.

"I'm asking that you check on her once or twice a week. I plan to be here before the baby comes, but from what I've heard babies aren't on anyone's time schedule except their own.

"Here's enough money to take care of her needs if Miz Goss cannot do so. Keep part of it for yourself. I'll be in your debt, Lasso."

Lasso's *lying low* scheme was falling apart. He'd never intended to get this close to any man, much less their sister. Worse, what would her opinion be of a poor half-Mexican cowboy? He was filled with a deep sense of honor that the cowboy who called him a friend, was entrusting his sister to him, a man with a stained past and mixed race.

Accustomed to camouflaging his fear of being detected, the dark-eyed cowboy's demeanor appeared unfazed. In a split second, his sentiment changed. Could this be his moment to seek redemption and make amends for his earlier misdeeds? Helping a woman in this way, was beyond his *fixing* experience. On second thought, he wasn't supposed to fix a problem, only watch over it for a short while. He'd been shoved away from niceties and disrespected the law, and now he was going to be responsible for a friend's sister. No one would know. But damned if a pregnant woman didn't scare him to death.

He ground his smoke out in a saucer. "I'll do this for you, Randy."

Randy released the breath he'd been holding. "Thank you, my friend. There's been some hurdles and more to go. I guess now it's time to find her."

Two days later, Randy assessed what he needed for his trip and what was unnecessary. After stuffing a small bag, and shoving it beneath his bunk, he walked to the boss's house.

He almost backed out when Mr. Sullivant opened the door, but he gathered his courage and walked into the cool, spacious hallway. He'd always been in awe of the stone and log construction, having had the chance to enter the big house before, and it never ceased to whisper to him that he'd have one like it one day.

William motioned him in. "Randy? Come in and have a chair." William was as fit as ever. He worked tirelessly, as most of his men. Despite a few gray strands in his hair, he showed no signs of a limp or any slowing down after the horrific injury that he endured years ago.

He led Randy through a door where a desk sat, and tall bookcases lined the wall. After settling on a leather sofa, Randy removed his hat.

"What can I do for you?"

"Morning, Mr. Sullivant. I've got a predicament I need to discuss with you, sir, if you have a moment."

Randy had prepared his story, but the first words didn't make it to his tongue. "It's a personal matter, Mr. Sullivant. I don't quite know how to explain it."

Randy was twirling his Stetson by the brim. While observing his actions, it reminded William of the story when Randy and his brother Finn were new to Memphis and were searching for lodging. Finn nervously did the same. Randy's story had made him laugh.

"Guess I'll lay it out the best I can. There's a girl. A lady that I'm quite fond of. She's had a rather rough time in her life. Uh, before we really, uh, understood how we felt about each other, she sold her farm and left town. I only found out from a mutual friend who bought the dairy."

William leaned back into the cushions. He knew of the dairy and the previous owner, but not the specific details. "Now, you want to find her?"

Astounded at his boss's assessment, Randy nodded his head.

William propped his elbows on his knees, hands dangling. "How long do you expect you'll be gone?"

"That's it, Mr. Sullivant. I just don't know. If I hadn't won the roping, sir, I wouldn't be able to go at all. But, if I had to guess, I'd say a month."

William nodded and pursed his lips. "I believe that each horse has their own style of bucking, Randy, and that men are the same. The best Broncs never give up. Any man who goes for the whole figure, risking everything to have what they want has bravado. A side of things you may have never considered. You've always been the wheel horse, Randy. Next to Rupert, of course."

A big grin crossed William's face. A smaller one on Randy's. "The ranch isn't short-handed. It could survive for a stint without its mechanic, blacksmith, and top hand. Who am I to interfere with a man's dreams?"

Randy took a minute to ingest William's powers of observation.

William stood, and so did Randy. He offered a handshake. "When you stop fighting, you die. Hope your luck holds out, and I'll see you in a month."

A big "yeehaw" was on the tip of Randy's tongue, but he stifled it to shake William's hand, then slammed his hat on his head. "I appreciate that, Mr. Sullivant. I will be back. That's a promise and thank you, Mr. Sullivant, for the compliment. Not sure that I'm that brave."

William smiled and walked the young cowboy to the door. "Oh, one other thing. When you bring her back, I'd like to meet her."

"Grace is her name. Grace Madden. And you will, Mr. Sullivant. You darned will!"

William smiled. "Go search for Grace, Randy!"

The walk to the bunkhouse provided enough time for the shock to subside. Everything had gone better than he ever expected. As soon as Lasso came in from work, there was another private conversation Randy needed with him.

Before long, Lasso did come through the door, took his regular chair, and lit a cigarette. He exhaled the smoke, sending it into the air. "I see you've packed. When are you leaving?"

Randy nodded. "Depends on when I wrap up things that need doing. I told my sister to look for the ugliest cowhand in Annona."

Randy wrote his sister's name and the boarding house address on a slip of paper and handed it to the man he prayed was capable of keeping his word. Phoebe had no one but Randy and Mrs. Goss to depend on.

One side of Lasso's mustache lifted over half a smile. "I will see to your sister as well as you have, my friend. Do not worry. I wish you well on your quest." Without looking, Lasso folded the note and put it in his vest pocket. He had spent his adult life concealing his existence and never sharing his past or dreams with anyone. Randy's trust was humbling.

"And Mr. Sullivant approved your leave?"

Randy whispered, "Yeah. He agreed to a month. Maybe it won't be that long." He quit talking momentarily when a cowboy shuffled through the door and out another.

Randy stood to retrieve something from a pocket, and placed a hand on Lasso's shoulder, palming three silver dollars into his closest friend's hand. They discussed random events, and gossip, and then idly tossed dice at the card table until they decided to turn in.

That night, he lay awake at a loss to know the reasons for her running away, and thought it was likely that she was hurting just as much as he was. He had no idea that her disappearance could cause him such immense pain. He shook his head as doubt washed over him that he'd find Grace.

CHAPTER SIX

The chill of isolation seeps into the bones.

Grace

The cats in the barns kept the feed bins free of rats. Grace picked up her favorite one and placed the calico in a large knitting bag. She likened it to taking a part of the farm with her.

After boarding the passenger train, Bea, unbothered, perched on the seat next to Grace, purring. Despite the cat's passive behavior, when the conductor approached their seats, Grace tucked her back into the knitting pouch. She held her breath as he walked by, but Bea stayed silent.

The buzz of conversation in the passenger car didn't interfere with Grace falling asleep. When the train slowed with a lurch, she awoke and leaned into the window to see their surroundings. The short time for the train to arrive at its destination was amazing. The car's comfort, the plush red seat they shared, and the phenomenal speed were all unfamiliar to her. So were the buildings at the East Dallas Union Depot surrounding a maze of tracks, and passenger and freight trains. A web of travelers, automobiles, and a variety of horse pulled vehicles filled the center of the station. She closed Bea in the bag, shouldered it, and grabbed her valise before the engine came to a stop.

As the car doors opened, Grace stepped onto solid ground. Pushing through the throng of boarders and greeters, she entered the Depot. A ticket agent was positioned behind a counter.

"Hello. I'm new to Dallas. Will you please direct me to a reputable hotel?"

He gazed at her over his glasses. After giving various directions on where to find rooms, he suggested, "Or you can take the nearest streetcar, which will stop in front of The Oriental Hotel."

Grace thanked him and exited the building. Bea squirmed in the stuffy bag. "Bea! Be still. I'm finding us a room." Bea meowed in complaint, no doubt hungry and thirsty. In a secluded area beside the building, Grace let the cat out for a moment on the dirt patch beside the train station. The streetcar tracks that the ticket agent pointed out were in sight yards away.

With the cat taken care of, Grace boarded a car and handed the fare to the conductor.

"I'm new to this area, sir. Do you mind alerting me when we are near The Oriental Hotel?"

"Certainly, ma'am."

She found the downtown Dallas trolleys, cars, and crowds unnerving. Her bravado was gone, and her heart filled with a deep melancholy tainted with regrets.

The conductor said, "Miss!" as the car stopped at the hotel, and he motioned it was her stop. Bea complained again as she exited the car. A fenced lot, with a cow grazing beside The Oriental, was the only thing around that looked familiar.

Grace released Bea from the bag a second time, and the cat found a suitable spot as Grace watched over her. Several workmen walked around the country girl wearing an outdated hat and shoes. With no familiar faces in sight, the realization sank in that she was on her own, with no one to turn to for help.

Then, Bea darted away. Similar to Bea, Grace felt anxious upon seeing the avenue's congested traffic of pedestrians, automobiles, and horse cabs. Her stomach knotted as she coaxed the worried feline into the sewing pouch again. Then, she continued across the narrow dirt drive to the entrance of the six story building.

Stepping through the doors of the grand lobby, she stared open mouth at the exquisite tile floor, the first of its kind in Dallas. The wide stairway was flanked with a balustrade of mahogany. Grandiose chandeliers lit by electricity hung from a high ceiling. As she paid for a room with a trembling hand, a stiff young man in a uniform appeared and picked up her small suitcase.

Her intention was to walk the steps to the third floor, but when he started in a different direction with her belongings, she followed. He stepped into a box where an operator stood ready.

"Third floor," said the porter carrying everything she owned. The cage lifted with a groan, covering the sound of Bea's yowl. When the lift stopped, the bellhop walked ahead.

She followed him to her door number; he unlocked it for her, handed her the keys and her suitcase, and wished her a good day. He waited for a minute, and she realized he was waiting for a tip. She raked the bottom of her handbag for coins and paid him.

As soon as he shut the door, she let Bea loose to roam. She lay her bag on the floor. An open door took her to a black-and-white checkered floor and a beautiful claw-foot tub against the wall. And it came with hot water faucets. She filled a clean cup sitting by the sink with water for Bea.

Bea completed her room inspection; she then discovered the cup upon the tiled floor. Nothing else interested her, and she leaped onto the bed to lie alongside Grace who had drifted into a light sleep as dusk was falling. After waking up in the dark, the cat's growling stomach reminded Grace that she was hungry, too.

Grace flipped on a light and straightened the hat still pinned to her hair. Then she checked her purse for money and, in the hallway, turned the key in the door lock. The elevator car arrived a minute after pressing the button. She gave a slight smile to the attendant. "Lobby, please."

On the ground level was a barber shop, a billiards parlor, and a cigar shop. She stopped in the arched doorway opening into a huge dining hall with ceiling to floor draperies.

The dining room reminded her of her date with Randy. It was silly to believe that distancing herself from him would diminish her feelings. She dabbed her eyes with a handkerchief, afraid she was going to make a spectacle of herself. She found a less visible empty table in a corner. The only single sitting at a table, Grace looked longingly around the room. Mixed couples and large groups of diners filled her ears with conversation and laughter. She stared at the empty chair across the table.

A waiter came and handed her a menu, to return three minutes later with a carafe of water and goblets. He whipped a pencil and notepad from a pocket and waited for her to order. After reviewing the menu for the cheapest dinner, she decided on a fish plate that Bea could share. A large glass of milk came with it. The waiter pivoted to go.

No longer able to push on and hold back her tears, she gasped, "Sir!"

The servant turned back afraid he had botched the order. "Ma'am?"

"I'm sorry. I've taken a turn for the worse and feel ill. Would it be possible, please, to have my order delivered to my room?"

The balding waiter in a black suit curled his lip and did everything to not roll his eyes. "Yes, Miss. What is the room number, please?"

"Thirty-four."

"Thank you, Miss. A porter will bring it to your room. I'm so sorry you're not feeling well." He turned and left the table, silencing her from saying another word.

Sure she had failed the big city societal rules of etiquette, she gathered her purse and found the elevator. Relieved when the doors shut, the lift's controls pinged, relaying a signal to stop at the second floor to pick up another passenger. She moved over as a gentleman, handsome in his day jacket and sweeping mustache, who was old enough to be her father, stepped into the lift and removed his hat. "Good morning, ma'am, or rather, good afternoon."

"Yes." Grace looked straight ahead. Not wanting to look a stranger in the eye, she studied the floor. She glanced at his fancy boots, tooled with red flowers. She had noticed a scar on his cheek, stark white, above his black mustache laced with gray. His words and face showed no emotion. Leery of slick strangers, she prayed that his presence on the lift was purely by chance.

Reaching her floor, she hurried through the lift doors, willing that they shut fast to block the stranger's stony stare. In the privacy of her locked room, she calmed her nerves. Then, she jumped at a sharp rap on the door.

She stood on tiptoes to peer through the peephole. She relaxed when she saw the porter.

Grace spread the dinner across the bed, using the bread plate for Bea's share of the fish. The food was good but did nothing to improve her mood.

She was floundering alone in the big city, not knowing her next step. She'd gone too fast and too far. Despite the circumstances, she had no choice but to face the next day and untangle the mess she created. Her options weren't the best, and she realized a smaller town was more in keeping with her inner self. She needed to make money as well; her meager savings were dwindling quickly. Working on a farm outside the city limits might help with her expenses. Or finding a job on a ranch. The dairy payments from the Turnbow's weren't available for another month.

Through eating, she moved to the edge of the bed, her bare feet touching the carpet. The floor was starker than a desert, the color of sand, dull and uninteresting. When she returned from her sabbatical, if she did return, she planned to roll in the grass at her house and throw dirt into the wind. No city life for her. Turning out the lights, Grace slept fitfully. She rose early, tired, but ready to dress in the remaining set of clothes she had for traveling.

It only took a second to sweep up her hair beneath her big brim hat. Grabbing the knitting bag and Bea, she picked up her small suitcase and walked through the cavernous lobby, and out of the hotel to hop onto a streetcar to the train station. Once there, she bought a ticket, boarded the train, and settled on a seat. Boiler steam from the engine stack obscured the Dallas skyline. At forty miles an hour, the thirty miles to Waxahachie would be fleeting. She knew nothing special about Waxahachie or had a reason to go there except the sparsely populated area was more likely to offer familiar ranch or farm work. Her spirits rose, though the town was larger than Clarksville.

Grace vacated her seat once for the bathroom. In the last set of seats, a gentleman sat hunched behind a newspaper, sleeping. When passing again, the man still slept, concealed by the newspaper. She looked downwards to avoid tripping over his stovepipe boots. Tooled red roses decorated the fine leather. He had spoken to her on the hotel lift. It was odd to see him again.

Back in her seat, through the window, the cotton fields flew by faster than she had sold the farm and then ran away. With a quick peep backward, the fancy boot man hadn't left his seat and was still sleeping under the paper. Or hiding. Acquainted with nefarious individuals in the milk business, she was leery of people she didn't know well.

The dull landscape offered no entertainment, so her mind wandered to the events in her life that had done nothing to boost her confidence. Among the few men she had known, Randy was a rugged cowboy unlike any she'd met. She fell hard and fast in love with his powerful hands, his deep laugh, and his handsome weathered face, lined with hardship and mirth. And more, he was an easygoing, gentle man who treated her with respect and adoration.

The sight of him in a doorway with another woman by his side had fractured her dreams into a million pieces. A chill of naivety washed over her when the truth slapped her across the face. All thoughts that she had of a future together seemed absurd. Thank goodness, she had learned of his betrayal early, sparing herself from further heartache.

The day was long and exhausting. The struggle and worry about money brought on another headache. Grace kneaded the space between her eyebrows with a thumb to ease the pain when the train whistle blew. Next, the train braked, and she knew they'd arrived at the Waxahachie station.

After stepping from the train, she boarded a mule pulled car near the station loaded with several other passengers. The slow-moving car passed a courthouse and an auditorium performance hall then weaved through a traffic jam of loaded cotton wagons going to market. She looked for signs of a hotel where she could settle before her work search. However, they had not passed any place she wished to linger.

Deciding to search on foot, she forced Bea's head back into the bag and held onto her heavy bag of clothes. Just yards away from a row of brick houses, she vacated the car and walked several blocks until she came across a 'room for rent' sign in a yard. The Victorian two-story house had porches that wrapped around all sides. It looked newly painted in a dark green and tan color and was spotless.

Accepted in, a deep sigh preceded her entry, where a kind woman outlined house regulations. Grace paid her for a two-night stay and noticed a stack of newspapers in the parlor. Lucky for her, she did not have to go out onto the street to hunt for one.

CHAPTER SEVEN

For better or worse.

Randy

Randy rode beneath a canopy of turquoise and peach colored clouds cradling a rising sun. It was a pretty sight, but the spindles of light falling over the dew covered grass was a deceptive prelude to the scorching heat. Already sweating, he dismounted his horse to take a drink from his canteen strung on the saddle.

He knocked on Grace's—or Alice's—door, unsure about the arrangement they'd made about the dairy. Only once before did he feel this uncertain about himself; after he left home before he discovered Red River Ranch. Being shot by the crazy Annona preacher was another terrible experience. Now, he was putting his livelihood on the line hopeful that Grace would come back, at least to Annona. Today, making an ass of himself was at the top of the list.

Alice peeked out the door, then swung it open. "Randy! Come in and have a cup of coffee. I see you got a piece of baggage hanging on your saddle. You're barreling off to find her?" She led him into the kitchen and offered him a chair at the table. After filling his cup, she poured one for herself.

"Yes." He ducked his head not wanting to go into detail and didn't want to stare at her missing tooth. If this chase became pointless, Alice Ann would know first. Then everyone for fifty miles around would laugh with her. The thought of not convincing Grace to come back with him, thus proving his father correct, was scarier than being left in the prairie for the ants. His father wouldn't be surprised if he failed because he always saw his son in that light.

"I'm sorry to say, but she hasn't sent another letter since the last one. I believe from somewhere near Red Oak."

Randy stood up anxious to be gone. "I remember. Probably it will be the first place I go. Don't know how I'll find out if she's up and left there, too, till I get there. Anyway, I'm glad she's not in Dallas." He stood and returned his hat to his head. "I appreciate the coffee, Miz Alice. I aim to find Grace, but if not, then I'll know at least I did the best I could."

Alice walked him to the door and took his hand and patted it. "You're a good man, Randy, and you deserve a good woman. You find her, you hear. I'm depending on you. Remember, Grace was struggling, being tied down here all her life. I don't picture it having anything to do with her feelings for you, though. You just bring her back. I'm depending on you."

He nodded. Unlike Grace, he wasn't going to cut and run; he'd find her.

Time was short. After adjusting his baggage behind the saddle, he mounted the horse and turned toward Clarksville. He spurred the horse into a quick trot, left it at a rental stable, and rushed to the train station.

* * *

The turbulence banging in every corner of his brain would outrun a Texas coastal hurricane. His plans ended as soon as he got on the train to Dallas. With his bag at his feet, he removed the Stetson and propped it on his knee.

Once he arrived in the big city, he had no idea where to go next. He'd always been good at doing things on the fly. This shouldn't be any different.

However, Alice had not convinced him that her assumptions about why Grace left were correct. Something else deeper had caused Grace to take off. It was more like a calf fleeing from a wolf.

His guarded nature made him question whether he could ever recapture those earlier feelings, uncertain as he was about her feelings for him.

But she started it, and he'd end it. He woke with a crick in his neck but refreshed.

The train slowed to a stop in the Dallas central business district. Rail tracks ran in all directions in the downtown area with stations along the lines. At Randy's destination, individuals appeared from the station house, joining the throngs of people leaving the trains, weaving in and out of the jumble of automobiles, horse taxis, and wagons. He found a horse cab once he broke free from the chaos of humanity.

The driver recommended a place to stay overnight that was not far from the station. Once there, he looked upward to the seventh floor of The Oriental Hotel. He paid the driver, picked up his suitcase and entered the huge lobby with a fountain centered beneath a chandelier. A counter of trinkets for the traveler to carry home and a tobacco counter lined one wall across from various arched doorways.

"Yes, sir? Would you like a room?"

Randy studied the part in the clerk's oil-slicked hair as he pondered how best to inquire about Grace. "For tonight. Not sure about tomorrow, but I will give you early notice if I decide to stay."

"Yes, sir. That will be one dollar. We have electric lighting and steam heat in our rooms. Our dining room is delightful and if you need any articles for personal use, our lobby has a lot of swell choices for sale for your comfort."

Randy handed him a silver dollar. "I wonder if you can tell me if you remember a young lady staying here a few days ago or she may even be here now. Uh, she is my fiancé and I've come to help her with her ailing mother."

"If you'd care to describe her, we don't have many single ladies staying at The Olympia."

"I'd say she was about this tall," he held up his hand, "and has very blue eyes. She is very slim and fit. Her name is Grace Madden."

The clerk started to turn the pages in the ledger of names and dates. He ran his finger down one page and up two more. "Here she is. I think it will be all alright to give you this information as you are engaged. Miss Madden was here on Wednesday last and checked out the next morning."

Randy smiled, relieved he'd been right about her choice of lodging. But he had no idea of where to look next. "I appreciate it, sir. I'm going to surprise her with my arrival. For now, I'll retire to my room."

The clerk nodded as Randy took the door key and chose the stairs to the third floor. There was not much else to do as the day was spent. The next morning he sat in a muddle on the edge of the bed not knowing where to start. If he knew why she ran away in the first place, he might have an inkling of her whereabouts. Who was he kidding? In no instance could he find a way to find out which direction she was headed. For some reason, she must have been disappointed in him. Then, it came to him that Grace was a farmer. She would be miserable in Dallas around so many buildings and people. How many towns were clustered around Dallas? He couldn't ride to all of them. But, her letter had been posted from Red Oak.

CHAPTER EIGHT

"Love is the absence of judgment." — *Dalai Lama*

Andelacio & Phoebe

Andelacio Slade was off on Sunday morning. If anyone needed him, they'd have to wait. Randy had ridden away three days earlier. Lasso couldn't postpone honoring his promise any longer. He studied his face in a mirror making sure he hadn't butchered his sideburns or mangled his mustache. He'd have to do.

I'm only helping a friend's relative while they're away. And I'm too damn close to Randy Jackson. I need to ride on. While he thought highly of Randy and hoped that his past was behind him, the law disagreed and might catch up with him if he stayed in one place for too long.

Ready to honor his word or get it over with, he knew where old Lady Goss lived. One of the oldest homes in town, it stayed the only one that took in boarders. The grounds were groomed, surrounding the house with the last green grass of the season before it became stunted and brown after a bout of frost.

After tying his horse to a heavy metal block, he gave his pants and gun belt a hitch up. While looking at his scuffed boots, the door opened a crack. "Umm . . . Miss Phoebe?"

"Yes, I am." She saw contemplation on his face. She wondered who he was expecting. "Are you Mr. Slade, who Randy told me about?" He nodded. "Please, come in."

Andelacio removed his Stetson, slicked back any errant strands of hair, and followed her into a room filled with furniture and every wall covered with books. After handing her his hat, she motioned for him to sit. The fine chair looked fragile, and he hesitated to sit down, fearing that one of its delicate legs would break under his weight.

Lasso's survey of the room ended as he watched Randy's sister spread her skirt behind and sit at the end of a sofa. She wore layers of clothes he supposed to hide her condition, but the little one she carried was still obvious by her round belly. But he didn't care about that. Her eyes were full of light with long lashes and dark eyebrows the color of her chestnut hair, curled high on the back of her head and adorned with a sprig of flowers, her skin looked like satin in comparison. She was not who he expected to meet.

He put a stop to his meandering eyes and thoughts, but doted on the one that pounded in his head. She appeared to be twenty at the most. He wanted to kill the bastard who violated this woman's virtue. What kind of parents would push their child away? *His father would and did.*

An uncomfortable silence rang across the room. Phoebe reasoned the cowboy across from her, being her brother's friend, was of good character. Familiar with cowboy whims, the hat she set on the table was a ten dollar Stetson. His air was proud. A red bandana stood out against his blue hickory cloth shirt that was tucked into darker blue denim trousers. The boots, however, were dusty and worn, but mainly comfortable. No cowboy relished breaking in a new pair of boots.

Neither knew where to start this strange conversation. So, Phoebe spoke first.

"I apologize we've put you into this uncompromising position, Mr. Slade. I do thank you in earnest for your willingness to provide such a service for my brother and me. Randy gave up his farrier business for a few days to take care of some business in Dallas. I pray, he is successful and returns happy." The sun-browned cowboy's intense stare, coupled with her own awareness of her state, made it impossible for her to look at Mr. Slade.

A smile tugged at the corners of his mouth as she shared her worry for her brother's well-being. "Please, don't say those things, Miss Phoebe. I am honored to help my friend. More so, since, I have met his family. Your brother is very protective. I know why. Your beauty is to be revered."

Phoebe looked at him and blushed. Beyond Mrs. Goss, Mr. Slade was the first person she'd met in Annona since the night of the assault; his presence felt strangely normal though a little personal. During their conversation, she felt so unlike a ruined woman, hiding from loose tongues.

Her emotions had been ungovernable, leaving her uncertain about her feelings for Mr. Slade. Did she feel accepted, or forgiven? No— forgiveness was not an option. She committed no wrong that needed anyone's mercy under any circumstances. She felt thoroughly examined by him, as men were apt to do, while his calm, objective comments helped lessen the impact of her ongoing trauma.

"Forgive me for not immediately mentioning my mission here is to see to your needs such as supplies, for now and later."

She understood the apprehension in Andelacio's voice. Though noble of her brother to help, who in their right mind would choose to be in this man's boots? Not being exposed to the public had been her utmost regard. A single cowboy shopping for goods for babies would start the gossipers faster than a brush fire. She shivered thinking of the shocking rumors intensifying and ruining her name.

"While I appreciate your direct approach, Mr. Slade, I think it would be best to let Mrs. Goss take care of certain needs." At least she had said it with some dignity.

Lasso nodded his head, relieved. He grinned showing beautiful white teeth against a jet mustache. He'd rather castrate calves all day than pretend he knew anything about babies. "Oh, of course, ma'am. Your brother wanted to give you money to cover everything."

Her heart skipped a beat. She'd rather he not smile. She blushed at how casually he addressed such intimate issues. "May I ask, where my brother got these funds? To my dismay, I thought ranch hands didn't receive high wages. I don't want to think he is penniless on my account."

Andelacio flashed another heartbreaker smile with just the right amount of shyness. "No, no, that is not the case." Lasso from the first had perceived a dormant strength in Randy. Although a calm man, he concealed an inner strength that Lasso predicted one day would unleash itself in a furious outburst.

"Many men are envious of your brother's skills. His blacksmith trade has seen a significant rise, and he is an excellent roper. One day, perhaps, you will see him rope. Your brother won a sizeable amount of money at the Red River contest that Mr. Sullivant, our boss, sponsored. His goal was to win enough to continue with your support. But he is too honorable to brag about his talents."

Phoebe's hands flew together in a gentle clapping fit. "Oh! Randy has always given his all to whatever he does. I am so proud of him!" She didn't mention he had always excelled at roping.

"He won enough, also, to fund his trip to Dallas or other parts nearby to search for a woman he cares about."

Phoebe frowned. "I'm confused. Who awaits him in Dallas?"

"You do not know her. They fell in love. Her reasons were unclear, but she changed her mind. News came that she was in the Dallas area. Your brother will not give up until he finds her."

Phoebe covered her mouth. Her brother omitted a lot of information about his trip to Dallas. *Randy has fallen in love?* Her gaze surveyed the carpet, a little hurt that he'd not confided in her. But, she didn't want to make Mr. Slade uncomfortable by asking questions and changed the subject.

She glanced at the impressive man sitting across from her whose smile made his square jaw line softer, his dark eyes brighter. Phoebe reined herself in. She was in no condition to present this side of her girlish personality. From this point on, she had to act her age and be more reserved, as mothers should. Expecting to be single for life, she would keep her child no matter what. Blame rested solely with the attacker, not the victim or child.

90

When the glimmer of happiness faded from her face, Lasso stood with a reluctance to leave. Shocked at himself for thinking this beautiful woman could want a poor, rough cowpoke like himself to stay longer was not worth considering. A woman's choice of husband usually involved finding an educated man with enough income to keep a home. However, he thought Phoebe Jackson knew neither of them could afford to be choosey.

She also stood, her guarded expression concealing her emotions.

"Senorita, may I return within a few days? You may have a feel for your monetary needs after talking to Miz Goss, which I will be happy to supply per your brother's wishes."

"Oh. Yes, I'll discuss *things* with her to decide how to go ahead." She led him to the door while he studied the lines of her torso from the back where no sign of a soon-to-be-born infant existed. She held out her hand. "It was lovely, Mr. Slade. I appreciate your taking your valuable time to pay a visit."

He held her hand in his calloused palm for a long moment.

The baby kicked. Heat radiated from her face giving it a soft glow. What should she do? She met his gaze with a smile. He turned to leave, and she shut the door softly and leaned against it.

Lasso didn't give a flying pig if no one approved his goodbye message to his ward as he thought of her now. He was untroubled by her past or her present predicament but troubled plenty over how he felt before and after meeting her. To him, he was taking a bigger leap than Randy ever thought about, and he couldn't and wouldn't change any of it.

CHAPTER NINE

Nothing to Lose

Andelacio Slade

Lasso rode to the boarding house for the second time two days later. Riding along, he removed his hat to scratch his head. He assumed Randy had no idea what it cost to give birth to a baby and the hoopla needed to care for it. Neither did he.

Andelacio Slade had nothing to lose except his freedom. At seventeen, he'd been free to do as he pleased after his mother's death. He'd ridden across the border countless times, but now, he refused to return south of the Rio Grande after he'd gotten into trouble and hunted by the law. Del Rio, Texas, was his birthplace, and all his Mexican roots had vanished.

Older and tired of wandering, he wanted to stay in one place somewhere forever. He considered himself lucky to have landed a cow puncher's job at Red River and avoided drinking hard liquor on a regular basis, gambling, and lots of questions. Being frugal, he had saved a few dollars for tough times. God knew he'd had enough of that.

Except for his mother, Lasso had never kept company with a woman like Phoebe Jackson. In his travels, he had *danced* a few times in some saloons that offered *dancing girls*, though he couldn't actually, for his life, dance. But they did give him lots of good lessons.

Miss Phoebe was an intelligent woman. A proper lady. Not one who flirted with love and gets with child. Raped, as Randy mentioned. No worse vile offense than a cowardly mad dog that would use a female in that manner. He came across plenty of worthless scum who deserved a blue whistler through the forehead for mistreating a helpless woman, including his father.

Arriving at Mrs. Goss', he tethered his horse to a hitching block and walked the yard to the porch to knock on the door. The landlady answered.

"Morning, Mr. Slade."

He walked in and tipped his hat. "Miz Goss, I've brought the funds for Miss Phoebe's needs." He pulled a drawstring pouch from his vest pocket. "How much cash is required for a fortnight's worth of supplies?"

She looked thoughtful for a moment. "Miss Jackson doesn't eat much, but mother and child need to be fed, so three dollars should suffice."

He placed four Liberty Dollar silver coins in her palm. "Here's an extra dollar in case something is needed later."

"I'm grateful, Mr. Slade. It's a kind thing you do for Mr. Jackson and his younger sister. Poor girl. Her family disowned her for something that wasn't her fault."

"Yes, a sad thing. I'll say hello to Miss Phoebe now and leave."

Mrs. Goss stared at him through spectacles that sat on the end of her nose. "I was hoping you could stay a little longer?"

Andelacio nodded. "Next time, Miz Goss, I'll allow more time. The ranch is short of help today. I will stop in a minute though." *And I'm just helping my friend.* He left the landlady standing and found his way down the hall to the parlor door.

Lasso stood in the hallway. He was finding it a challenge to see the slender woman as just Randy's sister. He had only known two pretty women personally: Mrs. Sullivant who owned the Eberly Ranch and her cousin, the wife of the ranch manager at the Eberly Ranch. Phoebe was *that* kind of woman. She lit up a room with her smile.

Pausing at the door, he looked her up and down. Despite her gown's failure to hide her pregnancy, her movements beneath a soft rustle of fabric displayed the lithe elegance of youth.

"¡Cuán feliz me haces!" he whispered. But no matter how happy she made him, he had to keep control; otherwise, there'd be some serious explaining to do.

Phoebe heard a sound, and then gestured for him to enter. She offered her hand with an intake of breath as his thumb's light touch brushed her knuckles.

His mischief left her conflicted, spurring a twinge of guilt. She questioned whether her response was proper for a pregnant woman. Or, was it because she was alone and terrified or something else? He had to hear her heart beating, but his calm expression gave no sign. The likelihood it meant something was nil, so she ignored his behavior.

Lasso held her hand as she seated herself in the cherry wood armchair. He sat across from her in a matching chair and hung his Stetson on the back frame.

"Mr. Slade."

"Oh, no. Please call me Andelacio, Miss Jackson. Or Lasso." As the hands called him that, he'd grown used to the shortened version. "I dropped by to give Miz Goss part of the money your brother said to use for your care. I believe you and she have a better understanding of what will be necessary when, uh…the time comes. And there's more. I'll drop by next week to check." When she didn't reply right away, he wondered if, in her condition, he had made her uncomfortable. But when she replied, she sounded serene.

"You asked that I call you by your first name. So, Andelacio, you can't grasp how much I appreciate your devotion to my brother's request. I wish there were a way to repay you."

He arched his eyebrows. She was clever.

"No, *es molestia!* There's no need for repayment. My actions stem from empathy for others' hardships. Isn't it true that everyone needs care from others sometimes? Now that I have met the sister, a fine and lovely woman, it's even more important."

Phoebe blushed. Because of her upbringing, she had never received such praise before and was unsure how to continue with the discussion. Single and eight months pregnant, sitting next to a male, and near stranger, was no small thing. After one night of fearing death by an attacker, her denial eventually became grief, which was replaced with anger. *I have no friends because of a man. But that's unfair. This is Randy's friend.* And she did not want to be angry with him. She noticed he stayed expressionless other than his brown eyes under heavy black brows that were soft with kindness.

Under the filtered light coming through the ceiling-high windows, Lasso hoped he had calmed her anxieties. As he was just lending a hand to his friend, he thought it best to keep it simple to lessen her erratic mood. He watched her fingers pick at her skirt before meeting his stare.

"I-I-that's very kind of you. I admire your friendship with Randy."

On this visit, she noticed his worn pants and boots with spurs and that he'd been a complete gentleman instilling a sense of protection, without a trace of shutting her out in his manner. Resting a palm on her enlarged belly was a reminder of dreams of the past that would never come true in her future. Her mother preached, that *no man wants a soiled woman for a wife.* But she was confused. *Was she really soiled now from what she'd experienced, or simply ignorant?* And so much so, that she must live tucked away like a sorceress from the devil!

She tucked her anger into a box in her mind. She hated feeling this way and had no reason to feel bitter toward Mr. Slade. If Randy befriended him, she'd best do the same. There weren't many options.

"Oh, please! You praise me too much! But I am very grateful." She deliberately pointed the conversation away from herself. "May I ask what your position is at the Red River Ranch?" Born on a ranch, Phoebe was familiar with a cowboy's function, but curious about Lasso's business at Red River.

Lasso sighed as he had nothing to brag about. "Regular things, Miss Phoebe. Rope. Trail. Herding. Branding beeves." He shrugged. It sounded mundane even to him, but it'd become a life he loved.

"Call me Phoebe."

Lasso smiled. "Phoebe." *Why would she be interested in him?* He brushed away the dust that had settled on his pant leg. He ran his fingers through his hair and reached for his hat.

"Allow me to come again. And to answer your earlier question, that alone will be enough payment."

She gave him a small smile and walked him to the front porch. She watched him mount his horse and rein it away before she shut the door.

He didn't dare look back and didn't mean to be abrupt, but he could no longer trust himself.

CHAPTER TEN

Avoiding danger is no safer in the long run than outright exposure.

The fearful are caught as often as the bold." – Helen Keller

Grace at Red Oak

Two days later, after securing a room in the town of Waxahachie, Grace had searched four of six newspapers in the parlor of the boarding house. Bea refused to leave her lap, content to hide beneath the rattling newspaper spread across Grace's legs.

There were no ads she cared to pursue for employment. She penned a letter to Alice Ann to relay her whereabouts and put Bea in her room. The landlady gave her directions to the nearest post office. Once there, with her letter on the way, she stopped at a bulletin-board filled with flyers. Thumbing through them, she found a short handwritten notice hidden beneath others for an opening at the Bar J Ranch near Red Oak for a hired hand. Only twelve miles away from Waxahachie. Though Grace was unfamiliar with the name of the nearby ranch, she wanted to return a telegram about her availability. The postmaster gave her directions to the Western Union office.

The day after she applied for the job by telegram, she received a response. Because of her experience with cattle, the Bar J Ranch hired her stating her salary along with directions to the ranch. They arranged for a horse to be at the town livery for her to travel there.

Relieved to find employment, she packed her few possessions and took another train to Red Oak. Bea was fussy when stuffed once more into the knitting bag, but quieted down once they boarded the swaying train that ultimately rocked her to sleep. In what seemed not enough time, the screeching brakes of the train and the cat's cries startled the already jittery Grace. The car had few passengers, and she found herself on solid ground in less than a minute. Looking around, she was the only disembarking passenger.

She looked the town over on a short walk from the small train station to the main street. As the telegram explained, a horse was waiting for her to use at the livery. The ranch owner gave the hostler written directions for Grace's ride to the ranch.

With her bag strapped to the back of the saddle cantle, she turned the horse onto a narrow dirt road with no significant landmarks. After thirty minutes, a scorched and weathered wooden sign, nailed to a post with the letters Bar J branded on it by a hot iron, announced her arrival. *Oh, my. How desolate and neglected.* A buzzard seemed to have read her mind as it rose with a noisy slap of wings and flew away. She reattached the barbed wire gap to the post and closed it from the other side.

Before continuing on, in the distance she studied the broken strings of wire, deteriorating barns, and sagging boards around the corrals, suggesting financial hardship for the owners. It was deathly quiet.

In minutes, she mounted the porch with missing floorboards, and a spare, gray-haired woman greeted Grace at the front door. "Oh, you're Grace Madden! Please, come in, and let me show you to your room. You must be tired. Feel free to refresh yourself. I'll introduce you to Mr. Jackson when you're ready to discuss your tasks. Supper is usually served at six o'clock."

Grace liked that Mrs. Jackson considered her wellbeing. Happy to settle into one of four bedrooms in the main house, rather than a bunkhouse, she later met Mr. Jackson who went over her duties during Mrs. Jackson's preparation of dinner. While he was gruff in questioning her, she found the Jacksons were a kind older couple. Within a few days, her daily activities included inspecting the cattle, tending to the corralled horses, milking the cow, and feeding the chickens. One afternoon at the dinner table, Mrs. Jackson asked, "Grace? Was there any problem moving the cows to another pasture today?"

Grace shook her head. "No, ma'am. I just swung my rope and separated the steers from the cows, and they walked peaceably from one place to the other. Herding older calves back across the fence presented the greatest difficulty. I enjoyed working cattle again, even sang a few songs to them."

Burnett's head snapped toward Grace. "Gal, you be mindin' what you're doing around them cattle. You'll get yourself hurt." *Women working cattle. Hell. Never thought he'd see that.*

She looked around sharply. It was the first time he'd given her instructions. "Yes, sir, Mr. Jackson. I wouldn't want that." Behind his curtness, she heard his concern loud and clear. After a few days, she learned not to give his words of warning much thought.

Finished with the noon meal, she returned to work and saddled the best horse in the corral to ride to Red Oak for supplies. She tied a crocker bag to the saddle horn to fill with a bag of nails, a bag of flour, and udder balm for the milk cow.

During the long, dull ride into town, Grace became curious whether a relationship existed between the elderly Jacksons and Randy, but she'd never ask. Thinking about answering their questions made her flinch, especially, if they asked how they knew one another.

Still having no friends in town, where and how long she stayed in one place depended on when Alice began sending monthly payments to Grace's bank for the dairy. She wasn't thinking of leaving. It was a peaceful place where she worked at her own speed, not bound to any specific activity at any specific time.

The outskirts of Red Oak came into view. Though she hadn't met many of the towns' people, it was a meeting place on the road where farmers and ranchers bought goods, went to church, and pitched horseshoes under the oaks. After tying the horse to a hitching rail, she tossed the empty bag across her shoulder. Grace dragged her heels across the floorboards and gave Mr. Sam a list. She strolled through the narrow aisles to see other items. Her small bag of clothes was causing her to wash daily. When she saved enough money, she wanted to buy another pair of trousers and a shirt. She paused at a stocked rack five shelves high. One particular thing caught her eye. The leather chaps hanging from a shelf brought Randy to mind.

Grace removed her hand from the soft nap of leather when she heard loud swearing on the other side of the tall rack. She stooped to the lower shelf and looked through. Two pairs of men's boots, scuffed and well worn, came into view through the opening.

One set of boots walked away and came back, their owner's voice loud and crude with annoyed curses. "To hell with this hole. He ain't got nothing here we need. I'm ready to do our business and leave."

"Just never mind, Carlisle. I'm thirsty. Let's see if there's some beer in this damn hole of a town."

The dusty boots had spurs attached over the heels, and red stitched stovepipe tops. She bit her tongue. Those boots were unforgettable. Petrified to see them in Red Oak in the same store, she prayed they and the man wearing them stayed on the opposite side of the shelving. She stood and turned to the wall to hide her face.

She pressed a knuckle to her lips wondering if he trailed behind her. Then, his words echoed loudly and she recollected the source of that unmistakable voice. At the hotel. A stranger spoke to her on the elevator and then boarded the same train. Confounded about why he was in Red Oak and why it was the third time she'd seen him, she held her breath in fear of his presence in the small store. *Why is he here? Is he following me?* No reason came to her mind. *Dear God, just get me home safe!*

Over her shoulder, she saw he was dangerously close to the shelves now. A hat covered with dust sat low on his head. His, and his friend's comments, were mirthless. After what seemed an hour, she heard the metallic jingle of spur rowels ring across the store, with the related dense thud of heavy steps moving toward the door. With her hand over her mouth, she waited for the two to exit the building, afraid of attracting attention. As the glass rattled in the slammed door, she then took in a large gasp of air as relief washed over her.

Though she knew the men were gone, her heart still thrummed. She forced herself into the open to peek through the front window. *What if he's... coming after me?* Had she known that the town of Red Oak was a hiding place for outlaws, she never would have answered the note for a ranch hand in that area. Not that she knew he was a cattle thief, a crook, or anything like that. Her biggest concern was that it seemed an improbable coincidence to run across the man in the fancy boots three times.

The two men were out of sight. She pivoted to find Mr. Sam waiting at the counter with her order. She calmed her breathing and approached his cash register.

"Alright, Miss Grace. Anything else I can fetch for you? I heard a rain was coming, and you might stock a few more things today to help carry you and the Jacksons over till the storm leaves." Mr. Sam took the money from her trembling hands and rang it up.

"We don't need more, Mr. Sam. I think we'll get by fine." She smiled cutting the conversation short. With the full croker sack in hand, Grace peeked through the window again to assure herself the outlaws were gone. At the hitching rail, she wrapped the bag's rawhide string to her saddle horn and placed a foot in the stirrup. She kept a watchful eye until she passed the last building out of town.

Regardless of why he was in the vicinity, as soon as she saved fifteen dollars, she'd buckle a Colt single action revolver around her waist. Old Mr. Jackson would have to teach her how to use it.

As she rode toward the Jackson spread a distant echo of thunder broke the deafening silence. Black clouds were gathering over the hills. The air weighed with the odor of moisture and decomposition, heightened her gut reaction of impending danger. Looking over her shoulder, she was afraid he might follow her, but no one was in sight.

Though it looked as though she was safe, her mind was in a fog. A growing unease urged her to go back to Annona. Better than buying a pistol, once she received her next wages, she wanted to be gone from Red Oak.

As the storm passed without a sign of rain, she relaxed in the saddle and released a sigh of relief when the sun popped out again. However, her attempt to avoid thinking of the red flowered boots failed, leaving her with so many questions. *Why are you even in this part of Texas? You have to go home!*

Her angst jumped higher as Randy would be there. She'd been waiting on him her whole life. Feeling her love unreturned and her struggles fruitless, she sought solace and guidance in prayer, hoping for a way to move forward.

The shuffling steps of the unshod horse and the little dust whirls that disappeared in the breeze interrupted her thoughts. She stopped at the ranch gate as she surveyed the sprawling acres and the outbuildings in need of repair. Stymied by the reason the ranch had fallen on tough times, she sighed. For sure, the red boots' appearance in Red Oak had shaken her, and so badly, the plans she had for future traveling were ending at the Bar J.

She, like the Jacksons, needed to learn that longing for the impossible is a futile waste of time. But like her, they loved something they had lost control of. Like her, maybe it was time for them to sell out and move to town.

Grace searched the stark beauty of her surroundings. Staring at the purple hues in the sky, she'd not noticed until now how much she'd ignored around her. A pale spark of realization made her dread a future weighed down by missed opportunities. It was then that she realized she was reliving the same old tale.

Tired of running from her problems, she lifted her chin, knowing no one could help her except herself. Unsure of her path, she knew she must stop fretting over a man. As soon as she put away the contents in the croker bag, she'd finish her chores, take supper in her room and, hopefully, decide which road was the best to travel. Definitely someplace where she'd never see red boots again.

CHAPTER ELEVEN

Guess What.

Lasso & Phoebe

Lasso knocked on the front door several times with no answer and worried about a possible incident. He balled up his hand and pounded it until he heard the lock turn. The landlady's flushed face appeared as if she'd been running.

"Mr. Slade! Thank goodness!" Hustling him into the house, she slammed the door shut.

Alarmed, he removed his hat. "It took so long to answer my knock, I was afraid something had happened."

"Something has happened! A little one is on the way! Head to the kitchen and wash."

His brow wrinkled. "What?"

Releasing his sleeve, she wagged a finger in his face. "I don't have time for stuttering! I need you to help me deliver this baby!" She scanned his hickory shirt, galluses, and rough trousers as if qualifying him for a nurse assistant. It satisfied her he was, at the very least, clean.

Andelacio backed away, his face ashen. "No, I can't!"

"Yes, you will *do as I say!*" Her voice was shrill. "You ain't the one having it, Phoebe is. And if she's capable enough to have it, a man ought to be capable of holding the hot water! Go ahead." She prodded him along with a pointed finger in the back. "After you've scrubbed up, bring it to me from the stove. We're in the right-hand bedroom at the end of the hall."

Unnerved, he found his way to the kitchen, slapped his hat on the kitchen table surface, and began to wash his hands in the sink. After restarting a roaring fire in the wood stove, he looked for something to safely grab the pot of boiling water.

What the hell? Miz Goss ain't going to scald the poor kid, is she?

He had never delivered a baby unless you counted calves. Though beyond his skills and capabilities, he *was* able to run errands for Miz Goss to make things simpler for her.

And Phoebe. With her in mind, he would bend to Mrs. Goss until the ordeal was over. Finding a dishtowel to wrap around the hot pot handle, he trudged along the hallway.

Surprised that Phoebe was alert and smiling, he sat the water on a side table and stepped back.

"Come over here, boy, and be useful. See this big spoon and this stack of towels? Rinse the spoon in the water and dip a towel in the pot to sterilize it. Set the spoon on it, and heat another towel. Then, stand right there in the corner in case you're needed again."

Andelacio did as she said, happy to be dismissed, and shuddered when Phoebe groaned through gritted teeth.

Mrs. Goss reached under the covers. "It's moved a ways, and I don't think it'll take long now. Mr. Slade, please fetch the sheets from the cabinet in the hall."

Lasso fled the doorway to retrieve the linens, happy *Captain Goss* didn't grab him by the ear. He took a deep breath before entering the labor room and, avoiding looking at Phoebe, handed the sheets to Mrs. Goss. "She needs a fresh gown, too. It's in the other bedroom, at the top of the stairs."

Galloping up the stairs, he searched through drawers until he found what he needed. He held a long gauzy white piece of cotton with lace around the low neckline and not much else to shield a woman's body from staring eyes. A momentary vision of her wearing the transparent garment flashed in his head before selecting a more conservative gown.

Given his experience as a seasoned cowboy helping with calving, he understood the challenges a woman faced. Water, blood, and the placenta were messy events. But this was Phoebe. He calmed himself. Lucky for him, it appeared Miz Goss had experience with delivering babies. It didn't seem such a major chore for a cow. He wiped a bead of sweat from his forehead and slapped the drawer shut, hurrying his way back to the bedroom. Now, Phoebe was panting through clenched teeth, clutching the sheets in both hands. She uttered a low growl and whimpered. The sound cut Lasso to the core, raising his anxiety. He hated seeing her in such pain.

"Hand me a hot towel," barked Mrs. Goss.

Andelacio dipped the cloth in the steaming water and turned his head to give it to her. Mrs. Goss grabbed it and put her hand beneath the sheets.

"Honey, you relax. The hot compress will help ease the pain. It's not much longer before your baby is here. That's it. Breathe in and out."

Phoebe cried out startling Lasso. Utter uselessness humbled him, unsure of what to do without being told. Clinching his jaw, every sound that she made put him on edge. He couldn't help ease her pain or make this ordeal any smoother than what he was doing. He just had to accept it and keep at it, following Miz Goss' directions as she yelled for him to grab and hold things for her. He rolled his shoulders, praying the child was fine, its mother, too.

"Push, Phoebe, push. The baby's coming. Bear down."

A yawl, similar to a baby panther's, broke the silence. "Aw. You've got a baby boy!" Mrs. Goss glanced at the helpless cowboy standing nearby. "Mr. Slade, I'd appreciate your wringing out and folding more towels in the kitchen for cleaning up. I'm going to cut this cord now." She raised her hand, managing the shears. "There we have it!"

Happy to be doing something, Lasso obeyed. When he returned, the small, but efficient landlady, had cleaned the infant and wrapped him in a clean towel. "Here, hold him."

Lasso wasn't sure he could hold such a tiny human without harming it. Cautious of its fragility, he took the baby in his arms.

He focused on his crinkled little face with a fist already in his mouth, a smattering of dark hair, and squinty eyes, and was bewildered by his whimpers. Not knowing why, a mix of joy and marvel swelled his chest.

"Mr. Slade, please leave the room with the child and close the door behind you. I need to make Miss Phoebe comfortable." Satisfied he wasn't near, she went to work on Phoebe, ensuring she passed the last of the placenta and checking the flow of blood. "A sweet baby boy. You must be proud! He's a beautiful child."

Phoebe raised her head. "I'm still hurting, Mrs. Goss."

"A natural occurrence after birthing. You'll be fine in two or three days." Mrs. Goss shook her head in admiration. "Child, you did well. Let's clean you up and change your linens and gown. Then you can hold your son. Have you considered a name?"

Mrs. Goss pushed Phoebe onto one side, then onto the other to remove her gown and pull the clean one over her head. "No. I haven't given it much thought. I didn't know he'd come this soon."

"Well, there's no rush. You're set for now. You don't need to be alarmed if we have to change you again. You've gotten through the worst, but expect more blood and fluid." She turned to the door and called loudly, "Come in now, Mr. Slade."

Lasso held the tiny child against his chest, mesmerized by the way his little arms flailed and his elfin face beamed with purity. The child's unfocused eyes darted, taking in the sights, sounds, and new environment. The doting cowboy felt the warmth and weight of the child against his chest, absorbing the scent of innocence and new beginnings. The baby made funny sounds that melted Lasso's heart. Back in the room, Phoebe reclined on two pillows, her hair brushed, held by a blue ribbon. This time, he thought his heart might burst. He passed the infant to his mother.

Phoebe looked at the disheveled cowboy. Andelacio wasn't smiling, but his expression was one of amazement.

Their moments together had been brief, but Lasso had a burning necessity to safeguard Phoebe from further harm. He pulled a chair closer to the bedside and sat. No training existed for navigating this road. He would have to let it unravel one step at the time.

Now Phoebe's face was burning hot. She felt vulnerable and embarrassed that a man and a friend of her brother's had actually been in the same room during her worst moments. She was fighting back the tears, swallowing several times while smiling at her son.

Lasso left the chair and kneeled beside her. *Madre Marie!* "Mi amor. I know it's been only a day or two, but I can't help myself. You are as beautiful as the moon and the stars. I will kill the devil who did this if your brother hasn't killed him already. Do not fear the future. I am a poor cowboy, but I promise if you accept me, I will move the heavens to take care of you and your little one." He rambled. He feared she thought him insane and was speechless, afraid of her reply.

Phoebe shifted the baby in her arms and fumbled for Lasso's hand. She sobbed quietly. She'd been holding her emotions—the fear, the hate for the attacker, the way her parents treated her afterward—for many months. Without a handkerchief, she loosened her grip on his hand and wiped her eyes with a sleeve. She smiled, sniffing between words. "I have found your name's meaning. Andelacio. It means compassion, inspiration, and that you are perfect."

He stroked her hair before leaning forward to kiss her on the cheek.

"It's only been a short time, but I already know I love you, and I accept you as you are. Now, we must part, *mi Vida*. Our friend, Miz Goss, will be back, and we must behave as if nothing has happened between us. I'd not have you suffer any gossip or mistrust of any kind. If our feelings are the same, for now, they stay just between us. I must find a means of support for you and the baby. Cowhands are not wealthy. We will be married if you say yes. No, no, not now.

I do not expect an answer until you have time to think about it. But I will protect you and the child always."

A veil of peace fell across Phoebe's shoulders at Lasso's words. How could this be happening? How could a stranger love someone he'd just met and in her condition? For now, it didn't matter. All she knew was she had a cowboy who cared for her and would protect her with his life. He was Randy's friend, a mysterious handsome man who loved her.

He offered to hold the baby, and they put themselves in order. He sat back in the chair. Unable to return to Mexico and wanted by the law, how would he support a family while working as a ranch hand? He would pray for an answer.

Phoebe decided not to dwell on his proposal any further. She knew what her answer would be. She'd lived through it and had a family. Mrs. Goss, Lasso, and the baby were her family. And Randy. Her brother and she were a comfort to each other through all their childhood difficulties. Wishing he were there, happy tears wet her cheeks.

CHAPTER TWELVE

An Unexpected Recourse

Randy at Red Oak

From the two week old postmark on Grace's letter, Randy wagered that she was likely still in Red Oak. After checking out of the hotel, several hours later on the outskirts of Dallas, he slapped his rented buggy horse on the rump with a rein to urge him into a faster gait. Red Oak was about eighteen miles from Dallas, and his calculations said he'd be there in about four hours.

By mid-afternoon, the largest part of Red Oak looked unchanged. Several older buildings in town had burned to the ground over the years, he thought, as a new bank and a dry goods store had taken their places. When he stepped from the buggy, he grimaced from a stiff back, eyeing a small wooden building. Before entering the Red Oak post office, he stretched with a groan.

He went inside, intending to question the locals. Someone could have a clue related to Grace. He knew that thought was absurd. He'd be lucky if he found her at all.

Alone in the post office vestibule, he waited on the mail clerk who finally looked up from his desk.

"Yes, sir. Do you need help?"

"I'm searching for a missing person. As post office personnel, I guess you see lots of folks."

The clerk's eyes widened. "Are you a Marshall, sir?"

"No. A friend asked me to inquire about his sister. She traveled through this stretch a while back. He's worried about her." Randy wasn't sorry for spreading the little white lie. No one needed to hear the actual story.

"Well, what can I do for you?"

"Let me describe her; it might jog your memory about whether she was here. She's about this tall." He held his hand mid-chest. "Her hair is a light brown, and she has turquoise-colored eyes."

"Turquoise?"

"Sort'a."

"Sorry. I'd be more helpful, but I'm new here." He rubbed his chin. "I ain't seen no lady of that description. I think I'd remember turquoise eyes. Someone else in town might've seen her. If there's nothing else you need, we're closing now." The clerk turned away with a smirk.

The unfriendly remark caused Randy's features to harden. Things hadn't started well. A deep breath helped calm his temper. He turned on his heel exiting the door before he changed his mind.

Back on a narrow dirt road, Randy drove toward the ranch. Whether the ranch house survived, he had doubts about stopping there. He didn't want any problems with his pa. The ranch became a financial burden about the time Randy turned thirteen. It was then that his father became abusive. He burned Randy's ears with scathing words until he felt ashamed for being born. And his mother never said a word.

Because he'd had no one else, his only remaining source of solace was Phoebe. It wasn't easy to leave her behind, but at sixteen, he had no choice. Now a grown man, he'd have no patience for the old geezer's foolishness. He pressed his lips against gritted teeth, bracing to receive the anger from his father for running away from home eight years ago. Tired of mulling over the past and giving himself a headache, Randy sped up the horse with a slap of the rein on its rump.

In a few miles, he stopped to give the horse a rest and to stretch his own legs. Wondering through the tall waving stems of Indian grass, he doubted he'd find Grace.

Why should I care?

She left of her own free will, and here I am, all reared up for her like one of Mr. Sullivant's stud horses.

Still pissed, and not fancying driving on, he mounted the buggy seat and told the horse to walk. He ran a restless thumb back and forth across the smooth harness leather reins woven through his fingers. With nothing but miles of grass and fence, he rested his elbows on his knees. Still, the scenery seemed familiar in the middle of nowhere. Then, in the quiet surroundings, the sound of an approaching horse caught his attention. Looking over his shoulder, a man was riding wildly, flailing a gun in his hand. Then, a bullet exploded from its barrel.

Baffled, Randy reached for his own gun, but he hadn't belted it on. He slapped the horse with the reins. Spooked, it jumped into the harness forcefully, throwing Randy backward. Catching his balance, he reached to retrieve the revolver from beneath the seat and managed the horse at the same time. A minute later, with the gun in his hand, he squatted low, leaving it to the horse to stay on the straight-away path, as he aimed at the shooter.

When Randy's shot blazed past the outlaw's head, the distance between them widened. He either wounded the gunman or he was a coward. Randy kept his horse at a slow gallop for a half mile.

When he was sure no one was following him, he pulled on the reins to slow the horse to a walk. Wiping his sweaty hands on his pants, he occasionally checked behind the wagon. No one was following. Fear had strange effects. Now, he was afraid of being killed before finding Grace.

Finally, at the Bar J, a sagging barbed wire gap prevented Randy's passage. The sun had reddened his face, and his mouth was dry. He stopped to take in his surroundings, hardly recognizing where he was. The Bar J looked haunted. Sage grass grew hip high in places, and it appeared a windstorm had upended several mesquite trees. Overgrazing had damaged parts of the pastures, and the fences were in terrible shape.

After releasing the wire gap to continue across the property, and then stretching it back into place, he cued the horse with a rein. Still unnerved by the shots fired at him, his hands trembled. Dusty corrals, and the enormous barn waiting for the wind to blow the structure over, spoke fully. Then, he saw the distant house, hoping it fared better than the barn. He wondered if his parents were even still alive.

Now parked in front of the house, he tied the horse to a post. He paused to survey the porch and stepped over the rotten boards. The front door paint had peeled away. He hesitated to knock, leery of what or who might answer if anyone. The place was silent as a tomb except for the rattling mesquite branches that clacked in the wind. If he were still a child, the noise would be enough to frighten him into running away once more. Randy fisted his hand to knock, but the door squeaked open. His mother stood there.

Her hair had streaks of gray, and her detached expression said she didn't recognize her son. "Mother?" he whispered.

"Randy?"

"Yes, it's me, Ma. Can I step inside?"

She looked confused as if she didn't understand. She swung the door open, and he stepped into a room that remained unchanged, only saturated with sad memories from the past. Randy glanced around in the gloom to find his father seated in one of the parlor chairs.

"Who is it, Rachael?"

"It's Randy."

"Who?"

His mother yelled at Burnett. "Your son, Burnett! Randy!"

Randy pushed back his hat wondering if his pa had gone deaf.

Burnett reached for a cane propped against the chair and struggled to stand. Slowly tapping his way to the door, he stopped within inches of Randy's chest, level with Burnett's nose. He reached toward his son and landed a hand on his shoulder, kneading it as if searching for evidence of his offspring who'd grown in height, width, and maturity.

"It's me, Pa. I came this way on business and thought I'd stop by. It's been years since I left here."

"Randy?" Burnett croaked. His thin hair and stubble beard had turned gray, and he needed a haircut. "Oh, my boy!" Attempting to wrap his arms around Randy, he started sinking to the floor.

Randy grabbed his father by the arms. The cane fell as the man Randy hardly recognized, beat him on the shoulders with his fists. Randy patted his pa on the back. After helping him back to his chair, he turned to his mother. She took him in outstretched arms as her tears soaked through his shirt.

Any doubts about his self-worth, along with the guilt of never measuring up as a son, faded. Never did he expect this greeting from the two who had driven him and his sister away from their home. Unexpected tears stung his eyes. He wiped his eyes with his fingers.

"Here, son, sit here." Rachael pulled up a rocker close to his father's, and she fetched a dining room chair to make a circle facing each other. She reached for Randy's hand giving it a squeeze.

Randy scrutinized them, one after the other, but they didn't meet his eye. "What's happened here, Ma? Last I remember, this place was flush with cattle and crops. Did you get sick, Pa? Ma?"

"Worse than that. We weren't doing well when you and your sister were young. Won't do any good to say more about it 'cause it's over and done. I've regretted for years how my children left home early. No way I'd be able to make amends this late. But I have written a will." Burnett Jackson had been tough on everyone, but life had been tough on Burnett. Burdening his son with stories of past difficulties was not likely to make a difference in their relationship.

His sigh filled the room, making the hairs on Randy's neck stand out. *A will? So what? What was in it? Nothing but the time-worn house.* He believed from the ground up, a bank takeover was inevitable. Driving in, he noticed a few skinny scrub cows nearby. It entered his mind he should take them to market for his father. If other cattle existed, they were out of sight. When his father mentioned a will, he knew the Bar J visit would not be a quick visit. He might have to postpone his search for Grace. Nothing had gone as he expected. A will seemed doubtful, but if one existed, he believed it would contain only their personal belongings. He waited for his father's next words.

But Burnett just stared at a window. Lost in an earlier time. "Where's the cattle, Pa?"

"The Longhorns made it. Had to sell the rest of 'em to keep 'em alive. Half were diseased—tick fever, then rinderpest, took a large part of the herd six years ago."

"Tick fever?"

Burnett nodded his head. "I sold out in a hurry 'fore all the cattle died. That damned anthrax is a problem in the southwest. Thank God we missed that one. There was barely enough money to replace some of 'em."

"So you and ma quit raising beef cattle?" Randy listened to his father with interest. His guarded temperament was gradually shifting towards acceptance of his parents' attempt to be civil. The conversation remained calm, with no rebukes.

"Naw, we didn't. We did our best but found no decent help. The hired hand ran off after one to two weeks. The girl we hired worked as hard as any man. Least she tried."

Upon hearing that a woman had been working there as a ranch hand, Randy jumped to his feet. Towering over his father, he asked, "Was she about this height, blue eyes?"

A man's voice pierced the air, devoid of its boyhood cadence. A stranger replaced the boy he once knew. Burnett's lip trembled. "I-I'm unsure."

"Randy," his mother interrupted, her hand on his arm, "she was a young thing. Said she owned her own dairy farm once. Her name was Grace something, I forget. Chores and working cattle weren't no problem for her." Rachael Jackson studied the tall stranger.

"What makes you–" Then she saw the disappointment etched in his face and understood. He hadn't dropped in on purpose to see them. He was looking for a girl. Wherever Randy had traveled from, she couldn't think of a good reason he'd roam across Texas. Unless he loved her.

"Damnation! Sorry, Ma, for the language." Rachael gave him a small nod. "She's a friend, umm, I've been looking for. She sent a letter to a mutual friend that was postmarked from Red Oak. That's why I came this way," he said lowering his voice. "I can't understand…"

Though she hadn't seen her son in years, the letdown in his voice was plain. "Well, son, the girl acted afraid, like someone had threatened her. No one lives around here for miles except for…" She cut her sentence short. In the area, there were cattle thieves and gunslingers, but as Randy had just come home, she preferred not to mention them. "Anyway, she said her goodbyes and she's gone. We don't know where to."

His experience on the road with a shooter made him acutely aware of Rachael's words. His mother likely hesitated to mention the outlaws near Red Oak, fearing he'd leave if she did. Since it had become a common thing, perhaps Grace had a good reason to quit and leave the area. The recent arrival of violent men in the area left him on edge. "Someone shot at me coming here. Is that why she was afraid? A gunslinger in the region?"

Shocked hearing that her son could have been killed, Rachael looked at Burnett and lowered her head, unable to say more.

Burnett shook his head. "I don't know. A man worked here before she came. Could'a been him. He wasn't no cowhand. That drifter was a thief. He was here a month ago. Later, I noticed cattle were missing. The law ain't good here, and I didn't want no trouble out of the bastard. Sorry, Rachael. So, I told him we didn't need him anymore. We ain't seen him since then."

"I reckon that's good. The owl hoots gone. Or it might have been him target practicing on me. How could it get any worse, Pa? I'm sorry y'all went through this."

"Randy," his father whispered.

He looked at his father and remembered him as the man he used to be. His voice reflected who he had become. And everything that had happened since he'd left home. "What in the hell can I do, Pa?"

"In case we never meet again, I need to tell you something 'fore you go."

Randy shot a look at his mother. It must be something important. She was sitting on the edge of her chair. "What is it?"

"After you and Phoebe... oh, God." Burnett sobbed into his hand. After a moment, he collected himself and continued.

"I realize it looks bad, this place, the cattle, the entire operation. But it's yours, son. Every bit's paid for and in my will."

Randy opened his mouth and shut it, speechless. He looked from his mother to his father. "How? How did you manage? Look at this place. It's falling apart."

Rachael reached over and squeezed her son's hand. The strength in his fingers stirred a memory of a little boy's hand she once held. Her voice caught in her throat. "It looks this way because we saved every penny to pay off the mortgage for you and your sister. The place is in your name, Randy. Your pa and I trust you will do right by Phoebe. She never cared for ranching. She's more of a city lady, I think." A tear tracked her cheek, and she swiped it away. "Is she okay? I mean..."

"She's fine, Ma. The baby'll more than likely be born before I get back to Red River."

Rachael's lips formed a downward smile.

"Red River. Is that where you got off to?"

"Yeah, Pa. I started off as a ranch hand, a cowpuncher. Then, I became interested in mechanics, and Mr. Sullivant, my boss, sorta promoted me to repairing the balers and equipment, plus the Buick."

"Burik?"

"Yeah. There are a few trucks, too. He's still in the cattle business, but his wife's set on raising race horses."

"I would'na minded raising a few cow ponies myself. Randy . . ." His father swiped his eyes with a handkerchief. "I've never said it. But, I'm proud of you, son, and the man you are. I wish..." His father stopped talking.

Randy sighed. Burnett was old and helpless. While he expected his bitterness to turn into anger, his travels and the passing years had mellowed him. As he grew older, he became weary of conflict with anyone. Besides, nothing was the same since he'd stepped into the house. And, his parents' ruination caused mostly by bad luck wasn't something he reveled over. How his parents kept the ranch was a miracle.

"It's alright, Pa. That time is over and gone. Everyone has their struggles. I started not to stop by, but I guess it's best for us I did. I have a lot of questions, Pa. What was your hand's name before Grace?"

"His first name was Robert. I don't recollect the last name of that worthless son-of-a-bitch. Sorry, Rachael."

Long used to Burnett's foul language, Rachel gave Burnett a reproachful look and touched her son's knee. "Randy, we have a little pork left. Will you stay for supper?"

Randy studied his boot toe for a second. "They got a telephone in Red Oak?"

"At the bank. It don't work most of the time."

"Yes, Ma. I'll stay. Tomorrow, I gotta reach my boss and let him know I'll be delayed. I'll take a chance that he'll have me back, considering I said I'd be back in a week. Now, I don't know."

Overjoyed that her son was staying, Rachael went to the kitchen to start their supper. Randy and Burnett moved to the porch step to sit in the breeze.

"Randy, I ain't got no money to help get this place back on its feet."

"Don't worry about that now, Pa. We'll figure out how or when, and when it does, I want your advice."

Burnett's face crumpled.

"It's gonna work out." Randy put his arm across his father's shoulders.

Burnett craned his neck to look his son in the face, "How?"

"I don't know. It just will. You, me, and Ma will bring it back to where it was. Until I return, I want y'all to live here now. Shoot, forever if you want. It's your place, too. Always will be. If you don't mind, I'm gonna clean up. I figure I'll have a pretty busy day tomorrow."

* * *

The next day, Randy sent a telegram to William Sullivant:

I have not yet found Grace Madden. I stopped by the family ranch. Parents aren't well. May have to stay awhile to get them on their feet. I understand if you have to fill my position. Will send another message when I'm able to leave for Red River.

The second telegram went to Lasso explaining his delay:

Ran into various problems. Unable to return yet, as originally planned. Please continue to watch over Phoebe. Someone took a shot at me outside of Red Oak. I may need your help. Something's not right here. I'll keep in touch.

Satisfied the messages were on their way to the intended parties at Red River, Randy drove through the Red Oak streets in search of lumber. Surely, there was a supply of lumber somewhere close by for patching up the barn. He stopped at a mercantile.

"Yes, sir. Drive a mile out of town that way," he pointed, "and you'll see a large area of felled timber. There's a portable sawmill there where the owners can set a price and cut planks for you."

Randy thanked him, then spun around. "I forgot to ask if you sell glass."

"Back this way, Mr.—"

"Jackson." Randy followed the store owner, putting him on his list of helpful citizens. You needed those kinds of friends when credit was involved.

"Are you from this area, Mr. Jackson?"

"Yes, sir. My father is Burnett Jackson."

The clerk turned to shake Randy's hand. "Of course. I remember you! You were just a kid back then."

"Yes, sir. That's right. And you're Mr. Sam. I'm glad to see you. As long as I'm here, Mr. Sam, I have a friend I've been looking for." Mr. Sam placed his hands on his hips, listening. "I once knew a woman who briefly worked at the Bar J. Then, disappeared. Did you know her?"

Recognition lit Sam's face. "Sure did. Miss Grace. The last time I saw her, she'd come in to buy supplies. Hadn't seen her since. She's a pretty woman, not from these parts, though. However, one thing stuck in my mind. That day, two hombres, bad ones, showed up. I thought they were going to beat the hell out of me. And I remember Miss Grace was awful cautious when she left the store."

Randy pieced it together. The same men had terrified Grace, too. "I appreciate the information, Mr. Sam. I have an idea they were the reason she cleared out of here."

Randy's eyes narrowed, hiding his fear for her safety. The elderly man started for the back of the shop. Unsure of the size, he bought a large piece and a blade to cut it if necessary.

With his purchases done and the wagon full of supplies, he turned the horse onto the dirt road. Overwhelmed by the many problems he faced and fearful that he may never complete his search for Grace, he let out a huff of disappointment. The opportunity to follow her while the trail was still hot was gone.

* * *

Four weeks had passed since Randy arrived at the Bar J. His father told him he was the owner now. His health no longer allowed him to manage the large acreage, and livestock, and keep up the structures that dotted the property. Randy's anger from his past waned after his father's apology. He wasn't a man who held grudges. The outlook for his future had changed.

The outlaw who took potshots at him might be the same lowlife who had stolen *his* cattle. And from what he'd been told, more trouble might erupt any time.

But at some point, he had to continue hunting for Grace, manage his parents and the ranch, and return to Red River. It wouldn't be right to leave Mr. Sullivant hanging wondering if he were returning. Grace was constantly in his thoughts. He thought his search for her had no ending, but, he needed to know more before he'd be ready to give her up.

Back to work the next morning, Randy worked for three days repairing planks on the porch, broken windows, re-hanging the barn doors, and other chores. His father, though unable to do much work, stayed at his side, making up the time they'd lost through the years. He sat on an old wooden chair in the barn's wide hallway, keeping up a conversation.

"Son, I started rebuilding the herd after the bovine diseases passed through. Wasn't long after I suspected my cowhand, Robert, rustled eight of the steers."

Randy stopped pounding a nail and glanced at Burnett. "And I suspect he's the one who took potshots at me, too."

His father started winding down after two hours. Through for the day, Randy lay down his tools and helped his father as they walked to the house. He prayed his sister would reunite with their parents. Then, she, too, may set aside the effects of the misery they had caused her as a young girl. Becoming grandparents could either make them more motivated to heal or create more challenges.

After leaving Burnett at the house, Randy rode out to check his cattle. Apparently, Grace had little trouble handling the herd. Seven to eight hundred head could be managed by one man, with two extra men to start restoring the ranch. Soon, he would invest in more cattle and more men. However, lots of hard labor had to be done before he'd be returning to Red River. Randy shook off any thoughts of the future. Today had enough problems.

CHAPTER THIRTEEN

Shoot Out at the Bar J Ranch

Randy

Time slipped away from Randy. He worked from dawn to dark on fencing, barns, and roofing, and guessed a month had passed. But, the herd of eight hundred cattle had priority, and he always rode out to check them twice a day. Rachael helped with a milk cow, a small herd of goats, and a coop of chickens.

Randy added the last of the heavy-duty door hinges to the rickety barn door. As he strolled past the barn, he saw unnatural colors moving through bushes and trees beyond the Bar J front gate, which was a compliment to the sagging wire stretched across the opening. When he saw a gray horse, it's rider wearing a red bandana, vanish into the woods, he shut the doors and windows of the barn. Then he circled its perimeter to shut and lock every building with a door or window that could serve as a hiding place for someone trespassing.

At the house, he fastened his gun belt and replaced the missing cartridges.

"Pa."

Startled, Burnett opened his eyes. "Son?"

"Are you sure the hand who worked here was rustling cattle?"

"Yeah, but I had no way of proving it. But it had to be him."

"Then, I think it's him I just seen riding through the brush. Do you still have your rifle and handgun?"

"All the guns are kept back there." He gestured toward the end of the hall. "Why? You expecting trouble?"

"Not sure. I saw men riding along the willows down the road. I couldn't tell which direction they were going. I want to be sure they ain't coming this way. Especially after you told me about Robert and the trouble he brought."

Burnett sat up. "You think he's dodging the law, hiding out around here?"

"Yeah, I do. Didn't you say the law here ain't trustworthy?"

Burnett picked up a spittoon and cleared his mouth. "They ain't worth a damn. Seen 'em turn the other way like they didn't see anything going on. And right under their faces!"

"Pa, you still pretty good with a rifle?"

"Don't know. Ain't used it for a while. But I'm game to find out."

Randy grinned back at his pa. "How's ma with a pistol?"

"I saw her hit a rabbit from thirty yards."

"Hmmm. I need to make a quick trip to Red Oak. While I'm gone, will y'all be able to hold down the fort till I get back?"

"Rachael!"

She hobbled into the room. "What is it?"

Burnett spoke up fast cutting off her complaints. "Randy thinks that thief Robert and his cohorts are watching the place. He needs to make a trip to Red Oak and wants to be sure we're able to take care of ourselves while he's gone. Can ya bring out the guns?"

"I'll try not to be gone more than an hour, Ma."

"Well, get going. I'll bring the guns from the back and we'll keep a lookout. Son, you be careful yourself out in the open."

"I will. I locked up the outbuildings as best I could. You lock the doors and windows."

Randy left the house and hot-footed to the barn to saddle a horse. Thinking they might set fire to the barn, he took a minute to turn the horses out of their stalls into the corral. Climbing into the saddle, outside he hid behind a corner astride his horse to survey the surrounding terrain. After a minute or two, he convinced himself that no one was nearby. With that assurance, he spurred the horse into a gallop to the gap. Making a quick dismount, the released barbed wire fell to the ground.

He rode as if he were in no hurry, trying to show he wasn't aware of the outlaws he saw earlier. Once in town, watching both sides of the road for signs of trouble, he tied his horse and entered the telegraph office.

Urgent message for Andelacio Slade of Red River Ranch. Please come. Hurry.

Need help. Take train to Red Oak. Send reply. I will meet you at station. Randy.

Upon returning to the ranch, he discovered everything was in order. His parents were still on guard, watching from the windows. They finished their normal tasks during the day, but he slept fitfully that night, waking at every sound.

He rode out again the next day to see if he received an answer to the telegram he sent to Lasso, which he did.

Two days later, he met Andelacio at the train station. After he mounted the horse Randy had brought along, they rode away from town. They shook hands when they were out of sight.

"I guess, you're wondering what this is about."

Lasso looked at him and grunted.

"You remember I told you about a girl? You suggested I should look for her."

His partner shook his head, his eyes narrowed with interest.

"I'll make it short, but it's a strange tale. My girl sent a letter to a friend postmarked from the post office at Red Oak. My family lives a few miles from here. Since I came down here for her and hadn't seen 'em in a while, I thought I'd stop by. On the way, I stopped in Red Oak, but hardly a soul in town recognized my description of her. Then, I found that Mr. Sam at the store knew her. He said Grace came in and while he was filling her order, there were a couple of fellas who walked into the store talking loud and mean enough to swallow nails. Grace stayed hidden behind the shelves until they left. Learning that, I headed on to the ranch, and an outlaw came chasing after me at full speed waving a gun. I reckon it was one of those men."

"He took a shot at you? Looks like he missed."

"Yeah. I ain't found no holes yet." With a lopsided grin, Randy exhaled smoke from his cigarette. "I returned fire, and he stopped dead chasing me. Don't know if I nicked him.

"Then, two days ago I was working in the barn 'cause my folks' ranch has fallen into bad repair. I glanced up and spotted three men riding through the brush on the hillside. You'd have to be blind not to spot the rowdy bandanas they were wearing. That's when I made sure my ma and pa still had guns in the house. Then I sent you a telegraph. Pa believes one hombre who worked at the ranch was stealing cattle. Seemed, the ones I saw riding the perimeter were watching the place. Maybe scouting to find the best time to raid the Bar J."

Lasso didn't reply. Randy wondered if he was listening. "Anyway, how'd Mr. Sullivant take it, about me being gone, and now you?"

"He told me to go. Friends are hard to find, he said. Cowhands are easier."

"Hm." Randy nodded not surprised. "The boss is a good man."

Close to the ranch, the two men fell silent, scrutinizing potential hiding places, searching for fresh horse tracks other than their own, and kept glancing behind them.

Standing at the wire gap, Andelacio saw Randy had not exaggerated about the ranch being in dire condition. New planks lined the barn's walls, catching his attention. The house porch, too, looked recently repaired. Randy told him to ignore the rifle barrel as Mr. Jackson removed it from the open window. As they sat on their horses, an elderly couple stepped through the door, guns aimed downward, and waved.

He waited while Randy told his parents they were going to put the horses up. His mother waved at Lasso as she turned to re-enter the house. His father was on her heels. Lasso fell in behind Randy and entered the big barn with a hayloft that held no hay. Randy, it appeared, had swept the barn's wide hall and nailed new boards to the horse stalls. Lasso dodged loose planks dangling from the loft where he dismounted his horse.

After graining the horses in the big pen, they made their way toward the house until Lasso put a hand on Randy's arm.

"Randy? I wanted to ask you in private—the girl you came to find?"

Randy propped his arms over the corral rail and took a deep breath. "I think I told you most I know. She mailed a letter postmarked with Red Oak to her friend. This was after she answered Pa's flyer for a ranch hand." He glanced at Lasso, who seemed unfazed by the bizarre sequence of events.

"Grace remained on the ranch for a couple of weeks. I asked some questions in town about her. The mercantile owner told me she was in his place and acted scared when two drifters came in. If she didn't know them previously, I don't know why she'd react that way. Somehow, I think it's the same man pa fired as a cowhand before Grace arrived here. Too, I believe that he's the same outlaw in each of these coincidences. Including trying to shoot me!"

Lasso nodded, seeing a link, too. "Where'd she go?"

"My folks don't know and neither do I. After things are under control here, I'll want to start another search. I have another thing I'd like to discuss with you. I'll bring it up later when times aren't so snarled up."

Though he'd not asked many questions, Lasso was curious about Randy's hint of something that needed further discussion and waited a few minutes to tell his own news. "I have something to tell you, Randy. Your sister has had a son."

"I'll be damned. I'm an uncle." Randy's eyebrows rose. "Are they doing okay?"

"Seemed fine to me, considering I know nothin' 'bout babies. The second thing is, I want to ask Phoebe to marry me."

Randy looked at Lasso unsure he heard correctly. But his dark eyes shone with intention and unwavering determination. "That's a big step for you, ain't it? A wife and her baby ain't nothing to kid about." If he didn't know Lasso, he would be more concerned.

"Who's kidding?"

"You're serious?"

Lasso nodded. "As serious as you are about finding your own woman. I love her. Your sister might have fallen off and landed hard, but she has a quiet determination to get back on.

"Don't know why she'd care for a broken-down nobody like me, but she does. I ain't asked her yet 'cause I've some planning to do before I can support the three of us." Randy raised his eyebrows, accepting the news better than Lasso imagined.

Randy was damned happy for Phoebe. "I may have beat you to that plan. We'll discuss it when we take care of the problem at the ranch."

Lasso frowned but decided to wait until later to find out about Randy's plan. "That's fair. Lead the way. Hope your ma is a good cook!"

At supper, Randy didn't mention the possible marriage of Pheobe and Andelacio. His parents finding for themselves the caliber of man he is, was the better choice. "Me and Lasso's going to the big barn where we'll hear better if anyone comes down the road. Pa, y'all should get a little rest before we return later tonight. We'll need to be awake if the devil shows up."

Burnett mumbled while retrieving his cane, and Rachael began clearing the table.

As night approached, the younger men retired to the barn and sat in their makeshift chairs. They drank a few gulps of corn whiskey and returned to the house for bed after midnight.

Following his impulses, the next morning Randy and Lasso rode out headed toward town, laughing and talking to alert anyone nearby they were leaving the ranch.

A half mile later, Randy cut to the right and followed a deer trail through the woods to circle back to the ranch. There, they dismounted and rushed into the barn, putting the horses in the stalls.

Watching through a barn window an hour later, his skin prickled when he spotted three men coming around the bend. They'd be through the gap in another five minutes. Lasso suggested Randy hide in the cow milking shed on the other side of the house. That way, if the gang started shooting, they'd be caught in the middle of the gunfire. Earlier, Randy helped his father settle in the outhouse with the rifle. His mother took cover behind the chicken coop.

With everyone in their place, Randy watched through the wall gaps in the milking shed. An urge to run shooting toward the outlaws quivered over him. But it was wiser to wait. The troublemakers slowed their horses, riding in at a walk, looking in every direction. A single whinny rang out from the barn while silence settled over the rest of the property. As one rider held the horses, the other two pounded on the door.

Any minute, hell was going to break loose. Randy checked his bullet supply again, and then a vision of Grace, as beautiful as a Texas sunrise appeared in his mind. *Grace, how'd I get myself into this mess? Where are you, girl? Pray for me. This might not end well. If I walk out of here, I'm coming for you, darlin'. And if I don't, God knows I've done everything I can.*

Each man walked a different side of the house, each one holding a weapon in hand. Shocked and incredulous, disbelief washed over

Randy as the scene unfolded. They came to kill his parents. *Where in the hell do men like this come from?* One rustler shot through the front door breaking the lock. A second later, another one fired a gun from the rear of the house. *From hell,* he answered himself. The two men sauntered through the house, returning to the front porch.

Lasso came from the shed in a slow walk, his rifle pointed toward the knot of men. "Hold it. You're under arrest for—"

He hit the ground when the outlaw still on his horse fired at him. Lasso fired back but missed, and the man spurred his horse into a run headed toward the road. Another shot rang out, he couldn't tell where it came from. A second explosion came, and one of the men on the porch fell wounded.

Andelacio stood up. "Drop your gun 'cause if my friend doesn't hit you in the back, I'll shoot your head off!"

Surrounded, the man dropped his gun to the ground. His battered hat brim covered his face as he stared at the ground.

"Get your hands higher! Higher!"

The outlaw stood, arms high in the air. He raised his head to meet Andelacio's stare.

Lasso stopped breathing. "Madre de Dios!" *It can't be.* But his memories didn't lie. He was ten years old again.

Andelacio dropped to his knees and wrapped his arms over his head. In a rage, the man standing over him drew his arm back and lashed the child over and over with a thick braided leather horse quirt. The long leather fringe on the end wrapped around Lasso's cheeks and nose that he couldn't protect.

A snarl crossed his father's lips. "You gonna shoot me, boy?"

His mother grabbed his father's arm. Livid, he turned and knocked her down and began using the quirt on her back. Lasso heard her screams and forced himself up. He grabbed the quirt, which was jerked out of his hand. His father drew back and slammed his fist into the boy's face. He didn't wake until hours later.

He had vowed to kill him his entire life. Deeply ingrained in his past, he was unaware of Randy and Rachael, standing in the sunlight beside the porch, holding Burnett's arms as he was too weak to stand on his own.

"You know this man?" Randy held his rifle in the crook of his arm. Adrenaline raced through his veins as he lowered his tense shoulders.

Spiritless, Lasso blankly looked at Randy, as he returned from his memories of violence. The outlaw's back faced the Sullivants. "Yes. I think first we need to get your folks settled back in the house. Next, we need rope to tie this murderer up."

"What about this one?" Randy nodded at the man lying on the ground.

"If he ain't dead, don't look like he'll be dancing soon."

Randy waved his parents into the house and left his mother to settle his father into a chair. He found strips of latigo cut for saddle and bridle repairs lying on a bench that were long enough to bind two arms. Back on the porch, he bound the man's hands behind him and swung him around to face him.

"Who is he, Andelacio?"

Lasso's nostrils flared. He wanted to do something terrible. Run away or lie. No love existed between him and the bearded asshole with a surly smile on his face. Shocked to see the man he'd hated for years, he began sweating and was breathless. He had no choice but to tell the truth. "He is my father."

Randy looked at the large man and then at Lasso. He could not put his friend and the fiend before him together as son and father. He cleared his head, ignoring the warm breeze brushing against his face and the distant sound of birds chirping in the background. Unwilling to make more of it than Lasso's simple confession, he

131

took a deep breath, filling his lungs. This had to be Lasso's decision about what to do with his pile of manure father who tried to shoot his son. He was sure he was the one who had frightened Grace in the mercantile. What if he was the man responsible for her disappearance into thin air, too?

"I heard you liked to shoot men in the back and frighten defenseless women."

"Go to hell."

A fire had been building inside Randy, and the poison bubbling in his brain ran over. Irrational, yet gratifying, he punched the murderous savage in the gut. "That's for my parents and this is from me. Dry-gulch bushwhacker!" He hit him under the chin falling him to the ground. "Where is she?"

Slade rolled onto his elbow to rest on his knees and bellowed, "Who?"

Randy knew he'd lost all self-control, but there was no time to analyze himself. His life had been regular to boring until Grace. His sister's problem, coupled with the overwhelming task of fixing the rundown ranch, was tempting him to run away again. But then, he despised people who took advantage of weaker ones. That was the flare that started the fire. He kicked the gagging criminal back to the porch floor. He glanced at Lasso. "I got an idea, if it's okay with you."

"Whatever it is, I'm in." Still in shock that his father had tried to murder the elderly Jacksons, Lasso's thoughts had scattered like chicken feed thrown into the wind. Without thinking, he grabbed Robert under his arms, and Randy helped to herd the duo toward the barn.

Randy's father kept one of his meanest bulls in a small enclosure next to the barn. His pa told him to stay out of the pen. The Brahman cross was too dangerous to handle unless you tied him down, and he refused to be herded, at least by an old man. Burnett planned to sell him one day if his health improved enough to get him to market.

Randy had use for the bull now. With the extra rope found in the barn, he created a loop and tightened it beneath Slade's arms. Facing the three men, the bull lowered its head and pawed the ground, sending dust swirling into the air. Next, he raised his muley head and let out a loud snort.

"Move him over here, Lasso."

Without a clue of what Randy was doing, Lasso shoved his father toward the fence where Randy had climbed to the highest rail to reach a pulley wheel hoist. He ran the end of the rope around the wheel, jumped down, and he and Lasso hoisted Slade over the fence and lowered him into the corral with the bull.

"What're you doing? Get me down from here! You're both loco!"

Lasso watched his father as he kicked and twisted, banging into the heavy rails of the corral. Despite his vow to kill him on sight, this wasn't how he pictured it.

The muley bull backed up a few feet watching the activity. Lowering his head, he pawed once and charged the dangling human in front of him. He hit Slade square in the butt swinging him through the air to slam into the fence.

Randy stood on the thick rails, yelling at the swinging figure. "What'd you do with the girl? I'll let this animal kill you if you don't tell me where she is!"

Slade, drooling saliva, bellowed, "I swear I know nothing about her! I saw her once on the road, but I never saw her again! Get me down!" He kicked in the air away from the fence alerting the bull again to his presence. The bull charged, throwing him out of the pen with such force that the rope jerked him back into the air, slamming him into the corral. "I don't know, I swear I don't know!" Blood was running from his mouth and several teeth were missing.

Randy thought he'd talk before the bull made a first move. He wanted Lasso's opinion first before the bull charged a third time. "What do you think? Is he still lying?"

"No, I don't think he's lying. He's too much a coward to let the bull hit him again."

"Is he why you ended up here in Texas?" Randy gave him a thin smile.

"He ran off before I could kill him. He'd beat my mother, then start on me. After she died, I got into some trouble 'cause I was a stupid kid. I left that part of my life behind."

Lasso's shoulders drooped. Randy gave him a slap on the shoulder and another crooked smile wanting to minimize the burden Lasso had to be experiencing. "Let's leave it in the past, partner. There's still another thing I want to discuss later."

Lasso jerked his head toward the house, mindful of Randy's encouragement. "Go take care of your family. I'll take the bastard to town for the sheriff to deal with."

"Pa said the sheriff wasn't much count. We may have to summon the Texas Rangers, but guess we better get him down before Killer makes another pass at him."

With a nod, Lasso looked at the sorry human dangling from the hoist and felt no remorse for the way they had treated him. His father was going to murder Randy's family.

Randy walked to the backside of the corral to open the gate leading to the pasture, hoping the Brahman bull would leave peacefully on his own. Once the bull was aware he was free to go, he trotted out the gate. "He's all yours. I'll be back in a minute. I need to check on the folks."

Lasso lowered his father and freed him from the rope. Slade tottered a few steps, then fell on his face. His son walked up and kicked him in the ribs. "Get up, asshole."

"I'll kill you, you little son of a bitch!"

"Get up and try."

"You were nothing but a nuisance, just like your momma—"

134

The rest of his sentence didn't make it off his tongue. Lasso hit him in the face with such force that his lip splattered, his nose bled, and blood was dripping from an injured leg where the bull had butted him with the force of a battering ram.

Slade struggled to stand. His arms freed, he staggered toward Andelacio, his hands curled into fists. "You do-gooder little bastard. I'll get you like I got that stupid little girl who lived here! You'll be a piece of raw meat!"

Lasso was unmoving, too stunned to reply. Slade took advantage of his son's conflicted pause and rushed him with fists swinging. Lasso fell to the left, drew his gun, and shot him in the chest, then he fired again to hit him in the groin.

He dragged himself to his feet and stared at the bleeding, motionless man lying on the ground. Something died within him, too. Without any forewarning before it happened, no feelings rushed to engorge his senses afterward. He'd killed a monster, but still his father. His mouth trembled, and he wiped his eyes. If he went to jail, he would do it gladly. He did what he swore he'd do if he ever found the man who hurt Phoebe. Still dazed, he realized he had to move. He holstered his gun and turned toward the house. As he sat on the porch steps, the reality of taking a life sunk in. Shame, grief, hate, and relief battled for dominance until he was reeling from what had happened. *Your own father.* Resolved to accept the outcome, he wiped his brow with his dusty sleeve. He jerked when the screen door slammed.

Randy stopped to stare at Lasso's back, slumped over with his hands between his knees, sure he'd heard a shot. He sat down beside him, waiting for Lasso to tell him about the gunfire.

"No need for a hanging now."

"What happened?" Randy caught only a whisper of his words.

"He jumped me and I-I—"

Randy's gut had kept him alive more than once and told him his friend wouldn't use his gun unless it was necessary. "No need to tell

135

me more. We did our best to stop them from murdering innocent folks." He patted his friend on the shoulder. They sat for a while longer. "You stay here. I'll take care of it. You've been through a helluva lot."

Lasso gazed unblinking, seeing nothing, until his voice broke, "I had a dream last night. About my mother. I couldn't tell where she was, but she looked at me, though I didn't see myself in the dream. She put her hands out and released a raven, black as sin. It flew straight at me. I heard myself yell." The omen had come true.

To make it worse, there was Slade's confession: he was the man who raped Phoebe. He would never forget his cold words nor ever reveal them to anyone, meaning no one could ever connect the two.

There was a long minute of silence where Randy searched for words that would help Lasso. "I'm sorry it ended this way." His voice was heavy with regret, and when he stood to go to the corral, it triggered an uncontainable outburst of emotion from Lasso.

With his Stetson off, he leaned over, his chin on his chest, and let the tears flow. The vivid memories of his mother's death, his abuser, and their shared suffering were overshadowed only by the enduring guilt he felt for killing his father; this guilt, he knew, would haunt him forever. He wiped his face and reached for his hat. "I must come with you." He had to help bury Robert Slade for the closure of his own wounds. And the secret he related to Lasso would forever lie in the grave with his father.

CHAPTER FOURTEEN

"New beginnings are often disguised as painful endings." — Lao Tzu

Randy & Lasso

The day after the shootout, Randy was woozy when he swung his legs to the floor. He balanced himself on the mattress with both hands palms down. The day before had taken a toll on his outlook on life and his resolve to act as though nothing had happened. He could only speculate on the turmoil Lasso must be having, while trying to align his actions with his moral compass.

He washed his face in the water bowl on the dresser and the nether regions, and put on clean clothes. Without further ado, he saddled a horse to ride to Red Oak to send another telegraph to William Sullivant explaining his and Lasso's delay in returning to the ranch. Per his promise to Lasso, he left out the tale of the rustlers. As the information would spread rumors about the shoot-out, it was their secret. After explaining that he had not found Grace, he informed Sullivant that he and Lasso had a short list of chores and repairs to do on the family ranch before heading to the Red River, maybe five days.

At the Bar J, Lasso poked at his breakfast, then shoved his plate away and went outside.

Later that morning when Lasso returned from checking cattle, Randy stepped from a ladder after nailing the last board needed to shore up the hay loft in the barn. Lasso had made himself busy putting the tack room back in order, and the saddles mounted on the walls instead of sitting on the floor.

Randy thought it time to present Lasso with a proposition as Mr. Sullivant may have given up on them returning to Red River.

"Hey, you got a minute?"

Work began at five a.m. Lasso shrugged. "Looks like it." Tickled to take a break, he sat with Randy on a large, exposed floor joist.

Randy spent the morning thinking about the way he wanted to approach Lasso with his ideas. A specific change in his outlook on life had appeared now that he owned something valuable. Mr. Sullivant's unassuming way of communicating with his hired hands was something Randy found admirable. Lasso was his friend, and he wanted to keep it that way.

"Lasso, you know that I trust you with my life. I assume you share the same sentiment. We'll never bring up the hell we faced here ever again. None of it. I want you to understand that. Coming here had positives despite the challenges. What I'm saying is this will prove beneficial to you, too. I didn't find Grace, but that doesn't mean I'll quit looking. I need to find her because my pa has willed the Bar J to me free and clear of debt. He wants me to come home and run it now."

Lasso leaned back, looking Randy in the eye. It'd be tough if the man he thought of as a brother gave up his job at the Sullivant ranch. Clearing his throat, he said, "I'm dumbstruck and glad for you!" Lasso slapped Randy on the back twice in congratulation. A sudden uncomfortableness tightened his chest. Did this mean the end of their friendship? If not for Phoebe, he'd ride up north to Montana if Randy quit the Red River.

"I'm returning to Red River and will stay awhile, if I haven't been fired yet. I'll search for Grace in that area, too. And I'll decide about my sister."

Lasso raised his eyebrows as his shoulder twitched. Though pleased for Randy, the comment about Phoebe left him perplexed; he nodded. "I already told you about Phoebe and my plan."

"I savvy. Just hear me out. When I return here, I want you to come back with me to be my foreman. For a while, it'll be you and me. We'll eventually build a place for you and Phoebe. If Mr. Sullivant hasn't fired us, I'd like to stay on at Red River long enough to find Grace, if she's back in Annona. After that, we'll be free to go—no matter whether I find Grace or not.

Lasso set his hat back on his head, not speaking for a minute, while turning the offer over in his mind. He had not yet formally proposed to Phoebe. However, working and living on the Jackson ranch could sway her decision. A cowhand was all he figured he'd ever be. After leaving home and crossing the border, he ventured through Texas, working for various cattle operations, small and large. He knew God was by his side. Though his young life had been brutal, a sizeable chance just came along for him. Given the circumstances, he found it impossible to decline such an offer.

"I'll do it."

Lasso stood facing Randy, his hand held out. "I'll do it."

After a minute, Randy believed Lasso was going to decline. Hearing his answer, he pumped his hand and slapped him on the shoulder.

"I need time to find Grace when we got back to Red River, but I have to get back here as soon as possible, too. It may be you'll have to come back 'fore me."

Lasso's grin was wide. As a foreman, he would have a chance to show his ability to manage and get things done. He was sure he had the experience to handle managing the ranch and working with other ranch hands. A moment ago, he climbed a rung in employment, not only managing cattle but also having a voice in decision-making which should earn a sufficient income to take care of a family.

CHAPTER FIFTEEN

"The busy have no time for tears." — *Lord Byron*

Grace

Her decision to go back home happened so fast, Grace was at a loss how to explain to the Jackson's that she was leaving. Of course, she didn't give the real reason that she was frightened of being followed by a ruffian all the way from Dallas. When she claimed homesickness, her words felt jarring even to her. This was true, but it felt slightly dishonest. In the end, they wished her well.

She gave Mrs. Jackson a hug and shook her husband's hand. She allowed several more days to ensure nothing remained undone to not be a burden on the Jacksons. They were not happy, but understood. On payday, she pocketed her wages and left early the next day for Annona.

* * *

Home by train during mid-afternoon, she picked up her bags, crossed the threshold, and set them on the kitchen floor. Stepping outside, she released the cat from the knitting bag. The feline stretched and yawned. When Bea recognized her surroundings, she sprinted toward the horse shed. "Tell the mice you're back," Grace muttered, exhausted and unsure of her next move.

In her own room at last, with a sigh of contentment, she pulled the drapes, removed her shoes, and sank onto the bed. The soft cotton sheet was cool against her skin as she covered her head.

Looking for peace, she closed her eyes to block out the world. But peace slipped away when she wrapped her arms over her breasts, gripping her elbows and willing her pressing fingers to be Randy's. Mockingly, a conversation with her sister, at thirteen, had unveiled the truth.

You will want love when you're no longer a child, because you cannot live without a man's affection and be happy.

Corrine, you are wicked. I'll never allow that to happen to me!

She would never forget being laughed at for her naiveté.

Nine years later, Grace understood it was true. Randy had awakened in her a gnawing hunger for his touch. With a frustrated sigh, she silenced the relentless inner voice berating her for the blinding jealousy she'd experienced that day. She sat up, tucking her knees beneath her chin, and ran her hand through her hair. Her sister in heaven was more than likely pointing a finger at her. *I told you so!*

After selling the dairy, she found no enjoyment in bustling cities and towering buildings. But none of her encounters had been as harsh as feeling alone. Although happy at the old folks' ranch, haunting prospects of the red booted stranger visited her nightly.

Still laying across the feather mattress, a bluejay squawked an angry warning. Grace jumped from her reverie, realizing it was late afternoon. Crickets were chirping in the maze of tall grass dotted with falling leaves, and there wasn't enough daylight to begin a large undertaking. She had wasted the entire afternoon. Unable to solve her problems in the bed's serenity, she jerked off the bedcovers and straightened the skirt that she had traveled in on the train ride.

For her to move forward, she must find something worthwhile to do to keep her occupied. She chewed her bottom lip. If she could lock her thoughts of Randall Jackson in a dark closet. She smiled at that. There were things she didn't know about him. But she was so hurt by the little she did know.

* * *

Awake early the next morning, she ran errands and stopped at the cotton gin to speak to an old friend of her mother. Mr. Roberts squeezed her fingers, and they talked for an hour. The elderly man in a straw hat spoke of past times and gave her the lowdown on everything that had happened there since she left. When he mentioned a doctor new to town who needed an assistant, she became interested.

Still arguing with herself as she headed toward home, she pondered if she should visit the doctor's office to introduce herself. She had no real nursing experience other than delivering calves and doctoring livestock. With the ranch wages spent, she needed to earn money, so she talked herself into taking a long shot. By one o'clock, she was knocking at Dr. Warren P. Woodcock's office door in the corner of the Pearl Drug Store. She skimmed over the many potions, elixirs, and tonics lining the shelves, then, the physician's door swung open held by a refined balding man with a mustache and full beard.

"How may I help you?"

"My name is Miss Grace Madden, Dr. Woodcock. My home is two miles from your office. When I heard you were looking for an assistant, I came right over. I'm searching for work currently. And here I am."

Dr. Woodcock did not expect a woman to come to his office or really anyone. He retired from his practice and moved to Annona, then kept his practice going instead of ending it. After spreading word of his need for a helper, he had not had one inquiry.

"Won't you step inside and have a seat?" After taking a pencil and notepad from his desk, he sat opposite her and started asking questions.

"I don't think we've met. Thank you for coming by. I'm Dr. Warren Woodcock, Miss Madden." He noticed her healthy, clean appearance. Her being single was a plus. A physician could be called to treat many illnesses and injuries at any hour. A married woman wasn't ideally able to just up and go.

"Thank you for your interest. Do you have nursing experience, Miss Madden?"

"I do and I don't, Dr. Woodcock. I feel compassion for the sick and elderly. I have no actual medical skills pertaining to humans, and my family owned a dairy for thirty years. I've helped our cows birth calves, administered stitches when needed, and applied an assortment of salves and drenches. I've had experience often in inoculating cattle, and I do not flinch at the sight of blood or an open wound. I understand sanitation's importance and am familiar with various medical conditions, including broken bones and gout. The main thing is I enjoy helping others. I would appreciate your consideration for the position. I am confident of meeting your expectations."

The doctor looked at the notes he'd been taking and smiled as he looked up. "I do find resemblances between humans and cattle from time to time," he chuckled.

Then, his demeanor took a serious tone. "Those are fine traits, Miss Madden. I find that in this part of the country, I do not require a helping hand who has attended a school of nursing. My fundamental requirements are steadiness, understanding instructions, and a soothing disposition." I think a trial period before permanently offering you this position is in order, Miss Grace, uh," he flipped his calendar. "Next Monday will do. I open the office at eight A.M. sharp. You understand emergencies can pop up day or night?"

"Yes, Dr. Woodcock, I do. Not unlike attending dairy cattle."

The portly, gray-haired doctor smiled and stood to walk around the desk to take Grace's fingers in his hand for a gentle shake. "Then, is everything settled? Oh, about the salary. Because you are a nurse by experience and not by certification, I'm happy to pay you thirty-five dollars for the first two months. Should your work be compatible with my requirements, we will adjust your salary to forty dollars monthly. If you accept my offer and don't have more questions, I will see you Monday morning."

"Oh, thank you for giving me the position." She stood with a smile on her face. "I shall see you early Monday next." He escorted Grace out. She turned and waved good-by, fighting back the urge to skip to her cart. She reined the horse toward her house, relieved to find employment that wouldn't deplete her strength and confine her to a milking parlor twice a day.

The boarding house was a short distance from Dr. Woodcock. She didn't notice if there were horses parked in sight under the enormous oak trees and really didn't care. Whatever had happened in the past, she would make it the key to the door of her future.

* * *

Saturday arrived. She planned to visit the dairy on Sunday. The Turnbow's weren't aware she had returned to Annona. It was only fair for Alice Ann and Garrett to know she was safe. She prayed she didn't run into Randy when she was back on the road, although she did owe him an explanation. But, he owed her an explanation *and* an apology.

After a good night's sleep, Grace set down her coffee cup and shoved her plate aside. The ticking clock on the shelf broke the tension. She stared out the window at waist-high weeds and unruly hedges along the fence row. While she was gone, no one tended to the mowing or clipping of the brambles and vines. She pushed from her chair and dressed in overalls, armed with a scythe and mower, she attacked the chigger ridden grass and prickly bushes.

When the sun was low, she wiped her brow while resting on the back door steps. A cramp attacked her leg. She rubbed it away with a lax arm. Exhaustion, though, didn't stop the past from entertaining her curiosity. *What if the Jackson's ranch belonged to Randy's kin?* An obstinate lift of her lip appeared. Wouldn't that be a trick on her? *Ha. Ha.*

CHAPTER SIXTEEN

"One great use of words is to hide our thoughts." — Voltaire

Grace

Sunday morning promised an early Fall. Yellow leaves littered the ground as they twirled a dance in the breeze to skip across the landscape. With the anxiety about obtaining work taken care of, Grace planned to visit Alice. And, she'd bring Coyote home.

After tying her other horse to a rail, she knocked on her—Alice's, door. Brown grass starved for water covered the yard. She looked around. The pasture behind the house and barn still looked quite green. The leaves rustled in the trees, more from the lack of water than from the cool air, then the door squeaked bringing her to the present.

Shocked, Alice squealed in delight at the sight for sore eyes on the porch. She wiped her hands with her apron and pulled Grace into a bear hug. Holding Grace's shoulders, she pushed her away. "Where have you been!" she squealed. Then, she whip-lashed Grace back into her arms.

"We've been so worried about you! Randy and folks in town have asked about you. Come, sit in here."

Grace sat in a kitchen chair. She'd forgotten how nice it was to have such a friend as Alice. She ran her fingers across the oak wood surface, finding peace sitting at the familiar table that had belonged to her mother. She was home at last and safe.

Alice poured coffee into mugs that she slapped onto the table as Grace fought the urge to ask about the gap in her friend's smile.

"Okay, I'll go first." She placed a finger where the tooth had been. "You remember that cow, 304? The horse flies were so bad this year that I s-stooped to pick up a bucket, and the big heifer s-s-wung her head in my direction to chase one away, and bam. Never did find the tooth. Anyway, we've been doing fine. We found s-s-ome wonderful help and business is doing well. Ethan's s-s-till doing the

145

run to the cheese processor and the milk deliveries. Now, you've learned about us-s-s. It's your turn!" She lifted her mug in a salute, waiting for Grace's answer.

Ohhh. Poor Alice Ann. She wouldn't say anything to hurt her feelings. But the whistling 'es's were funny.

"Not much to say. I learned a lot from using my bad judgment."

After Grace's self-criticism, Alice Ann squeezed her hand, wanting to boost Grace's spirit and encourage her to continue.

"I rode the train to Dallas and stayed at a grand hotel the first night. I had no idea how long I'd be in Dallas and soon left for Waxahachie." She shrugged as there was nothing to say as to why other than to get far away from the city.

"I stayed in a boarding house there and found a job advertisement in the post office. They answered my telegram I took a train to Red Oak. A nice old couple hired me to do odds and ends at their ranch. They were hanging on by the skin of their teeth even though they had quite a few cattle." She omitted the part about the hustler in the elevator, and that he had scared her twice by showing up in Red Oak.

"Before long, I realized that traveling the country wasn't for me," Grace said, patting Alice's hand. "I suppose I'm a homebody, a small-town girl at heart. I never thought I would return here."

"Yeah, it ain't a friendly place when you're alone in the world," Alice remarked. Grace's indifference regarding Randy created a significant gap in their discussion.

Alice thought that if they had met up, Grace would have mentioned it. Now, his lengthy absence was a worry to Alice, and she felt that Grace deserved to know everything that had happened since the time she left the farm.

"Grace."

146

Alerted by the gravity in Alice's tone, Grace searched her friend's face for anything readable in her expression.

"Randy was here after you left. He sat in that chair. Other than your letters, we couldn't pinpoint where you'd gone. I had never seen him so unnerved. He took Coyote to the Red River contest and won the roping. Then, he took a leave of absence from Red River and went to Dallas. He was using the prize money to search for you. It was nearly a month ago."

Grace blinked fast in disbelief. Randy's month-long absence stemmed from one agonizing truth: his pursuit of her.

"And, honey, he hasn't returned. Not a soul seems to know where he went. That little jerk, Jimmy, spread the word everywhere gossiping about how Randy just up and left. An' was saying Randy's searching for a woman who left 'em high and dry."

"Ohhh." Grace swallowed unable to reply, hurt by the gossip.

The expression on Grace's face broke Alice's heart. "And that ain't all. That cowhand they call Lasso followed Randy. And after Lasso left, word went around that he and that lady boarder at Miz Goss' place are married, and he ran off right after their baby was born!"

It was too much at one time to digest. Beside herself, Grace stopped breathing.

The woman Randy hugged in the doorway was Lasso Slade's wife! Not Randy's secret sweetheart? Grace was unaware of Mrs. Goss having a border. Not before she saw Mrs. Slade and Randy together.

When she released the spent air, it took a minute to calm her shaking hands. She'd wasted days and nights over a scene that had played in her mind since she left home. And for nothing. Like a frightened rabbit, she fled, pointedly avoiding questions about what happened at the doorway. She gathered her courage determined not to cry and asked a question.

147

"Isn't he a good friend of Randy's?"

"I think so. Must be true. I heard he's gone to meet up with Randy."

Half of Annona knew every cowboy's name on the Red River and the Eberly spread. While the name was familiar, she'd never met Lasso. She stared out a window deep in thought. Her head snapped around when Alice spoke.

Alice looked down, searching for the best way to finish her story. "But I sized up the actual truth. It was plain you two loved one another. That man seemed so torn up. It was me, Grace, who encouraged him to look for you. Course, it was his idea."

"Then, there's a different tale about Mr. and Mrs. Slade. Most deaths, births, and marriages are fodder for the gossip, but no one in town is talkin' about the mysterious border or about Lasso having a wife. I get the idea it's sort of a secret. I know, but I ain't talkin' to nobody but you. Miz Goss told me not to say a word about it while I was helping Ethan deliver dairy to the Annona customers. And I ain't."

Grace forced a weak smile, studying the cold coffee in her mug, her brows furrowed with worry. Ashamed, she hoped the gleam of tears in her eyes wasn't noticeable. "It sounds like a lot of excitement was going on in little Annona while I was gone. But I guess I started the fire!"

"Don't you worry about none of that! You're home and safe. That's all that matters. You and Randy will work it out. You'll see. He's a fine feller, Grace. He loves you."

"He must." Grace wasn't a girl who liked to go into lengthy conversations about her love affairs. Hearing Alice declare what she should have already known was embarrassing. Feeling like a simpleton, her spirit plummeted and made Alice's company difficult to bear. Needing time alone, Grace stood up.

"I only hope that he and his friend make it back and everything gets straightened out. Uh, I need to start for the house, Alice. Give Garrett and Ethan my regards, and I'll see them another day."

"Well, okay, if you're sure you can't stay a while more." Alice followed her to the door needing more time with a female friend. The hired hands and her two men didn't care for jawing over women's concerns.

"Wait. I forgot my news." Grace sat back down. "I have employment now. I'm going to be Dr. Woodcock's assistant."

Alice grabbed Grace's hands. "You're settling back in Annona, then! I've missed you and am so glad you're back to stay. When you come next time, I want you to tell me about your train ride and Dallas. I ain't been nowhere other than Clarksville. So be prepared to stay for a longer visit. And don't worry about Randy. He's more 'an tough. I just know those cowboys will be back before you know it."

They hugged and when Grace left, she stopped the horse past the old dairy house and looked back. The cows were noisy, lowing or bellowing. Too far away to hear the chickens in the coop, their activity was still visible. The horse, much older than Coyote, walked slowly away when Grace kicked it.

Her heart thumped slowly, dejected as the rest of her. She missed the farm but was also glad to be rid of it. Poor Alice. The missing tooth reminded her of the farm's relentless misfortunes. Her visit with Alice had re-opened the wounds she had nurtured, but differently. It was she who had wounded herself. She didn't know Mrs. Slade or that Mr. Slade was married. She doubted she could ever overcome her flawed assumptions, ending with Randy following her. To salvage some pride, she began planning her days. If Randy took Coyote to Red River, she would bring him home as soon as possible. She'd counted on that and her new job to help her discover a new, more fulfilling life.

Randy must think I'm crazy… he didn't understand and wanted to find me. Grace! You Are Stupid. Stupid. Stupid. He couldn't have possibly known she misunderstood his actions, resulting in her running away.

If they met again, she hoped he'd forgive her. Given the way she had treated him, she couldn't expect any more than that.

CHAPTER SEVENTEEN

White lies are many things, avoidance, encouragement,

and, also, the end of many things.—Cam Locke

Grace & Phoebe

On Monday morning, she entered the doctor's office ten minutes early. He was sitting at his desk.

"Have a seat, Miss Madden." The doctor glanced at the woman young enough to be his daughter. Then, clasped her fingers in a gentle shake across his desk.

"Please. Call me Grace."

He smiled. "Grace. Please." He waved at the chair.

Once she sat, he asked a few questions, then went ahead describing his routine. "Some days are filled with patients with broken bones to pneumonia. Other days are less hectic." He turned to move a leather medical satchel bag from a table to his desktop. "I'd like for you to familiarize yourself with the bag's content. It's imperative to keep the implements clean and sterilized."

"Yes, sir. I will."

"We'll discuss more tomorrow. At times, things have been pretty busy. Today, however, it's been slow." Dr. Woodcock was not called out the entire day. No one stopped by with any complaints.

The day dragged on. Grace, wanting to know everything, explored the office while Dr. Woodcock sorted through paper at his desk. She contented herself by looking over the containers of catgut for sutures and metal devices shaped like tongs, for bullet removal she thought. She took a thick book from a shelf and thumbed through it.

The quietness caught the doctor's attention. With his glasses on his nose, he saw his new employee absorbed in a medical journal.

He trusted that her enthusiasm stayed strong after they performed their first surgery.

"Mis—Grace. It's been a slack day and getting late. Unpredictable things can occur, however, there's no need for you to remain. So, go home and we'll start again tomorrow."

The next day, Tuesday, dawned clear and cool, a typical autumn day in east, with the sun warming the air.

After she arrived at the office, three patients filled the office. She simply observed to acquaint herself with the doctor's routine, and so the week went.

Returning the following Monday, she packed Dr. Woodcock's bags with every instrument and medical remedy that a home visitation might call for. His young helper, Johnny, had hitched the horse to the buggy.

"Today's first patient is only two months old. His mother needs assurance he is healthy in every way." He carried the medical satchel himself to the buggy.

At the end of Main Street, Grace spotted a white clapboard home standing at attention beyond the yellow and orange leaves that littered the ground. Her stomach knurled. She glanced at Dr. Woodcock who was guiding the horse up the narrow drive. She prayed he had made a wrong turn. When he stopped at the front door, Grace lifted her skirt and jumped from the buggy. She grabbed Dr. Woodcock's bag while he tethered the horse.

They waited on the porch after a loud rap on the door. A moment later, Mrs. Goss answered and waved them in. Grace knew the elderly woman; for sixty years she had lived there.

"Dr. Woodcock, please come in. Follow me. Mrs. Slade and her baby are in the sitting room."

Grace followed the two through the well-furnished home with a faint hint of lemon clinging to the air. Though Alice spoke of the Red River cowboy, Grace had never met the couple. Overwhelmed by confusion and uncertainty, she best let the chance meeting with the woman she had envied unfold on its own. She shivered with goosebumps though the mild fall days were warmer than usual.

"Dr. Woodcock, this is my boarder, Mrs. Slade. She is living here until her husband returns from a trip."

Mrs. Goss had rehearsed her lines well. Acting as Phoebe's guardian for three months, she shielded the girl's dignity by keeping the truth hidden. As Phoebe relayed, Mr. Slade had hinted at a proposal of marriage. And as far as she was concerned, the couple was married until a Justice of the Peace officially married them. She suggested that no one needed to know it was a little white lie.

She noted Grace Madden was Dr. Woodcock's assistant now. She'd known Grace's mother for years, who was as diligent as any man, keeping up that dairy. Word had spread that Miss Madden had sold the dairy farm to Alice and Garrett Turnbow. Then poof, Miss Madden left town. It was interesting that she'd returned and worked for the doctor now.

Grace watched as Mrs. Slade handed her baby to Dr. Woodcock. He sat in another chair with the infant balanced in his lap. After probing the child's limbs and his stomach, he ran his fingers across the tiny skull and looked into his eyes with a magnifying glass. Grace handed him his stethoscope about the time the fussing child let out a cry and passed gas.

"I'm sure he's feeling better now, Mrs. Slade," he smiled. "He looks to be in perfect health, uh, little—"

"We haven't named him yet. My husband had to leave for an emergency. When he returns, we can choose a name together." She smiled at the doctor and glanced at Grace.

Dr. Woodcock rose to place the baby back into the mother's arms. "Please ask if you need anything. As the child's mother, do you have questions for me? He's a healthy boy from my observations. About yourself, are you doing well?"

"Yes, Doctor. I am. Mrs. Goss is a remarkable nurse."

Dr. Woodcock handed the medical bag to Grace, then bowed to his patient in his old-fashioned way. "Yes, it seems so."

Grace, the last person to leave, looked back to smile and wave at Mrs. Slade, who returned the gesture. They hadn't spoken to each other. Somehow, Grace wanted to have a private visit with her. Out of Mrs. Goss' hearing.

The elderly woman led the doctor to the front door with Grace following. Stopping there, she touched the doctor's arm. "Dr. Woodcock, as Mrs. Slade's husband is not here, will you please send a bill to this address? It will be paid as soon as he returns."

"I will be happy to do that. Good day, Mrs. Goss."

Dr. Woodcock helped Grace into the buggy, and once seated, tapped the horse to walk. "Miss Grace, do you mind preparing a bill and putting it in the mail tomorrow? It's going to Mrs. Goss's address."

"Yes, of course. But I go by Mrs. Goss' place daily and can drop it off." She wanted to speak with Mrs. Slade, anyway.

His bottom lip curled as he nodded in agreement. "Thank you, dear."

She smiled, becoming accustomed to Dr. Woodcock's fatherly comments.

That evening, Grace pondered about Mrs. Slade and why her husband left town. Mrs. Slade didn't seem concerned about his being away. However, doubts of never seeing Randy again chilled Grace to the bone. She forced herself not to think about him being hurt or killed wherever he was. What if he was near Red Oak and that awful man was there, too? Wherever Randy was, it seemed probable that he and Mr. Slade were together. The two men, unlike her, were more capable of dealing with a gunslinger.

Still, she was worried. A friendship with Mrs. Slade could provide her with female companionship and conversation. However, she'd keep the possibility of a confrontation with an outlaw from Mrs. Slade. There was no need for her to worry, too.

If Mr. Slade returned soon, perhaps Randy would as well. She might ask the young mother later. Now may not be the right time to be so inquisitive. She shook her head at her naivete. *You're being stupid again. You must never assume anything.*

By Friday, the days had gotten busy. Doreen Thurman's eight year old son fell out of a tree and broke his arm. An hour later, Dr. Woodcock was looking down the throat of Gil Madison. Three house calls later, they closed the office.

Mounting her horse for the trip to the Goss house, her mind was bothered. Guilt repeatedly assaulted her solace, and she prayed asking God to forgive her for being such a bother to Randy. She had convicted a man she cared for without giving him a chance to explain.

At Mrs. Goss' door, she raised the knocker, her mind soothed for the moment, knowing everything was in God's hands. Mrs. Slade opened the door holding her baby. Phoebe's face lit up when she saw Grace. Her days were long and drab other than being busy with her little boy. Elated to have company, she led Grace to the parlor.

They started their conversation with the news of Annona, which wasn't too exciting, but it broke the ice. The baby waved his arms in the air prompting Grace to ask, "Your baby boy is precious, Mrs. Slade. May I hold him?"

"Of course." Phoebe stood to place him in Grace's arms. After returning to her chair, she watched the doctor's assistant hold little Slade. She was a slim girl in a split skirt for riding. Aware of her own physique, Phoebe was impatient to lose the extra weight she'd gained and to wear her normal clothes again.

Grace smiled into the child's face while he waved his arms and cooed. She marveled at his tiny fingers and toes, and for a moment, she forgot his mother was in the room. Tiny Slade had skin soft as down and dark eyes. *He must favor Mr. Slade.* Mrs. Slade was light-

155

skinned, unlike Grace who had spent days out of doors her entire life. Phoebe took him when he became fussy. His wobbly head turned toward Grace making her smile. Amazing, as small as he was, his dark eyes inquisitively searched the room from his elevated position.

"Is it a hardship without your husband here to help with a newborn?" Grace asked, unsure where the conversation would flow.

Phoebe smiled to disguise her fear of unwittingly disclosing her non-existent marriage. "Yes, it is. When this little guy doesn't sleep well, the nights are challenging. But if Mrs. Goss sees that I'm exhausted, she is being a dear and helps. But, yes, it's still hard without Mr. Slade. And you? Do you have a special someone in your life, or are you married?"

Grace was slow to answer. "Once I had feelings for a particular cowboy. But it didn't work out between us. I hope that it might change in the future. Right now, he's not present to test the waters, so to speak."

Grace at once liked Phoebe, though their differences were many. A graceful woman with a warm smile, she had dark brown hair. Her attractive oval face seemed familiar, yet her eyes were unique.

She watched Mrs. Slade's ladylike movements. Her soft Texas accent was calming, with mannerisms Grace would never have. "Are you from around here, Mrs. Slade?"

"Please, call me Phoebe."

"Alright. And please call me Grace. I haven't heard the name Slade, even in Clarksville."

"No. Our roots are from south of Dallas. Mr. Slade's reason for coming here was to work at the Red River Ranch." It was almost the truth. They were both born somewhere south of Dallas. One all the way to the Mexican border. Phoebe hated deception. *Will I forever live a life of lies?* Phoebe changed the subject before her new friend asked another question about Mr. Slade.

156

"Mrs. Goss said you owned a farm before becoming a medical assistant."

"Yes, my mother started it. After she passed, I ran the farm for years before I decided I wanted to travel. I realized I didn't care for city life. The traffic, the bustle was too much for me."

Though they just met, Phoebe realized Grace had skills she lacked. Phoebe wondered what Grace couldn't do. But she did want to stay friends. Her new young acquaintance had managed a dairy business, and now, she was a doctor's assistant. Grace's success, a potent mixture of ambition and freedom, and her mastery at running a business stirred a pang of yearning for accomplishment. Being a mother was a feat to envy, but the pursuit of her other interests was as far away as the North Pole.

Little Slade cried. Phoebe rocked him in her arms. As a mother, she loved her child, but she hadn't asked for him. Though reconciled with her fate, she did not deserve a mad man's wrath that had changed her life forever. She never believed that any man would marry her while she was carrying another's baby. But God was good.

The baby hadn't stopped fussing, so Grace stood to leave. "Phoebe, I should go to give you time to soothe your little boy. He's a beautiful child."

"Thank you." Phoebe ran her palm over the baby's mat of hair. She looked up at Grace. "Will you visit again?" She lowered her voice to a whisper. "With no one close to my age for company, I'm so alone here. I adore Mrs. Goss, but our age difference... I trust you understand."

Grace was more than understanding, sure she'd made a friend of Mrs. Slade. Grace rolled her eyes. "Yes, I do. I so enjoyed our visit and look forward to seeing you again. Here's your statement from Dr. Woodcock. I'll put it here on the table."

Disappointed that Grace must go, Phoebe showed her to the porch, the baby asleep on her shoulder. They chatted on the porch and agreed on their next meeting day. When they said their goodbyes, Phoebe sighed. Alone again, she longed for Andelacio to be by her side, so they could finally marry and put an end to the constant need for pretense. Not knowing him very long, but trusting her instincts, she believed he was a good man. She returned to the sitting room.

Mrs. Goss moved from her hiding place behind the hall door. Before Randy Jackson brought his sister to her boarding house, occupants in the past simply paid for their rooms and left. They were ghosts she never saw again. It was the closest she'd ever come to being a mother, since Phoebe had been boarding at her house. She did her best in keeping Phoebe from prying eyes and hurtful remarks.

Quiet as possible, she listened to the young women's conversation. Without knowing, Grace had become a new collaborator in the delusion. Mrs. Goss would learn about her and the Randy Jackson boy's relationship. She knew exactly who could tell her. Nothing this exciting had happened in Annona since a rearing horse killed Ned Applebee, bless his soul, in front of the mercantile.

CHAPTER EIGHTEEN

Danger Everywhere

Randy & Lasso

Randy sat on the porch steps with his friends, the stars. There was Orion, Aries, and Taurus. A sheer vapor dusted the rest of the sky, hiding most of the other figures in the inky black space. Many years had passed since he'd visited them after leaving home. He had come back changed. Here now, in the dim light, he felt less of his old self and more versed. He laughed. *More battle-scarred, was more like it.* He wondered what his future days, devoid of Grace's warmth and laughter, would mean.

Life was simple before meeting her. If the forge broke, fix it. The wheel broke, fix it. Previously, he had given little thought to his life's direction, but because of her, he had a clear vision of how he wanted it to go. However long their hearts remained unhealed though, there were unknown deeds that might be past mending, as the reason for her disappearance ate at him daily.

But he was surviving on his own and making decisions he'd never faced before. After being handed a ranch, he'd been working his ass off to bring it into some semblance of a business. All the while, continuing to search for a woman and shooting a man who tried to kill him. And worse, desperate to find her, he tortured an outlaw for information. Lasso's dismal need to protect himself from his father had taken a heavy toll on the son, despite the man's cruelty. He shuddered at the thought and needed to clear his head. *Shooting someone to save yourself wasn't simple to forget. A terrible loneliness washes over you... oh, shit, I've got to stop thinking about it.*

He ground his boot extinguishing his cigarette and opened the screen door. Morning came early. He had some notions he wanted to discuss with his pa.

* * *

"Pa, I'm going to get a bank loan on the ranch."

Burnett looked at Randy as though he said he was flying to the moon. "You can't do that, son. You'll be back in debt before a month's gone by. You'll go broke!" He leaned forward in the chair, shaking a finger in Randy's face.

"Just listen." He ignored his father's outburst. It was a throwback to the past, but his father was in no condition to follow up his bellyaching with physical abuse. The ranch was his now, and he was no longer under anyone's control, plus he towered over his father.

"Until we build back the herd and the drought is over, then hire another hand, this ranch can't support itself. My boss at Red River bought some registered bulls and upgraded his herd. His breeding program improved their weight, and they brought higher prices than the Longhorns. It's modern times, Pa. The railroads have changed the beef industry. Back east, folks are clamoring for steaks and beef ribs. It'll take some seed money and more help to turn things around, but I'm confident we can get this place back on track."

Burnett studied the back of his hands, knowing at his age and having poor health, he'd have to listen to his son. He stared Randy in the eye. "If you figure you can pull it off, I can't stand in your way. I'll support you the best I can, but I spent every dime I had getting this ranch on its feet. I can give you advice if you take it, but that's all I have."

"Your opinions are welcome. You've held onto this property and cattle, for a long time. I need you and your view point. It's as valuable as money. Almost."

"Hmmm," Burnett laughed.

Randy offered his father his hand. "We're partners, Pa. Always."

That afternoon, Lasso went with Randy as he drove to Red Oak. They left the wagon at a hitching rail and entered the First State Bank. After talking to Roscoe Billings, the president of the bank, they walked out with the assurance the bank would make a loan to restore the ranch, purchase cattle, and make a payroll.

Before they left town, they bought foodstuffs, grain and corn for the horses, the other livestock, medical provisions, and a few fencing tools and loaded the wagon. Next year, he could plant his own grain and sow a better grass forage.

On the rough road home, Lasso held on to the bench, leaned out, and spit to the side of the wagon. "It's been a while since we talked about this, but what's our plan about the women?"

Randy eyed Lasso whose cheek bulged with chewing tobacco. "Hadn't figured it out yet. I don't know where mine is, but I haven't forgotten about it. I still have no idea why she left everything behind. Once we get back to Red River and squared away with Mr. Sullivant, mostly cause I deduce I owe him something, I'll think what to do."

Lasso nodded. "Naw, it wouldn't be right to leave him high and dry. We need to give him an opportunity to find another cowhand, but replacing you will not be easy."

"Hm. Don't know 'bout that. Probably needs someone who'll stay put. Anyway, how would you fancy moving down here after you and Phoebe get hitched? If y'all can bunk up with the old folks for a while, I know it won't bother Phoebe, other than having to make amends with our parents. We'll get your house built as soon as we can."

Lasso's bristling mustache twitched in a quick smile. " Hmm. Does that mean after you find Miss Grace?"

"More than likely. I'll follow you as soon as I can. I have an idea she's in Annona, seeing how she skedaddled out of here."

When they arrived at the ranch, Randy unloaded the foodstuff and other supplies into the storeroom and kitchen. Then, he drove the wagon toward the barn to unload the grain and tools they'd bought. Lasso was in the corrals spreading feed and tossing hay to the goats, a few bulls, and the utility horses used for riding, pulling wagons, and plowing. The entire section, as far as he could see was turning brown.

"If the drought dries up the creeks and small ponds on the place, we'll have to sink a couple of wells to water all the stock soon. Another expense unless we dig them ourselves."

Lasso hung an elbow over the board rail. "Si. Unless the water table is too low for us to tap it. No reason to worry about it now, Boss. Look behind you."

Randy turned around. The sky had blackened over the horizon with clouds. "Huh. I guess things work out after all." He helped Lasso finish with feeding the livestock. Worrying about Grace was no use either, but he did anyway. The sooner he left the Bar J to find her, the better.

* * *

Randy and Lasso packed for the trip to Annona a week later. Burnett took them to the station. They waited outside the ticket office with Burnett who had made himself comfortable on the wagon seat. "I'd stand with you boys, but I'm staying where I am. These legs are 'bout give out."

"It don't want to leave you here with the place, Pa, just you and ma."

He scoffed and twirled his hand in the air. "Don't worry about us. You boys done a good job putting things in order. Me and your ma won't have much to do but throw some feed and hay to the horses in the corral and the chickens. Don't have nothing calving right now. Everything else can take care of itself till you get back here less we run outta water. And now with those men gone, we ain't scared of nobody bothering us."

"Stay alert, Pa. One of 'em ran off. So long as he doesn't come back to harass y'all, I figure you'll be okay. Could be he's part of that gang in the news lately, holdin' up trains and raiding baggage cars and robbing passengers, but I don't know if they killed anyone.

"Tell ma I love her, and I'll send a telegram to let you know when Lasso and Phoebe plan to move down here—." A whistle blew cutting off his sentence. "I hear the train coming. Don't drive too fast going back home. Ol' Pistol might decide to run off."

Burnett shook his head at the picture the swaybacked horse would make doing anything other than a shuffle. "Dan Patch he ain't, son!"

Randy smiled and reached up to give his father a shoulder hug. Burnett reached out to shake Lasso's hand. "I appreciate all you done, too, Mr. Lasso."

As he turned the wagon around, Randy watched him and prayed that it was the end of the terrible events that had happened at the ranch. He'd never hurt anyone before, or killed a man, and knew he'd never feel the same after the Bar J was attacked. The train pulled in on time diverting his thoughts.

Lasso followed Randy onto the train to find their seats. He removed his hat, hair plastered to his head, and glanced at Randy. A one-sided smile flashed across his tense expression. He hated sitting in the swaying car. It provided too much idle time allowing thoughts of regret, sadness, and worry. *What next? Surely, there's nothing else that can happen.* He picked up an abandoned newspaper. An image on the front page of captured thieves in shackles caught his attention. He put the paper on the seat and shuddered. It could have been him in his past life.

He'd put out the idea to Randy's sister about getting married. And though the Bar J had been her home, what if she didn't want to move to the middle of nowhere where her worst nightmares began? If they settled there, he pondered if a trip now and then to see the sights in Dallas would give Phoebe a sense of adventure away from the isolated ranch. Take her mind off the past. Maybe so. Luck had blessed him so far.

Previously, his nomadic lifestyle had prevented him from forming any lasting friendships. Until Red River Ranch employed him as a cowhand, he never stayed in one place long.

163

He respected Randy was an intelligent man, and happy in his own element of peace and harmony. But his search for Grace had caused a change in everyone's life, especially Randy's. A drawn face, dull eyes, and melancholy thoughtfulness replaced his easy laugh. Perhaps his woman could bring back the light in his eye, thought Lasso. If he finds her. With a muted sigh, Lasso placed his broad-brimmed hat on his lap and closed his eyes.

Randy tried the same, yet rest for him remained out of reach. Next time, the Texas Rangers could handle the murderers and cattle thieves. After rolling it over in his mind, he decided there was nothing else they could have done but what happened. Modern times had cooled off the wild in the West but reprobates still roamed the country like scavengers.

He didn't regret that his pursuit of Grace brought him back home. It resulted in a family reconciling; him gaining ownership of a large established ranch and providing a better life for his sister and the man she might marry. He'd been successful at Red River; nevertheless, he, himself, carried the burden of the Bar J and the outlaws. All had taken a toll on him, but he was still walking. *Thank God, it's over.*

He could see Lasso dozing from the corner of his eye. The timing of Lasso's arrival in his life felt like a stroke of good fortune. Finding trustworthy, skilled cowboys who stuck with you were hard to find.

On this favorable note, he willed his body to relax and pulled his Stetson low on his forehead.

No sooner than he'd dozed off to sleep, he and Lasso awoke together as the train lurched and screeched to a halt. Befuddled, Randy looked at Lasso who was frowning. The train was in the middle of nowhere, not a house or building in sight. He saw nothing alarming at the front of the car. Now sitting still, a hot wind came through the window, and the puffing smoke stack filled the air with black soot. Feeling like sitting ducks, both men slapped their hats on and prepared themselves for trouble. Randy swiveled, looking for anything out of place, or worse, a holdup. His answer came quickly.

A man stomped his boots across the metal vestibule floor; his hat brim obscured his eyes and a neckerchief masked his face. His clothes were above a cowboy's, but worn and wrinkled. If this was a robbery, Randy saw no horses waiting outside. A second later, he saw what he feared.

The outlaw waved a pistol in the air to make sure everyone knew he was armed. Then, he started down the narrow aisle with a sack in his hand into which male passengers were emptying their pocket contents. Women snatched off their broaches and other jewelry and dumped them into the bag along with their handbags. Another outlaw followed the first, waving his gun from one side to the other.

Lasso surveyed the back of the car. A third bandit with a drawn pistol stood at the vestibule, posing an added threat.

"Damnation, Randy," Lasso whispered. "Remember that feller? He's the one who managed to ride away from the ranch. Guess there's more of them cold-blooded murderers than we thought." *Nothing but killers who don't deserve...* He dropped what he was thinking. It was too close a reminder of that terrible day at Red Oak. Though he had no choice, the event had left an indelible mark on him. But no matter what had happened, now he had to survive for Phoebe's sake.

"Let's hope he don't recognize us." *Because if he does, he might want some payback.* Randy removed his gun from its holster and hid it by his side. Too late to plan much, all he needed was an opportunity to move quickly and aim straight.

Randy and Lasso slouched as much as possible in the confining seats. Their lowered heads hid their faces beneath their hat brims. Neither had more than a dollar in coin, and they retrieved what they had from their pockets along with string, a smooth piece of wire, and a few oats. When the two train robbers stopped where they sat, they dumped their belongings into the bag. Randy hoped they looked harmless as he slid his hand slowly to his pistol.

Andelacio's knuckles cracked faintly as he clenched his fists. His gun belt lay useless, earlier discarded next to him on the seat. Confronting life or death, his resolve soared to hard and cold, contrasting with the heat rising in his chest.

Just as the masked man started away, another piercing scream filled the cramped car when his partner snatched a necklace from a woman's neck. Heads snapped around, including the outlaw with the sack, looking back for the origin of the sudden outburst.

Except for Lasso's. He stayed focused on where his fist would land if the chance arose. In a sudden move from his aisle seat, he punched the gunman in the gut and kneed him in the groin. The injured man grabbed his damaged genitals, giving Lasso an opening to jerk the gun from his hand. Griping it, he smashed the butt into the man's temple. He fell across a passenger's lap as the other outlaw turned and ran firing errant bullets into the ceiling in his haste.

Lasso took aim. "Stop!" The sound hung heavily throughout the car, charging the air with tension. In the next second, a bullet brought the man to the floor. With passing minutes, passengers rose up from the floor, their heads appearing like gophers peeking from their burrows.

A couple of male passengers jumped from their seats to hold the wounded man down.

Randy pushed by Lasso and jumped over the outlaw sprawled on the floor and disappeared through the open door. Stepping to the ground from the steps, and seeing no others, he reentered the train car where silence greeted him. Other travelers had bound the wounded man in a seat and staunched the bleeding from his shoulder with a sleeve torn from his shirt. A few rows back, the crook who was felled by his own gun had been hog-tied and left on the aisle floor. When the gunfire quieted and the outlaws rendered harmless, the passengers made their way to their seats.

A train crew employee entered the car, made his way to the center of the aisle, and began speaking at full volume. "Ladies and gentlemen. The Houston and Texas Central Railway wants to apologize for the brief interruption of service. As you know, those two fast-thinking cowboys back there apprehended the men who performed this outrage. Let's give 'em a hand for their bravery!"

The passengers turned to look at the reluctant heroes, applauding, then quieted and sat down. Women opened their fans and wiped their brows with a hankie.

"We have telegraphed the next town sheriff. He'll pick up and transfer these men to prison for trial. We guarantee your safety until we reach our destination. Everything is under control." Through with his announcement, the man in an engineer's cap walked through the vestibule toward the smoking engine.

The conductor waiting for the engineer to vacate, walked through the car, offering help and assurances. The men nearby offered their hands to Lasso and Randy in thanks before the train moved again. Back in his seat, Randy checked his gun and returned it to its holster. Any thought of relaxing had been blown away. "Damnation. I think we're cursed!" He rolled his eyes to the sky. "You were quick, partner! Glad *you're* my ranch manager. Dear God, please let us get home alive."

"The third man?"

"By the time I made it outside, all I saw was a cloud of dirt. Too much for a horse to make, I think they were driving an automobile."

Lasso grunted. *Modern times. Lord, what'll come next?*

A combined murmur of *"Ohhh"* filled the area, as the train made a sudden movement forward.

"Amen," breathed Lasso. His racing heart finally stilled to a slow, steady thump against his ribs. He might learn to live with the last time he had to use his gun, but, Lasso was having nightmares about that day. He stayed in turmoil, consumed with guilt. Then, he had to suppress the truth from everyone that his father had abused an innocent girl and the outcome caused her to be thrown from her home. He wondered if the attempted train robbery were the end of the violence he'd suffered or if it would follow him for the rest of time.

The rough-spun fabric of his shirt felt scratchy against his skin as he gazed ahead, seeing nothing but the blurry haze of the late afternoon sun. He thought of Phoebe and how it would feel to hold her in his arms.

CHAPTER NINETEEN

Together Again

Grace & Phoebe

Exhaustion wore Phoebe to the bone. Dark circles beneath her eyes faded into the pink on her cheeks. She and Grace sat close by a lit fireplace chasing the chill from the room.

Seeing Phoebe was in no condition to dive deep into serious thought, Grace kept the conversation light. Little Slade had been fussing ever since she arrived. She strode straight to Phoebe, lifted the baby, and placed him over her shoulder to pat his back. Helping her friend, Grace had developed a soothing rapport with the baby. Grace handed him back to his mother when he had burped to relieve his tummy of gas.

Grace sat on the edge of a chair facing Phoebe. "Have you heard from Mr. Slade? I hope that his business will bring him back home soon so he can see his amazing son." Grace never questioned how the couple managed to live on a cowboy's income, but her support was coming from somewhere according to the Edwardian fashion Phoebe wore of high necklines and shirtwaist blouses that tucked into slender skirts that brushed the floor. She must have never worn a flour sack frock.

Phoebe lay the finally sleeping baby swaddled in a blanket next to her on the sofa. "Yes, I've been waiting to tell you as soon as this little rascal quieted down. Mr. Slade and my brother, Randy Jackson, are taking a train home. I expect them, perhaps tomorrow."

Blindsided, Grace clenched her jaw. *Randy's her brother?* She wasn't ready to face Randy with such short notice, if ever. Rather than expose she had never linked Mrs. Slade and Randy Jackson as kin, she said, "Wonderful! I know you're eager to have him back. Your family will be together again."

Nor did she feel it was time to make her relationship with Phoebe's brother known. Grace pressed down a show of her own elation while her feelings made themselves well known within her head. *I'm wanting him so, but I can't... I just can't. "*

The baby whimpered in his sleep catching Phoebe's attention. "It's been so long. And now that they're returning, Lasso will see how much the baby's grown and finally give him a name."

Grace, still shocked by the revelation of Randy's return, said as calmly as she could, "Phoebe, since Mr. Slade and your brother are close friends, why not give the baby your maiden name as a middle name."

"What a wonderful idea! Andelacio will like that. I'm sure he won't mind. After all, he has the honor of giving him his first name."

Grace nodded, lost in thought, wondering how she was going to visit Phoebe and not run into Randy. Her busy schedule might serve as a perfect cover for her for the moment. For now, she needed to leave to share Phoebe's news with someone else. They may suggest a better way to avoid the humiliation she was sure to suffer.

Troubled, she picked up her handbag, giving Phoebe a look of disappointment. "Phoebe. I've got to go. I enjoy our visits so much." She meant it, enjoying the serene time spent with Phoebe. And she loved to hold the baby. She walked to the sofa and kissed little Jackson on the back of his tiny head full of black hair. Though she had not met Andelacio, the child's resemblance to his father was plain, given his mother's lighter features.

"But you just arrived!" Disappointed, Phoebe's mouth turned down at the corners. She noticed Grace was always busy, a whirlwind of activity, and hurried goodbyes.

"I know. I'm sorry. I have to drop by the mercantile to get supplies for Dr. Woodcock's office. I'll lengthen my stay next time. Please, tell Mrs. Goss goodbye for me."

Phoebe stood and moved the sleeping baby toward the back of the sofa for safety. At the front door, she and Grace hugged goodbye, and Phoebe waved from the front door.

Grace's heart pounded as she crossed the yard. *Dear Lord in Heaven, I confess I lied again. It seems easier each time, but the weight of the situation is heavy upon me. And there's so much at stake.*

After mounting her horse, she smacked it with the reins to go into a gallop. He was out of breath when she tied him to a rail at the dairy. Grace pounded on Alice's door and waited. Impatient, she turned the corner of the house and saw Alice walking toward her.

"Alice!"

"Grace! Let's go in. I'm so glad you came to visit."

Grace shot her a feeble smile and sat at the table. Alice handed her the ever-present glass of water. "What brings you this way? How do you like your employer? Are you seeing lots of patients?"

"Dr. Woodcock is a wonderful man. He treats all sorts of folks with every ailment invented by the devil."

Alice placed her hand across Grace's in concern. The one-sided lift of Grace's lip creating a dimple said her friend was at her wit's end.

"Right now, I need some help. No, I didn't mean that kind of help, Alice. I'm doing all right. I found out Randy and his friend are coming back by train. Phoebe mentioned they could arrive as soon as tomorrow."

Alice pressed her lips together, resisting the urge to smile. Her prayers were being answered. Their love might re-emerge. She learned Mrs. Slade and Randy were kin when Mrs. Goss mentioned the secret marriage. Alice had her doubts the Slade's were married at all, but she would never say otherwise. *Her major concern was Grace, but was there anything she could say that wouldn't stir the pot?*

"Is that a problem?"

"Yes, it is. I was a perfect fool for leaving. I caused problems for everyone." Grace was breathing fast, on the verge of tears. "The mere thought of laying eyes on him fills me with a sense of dread. I'm fearful he'll hate me. Alice, why can't I just face things instead of running away? First, a man. Then, the whole darned farm!" Grace wiped the tears from her cheeks. *Why did she constantly cry over everything?*

Alice squeezed Grace's hand. "Aw. It's alright, Grace. Sometimes, we all do things we could have handled better in hindsight."

"Alice, I appreciate your effort to console me, but that's not the issue here. I don't stand up for anything. When Corrine passed away, I overheard gossip and appalling things said about my sister. Even though she may have been guilty, she was my sister. I stayed silent, aware of Corrine's inability to defend herself. I regret not silencing the gossipers." Grace gasped for air in between the sobs.

Alice stood over her and wrapped an arm around Grace. "Hush, honey. These things are just human. Please, don't cry. This is your opportunity for amends. If Randy loves you, he will understand. And if you love him, give him that chance. Despite the difficulty, we are strong women. Our lives have made us able to endure terrible things. Death. Lost love. Our best cow quits giving milk."

The tears stopped. Grace's shoulders shook when she giggled. Still, she was furious. At herself, at the world. She turned to hug Alice unable to hold back the smile on her face. "Of course, the worst is the cow's failure."

Alice laughs. "See. Things could be worse. Isn't that what they say?"

"I'm not sure who *they* is, but it's possible. I don't know what I'd do without you as a friend. And Phoebe. We girls have to stick together."

"It's gonna work out."

Grace wiped her face with the hem of her dress. "I've held you up long enough. Alice, you have been such an encouragement. Thank you, Alice." Stopping at the door, with a faint smile on her lips, she hugged Alice again.

On the way home, Grace thought over her predicament. The trials of her emotions made her angry with herself. Tired of being her old self; the compliant person who fled at the first hint of a challenging situation in her life. Alice informed her she wasn't the only human who made mistakes. True, but she was one unable to face life on their own. Well, great.

After riding another mile, she rethought Alice's words. She had traveled on her own, had taken care of a dairy that took expert skill, could ride better than a lot of men, read and write better than half the people she knew, and worked for a prominent doctor. More than most women could accomplish. She could be strong. She sat taller and then succumbed to the same argument that returned daily in her head. *Why does Randy Jackson care about me? I don't know why he thinks I'm worth saving.* A strange feeling clinched her insides from her shoulders to her knees, making her weak. It passed in a moment. She recognized that the reaction of her body was a normal, though lustful, longing that only a man may soothe. *Oh, Corrine! Grace, you can save yourself. He went looking for you once. If he loves you, he can damn well come looking again.*

Her victory in the argument against herself lifted her spirits. The rest of her ride was at a fast trot, wanting to put her new thoughts into action once home. That night, she slept soundly, with confidence.

Waking with a new resolve, determined to make the best of the day, she readied herself the next morning for work. She saddled her horse and rode straddle in a split skirt. It was a compromise between an ankle length dress and wearing trousers. This new style made it easier to harness horses to wagons and do other men's jobs. At Dr. Woodcock's office, she unsaddled her horse without help and put it into a fenced lot. After entering the office, the doctor looked at her once without comment about her clothing and returned to his papers. The moderately busy day dragged along.

With only one house call, no one had died or had a contagious disease. Grace sat beside Dr. Woodcock as he turned the horse to head back to his office. After visiting with Alice who assured her she was as normal as anyone, she had forgiven herself, but not her rash behavior.

A commotion on the street brought her out of her reverie. The horse snorted as it came to a startled, abrupt stop. A man on foot weaving through traffic, charged toward them.

"Whoa, Dixie!" said Dr. Woodcock, trying to settle the horse.

The winded man took a minute to catch his breath before speaking.

"Doc, come quick! A man who works in the yards at the depot walked right into engine No. 382 pulling in from down south. Cut his leg clean off!"

"Jump on, man!"

The messenger pulled his Panama hat down tight, then jumped onto the side of the buggy hanging on to a rail. With the man onboard, the doctor slapped the horse with his whip to hurry them down the street, trying not to run over any pedestrians or other conveyances. Grace clung to the seat, her eyes alert and mind racing.

At the railroad yard, the dapper gentleman hanging on to the swaying buggy jumped off before they stopped. Grace lost sight of him as he disappeared into a circle of passengers and other spectators. Dr. Woodcock climbed down from the seat to anchor the horse to a hitching stone.

"Where's the damned railroad's doctor at this hour! What good is he if he's not available?" Grace had a hard time keeping up with Dr. Woodcock. He sounded infuriated that the unfortunate soul might have already passed.

The angry doctor walked fast shoving through the gawkers to make his way to the center of the crowd. Grace was on his heels carrying a lightweight rolled-up stretcher. In her other hand was a case holding sterilized instruments, too large for the doctor's handbag. For Grace, it was a fresh experience: the first time she ever heard the doctor curse.

Comments about the incident circulated through the crowd.

"Damned fool."

"His own damn fault."

"You don't know that, Frank!"

Grace shouted, "Everyone, please move back so the doctor can work. Now! Please move back at once!" She swung the stretcher like a baseball bat scattering curious people aside like bowling pins.

As they had room now, she knelt beside the doctor opening the bulky bag ready to aid him.

The patient was alert, his head cradled in a man's palms who was on his knees. He spoke encouragingly to the railroad worker about ordinary events that helped keep him calm. Grace saw someone had tightened a belt above his knee that kept the poor soul from bleeding out.

Dr. Woodcock went about his business ignoring everything in sight except his patient. The doctor smelled whiskey on the injured man, thankful he was already drunk. Without anesthesia, he'd prefer for him to pass out. Three men stepped from the murmuring crowd, their faces etched with concern, and volunteered to help hold the injured man still. The doctor worked on his ravaged leg, and the air became thick with the scent of antiseptic and sweat.

Grace was attentive to Dr. Woodcock's instructions, passing scissors, gauze, cotton, a small saw, alcohol, and finally a curved needle, threaded for suturing the terrible wound.

Silence fell over the crowd. The cowboy at the prone man's head said, "You're going to be fine, Paul. Don't jerk around like that. The doctor is just about done. Said you were going to recover and hardly

175

lost a pint of blood. Here, Paul, have another drought of whiskey. That's right. You'll be good to go soon."

Grace recognized the voice without looking up. It belonged to Randy. She stopped breathing, no longer aware of the turmoil swirling around the train yard. She bit her lip stilling her shaking hands. Her previous day's bravado evaporated as quickly as a vulnerable deer in a hunter's sight.

She dared not look around, wanting to be anywhere else, but a man's life depended on the medical attention he was receiving.

Dr. Woodcock had staunched the bleeding, sanitized all affected areas, sutured, and bandaged the stump of the leg. Grace prepared the stretcher for easy lifting of the unconscious man. Doctor Woodcock stood and instructed the men how to ease the worker onto the gurney to prevent the wound from reopening.

As she gathered up the Doctor's tools and the soiled towels and bandages scattered on the ground, a pair of boots came into her sight. Randy took her arm to help her stand.

They stared at one another. It became clear they had to move as by-standers carried the wounded man away, and the crowd began to disperse. Randy released her arm, reached for the doctor's bag, and handed it to Grace. He held her gaze, noticing that her hair and face remained unchanged since their last meeting. But something had changed. He couldn't quite pinpoint it. Even after the terrible accident, Grace's calm demeanor impressed him as she worked beside the doctor, helping him with every move. He saw a woman who forced a mob back with a folding stretcher, waving it like a firebrand. Unafraid and aggressive, she now stood rigidly facing him. Was she afraid of him?

"I have to go," she whispered.

She sounded panicky. "Wait." He clasped her arm. "Will you talk to me? I mean, when we're alone and you're not rushed or working." He searched her face and recognized the drawn look of being caught off-guard. The injury to the station employee was extensive, yet Grace remained unaffected by the gory sight. However, he expected that the real shock was seeing him so close and without warning.

A simple "yes" was all she managed, uncertain how to continue. "We can meet at the dairy. Saturday at three." Grace wasn't ready to be alone with him. Yet, she desired privacy. Having Alice Ann nearby felt reassuring. She had to go before she started the damned crying again.

Randy nodded and released her arm. His anger surfaced, yet, it was an improvement over his current state, which was hellish. He had a notion that she didn't want to talk at all. But he'd be at the dairy Saturday.

CHAPTER TWENTY

"Taking a new step, uttering a new word, is what people fear most." — Fyodor Dostoevsky, 'Crime and Punishment'

Randy Jackson & William Sullivant

Lasso missed the incident at the railroad yards. As his feet left the vestibule to touch the ground, he headed to the livery to fetch horses to ride to Red River. Neither he nor Randy have any idea how Mr. Sullivant will receive them when they show up at his door to announce their arrival. Nor did they discuss it between themselves, thinking it best to prepare for the worst.

Randy stubbed his cigarette into his palm and threw it away. "I saw Grace at the train station." He continued when Lasso looked at him without question. "She's the assistant to the doctor in Annona."

Lasso raised his eyebrows with a silent, *What?*

"While you were at the livery, a roostered railroad employee walked right into a moving train. Lost his leg completely. Good thing he was liquored up. The doc and Grace worked on him, staunched the bleeding, and stitched him up. When they were done, I talked to her. She told me to meet her Saturday at the farm."

Lasso nodded his head. The brief report from Randy was all he needed to know to understand his brevity. They rode, looking down the road, for a few minutes before Lasso said, "When we get to Miz Goss' place, I'd like to stop to see the missus. Many things need our attention."

Randy gave him a crooked grin. "Fine with me. I'll go on and get it over with Mr. Sullivant." Randy waved him off when they passed the boarding house.

The scent of dry grass and dust did little to help Randy find the words for Mr. Sullivant. After unsaddling, he turned the borrowed horse in a small pen to return to the livery later. In the bunkhouse, he grabbed clean clothes and stripped in the shower staying as long as possible. The weather was still warm enough that a cold shower wouldn't chill him. Revived, he pulled on his clothes, gave his hair a rub with a towel, combed it into place, and used his hat to hide the fact it was still wet. A symphony of whispers and laughter filled with sarcasm greeted him as he walked into the bunkhouse parlor. The other cowhands told him it was about time he returned, each hearty slap on his back driving home their point. It felt good they were still friends.

Randy knocked on the Sullivants' door, looking around the veranda for any sign of Mr. Sullivant. A young Mexican girl answered the door. She turned away to search for his boss. While he waited, he admired the lake beyond the end of the house, wanting to make his inheritance a home and working ranch like this one.

"Randy, come on in! When did you return?"

Randy removed his hat. He followed William Sullivant into a room with a desk and pictures of Western scenes around the walls. The bookshelves were full of periodicals, papers, and news.

"Have a seat. Tell me about your trip. Did you achieve your goal?"

"I'd say yes and no." Randy tried to laugh, but choked, as he started his story, giving him a moment to regroup. After clearing his throat, he tried again. "I found the girl I was looking for. She came home to Annona."

William looked at him wanting to know why his mechanic was gone for six weeks. He offered Randy a smoke and lit it for him. They settled back in their chairs as Randy sorted his thoughts.

"Grace had settled in the Red Oak area. That's near my parents' ranch." He dragged on the cigarette and began again. "I haven't seen my parents in a few years, Mr. Sullivant. As I rode in, the barns, fences, and the entire place were in poor shape. I worked on the ranch for a few days and found out that a dangerous man was stealing cattle from my father. That's when I sent a telegram to Andelacio for help.

"Grace had already left the ranch—"

179

"The ranch?"

Randy nodded. Being as direct as possible, he hoped his story was believable because it *was* the truth.

"I'm pretty sure that she had traveled there in search of employment and ended up at my ranch."

"Your ranch?" William repeated.

"I'm getting to that part, Mr. Sullivant. Grace got spooked when a thief tried to run her down when she was riding back to the ranch from Red Oak. As far as I know, she didn't realize the Bar J belonged to my parents." Randy took a deep breath. "Look, Mr. Sullivant, I know this sounds incredible, but I'm telling it straight."

William propped his elbows on his knees as he hung on every word. He waved his smoke through the air. "No, no. I'm listening, Randy, and I believe you. Keep going."

Randy fingered his hat brim, turning it in a slow circle between his legs. "Honest to Pete, Mr. Sullivant, I was relieved she'd gone somewhere else after what happened."

William smiled. "Go on."

Randy ground his cigarette out in the fancy stand beside his chair. He chanced a look at the Navajo rugs laying across the floor. They symbolized a notable chapter in American history. He felt the same pride in his ranch as well. A nearby pasture carried the faint calls of cows separated from their calves for weaning. More than ever, he yearned to be at the Bar J.

"One morning while working on the barn, I spotted three men ridin' through the brush near the ranch. I figured it was the same man my pa fired after he caught him stealing cattle. Only it was three of 'em. I asked Andelacio for help, and he had arrived by then. We sheltered the elderly in sheds, and ourselves in the barn. Well, all of us survived, but we killed one of them, wounded another, and one escaped. It was self-defense, Mr. Sullivant." Randy had given too much information without intending to, relieved to see his boss understood.

William pursed his lips and nodded in agreement. He watched Randy drop his gaze and waited for him to tell the rest of the story. If his mechanic were to leave, he'd have a hard time replacing him. "Are you and Lasso back for good now?"

"This is the thing, sir. My father has given me the ranch. It's solvent. I took a small loan to repair the barns and fencing. My parents are not in good health. And that, sir, is the reason I have to leave Red River. I made sure before I left they had plenty of supplies for themselves. And my pa wouldn't have to worry about our livestock starving." He watched his boss sit straight and prop his boot on one knee.

William's hair was turning gray around the temples. He was sure losing Randall Jackson would turn it white. Randy rode to Red River Ranch when sixteen years old. Even as a boy, he was one of the best cowhands he'd ever hired. For a moment, he was grim over the news. Then, he realized he had the privilege of watching him grow into a fine young man. As the sun set on the horizon, casting a warm golden glow over the room, he couldn't help but feel a sense of pride wash over him. With a mix of emotions, he asked, "When do you plan on leaving?"

Randy's stomach turned. Red River had been his home, but he had gained back his rightful home. Surely, Mr. Sullivant understood. Randy had heard that his boss' young life was not much different from his own. "Here's the rest of it. Lasso is going to be my ranch manager. But you can be darn sure we won't be leaving here until you find suitable replacements. Red River's been awfully good to both of us and we won't leave you in a lurch."

William stood suddenly making Randy flinch expecting a punch in the face for his unlikely story and for leaving Red River, plus taking another hand with him. Instead, his boss stuck out his hand.

"Congratulations, Randy. I'm glad for your family that you'll be there to take care of them and, boy, you've become a cattleman!"

Randy's broad grin matched the gusto of his boss' handshake. He couldn't wait for Lasso to ride in and hear the news. He strode with confidence to the bunkhouse expecting to have the best future a man could know. Except for not having her.

Though good fortune smiled on him, the familiar bleak landscape offered no visual comfort. The scent of missed opportunities and unfulfilled dreams still lingered. He craved her, as he deeply needed her. She was impulsive, smart, and beautiful. He hadn't figured out the rest, but, she had gained nothing by leaving Annona.

CHAPTER TWENTY-ONE

How long 'longing' lasts, depends solely on you.— *Cam Locke*

Randy

Saturday morning, Randy shaved, tamed his hair with Vaseline and brushed the dust from his hat. The lines he rehearsed, he hoped, would straighten any misunderstandings between them. *Must he assure her his intent was honorable? That he thought highly of her? And loved her? Was she able to understand that he spent weeks searching Texas in an attempt to find her? If she did not appreciate what he had done, it would chafe mightily.*

He mounted the porch steps after tying his horse to a rail at the back of the house. After three raps on the open door, no one answered. Dubious, he turned around. Alice was striding toward him from the barns. She invited him in, and they sat at the kitchen table.

Strange, but she looked as though she might cry. Randy removed his hat and prepared himself for another shock to his system. *What now? I don't know how . . .*

"I'm sorry, Randy. Grace ain't here. She sent the messenger boy who works for the doc out here with this note. The doctor had a huge emergency and needed her."

Alice held it out. He reached for it not wanting to know the message.

Randy, I'm sorry I cannot be there for our meeting. An emergency called Dr. Woodcock away, and I was summoned to help. Please forgive me. Perhaps another day?

Only the second day of his return, she was the entire time unavailable, hindering their progress to resolve their differences. Not unusual that women had resorted to earning their own wages. Especially if they were single. It seemed worse than owning the dairy. He decided not to quit his quest completely, however, if she wanted him, a compromise from her was essential for them to reconcile. He planned to leave right off for the Bar J. The twist in his gut tightened realizing it may be without her.

Randy nodded at Alice, and saying nothing, mounted his horse unsure of seeing Grace again. Since Grace was back home and safe, another day pursuing her was not in his plan. Unless there was a good reason. Thinking of Grace was an unrelenting, bitter-sweet perpetual pursuit of a beautiful bird over the horizon.

Though he cared about her, he needed time to come to terms with the ugly thing that occurred at his ranch. He proved to be an excellent shot but never thought he'd have to use his gun to shoot someone. It ate at him daily.

Lasso, too, had been untalkative on the train, which reinforced Randy's belief that the brutal behavior of his own father scarred him.

He stared at the sky knowing God orchestrated everything. *You brought me back to my parents. My parents have given me the ranch. Lasso, my best friend, is marrying my sister. The result was clear to You from the start. It'll be interesting to see what You have in store for me now.*

He mopped a sheen of sweat from his chin with his handkerchief. The horse walked on as he removed his hat to run the damp cloth across his forehead. How could the sun be so hot and the early autumn breeze so delightful? He guessed it was just Texas.

Back at Red River, he unsaddled and took care of his horse. His stomach loudly complained, taking his mind from his worries, and he came to realize his love of the life at Red River, working cattle, and, now, he was a mechanic over all equipment at Red River and Eberly. Equally, other factors existed he had no control over.

Randy wrangled leftovers from the cook who fussed at him in Chinese for coming in late and dirtying more dishes. Randy apologized as best he could, as Chu knew little English.

While finishing up his plate, Lasso came in, dropped his hat and gun on the table end, and helped himself to the leftovers, ignoring the cook's hard looks.

The two cowboys ate for a minute then spoke together. Smiles broke out. Randy felt tension in his muscles relax as he scanned the area for eavesdroppers. "Lasso, you first. How's Phoebe and the baby?"

"Phoebe remains as beautiful as ever." Then he taunted, "Unlike her ugly brother."

"Gee, thanks. Just remember I'm your brother-in-law and soon-to-be boss!" He waved his fork in Lasso's direction.

"Si. As I was saying. The baby doesn't have a name yet, at least an entire name. Grace and Phoebe decided on the middle name Jackson in honor of his uncle."

"I *am* honored," Randy smirked. "Andelacio is quite a mouthful."

Lasso looked at him, his eyes rolled back in his head. "You *should* feel honored, my friend." Remember, it was Andelacio who rescued your ass when you needed it!"

Randy laughed and asked, "When will you and Phoebe seek a preacher? I assume you plan to after all you've said."

A crease appeared between Lasso's eyebrows. "We plan to take the train to Clarksville. Most of Annona believes we're married. Our being together oughtn't cause a commotion. I trust you don't mind me telling her that your parents left the ranch to you. The news appeared to suit her that we'd be living there, too. Did you and Mr. Sullivant talk over our leaving here?"

"Yeah, and he congratulated me and wished us luck. But I told him we'd not leave till he found a couple more cow punchers. It ain't right to leave him short-handed."

"There's one other thing I should mention. Phoebe would like to have her brother be there to give her away, as her pa won't be. I ain't never been to a wedding before, so I'm not sure how important that detail is."

"It sounds important to Phoebe. I wouldn't want to disappoint my sister. You tell her I'll be there. Good grief. You do know we're gonna be brothers-in-law?"

"So, 'sides us being related, you're my boss, too? Damn, that's tough." He made a sad face.

"I'll tell my sister to go extra light on you so you don't get all balled up."

"Huh, huh. Thanks." As Lasso listened, the jovial lilt of Randy's banter was a sharp contrast to the flicker of something dark in his eyes.

CHAPTER TWENTY-TWO

Better a broken promise than none at all. — Mark Twain

Grace & Randy

Grace didn't plan to avoid meeting Randy at the dairy. She had no choice when Johnny, Dr. Woodcock's errand boy, rode up to the back door. Dr. Woodcock needed her in town. She scribbled a note and asked Johnny to deliver it to Alice. She simply explained the situation, too rushed to say more.

After she arrived at his office, they set off on a three-mile drive to the patient's home. In the future, she might follow on her horse to avoid the jolting buggy seat on the pothole filled road.

"Grace," the doctor began as his derby tumbled from his head. He caught it and jammed it on his head. "Old Weasley T. Thompson was about gone from a case of DTs. His son found him on the side of the road on his way home."

She nodded. After turning up a dirt trail, they stopped where a shack stood. They followed young Thompson through the only door. Grace noted that Mr. Thompson's only son looked nearly twenty years old. No women were there; two men were the only occupants.

His father, Weasley, lay in bed amid a swaddle of rags. Worn, yellowed long johns were the only clothing he was wearing. His face was deathly white face poking through the neck of the stained undershirt.

After looking Mr. Thompson over, the doctor turned to Grace. "Miss Grace."

Grace clenched her teeth against the odor of decay. "Yes."

The doctor turned toward Billy Thompson. "This gentleman has a case of rum fits that are a manifestation of withdrawal from liquor by a chronic alcoholic."

The young man nodded his head, thinking he already diagnosed that himself. However, treatment was out of his element of expertise. Billy had never seen his father sober or bring home a complete paycheck. Weasley stopped daily on his way home to spend the majority on whiskey.

"Billy, how long has he been in this state?"

"A full day and night, sir."

"As you see, your father is sweating profusely. He has dilated pupils and is suffering from confusion and tremors."

As if to refute the evidence, the old man's eyes popped open. He struggled to sit up as both men held him down by the arms. The doctor glanced at Billy while blocking Weasley's fist from hitting him in the face.

Finally, Weasley lay back down. Doctor Woodcock said, "Keep him hydrated, son. Anything you're able to get down him except alcohol. Keep it as dark in here as possible. In this condition, he'll have sensitivity to light and hallucinations." He glanced at Billy and Grace to be sure they were listening to this lesson.

"I'll do my best, Doc, but I go to work early and come home late."

"Do you know anyone who will check in on him? He needs water during the day."

"Yes, sir."

The old man calmed down, and the doctor forced a sip of water down his throat. Half of it ran down his chin. The doctor pulled a vial from his case.

"This is laudanum, Billy, to help him sleep, but don't give him too much or he will sleep permanently. Relay to anyone checking on him to follow these identical instructions. He'd be better off with a change to a nightgown or clean clothes, too." the doctor checked his watch, "I'll check back with you about this time tomorrow."

The young man was staring at his father, still holding his hand. "Yes, sir, I'll be here."

Grace gathered the medical instruments and left a spoon and laudanum on the dresser for Billy to administer.

"Alright. For now, I'm leaving it with you to take care of your father. And I'm sorry, son. But we'll make him as comfortable as possible." The doc nodded at Grace signaling he'd done all he could.

Billy nodded. His mouth was a grim line.

Once settled on the buggy, the said, "It's a shame about that family."

"How exactly?" Surprised, Grace had never heard the kind man talk about any of his patients.

"Young and in love, Thompson and Sue Ellen Cully were married at the end of a shotgun. Sue Ellen died from complications after their son was born. Old Weasley never forgave his son. He blamed his wife's death on the child."

Grace remembered Billy holding his father's hand. "That's both awful and sad."

"Yes. That's when Wes started drinking, and I think Billy was much neglected by his father. Such a loving and wonderful young man is a rare find. Life certainly doesn't treat everyone the same."

Deep in shuffled thoughts, she chewed on her bottom lip, holding on for life on the rutted road. Arriving at the shared post office, Grace bid Woodcock goodbye. When saddling her horse for the ride home, she whispered a prayer for the Thompsons. Staring into the clouds that floated across the majestic, open sky like enormous ships, nothing came to mind solving her problems.

A rider appeared at the top of the knoll. The man's torso towered above his horse's ears. Closer now, she recognized Randy's Boss of the Plains Stetson with its deep center crease. Dust coated his chaps and hat. It puzzled her why he'd be riding toward town.

Randy would not be on the road if there had been another way. He had ridden over to convey that Lasso and Phoebe were getting married. Grace was to be at the wedding, too. Randy pushed his hat brim up and put his hand over the other on the saddle horn. "Hello, Grace," he said with a measured voice, devoid of any joy or disappointment. Though tired, he also gambled that having a meeting with her might help him sleep that night.

Still uncertain about meeting with Randy, Grace stopped her horse when he pulled up beside her. Up close, he appeared thinner than at the train station and in need of a haircut. Now, close enough to touch him, Grace nodded. He was a fine-looking man and there was nowhere else to look. His piercing stare held her speechless. "Hello." Hadn't she wished every day to make amends for her behavior? Now, she had no words. She waited for him to speak.

"It seems you spent most of your day with the doctor."

"Part of it with an ill patient. It was a sad day. I apologize for being unable to join you earlier. And you? Did you work cattle all day?" He didn't sound vindictive, but she worried he would turn around and become angry with her.

When her mouth trembled, he took a deep breath through his teeth, then let it out with a whoosh. She spoke with restraint as if he were a mere acquaintance she had just met. "Most of it. At least till the other men showed up to take over. Thought I'd ride over to see if you were home. Since we're standing in the middle of the road, have you got time to talk to me now?"

He found being pragmatic brought better results. But being intimate with Grace before, blocked his best reasoning. Once upon a time, he longed to kiss those beautiful lips.

There was a hardness in Randy's eyes, a potency she'd never seen before. Deep down, she knew she wasn't able to deny him an audience. Alongside inviting him in, she found it impossible to suppress the overwhelming fear of being rejected. "I will make the time. Shall we ride to my house instead of making spectacles of ourselves on the road? I bet you could use something to drink."

He agreed by nodding. She could never accuse Randy of being a whiner. Turning their horses in unison, they headed toward her property. Resigned to making conversation, she looked at Randy. "I heard about you and Mr. Slade's terrible ruckus on the train. The robbery."

She knew, which surprised Randy; his head gave a little shake, and his expression was curious.

"Y'all were quite the heroes. It was all anyone talked about in town. I've been worried about you and the outcome of the charges. It was a relief that no one killed anyone."

She sounded sincere. But the day he stepped from the train, they set a date. She missed their meeting. After feeling ignored, to avoid the pain of loving too much, he chose to distance himself.

"My lucky day." Sarcasm covered the anxiety. But discussing the outcome with her was better than keeping the scab over the wound. More the reason he needed her. "We're waiting on a court date to clear us shooting one of them. But it was self-defense. Shouldn't be too hard with a carload of passengers to vouch for us." Randy fidgeted with the rope tied to the saddle as a reason to not look at her. Anyway, her gaze stayed fixated on the ground as if she were asking it to swallow her.

"I'm sorry that happened—I mean, on top of everything else," she muttered.

She was hard to hear, yet he sensed regret in her voice. In his approach to mending whatever was left to salvage from their brief relationship, he refused to be spiteful. Dismounting at her barn, they tied the horses to a post. Not to waste time getting down to their state of affairs, they left the horses saddled beneath the lean-to.

Grace's reactions were apparent to Randy. Her hands were shaking as she tethered her horse. Coyote stuck his head across the fence, but she paid no attention. Her movements were deliberate,

191

her back stiff. He wanted to have something more than pity for her, but the high walls he'd built were too strong to offer her even a hint of how much he loved her.

Through the back door into the kitchen, he sat at the table and removed his hat. His fingers moved through his errant hair. She chipped an ice block to cool the water in the glass she sat on the table. She moved as easily as her name implied, grace in every step, her hair undone from its pins because of the steady breeze while they traveled on the road. She re-pinned what she was able to, still not meeting his eyes.

Randy sighed while rummaging through his mind. Full of regrets and images of the terrible events that had happened in the past four months, he thought the worst was over. The woman he thought to share his life with, sat at the table staring into the oak top as though waiting for the hangman to tighten the knot. *Did she run away because she wasn't ready for the responsibilities of a married woman? After all, she had shucked an entire farm because it had become a burden.* The new thought was intriguing. Though it didn't particularly trouble him, he would find out.

The distant sound of rain tapping against the windowpane, echoed the palpable tension in the room. "Grace." She didn't look up. He reached out and wrapped his big hand around her wrist and drew her arm across the table. He grasped her hand with both of his. "Grace, please listen to me."

Her sigh filled the silence and her breath made the candle flicker. Then she said, "I'm so sorry to have caused you such worry."

As she apologized for his mistreatment, he stared blankly at her. "I'm not angry, Grace. I swear. But, you ought to have talked with me. I couldn't grasp your reason for leaving without saying anything. I'm a good listener. If you'd told me I ain't worth the sweat off your brow, I would'na been half as worried about you and how you were doing out there, somewhere by yourself."

There was no way to justify her innocence. She watched the movement of his thumbs as he stroked her palm. "I-I have loved you, Randy, from the first day we met when you shod Coyote." His dark mustache frowned along his top lip before it dipped toward his chin at each end. A beating was preferable to his tormenting patience. How could she say the words without sounding ridiculous when he looked so solemn? When he knew how frivolous she was as a human being, he would laugh at her and leave. Breaking her. A tear rolled down her cheek as she prepared to lose the love of her life.

"So you understand, Randy, in the past, a handful of men… a couple of cowboys, crossed paths with me at various times, but our life goals never aligned. Then, they'd become smitten with Corrine who culled them like black-eyed peas on New Year's Day. It was difficult to acknowledge that I, for myself, was not enough. It hurt, more so, as she was my sister."

When Grace stopped talking, his mouth lifted to one side. He offered neither advice nor criticism. "I'm listening, Grace."

Still unable to meet his gaze, Grace looked at his red neckerchief tucked beneath his shirt collar. She said, "As we became better acquainted, I loved you more. Early on, I prayed you'd ask me to marry. Now, I'm confused about marrying at all.

"In short, when I tell you, if we're together or go our separate ways, I'm asking you to forgive me." Knowing she was admitting to raging jealousy, Grace stared at their hands, and tears flowed freely down her face. "I was on my way through town to the dairy one day. It was the day young Ethan made his first run to the cheese factory and delivered milk around Annona. Headed back home, as we reached Miss Goss' place . . ." Her heart hammered with shame as she strove to expose her flaws.

Randy said nothing but rubbed her hand with his thumb. His curiosity had grown, as he could not fathom where her tale was going. He did not intend to judge, but to move past the past.

Grace cleared her throat and started again. "And, uh, I saw you, 'cause I'd know you anywhere. A woman stood with you near the entrance. Then, *then* you embraced. Like lovers. Randy, I loved you with my heart and soul. I thought you... I thought you cared about me the same. After the other men—the disappointments. Of all of them—now you! I thought I might die. And, I didn't know *it was your sister* until later! It was because I loved you, I behaved the jealous fool. Then after, I thought... you had deceived me, and I begin to hate being tied down at the farm."

At length, Grace stopped speaking, shattering him as he watched her empty her heart. Grace pulled her hands from his. With palms down, she propped her forehead on the back of her hands. She cried wiping her face with her sleeve.

Humble and teary, he let her cry for a few moments more. He underestimated love's blinding power. Not only did he still love her, but he also knew he should thank her for leading him to the Bar J and his family.

"Grace," he called out, but she kept her head down. He raised his voice, imploring, "Grace, please, meet me halfway." Randy offered her his neckerchief to wipe her face. He wondered what it would take for her to look at him. He heard her out. How could he convince her he was not angry if she refused to listen? His chair creaked when he shoved it back and rounded the table. Not knowing another way, he pulled her up by the wrists from the chair, sat in her place, and forced her into his lap.

Grace pushed on his arms, only to feel his arm muscles tense. There was no escaping his hold. Randy put his face close to her hair and took a long breath. When he loosened his grip, they were inches apart when she looked at him, and she gave up the struggle. It wasn't the way his hair covered his ears like a small boy's. Or the day's beard that softened the set of his jaw. He was far more tolerant than she was capable of being.

"Randy." She moaned the useless objection as his muscular arms pulled her closer. He held her in an unbreakable grip and spread kisses along her jawline. These moments were the ones she prayed for. She did love him. Staying in love for life was the question. His powerful arms pulled her in, drawing a whisper of 'Randy' from her.

"So, help me, you taste good." He pushed her hair from her wet cheeks. "It's over, Grace, we found each other again. Let's begin anew. I never thought I'd hold you again," he whispered as he kissed her ear. Filled with a mix of joy and apprehension, he kissed her lips, pulling her softness against his hardness. His hands roamed down her hips and explored the curves of her back.

The subtle scent of male, dust and hair oil enveloped her. His shoulders were broad and his arms were those of a man who worked hard for a living. Every touch, every caress, ignited a symphony of sensations that left her breathless. Grace wrapped her arms around his neck. The buttons on his vest pressed against her.

When they separated, she whispered in his ear. "Are you sure about this, Randy? I figured you'd never forgive me for making you go on a wild goose chase." She pushed away studying his face.

"Just so long as you pay me back, Grace." They were so close he saw black specks in the bluest of eyes.

"Pay what back?"

"The same 'grace' as I paid you. I reckon everyone does unfortunate things once in a while. I've loved you, too, from the first day. The hardest experience of my life was when you disappeared without a word or explanation. I never felt this way about anyone." He stopped speaking, arguing with himself it was best if he turned in a different direction. From what he learned in the past hour, Grace had changed, much wiser and with greater self-reliance. The physical contact of her breasts against him was enough for now. But what he wanted, her, was impossible.

He loosed his hold and smoothed her disarrayed hair covering her back. He put his hands on her face to pull her mouth to his lips and only let go when they were out of breath. She pressed her face into his neck and kissed him, caressing his long hair.

A swell of lust heated his crotch as her soft buttocks bore down on him. He knew she felt him as a flush of pink colored her cheeks. His breathing slowed, and he relaxed as much as possible. He thought it unwise to press her further knowing a committed physical relationship and marriage were both out of the question for her for now.

After the attack on the ranch, weeks of traveling, carpentry, and fencing at the ranch had worn him thin. From the time he left Red River, nothing had gone the way he expected. A conundrum for him, he had to let her find her own way to an end of their love. Or come to him offering everything.

With that mix of objective understanding, he settled for their being wrapped in each other's arms. He intended to share news of his father's ranch inheritance. Then, he decided the time or place to go into it wasn't right.

Before he thought about it further, a flash of lightning filled the open window with light. Grace stood from Randy's lap. He glanced over his shoulder as the wind picked up, irritating the curtains into a fluttering dance. The next clap of thunder came with more wind, this time pushing the curtains further out from the window casing.

Grace watched him stand to close the window and grab a dish towel nearby to wipe up the rain that had covered the sill. He removed his chinks. He was tall and lean, with slim hips. She swallowed and continued her search for matches to light the kerosene lamps.

"I'm going out to unsaddle and feed the horses."

"Alright. If you're hungry, I'll make up something."

Randy felt in a strange place. Like he'd just woken up in a rowboat loosed in the sea. He walked to her and ran his fingers across her cheek. "That's fine, Grace. I'm pretty hungry." At the door, he stopped. "You'll be here when I get back, won't you?" A wicked grin slashed his face.

"Randy Jackson!" Despite her precarious footing, Grace smiled through the tear tracks on her cheeks, watching him hurry down the steps.

She emptied the small pile of dry wood in the bin beside the stove. After starting a fire, she whipped up some flour and buttermilk to make flapjacks. Thick sliced bacon was sizzling in the skillet when Randy returned. He cracked eggs in a bowl he found on a shelf and beat them into a fine lather with a spoon.

"Before long, it'll be pitch black outside. The storms picked up wind, but you never knew about Mother Nature. I've never been able to outguess her."

"No one can." Grace twisted the wick raiser knob on the lamps, lengthening the cotton wicks for more light. Another clap of thunder made her jump while she was taking plates down to load up with the bacon and fried cakes. She was thankful for Randy's company. Storms made her uncomfortable, but Randy reassured her. She had never shared this experience with a man and found it as natural as rain.

He removed the butter from the larder, and she took the honey jar from the shelf to the table. "This looks good, Grace." Her tears had shaken him to the bone. But, he wasn't ready to surrender the fort that his heart had built to protect it from the arrows of warning she released over marrying him.

They ate in silence. Grace watched him eat like a starving wolf ignoring the plunk of heavy rain on the roof. She felt bad that if he rode home, his saddle, gear, and the poor horse would drown in a minute if either of them looked upward. The ranch lay at least five miles away. Another clap of thunder rattled the windowpanes.

"Randy."

He looked up when she called his name. The lamp light was dim causing shadows to flicker on the wall. Grace was as beautiful as a freed bird who'd left her surroundings only to find she didn't belong anywhere except in the gilded cage she'd come to despise. Tonight, she looked at peace and content.

Another streak of lightning lit up the sky. Two seconds later, an explosion of thunder followed that made Grace wince.

Randy reached across the table to hold her hands. "It's alright, darlin'. We're safe here. Let's ride this storm out in the sittin' room, away from the windows."

Grace stood up, and with his hand against her back, he guided her to the settee. When they sat down, Randy wrapped his arm around her shoulders and pulled her closer. She lay her head on his shoulder, then raised up, her eyes searching his face.

"It's a terrible night, and it seems like we've only just met. But, I'm afraid for you to travel in the storm. The lightning kills cattle and destroys trees, but it's worse if it hits a man on a horse. A man who lacks even a slicker tied to his saddle!"

Randy chuckled.

"Oh, don't look at me like I'm daft! It has happened before."

"Why don't you say you want me to stay tonight or at least till the storm passes?"

Grace squealed at his wisecrack and punched his arm. After the shock wore off over his directness, she said, "Are you serious?"

"Yes, ma'am. I'm perfectly content here on this settee."

"Can I trust you?"

"You think I would hurt you?" His eyes crinkled at the corners, insulted.

She had to think. "No. Not physically."

Now he understood. "Grace," he whispered, I have never loved another woman, didn't know what it would be like." He pushed her hair behind her shoulders. "I know now. I know love can be painful, and brings up a terrible fear you might lose the person you'd die for. Look at me." His finger under her chin lifted her face. "I'm *that* man."

For a moment, she basked in his words. Throwing herself into his arms, she gripped his hair in her fingers. "I do love you, Randy, I do!" Her cheek rested against his shoulder.

"I'm not afraid of waiting awhile, Grace." He ran his finger down her jaw. "Does that suit you?" *If you can just decide before I leave, that's all I ask..*

She gave a weak nod with a sniffle.

"Come on, I'll help clean up the kitchen."

If Randy caught pneumonia in the rain, she'd never forgive herself. She gave in to him sleeping on the settee wrapped in a blanket. With his head on an extra pillow, stripped down to his long johns, his legs hung over the end of the short sofa. Down the hall, she shut her door and dressed for bed.

* * *

The sun was shining through the bedroom window when Grace woke up. A heavy weight pinned her to the mattress. Randy's arm lay across her. He was so warm and smelled like the outdoors in the spring. She shut her eyes not wanting to wake him up. His body was lanky with long muscling on his shoulders and arms. She knew he was an above-board man. No one she knew ever had a bad thing to say about the blacksmith. She'd not felt this safe since being chased by a crazed man shooting a gun. Because of Randy, she didn't wake up one time during the storm.

She gently lifted his arm, then he moved it on his own and put it behind his head. His eyes following her every move.

Grace covered her breasts with the sheet as her gown did little to conceal the goosebumps caused by his intense gaze, making her nipples visible. She jerked the sheet from the bed wrapping it around her shoulders, then turned toward him.

199

"What in tarnation are you doing in my bed, Randall Jackson?"

She looked wonderful with her hair in a pigtail, parts of it loose, fluttering with her exaggerated movements while scolding him. "Taking care of you, my beauty. You were crying out in your sleep. I was hoping it was for me, but I think it had more to do with the storm. So, I acted a gentleman to ward off your fears."

"Hogwash." She stomped from the bedroom and sat on the settee pulling the sheet tightly around her. There was a delightful feeling coursing through her hips and pelvis. She knew he had made it happen just by looking at her in her nightgown. She'd wait where she was until he removed himself from her bed and went elsewhere, hopefully, to feed the horses. Her hope came true when he walked barefooted and shirtless, wearing only his long johns, to the settee to retrieve his pants and boots. She refused to face him but could see him dressing from the corner of her eye. His shoulders bent, his back curved as he pulled on his boots. Just watching him dress started the goosebumps again and awoke those spasms that brought a blush to her face and hastened her breathing. She turned her head to hide her flushed face and to calm her breathing.

He stood with his boots on, fully clothed, grabbed his hat, and walked to the door. He stopped with a sly grin on his face. "I'll be back shortly. Got things to do outside."

She watched him shut the door and she started to turn the lock. *It would serve him right, sneaking into my room in the middle of the night.* A shiver went through her, reminding her how warm his body had been, how comfortable she felt next to him, his arm protecting her from an unseen threat. She dressed quickly in the most unfeminine clothes she could find in the armoire, baggy pants to her ankles, a white blouse with a lacy collar was all she had that was clean, and brogans. She bought the trousers at the mercantile in a boy's size because there weren't any for women. She at least owed him a meal after feeding the horses, the chickens, and the goat.

There was a fire in the stove by the time he made it back into the house. As she cracked eggs in the skillet to fry, she appreciated him knocking the dirt off his boots on the porch before entering the house. To her surprise, he didn't sit in the parlor, he entered the kitchen, went straight to the pantry and set the table with plates, forks coffee cups, and butter for the biscuits he could smell rising in the oven.

They sat at the table without speaking. Randy devoured his breakfast while Grace poked it with a fork, but hardly ate. Randy was the first to arise and, as before, began to clean the table. Grace watched for a moment before removing the plates from the cabinet top to the sink.

Randy left the kitchen and returned with his hat in his hand. "It was awfully nice of you to allow me to stay the night out of the storm. He wrapped his arms around her and kissed her. The next kiss was longer and wetter. Grace gripped his arms pulling him down to her as she stood on her tiptoes. Their touching lips lingered like a butterfly touch until Randy slid the tip of his tongue across hers. She opened her mouth to his tongue igniting a wave of electric sensation down his spine. His arms pulled her hips flat against his as if claiming every part of her. He had been through hell, and she was going to heal him.

They slowly separated, he with a kiss on the corners of her mouth. He regretted having to leave but had a job to do. First, he needed to pass along the information he came there for. "I heard you and Phoebe had become close friends. I wasn't privy to your and her discussions, but there's one thing lacking between her and Lasso."

Grace leaned back. "What one thing?" Phoebe and she had become close, but she never talked in depth about their marriage. Nor ever asked if he fathered the baby.

"A marriage."

"You mean—"

"Yep. No one knows but us five if you count Miz Goss. So, we talked it over, and they set a date to go to Clarksville. We'll get rooms at the hotel, find a minister, and come home the next day. If we're lucky, nobody will suspect a thing.

"I had an inkling, but it didn't matter. Phoebe's my best friend."

"Sis wants you to be in her wedding, Grace, and me to give the bride away."

"Oh. I'm flabbergasted and honored that she wants me involved." Aghast at the entire sordid chain of terrible things that happened after she left Annona, hearing that Phoebe and Lasso were getting married lifted her spirits, so much that she felt normal again. She took Randy's hand and gave it a squeeze. "Of course, I want to be there. Is there a date set?"

"Not yet. As soon as I find out, we can discuss it further. I need to go before the ranch is searching for me."

A rooster crowed, and they broke apart again. She lay her head against his chest as he rubbed his chin against her hair.

"Tomorrow, I'll be in Annona to do mechanical repairs for my customers. Maybe shoe a few horses. I'll be riding by about dusk. I'd like to drop in if you're home and not away assisting the doc."

"Alright." His eyes bore into hers.

"If I'm here, I'll have supper made."

He kissed her, gave her a hug, and left.

With arms wrapped around herself, her shoulders relaxed as relief flooded through her veins that he was gone. With him there, it was too easy to give in. She wanted to and was glad he was not there to tempt her further. Then anxiety swept in as he rode away, leaving her alone again. She felt something awakened within—love sparked an additional need, not a need for love, but a need for him because of it. Powerful and demanding, she couldn't deny it anymore. She loved him more than ever.

Later as the sun set, concern about the future filled her with questions. Common sense said they needed explaining. Where were they going with this *flirtation, infatuation, whatever it was*? He was a cowhand making money on the side as a smithy. If she had a husband, her working would be unmanageable. She liked her job. And a cowboy's salary alone would not support a family and rent. The ranch he loved so much had a bunkhouse, but nothing for a husband, wife, or children. The cowhands at Red River were single.

She believed he probably worked too late to stop to visit. All the thinking gave her a headache, and she left the kitchen for relief. Being alone didn't affect her before. But ever since Randy rode away, her loneliness had magnified a hundredfold.

CHAPTER TWENTY-THREE

Something to Think About

Grace

The next afternoon, a familiar frantic knock on her door cleared her mind. Dr. Woodcock used Johnny as a messenger and dispatched him to her house when he needed her. After hearing his message, she rode into town, her horse gouging holes in the dirt in her haste. When she arrived, the doc was waiting for her with every portable medical device loaded in the buggy. His Percheron Mule's long stride shortened the trip to a sawmill on the south side of town.

"What happened?" Grace asked.

"A pine trunk rolled off a farmer's large-wheeled cart when his mules bolted, pinning the unlucky farmer beneath it. I was told the other loggers moved the log aside, but I'm not sure what we'll find."

"Oh," she braced herself, breathing a joyless sigh.

When they arrived, the man had breathed his last breath. Dr. Woodcock wore a calm expression. Grace never knew what he was thinking. After examining the injured man, he attributed internal injuries as the cause of death. The farm workers circled the doctor as he explained how best to load the body into a wagon for transport home. After it was done, Grace re-packed his medical bags to return to the buggy and start for the office.

Dr. Warren P. Woodcock III looked at his assistant. With no children of his own, he had become fond of her. Grace was staring off to the side as he maneuvered the horse around a jackrabbit darting across the road. "You have said little, Miss Grace. Please, don't be upset about Mr. Whittaker. That's not to say, his death wasn't a terrible thing, but death is a part of living. We go forward the best we can and enjoy those we love while we can."

It was as though he read her thoughts. A man's life came to an abrupt stop without warning. Or a chance to say goodbye. That was the worst part. What if something terrible happened to Randy? He

204

worked on heavy machinery. Was even shot at. A tingle of foreboding scampered down her spine.

"I do believe that, Doctor. Sometimes it is hard to accept. Poor Mrs. Whittaker. I bet she and Mr. Whittaker had children. It's the ones left behind who will be hurt now."

"It's nothing we can control. Humans grow more accepting of life's only certainty with age. One day we all will cross the heavenly Great Divide."

Despite the sensible explanation, Grace said a prayer. *Please, keep him safe.* Grace looked at the watch she wore on a chain around her neck. It was two P.M. She aimed to see Randy riding down her drive by late afternoon, assuming no more emergencies arose before she mounted her horse to ride home. She looked at the doctor. "It's not something one wants to dwell on often. I think it would be bad for the spirit."

"That's right, Grace. Young people are more resilient than their elders." *And they never think about dying.*

Back at the tiny postal building where the doc maintained a corner office, Grace bid him goodbye. She saddled and turned toward the road home. At home, she removed a steak from the cooler. After cooking the rest of the meal, she placed it in the warm oven until Randy arrived.

By seven-thirty, she gave up the possibility of seeing him, set her place on the table, and ate. Not yet dark, the vacant chair was striking, the lack of another's voice thunderous. Over the past few days, she had learned not to judge others too fast. And she never wanted to repeat the loneliness she felt in Dallas. Randy was many things. A mechanic, cowboy, a modest man. He was too busy to come over. She stored the leftovers.

An hour later, Grace lowered the windows. The frogs croaking by the pond and crickets singing their nocturnal lungs out brought a smile to her face. Once in the bed, she blew out the lamp. She shut her eyes and, envisioning Randy lying beside her, she placed her palm on top of the spare pillow. *Please, don't do something stupid and get hurt. Why didn't you come today? You said you would. I expect you to burn the breeze next time you travel here.*

* * *

Randy & Lasso

That night Randy drove to Red River under a full moon. He leaned forward, bracing his elbows on his thighs as he rolled a cigarette. After lighting it and taking a long breath in, he stopped the wagon horse as he approached Grace's house, and exhaled. The shades covered the dark windows. He worked on a Caterpillar track-type tractor until dusk for a cotton farmer outside of Annona. Too late to make it for dinner.

"To think, I was in bed with her last night." He imagined the possibilities of their activities in bed that night if her feelings matched his. She must be wanting to smack him in the head with a skillet for not showing up. But no matter how he longed to see Grace, he couldn't stop in the middle of fixing that contraption and the farmer needing to use it.

Ain't life funny. He slapped a rein on the horse's rump and craned his neck to see the house until it was out of sight. Tomorrow he will find out more about Phoebe and Lasso's plans. Marriage ceremonies were not in his purview. He'd know soon enough when they traveled to Clarksville for the marriage. He had explained bits of the wedding plans to Grace but planned to talk with her again tomorrow. He had no jobs the next day, other than regular ranch work at Red River to hinder him.

He unhooked the horse from his work wagon and fed the gelding in a small pen alone so the other cow ponies wouldn't steal his grain and hay. He rinsed his face in a watering trough and shook his hands dry. The bunkhouse was dark, the cook had gone to bed. He saw a plate on the table with a napkin draped over it. It had a round of steak, potatoes, beans, and a slab of pan bread on it. Lasso.

Early the next morning, he rode out with Lasso to check on some heifers. They determined after a head count that none of the young cows were missing. They continued their ride along the fence line for downed wire.

"Thought I better ask if you and Phoebe had come to any agreement on how you want to— you know, and when you want to—"

Lasso looked at him. "Now, you have a problem with me marrying your sister?"

"Naw. Not at all. Just hard for me to get used to the married thing and you being my brother-in-law."

In fun, Lasso elevated his voice to tenor. "Aw, amigo. We could jump into the fire together. We can give solace to each other when our wives don't like our having poker night. Ask your girl to marry you, eh? We can have a double wedding in Clarksville." Lasso gave Randy a sly smile. "Are you backing out now that you found your lady?"

"I was mainly talking about my little sister and you, you big bag of horse shit! I'll do my own asking when I'm good and ready."

"Si, boss." Lasso grinned from ear to ear. "Getting back to what you asked about the *married thing,* it'll be a couple of days 'fore Mr. Sullivant can do without his best hands. That's us."

"Hmmm. Not sure about that." Randy shook his head. "Just give me a day's notice, okay? I'd like to get things in order. I can't just up and run off on a minute's notice."

Lasso nodded, stopped his horse, and stepped down to take a closer look at a strand of wire that needed splicing.

* * *

The Big Day

Phoebe spoke in a whisper with two fingers across her lips. "I barely had enough milk to leave with Mrs. Goss for Daniel. I can't wait to get back to my baby. I miss him so much."

"I understand how difficult it would be for a mother to leave such a sweet child. I'm so happy for you, though, that now he has a daddy. And you. Someone who loves you and Daniel so much."

Grace and Phoebe left the side of the baby's crib and gently closed the door. They tiptoed away to wait inside the front door for Randy and Lasso to arrive. When they heard the horseshoes in the drive, they rushed outside with their luggage. The two couples arrived at the train station early, giving time to leave the horse and buggy with the hostler at the town stable.

* * *

Phoebe wiped happy tears from her eyes, then peeked over the seat and smiled at Lasso. Her brother was seated by the isle staring out the far window.

Once in Clarksville, they stepped off the train and walked twenty minutes to the hotel on the public square. After checking in, Lasso unlocked the door to the girls' room, pushed it open with his boot, and deposited their bags near a large dresser. When Randy and Grace stepped back into the wide hallway, he took Phoebe's hands in his and kissed her palms. She gently touched his black hair and smiled.

Lasso set the Stetson back on his head at a jaunty tilt.

"I will fetch you at three o'clock, provided you're ready?" His voice was a whisper and his eyes soft.

"Yes, that's fine." Phoebe sighed.

Lasso kissed her on the cheek and headed to the door, looking back as he left the room.

Randy and Grace waited in the hall, his hands set against the wall next to Grace's shoulders. He leaned in close as Grace glanced to the side to see Lasso come into the hall. "Oh."

Randy followed her gaze. His hands fell to pick up his own bag, and he walked Grace back to her room. "Lasso set the time at three to leave here. He asked the desk about a church we passed down the street and was headed there to set up the ceremony. When he gets back later, we'll come for you ladies around three. I'll see you then." With no one looking, he leaned in and kissed her.

After examining the room's bare necessities, still dressed in traveling clothes, Grace and Phoebe lay out their fineries to shake out the wrinkles. Phoebe sat on the bed to remove her shoes. "I'm exhausted and didn't sleep well at all last night."

"It's typical on a big day in a woman's life." Grace unlaced her shoes and let them drop to the floor, fluffed a pillow, and lay back. "At least, lay down, Phoebe."

Phoebe lay down and reached for Grace's hand. "Thank you for coming with us."

"I'm so joyous for you, Phoebe. You're my best friend. I know why sleep is impossible. I can't either."

A drawn shade covered the room's one window, letting only a sliver of sunlight through, which warmed the worn wooden floor. The moment offered her the only chance to discover the truth. In her parents' house, if she asked questions, she received no answers. Muffled sounds through the window interrupted her thoughts for a moment. *If not now, talking with a trusted confidante such as Grace will vanish.* She clasped her hands together beneath her chin with a glance at Grace who was staring at the ceiling.

"Please, forgive me, Grace, for what I am going to say. I've never talked about this to anyone, but I have to know. I'm a little frightened, Grace."

Grace propped up her head with her palm, wide-eyed.

"When I—it happened, I wanted to die. I wanted to. I prayed not to be pregnant. When I discovered I was, I contacted Randy, as I knew my parents would rather I disappear than have my condition made public. And it has made me afraid of my to-be-husband. It was violent and hurtful. Does this happen after we're married?"

Alarmed, Grace raised up on her elbow. Phoebe had shut her eyes, her head moving slightly from side to side, as if denying it ever happened. It wasn't a question. It was a statement of fear. On a cattle ranch, Phoebe grew up surrounded by livestock, including chickens, goats, and cattle used for breeding. How callous to not have anyone to explain life to you. Dumbfounded by the Jackson's treatment of their own flesh and blood, Randy must have suffered likewise. She couldn't accept that the ranch near Red Oak could be home to the same kind, sweet Jacksons she knew.

Phoebe spoke again before Grace could answer. "We suffered when momma and daddy argued. Then my parents took their anger out on Randy and me. Daddy was especially hard-fisted with Randy. Especially, when the cattle market wasn't doing well. He'd belittle him, beat him, curse him." Phoebe glanced at Grace. "He may disapprove of my sharing this with you, but if you and my brother are in love, you will understand his childhood experiences. I suffered, too, from a silent mother who ignored her children's suffering and upbringing.

"Not yet twenty, Randy couldn't take more punishment and left. I had no one to talk to. By the time I'd adjusted to his absence, I took a walk in a near pasture, under a dark moon, but the stars lit up the sky. A stranger attacked me. By his height and the few words he spoke, I deduced it was the hired man my daddy had fired. He violated me, Grace, in the most horrible way. I was too afraid to tell them I suspected it was the same man. After it happened, my parents were angry that I went outside so late at night and stopped speaking to me, and that's when I had to leave. They stopped talking to me!" she cried. "And, Grace, I did nothing to make it my fault." Phoebe was close to throwing up. Reliving each word as she relayed the story to Grace had stripped her of the single thread of pride barely clinging within her since it had happened.

Grace's heart was bursting. "Oh, my love! She pushed her arm under Pheobe's shoulders and held her close. "Please, don't cry. You have been so strong, Phoebe, that I envy you. You've had the worst thing happen to you, but you've held your head up high. Still, you survive! A man has asked for your hand because he adores you and Daniel."

Phoebe whimpered. "I would never burden you with this sordid story. And I wouldn't normally, but nothing has been normal for a long time. It all leads to this. What is happening today? Will it be terrible like before? As a married woman, what is the appropriate response when, you know... in certain situations?"

Grace had no words. Corrine could have helped with some advice. She smiled at the picture of her sister teaching her and Phoebe the art of love. "No, no, no, Phoebe. Love is different. Humans, anyway, are different animals, capable of much more than raw instincts. Love, parenting, a shared life. Other than that, I have no idea. Mother bore two daughters. You have a brother. Other women I've known are quite happy being married, and I can only imagine. I sincerely have faith your fiancé would do nothing to shame any woman or hurt you."

Grace hesitated, biting her lower lip, unsure she had answered Phoebe's question. No one discussed such a singular topic, not that she knew. Except for her sister. "I'll say this, but I'm a little embarrassed. Randy makes—no, not makes me. His male advances are loving and gentle. He heightens my desire to follow his lead. Isn't it the same for all living creatures? Even the fragile flowers require bees. Like a flower, as a woman, you will welcome the honey bee who will never sting you. Andelacio is a gentleman." Grace smiled and hoped she was saying the right things to ease her friends fears. "Well, as much as a cowboy can be."

Phoebe wiped her nose and stopped crying. She had just entrusted her fears and doubts to her friend's ears that she dreaded consummating her marriage. She now understood the daily burden and suffering she bore that was caused by keeping her secrets. Her trust in him as a guardian of her love, and pleasing him without fear of his wrath or judgment was stronger, but she knew the time to give him all he wanted was far away.

"Thank you, my dearest friend. I understand more, and many of my fears have been relieved. Thank you for sharing these things with me." Her face brightened as she looked at Grace.

"There's a bit of news, Grace. I did something I'm not sure Randy will approve."

Grace's expression asked the question *What?*

"I haven't told Randy. So please allow *me* to tell him that I wrote a letter to my parents explaining that I am getting married. I received a letter from my mother in answer. She blessed us, professed her love for me, and prayed for my happiness."

"Phoebe, that's wonderful. I am praying for your happiness, too. You and your mother will unite, and I allow she will make amends for the past. This is turning into the best day I've ever had!"

Tears stung Phoebe's eyes and brought solace after sharing her anxieties with Grace. How much time it will take time for the pain to heal, she didn't know. Moreover, it was time to stop imagining herself as an adulterated woman and recalling the night that changed her life forever. It was obvious Lasso saw her heart and not her broken body.

"I am better now but exhausted. Should we try to sleep a while to refresh ourselves?"

"Great idea." Grace plumped her pillow. "You will be the loveliest bride ever." Turning to her side, she reached behind her and patted her friend on the back.

An hour later, after washing up as best they could from a pitcher and basin of water, Grace finished pinning up Phoebe's hair and centered a brimmed hat with an array of Camellias on one side. "You're ready. Look."

Phoebe walked a few steps to the dressing table mirror. She covered her mouth with her hand, squealed, and bounced a few times on her toes.

Laughing with Phoebe, Grace stood next to her with a grin. "You are so beautiful, I think I'm going to cry now."

"No, you can't mess up my wedding day with tears." She shook Grace by the shoulder. "It's five 'til three. I daren't sit and mess up my dress. It was the prettiest outfit in the mail-order Philipsborn Catalog. Mrs. Goss subscribed to it for me." The floor-length skirt was a deep purple that hung in well-pressed pleats. The modest off-the-shoulders linen top matched the camellias on her hat.

Neither woman could stop smiling, though Phoebe wrung a handkerchief in her hand.

When Lasso knocked on the door, the girls jumped, then giggled. Grace opened the door and bowed as Phoebe walked through the hall.

Lasso's breath caught in his throat, and a thread of sweat worked its way down his back. *How in the hell do I deserve this?* He swallowed as he prepared himself for the biggest day of his life. He stood aside for her to take Randy's arm. Grace joined Lasso as they regally went down the stairs.

Grace took in Lasso's persona, which was not his usual self: a new white Stetson and shirt with a silver silk scarf tied around his neck, shiny black knee height, three inch heeled boots. Not as tall as Randy, he was a handsome man with soft brown eyes, a sharp contrast to his lean, hard body. Although he had shaved, a dark shadow of a beard covered his chin and cheeks. With practiced attention to detail, he had meticulously trimmed his thick mustache. He was night to Phoebe's day. If not so obvious, she'd steal glances at Randy in his shiny boots and silk vest.

The front doors to the small white clapboard church stood open. The preacher, dressed in black, greeted the two couples, introducing himself. His wife directed the couples to their place, and the ceremony began. It was a brief service, unrestrained by a sense of propriety followed in Eastern society for social standing. Randy did his best not to stare at Grace standing next to his sister. Happy for Phoebe, he experienced a sense of freedom and relief, no longer worried about his sister's survival if anything happened to him.

After Lasso kissed his bride, Randy shook his friend's hand and kissed his sister. Grace gave the new couple a hug.

Phoebe giggled. "Did you hear my vows? I'm sorry, Lasso. It was a dreadful thing to say! Not very Christian."

"I thought it was clever, Sis. Lasso needs to obey, as well. It won't hurt to put him in his place from time to time."

"Everything is fine. If I can endure your brother, my beautiful wife, I am well prepared to deal with my wife's every wish."

Although everyone was joshing, the underlying sentiment touched Phoebe's heart. She wanted her new husband to hold her, but it wasn't proper in public view, so she squeezed his hand. He smiled at her, his eyes saying more than words.

"Shall we eat now?"

"It's the new couple's choice."

"I think we should go to the hotel's restaurant." Randy glanced at the dark sky. "I know the ladies do not want their beautiful dresses to get wet."

The giddy friends decided to celebrate at the hotel restaurant for a wedding dinner. They teased each other mercilessly. Phoebe laughed a lot to hide her jitters. She ate a few bites from her plate, and pushed the rest aside, afraid to distress her stomach causing a horrible ending on her wedding day.

Lasso studied his bride while keeping their conversation light. He saw her fork waiver a few times and realized she was avoiding looking at him. Already, he recognized the too careful way she laughed with her mouth closed as if she might give away a secret. *She's scared to death.* He believed it was a natural reaction after being attacked… he let the incomplete thought drift away and never wanted to rethink it again. He loved her. Would do everything in his power to make her happy. Learning the truth from his father, he owed her that.

The setting sun cast a harsh glare through the hotel windows. Randy called the waiter for the ticket to pay for their meal. His small gift to his sister and brother-in-law.

"Grace mentioned walking a bit, maybe visit one of the shops."

Lasso appreciated the signal Randy shot his way. He looked at Phoebe. "Do you want to join them, Phoebe?"

"I wouldn't mind resting for a bit. It's been a wonderful, hectic day."

The men pulled the chairs for the ladies. "Perhaps, we should meet here for breakfast, then be on our way back to Annona."

The men shook hands. Grace and Phoebe hugged one another.

CHAPTER TWENTY-FOUR

Andelacio & Phoebe

Randy & Grace

After shutting and locking the door, Lasso set his hat on a small table. He sat in a chair and pulled off his boots and neckerchief. Phoebe hadn't moved. He walked over to her and took her hands in his. "I love you, Phoebe. I vow to you I will never hurt you. I'm always here to listen, but there's no need to focus on the past unless you want to talk about it." She said nothing but nodded her head.

"I'm going to sit on the bed while you change your clothes. If you want to. Perhaps we can lie down and talk. As your husband, I will protect you and our son with my life. You will always have a home, food, and me with it, if you can stand me." His grin was unpretentious.

His soft-spoken words were more than she had hoped for. And selfless. Phoebe pulled her hands away to wrap her arms around his neck, looking her husband in the eye. "I love you, Andelacio Slade. You are a kind, hardworking man. I want nothing more than to be your wife and to care for you." After she removed her hat and gloves, she watched Lasso remove his belt and walked to him and turned away.

Of, course. She was asking him to unbutton the tiny buttons down her back. He accomplished it within a few seconds and placed a light kiss on her neck. When she faced him, he placed his palms beside her face and kissed her on the lips. He smiled and let her go, then he stretched out on the bed facing the wall giving her privacy to change. There was a rustle of fabric as she removed her clothes. Her back turned toward him, she pulled a nightgown over her naked body to fall around her ankles. After donning a lacy robe, she lay beside him.

Overjoyed, he smiled at her and without a word stood to slide his galluses over his shoulders and shove his pants to the floor. Lasso

216

gathered her against his chest and wrapped his arms around her, stretching the length of his body against hers. Propping himself over her with his elbow, he smoothed her hair. "Eres Hermosa, por dentro y por fuera."

Beguiled, his dark eyes reflected a gleam of light from the window. Thick black hair had fallen across his forehead. She lay still afraid to move, but a minute later when nothing happened, she put her hand against his cheek. She eyed him curiously.

"You are so beautiful." As her eyes betrayed her fear, he would not ask any more of her than to sleep with him. "You will learn about me in your heart within a few days. You will let me know then. Hmm?"

Phoebe nodded as she ran her hand across his hair. His muscled arm lay across her ribs. Exhausted, her eyelids grew heavy from the day's stress, but she felt safe and loved. For her, this was forever, but tomorrow always brought uncertainty. Before closing her eyes, she prayed her brother found a woman for himself who brought such happiness into his life.

* * *

That evening, three rooms down the hall, Grace answered the knock on the door in her robe and gown. As Randy rushed in, she backed a few steps away before he picked her up, her legs dangling.

Breathless, as he sat down on the settee with her in his lap, and she wrapped her arms around his neck. The leather and tobacco scent of his daily wear was familiar, and she liked its pure outdoor allure.

"Why are you here? Your sister and her husband are down the hall. If they need something and knock on the door, what will—"

Three raps sounded on the door. Randy groaned as Grace jumped from his lap. After straightening her wrap and nightgown, she motioned for Randy to hide somewhere. The only large piece of furniture was an armoire, and he flattened himself against the wall at the end.

Glancing back, she saw he was well hidden. Grace smoothed down her hair and put her ear to the door. "Who is it?"

"It's room service, ma'am."

"You've got the wrong room."

"Oh. Begging your pardon."

Grace listened to footsteps and the tinkling of glassware until they faded. She thought her heart was going to burst at the sudden interruption. She turned to find Randy sitting on the settee. "Randy, what are we doing? Imagine if that had been Lasso or your sister. I don't know how we'd be able to explain why you'd be in my room." She watched him look around the room like nothing had happened.

"My sister and *her husband* I am sure are busy right now. I can't think of a thing they'd need outside of their room."

Grace turned red and pulled her wrap tighter and crossed her arms over her ribs. Her brows were drawn down, appalled by his suggestion.

Her embarrassment was all over her face. Randy grabbed the Stetson and walked over to her. "Alright, Grace. Have it your way. But it will happen again, more 'an once, and I ain't leaving next time." He put his hand on her hair and gave her a kiss. Her arms fell to her side, and he hugged her. She pressed into him, her breasts firm against his shirt.

Grace looked into his eyes with a saucy expression on her face. "Alright, mister, so you think, but you have to leave now before someone else knocks on that door. Annona is…" She sighed before finishing her sentence, "a safer place," she said, looking into his eyes.

Annona, safer? Was she saying he could stay all night again? He grinned. "I'll see you in the morning." He nodded toward the newlyweds' room. "I don't think they'll be up too early. In the morning, we'll eat downstairs in the restaurant while they're getting dressed."

218

Grace stood on her tiptoes and kissed him on the cheek. He returned it with a full-lipped kiss goodnight and shut the door behind him. He walked away in no hurry thinking she was the most complicated woman he'd ever known.

She turned the key in the lock and walked to the bed with her fingertips over her lips savoring their last sweet kiss. At that moment, her senses came alive. The darkened walls were vibrant and the moonlight shimmered through the window curtains. The air carried a subtle hint of a pine essence from his skin and hair, a scent that intoxicated her senses. Every touch, every caress, ignited a fire within her for Randy with an intensity she had never experienced before. She turned on her side and reached for the extra pillow hugging it, a pitiful excuse for the man who just left her. Things were better—a development she deemed impossible.

The next morning, Randy was waiting for her, leaning against the banister enjoying a carry-over memory from the early night when he ignited her emotions. As she closed her door, her cheeks flushed as he smiled. Beautiful and smart, he found it difficult to read the direction of her '*thought of the moment.*'

A determined man with his own purpose, he wanted her to share in his endeavors to make his dream come true. He'd honed a grand scheme of becoming a known cattleman south of Dallas. He didn't intend to hinder the pursuit of her dreams, either. So far, however, their relationship was stuck in a slew.

But today was a celebration for his sister, best friend, and new brother-in-law. He removed his hat and followed her down the steps and into the restaurant, surprised to see his sister and Lasso already seated. After pulling a chair for Grace, he hung his hat on a rack and sat down.

"Thank you both for attending my wedding."

"Wouldn't have it any other way, Sis." He looked at the gold band on her finger and smiled. Lasso was staring at the tablecloth and nodding his head. "Hope y'all had a good time yesterday. Ready to travel, I guess?"

"Yeah, reckon we should get back to Red River 'fore Mr. Sullivant sends us packing. I'm ready to get back to Red Oak, anyway, and I told Phoebe it won't be long 'fore the place will be ready for her and the baby to come down."

Red Oak. Phoebe? Grace and Randy locked eyes, but her intense gaze and furrowed brows conveyed her message: *What haven't you told me?*

Randy read her silent message. He wanted to discuss his plans with Grace once they were alone. Last night, in the dim lighted room, he whispered every intimate detail about his love making desires, aware of her own desire filled with a mix of anticipation and love. However, he craved more, wanting to delve into the depths of her thoughts and aspirations for the future. Lord, what if she didn't want to leave Annona? Suppose she wasn't even ready to get married. He had left her room before mentioning the Bar J and his vision for their lives. He turned his gaze toward his sister.

Phoebe was busy twiddling with a fork, and Lasso had eyes for no one except Phoebe. The conversation shifted to breakfast and the successful wedding. The preacher and his wife were the sole couple in the small church, and the kind woman had prepared a cake for them. Grace had wept, Phoebe beamed nonstop, Andelacio perspired, and Randy thanked God for his sister's marriage at last.

After breakfast, they spent idle time sight-seeing. Closer to time for the next train to Annona, they retrieved their bags from the hotel. After walking four blocks to the train station, empty seats in the car for the four were not available.

Seated six rows from Phoebe and Lasso, Grace spread her skirt before taking a seat. She defied anyone's opinion and unfastened the pin holding the hat in place. Despite its simplicity, she purchased it because it was cheap and unlikely to be worn again. Only sun and rain protection made a hat worthwhile.

220

Grace's smile disappeared when they boarded the train. Idle time found her angry again, disgruntled that Randy had not shared his plans with her. She didn't totally understand whatever it was Lasso had referred to in Red Oak. He said 'We.' Were they returning to Randy's parents' ranch? Why had he not mentioned it to her? She pursed her lips to keep from frowning. Maybe he was hoping to exploit her affection for him and then abandon her for Red Oak.

She sat straighter in her seat, staring out at Clarksville until only fields and grazing cattle remained. Randy took her hand in his. She didn't resist, but she wouldn't beg to know more about his plans, either. He looked at ease when she glanced at him, and he squeezed her hand.

Randy had more to discuss with her, that he'd inherited the family ranch, and maybe get up enough courage to ask for her hand. But similar to the earlier trip, cigar smoke filled the air, and the hum of voices in conversation interfered with his state of mind. It felt wrong. There'd be another time with just the two of them when he'd lay everything out and ask her to marry him. Time, however, was short. The Bar J needed him. He took a breath, feeling pressed. Yet, content with his efforts, he took off his hat, placing it on his knee, and leaned back in his seat.

When Grace turned from the window, she saw he had fallen asleep. His chiseled face had perfect planes and creases that created a handsome man's face. She pulled her hand away and huddled by the window, unable to relax.

Randy woke first, returned his hat to his head, and shook her awake. Surprised she had fallen to sleep, she looked around remembering they were on the train to Annona. The train had slowed, and Randy was standing, holding out his hand to grasp hers, drawing her to her feet.

Randy looked at her as she stood, her face inches away, as if searching for something. Was he waiting for her to whisper her love for him? As he didn't share his plan with her regarding Lasso's puzzling comments about going to Red Oak, she felt overlooked and excluded from his life. A small thing, but hurtful the same. Until he told her himself, she would keep her cards close to her heart.

CHAPTER TWENTY-FIVE

Take the time to think it through 'cause nothing good comes by acting a fool.

Randy & Grace

Randy retrieved the horse and a double bench buckboard from the Annona livery. He dropped his sister and Lasso off at Miz Goss' house relieved, knowing Lasso would treat her and the baby well. Happy for his sister and child, his only worry was himself now. Randy glanced at Grace with hands folded in her lap, and asked, "Did you have a pleasant time, Grace?"

"It was a beautiful time, the wedding and being with our friends." Grace stopped herself from saying too much about the trip. It was fun and necessary for Phoebe to come out from hiding. Her curiosity about Randy, Lasso, and Phoebe returning to Red Oak was overpowering her vow not to mention it. Why would any of them want to go to the Bar J? But, if he wanted her informed, wouldn't he have told her already? Left out of the discussion and irritated, she developed a headache. Her chaotic thoughts were bouncing around like disruptive firecrackers. It was a small detail, but her being last to be told was a big detail. If he cared for her as much as he said, shouldn't she be the first one to know his deepest secrets? But she learned her lesson before about jumping to conclusions.

Randy reversed the horse at her home's rear entrance. He turned to her. "Do you mind if I come in? I'd appreciate your company," he said and wrapped his arm over her shoulders. He'd be tickled to start where they left off in the Clarksville hotel room.

Grace rubbed her temple and avoided his gaze. Because Randy had kept his undisclosed wish to go back to Red Oak from her, she was unsure of her own place in his plans. She needed time to think. "I started a headache while on the train. I'd rather go in and rest."

Grace yearned to be with him, her heart ached for his touch. There were consequences of being weak around him. If he only

223

understood, she had to lie to keep from losing her moral principles. Next, every indication was that he was the son of the Jacksons at the Bar J. And he kept it from her. She felt sick realizing her imagined romance was becoming no more than friendship and her role as his fancy woman.

Knowing her to the marrow, a slow breath escaped Randy's lips. Something other than illness was affecting her. Again, she wasn't trusting him to express her concerns. He kissed her temple where her fingers had been and breathed deeply to catch her fragrance. "Let me walk you in." He fastened the horse to a nearby tree and escorted her up the steps. She stopped at the door and turned toward him. He knew what she was thinking. But he would never let that happen. "I'll check on you tomorrow to be sure you're feeling better." Randy gave her a hug that she hardly returned. He opened the door, and she went through, disappearing without looking back. He returned to the buckboard bench and flicked the horse with the buggy whip to speed up his arrival at Red River. He cocked an eyebrow as he finally understood her reluctance.

A wing whistle from a mourning dove caught his attention as the bird lifted from the ground and flew over his head. It dipped and darted landing on a fence post. Its coo went from soft to loud. "Me, too, buddy. Only I ain't looking for another mate. Can't talk the right one into my nest, either. Not yet."

Randy never wanted a forced marriage because of his lack of control that would ruin Grace's reputation. He sought a proper, honest marriage. As a man, he understood the freedoms whores enjoyed and why men frequented saloons with prostitutes. But he wasn't getting younger and wanted a family. His eventual destination was the Bar J, with or without Grace. She just needed to show she wanted that, too. He wanted to explain it today to Grace, but for some reason, she wasn't ready for a discussion. He figured, too, that she knew he and Phoebe were the offspring of the Jacksons at the Bar J. As his relationship with Grace was above his bend, he'd let it be for a while.

* * *

Lasso

The next morning, Lasso trotted his horse from his new home at Mrs. Goss' to Red River and showed up early for breakfast. He found it agonizing to leave his wife with her long, wild hair in a halo on the pillow. He left her a note and tiptoed from the bedroom, closing the door behind. Phoebe took care of Daniel, or Dah-night as Lasso pronounced it, at least two times during the night. Unaware of anything else and happier than ever, he slept soundly the rest of the night.

Time was getting close to deciding when he and Phoebe would move to Red Oak. Mr. Sullivant had hired one lanky cowboy who rode down all the way from Montana. For the last couple of days, he complained constantly about the Texas heat. One cowhand told him to shut up or get out of Texas. After that, no one mentioned a word about the weather.

Lasso tied his horse to a post, glad to see the cook was still serving breakfast. He glanced at the slice of sun peeping over the treetops. Clear skies; another dry day. Twelve hours until he'd ride to Annona again to be with his family. He raised to his full height, proud he'd risen above the life he'd led before.

Lasso appeared from the kitchen, plate in hand, as Randy looked up. "How's the family?"

"Couldn't ask for nothin' more. They was asleep when I left." *I love her more than life, amigo. My desire to cure my wife's anxieties haunts me daily.* Even if Randy was filling more than one role, that of brother-in-law and boss man, Lasso did not want to sound weak or discuss Phoebe with anyone, not even Randy. With nowhere else to go with his thoughts, he gritted his teeth dragging his teeth across the fork.

"Good. You better chuck that down fast. Rupert wants us and three of the other boys to check for missing heifers and mend the fence. A few escaped a day ago. A high wind blew a tree over a stretch of wire. He told Jimmy, that guy from Montana, and Ash to go with us. Those who ain't checking cows and calves are staying here to break out a few more of the Thoroughbreds, along with some cow ponies. Rupert says they got a fast son-of-a-gun and they're getting ready to take 'em to Montgomery Park in Memphis. I'm thinking they'll take a few others with 'em to enter in the claiming races. Guess Miz Lilli and Rupert are traveling with the horses. She sure loves that colt."

"Think I'll stick to cattle," mumbled Lasso. "I'm ready to ride out if you are." Lasso shoved his plate to the side. He barely heard Randy talking about Miz Lilli's racehorses and put his own problems aside till later. *Have to. Keep my job to feed us.* He was sure she'd eventually see that he wasn't like that other man. The thought made him shiver.

Randy looked at Lasso. He looked okay, but sounded a little disgruntled. None of his business, but he prayed whatever was bothering him wasn't terminal.

Lasso joined Randy who was walking toward the horse barn to saddle up. He picked up speed and kept in step with his brother-in-law's long stride. The other cowhands were sitting on barrels waiting for Randy and Lasso to join them. The men loaded the wagon with wire and fencing tools to repair the downed fence. Only Randy and Lasso rode horses. The others hopped aboard the wagon and headed out to Section 7. They passed the stable built by William Sullivant for his racing Quarter Horses, the cattle barn for breeding special bulls, and the small oval track where they trained the colts and fillies to run.

The short drive across the pastures revealed a landscape scarred by past wagon wheels. The four men jumped to the ground as the wagon rumbled to a stop. "See y'all later," Randy said with a wave. "Better leave a fence gap to get those heifers through and back on your side of the fence when we find 'em." The cowhands waved the two on horses away and started unloading fencing tools, wire, and posts.

The sky had grown dark in the west. Lasso followed Randy through the sizeable gap in the fence, thinking the slow breeze would break into a gale soon. Only the mangled barbed wire, a few tracks, and other natural signs pointed them to the cattle.

"How's it going?"

"You and Miss Grace doing okay?"

The two asked in unison. Lasso waited for Randy to continue.

"I have a crazy idea in mind if you'd like to hear it." Randy glanced at Lasso to see his reaction.

"I'm listening."

"I'm thinking you and Phoebe ought 'a move on to Red Oak. Your belongings won't be too hard to pack. If you don't mind, y'all can live with Ma and Pa till I see my way to get down there. In time, we'll get a place built for you and Phoebe. When we get you resettled in your new place, I can stay on with the folks."

"Ain't you forgettin' something?"

"Naw. I ain't forgot. I'm working on it, just not setting a deadline. Times are changing, Lasso. Women got their own ideas about gettin' things done. They're not asking either—their telling. Grace likes her job with the doc. Fills some kind of notion she's got 'bout doing good deeds. Or making their own money can make a woman feel she doesn't need a man's help." He didn't mention his other thoughts about Grace.

Lasso cussed under his breath. "I ain't a woman. I don't know how they bear having babies, but I damn sure wouldn't want to. That's that. We got enough tasks to fill a day doing what we do, but damn, Miss Grace ran a farm. She worked as hard as most men. Could she have had enough of it and want time to just be herself?"

Randy nodded while taking in his words. Lasso sometimes spoke with the wisdom of an old man. Maybe Grace just needed time to herself. Maybe he'd give it to her.

CHAPTER TWENTY-SIX

"Good decisions come from experience. Experience comes from bad decisions." - Mark Twain.

Randy & Grace

The days rolled by. Each repeated itself with little change other than a quick cloud burst that likely flooded low places with the downpour of rain. Red River seldom had flood issues. However, the meandering creek ran over into the pastures, which helped the grass grow.

Like the sun, Randy always arrived on time. By one o'clock, he'd shod five horses and two mules in a large barn at the Clayton Farms. A favorite client and place, he worked in the breezy end of the barn and stayed dry in its wide hallway when it rained. Through working for the day at his last stop, he loaded his equipment in the wagon, headed for town, and stopped at the emporium on the outskirts of Annona. He parked his wagon by the boardwalk where Johnny was playing with marbles and made a wide berth around the boy to enter the store.

Randy flipped a coin on the counter to pay for a bag of tobacco and a bottle of liniment. He used the medicine on the horses, but he had exhausted his supply. One of Mr. Clayton's horses kicked him when he was putting on its rear shoes. Then, the wagon rolled over his foot when a loud noise startled the wagon horse. He had forgotten to set the wagon brake. The liniment was strong, and he used it on himself for injuries such as today's.

He gathered his belongings and headed out the open door. He nodded his head at Mr. Armand and said, "See ya later, Johnny!" He turned to hand a nickel to Johnny who was hot on his heels. The youngster ran errands and did odd jobs for Dr. Woodcock to help feed him and his widowed mother. The boy flipped the coin and caught it in his pocket. Randy laughed and climbed onto the wagon bench.

Despite scattered storms, the packed dirt road from Annona to Red River was still dry. Any disturbance by wheels or hooves coated the wagon wheels, hubs, and the seat of the worn wagon. Even his horse had a dry sprinkle of gray dirt across his rump.

A mile away from Grace's, he warred with himself on whether to stop in to see her. He lost the battle of common sense to reach the ranch before dark. Turning into her drive, a gentle breeze fluttered the leaves in the trees, then turned into a gust that almost blew his hat off.

You horny bastard. Here he was with a bum leg and a bruised foot hobbling up to her door. He thought of her constantly. He yearned to become a significant part of her life, picturing his arms around her, and excited to feel the rhythm of her breathing against his chest.

He eased himself from the high wagon seat and hobbled one step at a time to the door. He carried his weight on his left leg. The right one was assaulted twice in one day and hurt like hell from his thigh to the arch in his foot.

Grace arrived home two hours before she heard a wagon rattling up the drive. She took a moment to rush to the mirror to tidy her hair, knowing it had to be Randy. No one ever visited at that hour.

As soon as the door opened, he pushed his hat brim up and reached for her. With his arms across her back, she put her hands behind his neck, her fingertips moving through the hair on his neck. As she looked up, he kissed her. She leaned into him expecting another kiss, a passionate kiss. Instead of a kiss, she opened her eyes. He was staring at her.

"Grace."

Puzzled, she stepped back though he was reluctant to let her go. She took his hands in hers. "You seem bothered, Randy."

"I have been standing most of the day. Let's sit in there for a while," he said, pointing to the parlor, He led her by the hand toward the front room with the sofa. Grace sat. Randy limped to a table and lay his hat there, then limped back to sit at the end of the settee. He braced on the back and the armrest to sit, one foot flat against the floor, and the other leg propped heel down in front of him. It hurt like hell.

Grace watched him lower himself with a groan. When he didn't move closer to her, she realized he couldn't without causing himself pain. She faced him, her palm on top of his hand.

"Are you hurt, Randy?"

"It's nothing."

"I don't believe you." She poked him in the thigh with a finger.

"Yeow," he said with a grimace.

"What happened to you, today?"

"Nothing." He wanted to discuss his ideas, not his injured leg.

"I'm not a nurse, but I am a doctor's assistant." She raised her eyebrows to make sure he respected that. "That face," she pointed, "shows pain. Please, tell me. I want to help you. Does it disturb you that I, a woman, am trying to ease whatever is hurting you?" Women couldn't even vote, which she took umbrage with. Then, she was sorry for implying that he thought she wasn't capable as a woman, of helping.

He smiled at her temperament. He wasn't thinking about what she described. Now, she was pleading with him. He had no notion what she could do about it but was certain she wouldn't relent until he gave in. "It's not like I got shot. I just got kicked by a horse I was shoeing. Then, got my foot run over by the wagon wheel. Not sure my boot will come off."

Grace jumped up and dragged a footstool close to Randy's leg. She reached down and lifted his booted foot. Her hands gripped the back of the leather heel and the toe. She worked the boot to ease it off, but it refused to budge. "Randy, this is going to hurt. If you wear this boot any longer, it'll have to be cut off."

He watched her leave to return with matches to light kerosene lamps scattered in the room. The sun had vanished leaving the room in gloom. This time she straddled his leg, her back to him. The simple skirt she wore even with petticoats left little to his imagination with her hind end so close to his face. The added wiggle held his attention while she struggled to work the stubborn cowhide over his arch. "Take your time," he said, feeling the pain was worth it.

The boot finally gave to the constant pull, and she rolled his sock down and worked it off, throwing it next to the boot.

"First, I'll take care of this, then I'll check your leg. Don't wear a boot on this foot. Not until the swelling goes down." She left to return with a piece of raw steak in her hand and a roll of gauze. "There's not enough ice left to be of use. I think this," she lifted the meat, "is cool enough to help shrink the swelling."

The cold meat was a jolt but brought a little comfort to the bruised area of his foot. "If you're able, will you lay on the floor to work out of your trousers to give your leg a look?"

Seeing his naked leg wasn't shocking. But a pang of jealousy, like a swift arrow, darted by as he wondered if this was what she did normally for Dr. Woodcock's male patients.

She held a candle close to his thigh to examine the bruise. Black and purple, and shaped like a hoof. She poked it with a finger again.

He yawled a second time. He watched as she worked, oblivious to the bare leg in front of her.

Absorbed with slapping another piece of beef on his thigh and wrapping gauze around his leg to hold the piece of meat in place was a learned skill, only ice was better. "I'm all done. I'll go in the kitchen while you get dressed."

She had dressed other men's wounds without a thought, but this was Randy. She had to bite her lip to keep from breathing as she straddled his leg, wrestling to remove his boot. The sight of his muscled thigh with nothing but a towel covering his groin, made her question their ability to keep at bay what they both wanted. The crazy impulse made her giggle at the irony.

He stood and struggled to pull his trouser leg over the bulging chunk of red meat and the bandages. "Okay, Grace. I'm decent." He limped to the sofa where Grace joined him. Her face lit up with a smile; it was clear she found the most joy in helping others.

Though he'd chased her over Texas, he had to know if she even wanted to marry him. Ranching was not a simple life. Rain, drought, disease, and market prices could bring disaster. And bringing the ranch back to its best was a lengthy undertaking.

"Grace," a one-sided smile lifted his lip, "before you insisted on being my personal nurse, I wanted to talk to you about... something."

Grace noted Randy was no longer the patient, but the white knight. His hesitation signaled he had something pressing to say. She rolled her shoulders, sat straight, and tucked her calves beneath her. "What, Randy?" Her voice was soft and meek.

He wanted to be close to her, but moving risked losing the awkward meat chunks. He had no idea how long it would stay cold, but he was enjoying the relief it was bringing now.

"You know how much I love you."

She nodded 'yes,' focusing on his words. His deep voice was assuring, matching the decency in his character. With little effort, he held her attention as his eyes searched hers for validation of her love.

"I've kept nothin' from you to befuddle you. Maybe one thing, as the ideal time never appeared," he admitted. "I honestly can't read you very well." He laughed as his fingers skimmed down her cheek, his eyes lit with adoration. "You're unlike any woman I've ever known. In a good way. You're beautiful and down to earth." He gestured at his injured limb. "And I can testify to your resourcefulness."

Grace reached for his hand. The palm was rough and calloused. His praise heated her face. "I love you the same. I dream about you, Randy." She smiled and mimicked him, "In a good way."

"Huh," he chuckled. "Glad to hear it. I'd hate to think I chased you over Texas for nothin'."

She grimaced and shook her head. "No, you did not," she said with a pang of guilt over the half lie, half-truth. The truth part was, "I've loved you since I first found you in the heat of the day taking care of Coyote."

"Damn, Grace. You never showed it."

"That day you came back to my kitchen door and found me in my robe?"

Astonishment silenced him for a moment. He looked her up and down. He never figured her for a tease. Or seen her behave in that way before or after. It scrambled his brain finding out she used those tactics on the day they met. He wished he'd acted on his impulses if only to see her reaction.

Goosebumps covered Grace's legs. It was impossible by his expression to tell if he was angry or pleased at her brazenness. She hadn't planned on his coming back that specific day, but she wasn't sorry she showed herself in a less than lady-like way to get his attention.

A broad grin answered her question. "Glad you did. I've carried that image of you in my head for months. I had ideas about us when you first showed up in those men's pants and a lacy lady's blouse. I knew you was special. You're someone who aimed to succeed in life doing grand things. That's what I loved about you."

Warmth spread across her face. As her heart surged, she scooted next to him and held his face in her hands. She kissed him with a passion she'd not felt before. Her need doubled when he placed his palm on the back of her neck and leaned into the kiss.

Unaware of the depth of his declaration of love for her, he wondered why he deserved such a passionate response, but for whatever reason, he was happy about it. He whispered close to her ear. "When I can get on my knees, when I can get the ranch my daddy left me up and running again, I want to ask you to marry me proper, Grace. No, don't answer now. You're a wonderful nurse and woman. For now, keep doing what you like."

She would wait as long as he wanted before proposing. She sat back as he relaxed his grip. Grace was right. Randy was the Jackson's son. Not an actual surprise.

"You must know you were on my family's ranch at Red Oak."

Grace nodded. "I never asked, but I thought it."

"Give me time to get the Bar J back on its feet. Then, if you say yes, we'll get married." Well aware that he had told her to keep working in the medical field, it was unlikely she would go back to the Bar J. But he not only wanted to bring his ranch to financial independence, but he also had to. He was born on that ranch and it was his calling. Time might show it wasn't compatible with her desires, but he would let it simmer.

"I'll say *yes* anytime you ask. I love you." She moved inches from his face. One eyebrow cocked at an angle. "But I'm confused. Do *you* own the Bar J?"

"I intended to tell you, but the time was never right. The ranch was willed to me by my father." After holding his thoughts so long, he was relieved to get everything off his chest. He let out a heavy sigh.

"That's what you and Lasso meant in Clarksville about moving to the Bar…"

He nodded. "Yeah. I've hired Lasso as my ranch manager. He and Phoebe are moving there soon."

The tight hold she had on her tongue loosened when she heard his story. A melting sensation spread through her chest; the reluctance and misgivings she had carried slipped away, leaving her feeling limp and foolish once again. It became evident that he wanted to share the news when they were alone. The future it presented—one that involved living out her life in Red Oak—troubled her deeply. Married and working outside their home would raise questions about his ability to be the breadwinner for their family, making her seem like an unfit wife.

Although she was certain she loved Randy, she had given little thought to leaving her job. While she wanted him to propose, she hadn't fully considered the implications of returning to Red Oak.

She lay her head on his chest. Wrapped in each other's arms, the lamps flickered in the darkness. "It's getting late. Guess I better get to Red River while I can still see the road."

This time, Randy lowered his pants in Grace's presence, his shirttail creating a cover over his hips. She removed the gauze and the beef from his thigh and looked up. He was gazing away at nothing. She stood to brush her fingerprints across his mustache and mouth catching his attention. He grabbed her hand and kissed it.

Then, she began pulling his sock back over the injured foot. "I think the bruising has receded a bit."

Randy finished pulling on his sock but didn't wrestle the boot on. She handed him his hat and supported his arm on her shoulders as he limped to his wagon. "Randy, please give this swelling time to go down. Riding and hanging your leg in a stirrup will make things worse."

"Can't promise. It might be another day at least before I'm slapping this leg over a hard leather seat." After giving her a long kiss, he pushed himself up to the wagon seat with his good leg. She stood on tiptoes as he bent down and kissed her again.

"I'll stop by shortly. You be careful out there amongst the sick folk. Please let nothing happen to you."

"I'll be fine," she laughed. "Looks like you're getting all the short ends. Thankfully, you broke nothing. I love you. Please, hurry back."

He looked behind as he slapped the reins for the horse to move. "I love you. I'll come over as soon as my leg's healed enough to stand on. And I get back to work. I can't wait to see you again."

She waved until he was out of sight. Inside the house, she leaned against the wall, her head bowed in thought and her hands clasped behind her back. She thought that Randy would eventually propose and that he expected her to follow his lead.

She sat at the table and stared out the window. *He is so unaware of the consequences I would face by moving from here.*

CHAPTER TWENTY-SEVEN

"Nothing is more difficult, and therefore more precious, than to be able to decide." – Napoleon Bonaparte.

Phoebe & Lasso

Dust blew in the faces of the five men sent out from Red River to brand calves. They pulled their neckerchiefs over their face up to the eyes. The unwelcome breeze was as hot as the devil's breath. Fall was masquerading as Summer.

Lasso wiped away sweat seeping through his eyelashes, burning his eyes. The calf bawled as he backed his horse to keep the rope taunt around its neck. A second cowhand caught his two hind feet and stretched it out on its side. A third cowboy pulled the branding iron from the fire and hurried to the calf's side, bent over, and hit the spot he'd aimed for.

Spurs urged the horse to walk forward a few steps to loosen the rope. The cowhand flipped the rope from the calf as it struggled to rise to get back to the momma cow.

Lasso was tired and doing chores by rote. His eyes were dry and scratchy. He felt poorly, less from dust, more from lack of sleep.

Two weeks had passed since he said, "*I do,*" and nothing had changed much in his wife's reactions to his romantic advances. The mental scars from the nightmare she had experienced brought whimpering and tears, though he had been slow and gentle. He never showed cruelty to prostitutes or other women. His mother had told him never to treat a woman the way his father treated her. He had given Phoebe time to heal the humility and pain she harbored. And sometimes she acted afraid, as if she thought he would harm her. It ate at him daily.

She and Dah-nyehl were his life, the family that he loved. The child was stronger. Dah-nyehl could hold his head up and make eye contact. His little smile melted Lasso's heart when he played with him. As he chose not to think about it, he seldom thought of Dah-nyehl as his half-brother. It was a niggling reflection, but less frequent with time.

The day's final calf received a brand and vaccination. It was getting late. The mix of men, mostly skilled cowboys, had finished branding. They doused the fire used to heat the irons. Lasso gathered them scattered on the ground to clean for use tomorrow and set one aside. "Heads up. This 'un's wore out. I'm putting it here by itself, so when you load it with the others, it won't get mixed up with the good ones."

The less experienced cowboys looked up, took note, and went back to whatever they were doing. The calves had trotted away from the humans and disappeared into the brush.

Back at the bunkhouse, some men fed other stock, or checked on the cows kept close by that were close to calving.

After taking care of his horse first, Lasso told Randy he was riding to Annona after cleaning up. He didn't want to approach Phoebe with dirt, sweat, and a smell about him that might offend her.

With his back to the steady stream of cold water, he rubbed his neck. The water followed the sculpted rifts along his back and shoulders, dripping from his hair and fingertips. The water drained, and his tension was gone. Bracing a hand against the wall, he turned off the water and shook his head like a dog. A memory surfaced. *The river. I played in the shallows with mother watching me.* From nowhere, a vision of Phoebe rising naked from the shallows shook him enough to grab a towel before forgetting where he was.

Randy looked up when Lasso walked out of the concrete shower. "Hey."

Lasso tightened the towel around his waist hesitating to see what Randy wanted.

"Are you and Phoebe ready to go to the Bar J? Is the baby strong enough to travel? I wouldn't want to stress my sister by rushing anything."

Lasso knew the time would come. He was ready to move on, hoping the change would somehow work a miracle in his wife. "Let me talk to her. I'm okay with it. Just want her to be happy."

"I appreciate that. Let me know."

"Sure."

When they parted, Randy entered the shower. Lasso sat on his bunk to drag clean clothes from a trunk of personal items. He saddled a fresh horse for the ride and trotted down the long drive to head to Annona.

Phoebe fed Daniel early. The baby was growing fast and wanted to explore along the carpets inching along on his tummy with his hands and knees. He required watching outside his crib.

Lasso would be home soon unless a problem on the ranch detained him. She quickly learned all his habits not long after they married. Never raising his voice, the feeling that she had to protect herself was gone. He took her rebuttals quietly, never insisting or angry. Never dirty or smelling of cattle when he arrived home, was one thing she liked. Occasionally he stopped along the way to Annona to collect a handful of wildflowers that delighted her. And now, seeing her husband in long johns had become routine. Curiosity and a quiver of longing for his attention had replaced her fear. Her hands no longer shook when she lay beside him in bed. The steady look as he watched her in her nightgown no longer embarrassed.

I made vows to have and to hold, for better or worse.

Somewhere along the way of sharing life with him, her heart had opened to love, replacing doubt. The urge to meet his wants in every way grew stronger with each goodbye kiss, and watching him play with Daniel as though he were his own, was a blessing.

I love you, my husband, for who you are, and ready to show you in the most intimate way a woman can.

Seeing him ride up the drive, Phoebe met him at the door and took his hat. A smile covered her face when she placed her palm on his cheek. "You've shaved. You're even more handsome now."

Lasso followed her to the dining room. Two plates were on the table. "Miz Goss not eating tonight? Where's Dah-nyehl?" Phoebe's face was rosy.

"Mrs. Goss is taking care of the baby tonight." Part of her wanted to be somewhere else. But it was time to come out of hiding, to stop punishing a man who made a promise to love her forever. "Don't you think we need some time to ourselves?"

Lasso's eyebrows shot up along with the rate of his heartbeat. He rubbed the back of his hand across his chin. He'd never been called handsome before. Candles lit one end of the table, her chair pulled near his. His wife had turned into someone else. He nodded with a small smile.

"I would like that. We seldom are alone." He emphasized 'alone' with his fork waving. Dinner at noon at the ranch seemed hours earlier. His stomach welcomed every bite Phoebe ladled onto his plate. He took nothing for granted but was curious about her comment. They had moments alone many times when Dah-nyehl slept—unless she meant...

She whirled around after taking his plate from the table.

After she cleaned the table, they sat in the parlor making small talk. The lamps burned low. He studied his wife, his elbow on the chair arm, his hand on his cheek. He yearned to cover her with kisses.

No. None of that. It won't work. He'd be slow and easy like taming a skittish filly.

The clock chimed eight o'clock. Five in the morning came early. Four-thirty for the extra time to ride to Red River. He rose to pick up the lamp and distinguished the flame. Not quite pitch black outside, the light coming through the windows was enough to find their way to the bedroom without falling over the furniture.

240

The undressing ritual was the same. While she disappeared behind a screen, he sat on the bed to remove his shirt, belt, and trousers. Clean ones lay over a chair to wear the next morning. After laying the gun and belt across his clothes, he propped a pillow on the headboard and leaned against it. Any minute she would come to bed. He liked to watch her walk across the room, step on a stool to climb onto the mattress, and lift the cover.

Phoebe had ordered a simple nightgown. Most had high necklines and long sleeves, but she searched the catalogs. It was too hot to sleep in long sleeves, but she could always unbutton the high-neck collar. When it arrived, she cut the sleeves completely off. She sat at her dressing table taking down her long hair and brushed it. She glanced at Lasso intently watching her, as if fearing she'd disappear. Determined to block out terrible memories and not to tear up, she took a deep breath. It was time to become one with her husband.

One kerosene lantern cast a musty light of shadows across the room. She stopped to blow out the flame. Here she paused, uncertain. The darkness gave her courage, though, as she slipped into the bed beneath the cover. She lay there until Lasso ran his hand along her arm, his fingertips trailing the side of her breast. An uncontrollable shiver ran through her body.

He lay on one arm propped beneath his head. She looked at him with a sweet smile. "I love you," he breathed against her cheek. His arm lifted her closer to him. His filly hadn't flinched. His hand caressed her shoulder, his free hand cupped her cheek. *Did he dare kiss her?*

He pressed her lips with his, spreading tiny kisses along them. Phoebe opened her mouth, her breath caressing his cheek with warmth. *Dare he touch her elsewhere?*

Phoebe touched his hair, as dark as night. She followed his gentle movements and raised her hand to touch his lips. A rancher's daughter, she'd seen it many times. He had swelled like the bulls that bred her father's cows, like the stallions that bred his mares. Would it be painful like before? Surely, if other women didn't mind it, it wasn't as terrible as her assault. She found herself in an unexpected place. Responsive to his exploration of her body, she moaned, cuddling next to him, held in his muscular arms, wanting more.

"Phoebe," he whispered.

"Yes."

"Would you be agreeable if I…"

"Yes. I am more than willing. I want to learn more from you, my love."

CHAPTER TWENTY-EIGHT

"This is the beginning of anything you want." –Unknown

Randy & Grace Lasso & Phoebe

Until Randy could wear a boot again, Grace thought he would not come around for a few days. It was just as well, as Johnny galloped up with a message that Doctor Woodcock needed her. Someone shot a man in the saloon.

"The doc says to meet 'em at the saloon, Miz Grace."

She shook a finger in the boy's face. "Johnny, how'd you find out about the shooting? You have no business in a saloon."

"That's what my ma says, Miz Grace. But that's where I hear most of the news around town! Sometimes I make thirty cents a day off'n folks 'cause I know the news circulating about town. Anyway, my ma depends on what I bring home every day." he wailed.

"Okay. Just go somewhere else now. You don't need to see or be around a place where a shooting occurred."

"Yes, ma'am." Johnny jumped on his mule and rode toward town.

Not far behind Johnny, when Grace pushed through the swinging doors, the doctor was on his knee, leaning over a man lying face down on the floor. Blood pooled round his body. The doctor looked up when he heard her footsteps.

"Give me that wad of cotton to staunch the bleeding, please, Miss Grace. But that's not the worst thing that's wrong with 'em. Anyway, everyone ran out of the saloon when the shooter drew his gun. That's why the tables and chairs are vacant. Except for that fella over there." The doctor nodded toward a cowboy in a battered brimmed hat pulled low on his head.

She glanced at the cowboy, then watched the doc press the cotton as hard as he could against the man's chest wound. Levi, the bartender, had hidden behind the high counter where he had ducked down when the fight started. Still behind the bar, but now standing, he told Grace, "The shooter ran out the side door."

In answer, she gritted her teeth and nodded. She bent over and saw the bleeding man on the floor also had a large gash on his forehead. Dr. Woodcock put his ear to the man's heart and stood up, shaking his head from side to side. "He's dead."

The shooter's partner took a swig from the liquor bottle, then shoved his chair away, to sidle up to Grace. Getting too close for comfort, his snarly smile and red eyes spoke loudly about his character. His unwavering stare caused her to step away from him. His breath reeked of whiskey.

"Step back, please. Give the doctor room to do his work. In fact, you ought to leave."

The man spit and missed the spittoon. "Ain't you the bossy one! The doc's taking care of my *friend* looks like to me. You and me can sit over there," he looked at a vacant table. The drunken cowboy grabbed her arm to spin her around. Grace jerked away and stomped his foot. Her eyes widened and her breath hung in her throat when he bellowed in pain.

"You stupid bitch!" Before his fist did any damage, Randy grabbed his arm and punched him in the face. He staggered backward and just missed the doc, who was caught in the middle, hunkered down over the dead cowboy.

"Watch out! Gun!" Grace screamed.

Randy punched the drunkard again who was fumbling for his gun grip. This time he didn't get up, and Randy took it and stuck it in his own belt. He looked the outlaw over but didn't know him. "Levi, you got time to run to the post office and telegraph the Clarksville sheriff to come pick up this asshole?"

The bartender came around the end of the bar, placed his shotgun on the bar top, removed his apron, and sprinted toward the door.

COWBOY IN SEARCH OF GRACE AND THE LITTLE WHITE LIES

"You betcha! Be back in a minute!" He disappeared, leaving the doors swinging in his wake.

Dr. Woodcock took the gunslinger's Colt Buntline from Randy to stand guard over the unconscious man on the floor. Randy went to the back room to search for rope or anything to tie the outlaw's hands. He returned with a roll of strong cord and secured the man's hands and feet. Then, he turned to Grace a few feet away, frowning and silent.

"Are you alright, Grace?"

"I believe so." She looked at Randy, biting her lip. "I've never been so frightened. I'm not sure what might've happened if you hadn't arrived when you did."

"I saw the doc's buggy and thought you might be here, too. It's over, darlin'. He's going to jail. I'm on my way to Miz Gozz' to help Lasso and Phoebe load their belongings." He looked at Dr. Woodcock. "Sorry, Doc, but I'm needed somewhere else."

Dr. Woodcock waved him off.

You're leaving? Coming out of her daze, she remembered now. The Slade's were headed for Red Oak. "You go. It's best I stay here with the doctor. I'm going to be fine. But, I'm going to miss Phoebe and the baby. And Lasso." She'd already said goodbye to the three and grieved their absence. Besides navigating the scene in front of her, one more grievance loomed ahead of her. What if Randy left without her?

He nodded and squeezed her hand. "I'm not needed here. The shooter's plumb outta Annona by now. The doctor and Levi can hand the outlaw over to the sheriff." He looked around. No one was paying attention to them. He ran his hand down her arm and turned to go. "I'll see you later." He looked back at her from the swinging doors. She gave him a wave. Lasso and Phoebe's move was underway.

* * *

Lasso and Phoebe

Lasso filled his valise with his underwear and some baby clothes. An old suitcase donated by Mrs. Goss held Phoebe's day clothes, her nightgowns, Lasso's trousers, clean long johns, and shirts. His saddle and tack stored in a wooden box, lay in one corner of the buckboard. Randy entered the front door to bring out the large suitcase bursting with clothing and other items.

Mrs. Goss bounced Daniel in her arms to keep him occupied. She cried most of the night over the Slade's moving to Red Oak. Now, she breathed in every essence of the baby to remember him and followed Phoebe's every move as she sifted through the belongings they could pack, leaving others to stay behind in the old house.

Lasso had finished loading the heavier suitcase onto the wagon. They sat in the parlor to say proper goodbyes to Mrs. Goss who still held the baby in her arms. A half-empty tea service sat on the coffee table, but the tea cakes went uneaten.

"I'm so grateful to you for taking me in. I had nowhere else to go." Phoebe squeezed Mrs. Goss' hands, then wiped a tear from her cheek. They sat apart from the men who were discussing the Bar J and the plans to be carried out.

"My dear, you have given me a reason to be here." Mrs. Goss' lip quivered as she put on a small smile. "I pray for your happiness and sweet Daniel's. I don't know that you would have a reason to come back here, but should you..." She broke down and stifled a despairing sob.

Since Phoebe had agreed to return to the family ranch, her mind galloped down two roads: one of optimism and one of misgivings. While excited to be moving back to her childhood home where her husband would be the ranch manager, she had reservations about leaving the elderly woman who treated her so well for months. "I'll never forget you. And we will write, and I will send you a photograph of Daniel as soon as possible." She patted the elderly landlady on the shoulder noting a tear tracked her cheek.

And, according to Randy, their parents had changed. Feeble and aged, they had suffered loneliness and guilt. He had forgiven them. She had changed, too. With a child of her own and a husband, Phoebe was happy that they expressed their guilt to Randy. Until she saw for herself, she settled for not passing judgement.

She broke from her reverie and noticed Lasso and Randy were fidgeting as time was drawing near to making it to the train station while still staying polite.

With Daniel on her shoulder, she met Mrs. Goss with an arm outstretched to hug her. She drew back to wipe the tears away and promised again to write and visit from time to time. When the women parted, Lasso gathered up a carpetbag of additional baby clothes and diapers. Inside the leather-handled bag, a draw-string silk bag held Phoebe's hairpins, combs, hairbrushes, and a few pieces of jewelry, gifts from Mrs. Goss.

Randy kissed Mrs. Goss on the forehead, then Lasso kissed her cheek. Going outside, Randy sat on the box that held Lasso's saddle, his elbow propped on the top of the bench back. Lasso held Daniel, and with one hand, assisted Phoebe to the bench. She reached down to kiss Mrs. Goss, too, who was doing her best not to cry again.

Once everyone settled in the wagon, Lasso slapped a rein over the horse's rump, and within minutes they were out of sight of the Goss house.

"Pa's going to fetch y'all at Red Oak. Ma's got your room ready. Said she dragged out the baby crib from the loft and cleaned it up. I'll be there as soon as I tie things up here. We already talked about things that needed taking care of first at the Bar J. I know it's a gigantic task. Lasso—just do what you can. It'll get better as soon as I get down there.

"I left instructions with the bank that you're my foreman. They're to give you whatever cash you need to take care of the ranch. Meanwhile, if we need to discuss anything, you send me a telegram or call the Sullivant's telephone if necessary."

"Okay, Boss."

"Too, if you got time, order the lumber needed to build your house. Maybe get started on it?"

"I'm sure Miz Slade will think that's a fine idea. I'll get to it right after checking the cattle for brands, disease, and vaccinations, and fencin'. I reckon that should come first."

The sarcasm in Lasso's voice was heavy. He and Randy exchanged glances. Randy shook his head.

The train ride was uneventful. Mr. Jackson met them at the train depot as planned and wrapped his arm around Phoebe's shoulders. After introducing Lasso to her father as her husband, the three crowded themselves onto the wagon seat. He tried hard to think of something to say, but the words wouldn't come. He didn't want his daughter to hate him. But he felt he deserved to be.

Phoebe knew a day of reconciliation would come. But, for now, she thought her father wise to be silent. They could hash out questions and answers later.

Almost home, Phoebe recognized the small bluff on the right. As a girl, she hunted for seashells in the loamy bank. Now, the Texas sun was doing its best to fry all of them like donuts. She placed her palm across Daniel's eyes protecting them from the sun. Looking ahead through the gate gap, she noticed little had changed in the months she had been gone. But Randy and Lasso's work was clear everywhere. They'd restored the house to its former charm with its repaired porch and cleared the brush and sage from the yard space. Lasso also told her that he and Randy had done a lot of carpentry work and fencing when they were there. Not knowing what to expect, her mother would be the last surprise. She bolstered herself against bitter behavior. Free from childhood constraints and answerable only to her husband, she placed her faith in her own capabilities, deciding to rely on no one but herself.

The minute Rachael heard the squeak of wagon wheels and weathered wood, she hurried out the front door and watched the wagon as it grew from the size of a large dog to full dimensions. She could clearly see three people on the buckboard seat. A gust of wind billowed her skirt leaving a film of dust over her shoes. She stuffed the wadded handkerchief in her hand under her belt, kneading her fingers. *Phoebe was home!*

Pulling up to the porch, Lasso jumped from the wagon. "If you're okay, *querida*, I'm going unhitch these horses and put 'em in the barn. I'll unload the stuff in the back of the wagon when I return." He held the baby in one arm and held his wife's hand until she was safe on the ground.

A smile lifted the corners of Phoebe's lips. He called her *darling* many times a day. He was, indeed, a romantic man. "Hurry back, my love," she patted his arm when he transferred Daniel to her arms.

Rachael steered clear of Lasso and the horses as he passed by. She ran the few steps to Phoebe and hugged her, the baby between them. "Oh, I've missed you," she sighed in Phoebe's ear.

"Oh, Momma. It's so good to be back."

They walked to the door, leaving her father standing by the wagon waiting for Lasso to return. In the house, standing at the bedroom door, Phoebe hesitated as she surveyed the room that had been hers since childhood. It now belonged to the Slade's. At least till the men had time to build a house for them. She stood in the doorway with her fingertips over her lips. Rachael squeezed past her daughter to lay her grandson in the middle of his great-grandmother's four-poster bed and joined Phoebe at the door.

"Momma!"

Rachael pulled Phoebe into her arms. "Don't cry, please don't cry. I'm so happy you're back. I've missed you so much. We didn't know where you'd gone for the longest. Here, here. Shush. Everything's okay now." Rachael pushed Phoebe back a step. "Now, tell me about the baby and that handsome man you married."

"As you know, Momma, Lasso is Randy's friend. We met when he did a favor for Randy, looking after me, the time Randy traveled back here. We fell in love very fast. You will not believe that he helped deliver Daniel."

"Nooo!"

"Yes, he did. With Mrs. Goss' help. She's the lady who took care of us."

"I met Mr. Slade when your brother traveled here looking for, uh…"

"Grace?"

"Yes. We had some problems with… the cattle. Thank goodness they were here to help." Phoebe looked none the wiser. Rachael did not want anyone, especially her daughter, to know about the danger they had faced.

They sat for a few minutes on the high mattress facing each other. "Phoebe," she nodded toward the baby, "it should have been me there with you. But your pa—"

"Don't say anymore, Momma. Let's be a family and not think about that." Phoebe stood up. The baby crib caught her eye. She walked over to it and ran her fingers over the side rails. "You've kept this all these years?"

"Yes, and hoped you'd have a use for it one day. Not under the best of circumstances, but it doesn't matter. You're our daughter. Little Daniel is our grandson. Anyone says any different and I'll shoot 'em. I swear I will. Hmm, does your husband—"

"Yes, he knows. No one should ever say he's not his son to his face or he'll be the one who'll do the shooting."

Daniel was becoming increasingly fussy and loud. Rachael hurried over to pick him up.

"Well, I best see if I can help Lasso—least that's what the cowboys called him. They said Andelacio was too long to pronounce. Anyway, do you mind tending to Daniel while I get busy?"

"Of course not." Rachael picked him up, tickling his chin to make him smile.

Returning from the barn, Lasso climbed over the seat back and into the bed of the wagon. "Damn!" he swore under his breath as he dragged the ancient trunk to the back gate of the wagon. *Thing must be made outta of lead.* After undoing the heavy pins in the tailgate, he lowered it until it lay level, held up by chains attached to each side. He heaved the trunk from the wagon setting it on the ground.

Lasso pulled himself once more onto the buckboard and handed Phoebe a few of the lighter weight articles. Daniel was asleep in his crib when she returned to their room.

Phoebe directed her mother to leave the trunk where it sat knowing it was heavy. There were additional bags piled on the oak floor to be unpacked, too. She put her hands on her hips and looked at her mother.

"Think I'll go see what to fix for supper. Take your time to unpack. I'll holler when it's time to eat."

Her mother headed to the back of the house. Phoebe looked outside through the front door. The corralled horses were stirring in the pen. A cow somewhere near the big barn bellowed. The faint bleat of goats joined the chorus. Phoebe was at peace.

The setting sun cast orange rays through the clouds as Lasso pumped cold water into a bucket and rinsed the sweat from his face and arms. Though dust from the day remained on his clothes, he was sure he felt better than he looked. Not that he cared what his in-laws thought of him. Only Phoebe. Something had changed about her when she overcame her fear of men. She never denied him again. He knew she loved him, else why did she seem to enjoy his exploration of her body? She gave him a reason for living. She and Dah-nyehl.

Since meeting Randy and Phoebe, after all that had happened at the Bar J, his new position was making him uneasy. While he knew cattle from their snotty noses down to their cloven hooves and the diseases they might carry, he knew nothing about running a ranch. As he walked to the house in the dusk, he settled on practicing what he'd done at Red River. He'd check with Mr. Jackson tomorrow to see if he kept any records regarding vaccines and cow-calf production. If not, though unfamiliar with record keeping, he'd have to try to manage his own books.

* * *

Dusting his pants and stomping his boots on the porch alerted Phoebe that Lasso was back after taking a tour around the ranch for anything that needed tending. She'd prepared a pitcher of water and a bowl with clean towels for him to wash. Clean clothes for him to wear to supper and use again the next day, lay across the bed. She liked to watch him strip down. His heritage and the sun had turned his skin into a soft doe color, and she loved to run her hands across his muscled back, washing it for him when she wasn't busy. While he liked being clean, he enjoyed it more when she helped.

They ate at the kitchen table, as it was late. Her parents had already retired to their room, which gave her more time with Lasso alone.

"What's troubling you?" Phoebe placed her hand over the back of his.

"Nothing much. Tomorrow I thought I would take a head count. This is a small spread. Still, I'd like to see any records your father may have kept on expenses, income… business associates. Randy spoke to the bank and took out a loan. So, I want to learn as much as I can before he comes here for good. Least I can do is to be savvy on what still needs to be done that involves spending money and have a record of how much he spent already."

"I can help you."

One dark eyebrow dropped downward. "You're awful busy nowadays, Phoebe. Dah-nyehl, plus helping your ma with your daddy? I don't know how you could help."

"That's the point. I'm here most of the day. Pa's not doing too well, but I bet I can get him talking about the ranch and where he keeps his records. I can look them over to learn how and sort out everything that needs to be brought up to date. I want to help, Lasso. I still have my arithmetic lesson book, and Pa can show me how to do the taxes."

Always wanting to learn more about his new wife, it made him proud that she could read, write, and do numbers. He felt blessed to have such a woman. "I'd like that. Tell me how I should keep up with the daily expenses for you to record in your book."

Phoebe stood and walked across the room to a sideboard with shelves and cubby holes attached to it, reaching the ceiling. She rummaged through its drawers, found something, and walked back to the table behind Lasso. She leaned over, her arms across his shoulders, and lay two small notebooks and several pencils on the table.

"Keep a daily record in your diary and give it to me to put in the ledgers. Be sure to keep all invoices."

Lasso heard her voice, but the words weren't making sense. Her breasts pressed against the back of his neck, and her breath was warm on his cheek. He grabbed her arm pulling her to the side of the chair. When she put her hands on his shoulders, he ducked down to gather her in his arms.

She looked back at the table as he walked to their bedroom wondering what excuse she'd give her mother for leaving the dishes on the table. When he started unbuttoning the back of her blouse, she removed her belt. Turning around, she loosened the kerchief around his neck. When her skirt fell around her ankles, she tiptoed to check on the baby and lowered the wick in the lamp.

Lasso turned down the coverlet, his eyes never leaving hers.

CHAPTER TWENTY-NINE

Avoiding a problem won't solve it.

Randy

Randy spent half a day Monday bent over with at least sixteen hooves between his knees. Farriers were in enormous demand to shape shoes, trim hooves, and treat ringbone or other debilitating conditions that horses suffered from. Ringbone was incurable. It was crippling Susie Jenkins' favorite pony. To make the ten year old feel better, he left her with a bottle of liniment to use on its sore legs, doubting it would do the little horse any good.

As the sun sunk low in Annona, he thought it was the perfect time to head to the saloon. Gossip, socializing, and his weekly shot of whiskey were the best part of the day.

Levi slapped the bar top. "Hey, Randy! Same old thing?"

"Yeah."

With his usual finesse, Levi served up the jigger. "That all?" He already knew, yet still he asked.

"Yeah. Thanks." Randy checked himself in the long bar mirror. He could see a ruckus being raised at a table behind him. A poker game filled one corner; cigar smoke hung over the table. Randy eyed it with little interest until the fourth man lifted his head enough to show his face beneath his broad-brimmed hat. He was the bad egg he'd punched in the saloon for pestering Grace. He must have just gotten out of jail.

The game was nearing its end. Two gamblers threw their cards on the table and left. The two still seated, leaned in, talking low, and never looked his way.

To avoid a fight, he ignored the situation, but not wanting to push his luck, and through with his drink anyway, he flipped a twenty-five cent piece on the bar top. He noticed the two men left sitting at the table were downing drinks.

254

He left unnoticed and mounted his horse, giving the mule loaded down with his smithy tools a tug, and headed out of town, leaving its problems behind. The days had grown shorter, the nights a little cooler. Randy was eager to be on his way to his own ranch. Though Lasso had written saying all was well at the Bar J, Randy thought he should be there to ensure things ran smoothly. More than anything, he wanted the ranch to excel as a successful business. The next thing that fed his appetite was convincing Grace to come with him. Getting married had been mentioned. But since he told her the ranch was his, she'd not said she'd follow him there. He grunted with worry she would not. He planned to stop at her house to find out what she planned to do in the near future. If not coming with him, there was nothing he could do about it.

* * *

Billy Thompson

"Hey, young Weasley! Levi waved a hand. Come over here a minute."

Billy stopped rolling a wooden barrel to the storeroom at the bartender's call.

"Yeah, you!"

Being called by his father's name was degrading. He'd died from drinking whiskey, moonshine, beer, and sometimes sarsaparilla if his arthritis were bothering him. It happened a month ago, relieving Billy of tending to his pa who was suffering from the DTs. He walked up to the bar and leaned an elbow on it, attentive to the bartender's instructions.

"You were hired to work here to sweep and clean up behind these drunks and no-goods. That means them spittoons sitting 'round, are about to run over with whatever the yahoos spit in there."

Whine, whine, whine. Billy sniffed, bracing himself for another tongue lashing. "Yes, sir, Mr. Levi. Anything else?"

"Those windows need cleaning, too. So get with it and quit resting on the broom handle!"

"Yes, sir." Billy sat the broom in a corner of the room and the barrel upright against the bar. Going down the line at the bar, he snatched the spittoons from between the booted legs of the regular cowboys, buckaroos, and passers-by waiting on the train having a shot or pouring from a bottle.

He dumped the brass containers in the lot behind the bar and dipped them in the water trough to remove any excess tobacco juice and spit. Two more were under a table occupied by four men playing poker. When he returned to fetch them, only two men sat at the table, leaning across it in heavy discussion. They weren't locals, and Billy had never seen them before.

When he dropped to his hands and knees at their table, they never looked his way. He reached beneath and drew one spittoon out. The second spittoon sat next to the wall behind the man wearing a high-crowned Stetson with a bullet hole through the crown.

* * *

"Aw, go to Hell you long-legged son-of-a-bitch." —Tom O'Folliard, rustler and best friend of Billy the Kid, age 22.

Callahan

John Murphy Callahan uttered a curse as he folded his cards. Two players, fearing the armed man's drunken aggression, abandoned the game and left the saloon because of his foul temper.

The man facing Callahan finished his beer, dropping the empty bottle to the table. "What's the deadline for this job?"

"As soon as possible."

"Exactly wha' cha want from me?" The wiry man pushed his hat to rest on the back of his head and leaned on the chair back with arms folded across his chest. His cold eyes bore into Callahan's discouraging any fast moves.

John Murphy Callahan had waited a long time to execute his revenge. "Just a little rough stuff, nothin' deadly. That cowboy bastard needs a lesson about messing around with something that wasn't none of his business. His girlfriend should be easy to handle. Wouldn't hurt my feelings if you found a pile of money lying around that whore's house. I need paying back for the fine charged me by that crooked asshole of a judge just because I asked the girl to sit with me at a table."

"Won't be nothing to that. What if her boyfriend shows up?"

"Shoot 'em. Makes no difference to me. There's another 'un if I can find 'em. A half-breed Mexican. The two of 'em killed all my men down at Red Oak."

Billy made out a few words of their conversation. *Girl, sit with me.* He glimpsed the man's face when he stood with the spittoons in his hand. Billy's mind glazed over and his mouth went dry. The scene reassembled in front of him when the outlaw grabbed Miss Grace's arm. Randy Jackson pushed through the swinging doors and slugged him for harassing his girlfriend. The other man sitting at the table now was not familiar.

They'd add him to their list of folks to hurt if they noticed he was listening. He kept his eyes to the floor carrying the nasty brass pots through the back door. He was stumped. *Should Mr. Randy be told first, or Miss Grace?*

Billy stayed until dusk, drying glasses behind the bar. He changed the used hand towels hanging below the bar and did any other chore he could use as an excuse to hang around until the locals had gone home. A few drunks remained at the bar, and the two men at the table had ordered a bottle and were finishing it off.

He occasionally glanced their way as they pushed back their chairs, picked up the half-empty bottle, and laughed at something one said. Then they were on the boardwalk. Billy moved close to a window, wiping down the tabletop, and straightening the chairs. They weren't laughing anymore. The one who'd bothered Miss

Grace was waving his arm in the direction of Red River, which was also the route to Miss Grace's house. The stranger left: the bottle stayed in the other man's hand. The 'hole in his hat' lifted the bottle to his mouth as he turned toward the stable and disappeared from Billy's sight.

CHAPTER THIRTY

Why it has to end.

Randy & Grace

Still warm enough to work up a thirst, Randy offered his horse and mule a drink from a water trough outside of Grace's barn. Coyote, hearing company, came galloping up from the back pasture to inspect the strange horses guzzling water in his water trough. Randy gave him a pat when he stretched his neck across the fence, then tied his horse and mule to the usual tree.

The four-foot pattern of hooves caught Grace's ear. She had returned home an hour earlier. He was on his way up the stairs as she started down them. A smile lit up her face as she backtracked through the door holding his hand.

"What brought you here?" she teased, looking into his hazel eyes, the gold in them reminding her of a precious stone. "Seems you haven't been here for days."

"I can't stand being away from you for more than two days." He pulled her by the hand to the settee. He wished she were closer than the opposite end of the small sofa. He reached across her lap and scooted her as close as possible to him. "What did you and the doc do today?" He nuzzled her ear.

His tongue touching her neck caused her to shiver making it impossible to answer him with clarity. Pushing away, she faced him. "It was a fairly quiet day. No one broke their bones, broke out with chicken pox, or expired. The day went well."

"Hmmm," he answered, not listening, his mind diverted elsewhere. After pulling her legs across his, he lifted the bottom of her dress and chemise to her knees. She often refused to wear layers of petticoats which hindered her in assisting Dr. Woodcock. Randy thought she looked modest and beautiful without the bulk of layers of underwear. From the first, when he saw her in trousers, he knew he wanted her forever.

259

His fingertips trailed upward from her laced shoes to her stocking clad knees.

She pushed against his biceps. "Please, have pity on me. I won't be able to resist you if we dally even more. I love you. Thinking of you leaves me breathless."

He removed his hand that had traveled above her stocking to her garters. His calloused fingers stopped their gentle play against her bare skin.

Randy gritted his teeth while her warm breath heated his neck. He swallowed and moved his hand to the hem of her skirt. He smoothed it over her legs and wrapped his arms around her. The sun warmed their backs through the window though nightfall was near. So little time remained.

"I don't want to leave, Grace."

"I know," she whispered. "Will you stay the night?" She blushed. "Here on the settee?"

"No. You and I know what would happen. I can't promise to act like a gentleman. But that's not exactly what I meant."

She raised her head from his chest. "What did you mean?" She pushed further away to repair her hair escaping from the pins when Randy pulled her to his lap.

"You know Lasso and Phoebe are settled at the Bar J. I can't leave him alone any longer doing all the work."

"Have you heard from him or your sister?"

"He sent me a long letter. Looks like Phoebe penned it." His sigh was long. "They're doing well. Still, I have to leave soon permanently. You know what's involved in running a cattle operation."

"Yes, there's that." She pushed away and stood up, straightening her skirt. Though aware of his eminent return to his home, her mind refused to acknowledge he was leaving. "In truth, Randy, I left the

Red Oak area due to the violence. The memories of a man chasing me with a gun in his hand on my way to the ranch still haunt me as though it were yesterday. I thought I was going to die. And, then, the entire move, selling my property, resigning from my job—I have yet to understand how to accomplish all of this in such a short time." Not wanting to say it out loud, she wasn't certain she'd adapt to living with his family or on the ranch.

Randy looked at her, one eye squinting, lips parted. After her abrupt move from his side, he figured it had to do with the Bar J. Didn't she understand they'd be living near Red Oak when she earlier said yes? After all, she lived there for a short time. Hadn't he been clear that he had a business to run? Of course, he'd be there to help with her move. If a move was her biggest concern, he was out of suggestions. Feeling battered and fed up with being put off, he ran his hand through his hair.

"Grace, as for your being shot at, that gang ain't around the Red Oak area anymore. I understand it was awful and scary. As for the rest, we can take care of it in time." He slapped his hat against his leg. "Anyway, I thought I'd drop in to check on you. There's more for me to do before I leave Red River, so I guess I should get started."

Not knowing what else to say, he left the settee and hugged her. "And soon, I'm off to the Bar J. But, I'll come over in a couple of days before I leave. Perhaps then you'll have a clearer vision for your future. After that, I just don't know." He gave her a quick, hard kiss, pulling her against him. "I love you, Grace." Before she could speak, he turned to the door.

Stunned by his abrupt departure, she watched him turn and leave without another word. Following him as far as the top step, it was all she could do to keep from running after him. He settled in the saddle and kicked his horse forward into the sinking sun.

Not understanding what just happened, she was back at the kitchen table. She had rambled, unable to speak to the problem. It came to her that she feared being dependent on anyone other than herself. She'd been doing that for years.

It was nearly dark now. She forced herself down the steps. In the feed room, she blocked out the bleating of the goat, the chickens scurrying in their enclosure, and the horses banging their hooves against the trough for grain. She filled two coffee cans with horse oats, dumping it into the feed trough. The goat got a smaller amount, and a few chickens received handfuls. She managed to have a blank mind while her hands were busy.

Back in the house, she plopped into a kitchen chair, torn and unsure of anything. Her hands shook. Her heart hammered. She couldn't even remember which animals she'd fed or forgotten. Randy said he was resigning his job at Red River and returning to the Bar J for good. All she could think of for the past hour was him. The house was eerily quiet. Loneliness filled the house. Utterly wretched, she began questioning herself.

Would it be that bad to be a rancher's wife?

There weren't any answers. She loved working in the medical field. Until Randy awakened the woman she'd left behind at the dairy.

If I stay as an assistant to Dr. Woodcock, what about me? Who will love me, care for me? Give their life for me? Dear God, what should I do?

When he returned, it would be the last time. Giving up her life's work left her struggling to understand her feelings.

* * *

The inside of Randy's head was as dark and unfathomable as the road in front of him. Not one star was visible, nor was the moon. He had to keep his eyes on the raggedy strip of grass that somehow survived in the middle of the busy dirt road to keep from wandering off the road. The excitement of bringing his ranch back to its former self left when Grace voiced her feeble excuses.

Deep in thought, his eyes partially shut, all he could figure was the dairy soured her on being tied down to a herd of cows. Could mean she didn't want to settle down on a cattle ranch near a town not much larger than Annona, either. She could be anything she wanted to at the Bar J. A wife, cook, housekeeper, laundress. Maybe she'd rather rope steers for branding or chase strays that got through the fence. Hell. So long as she was with him, he didn't care. That's all that mattered. He willed his mind to go blank. Fretting wouldn't help her change her mind. And it sure as hell didn't soothe his.

At Red River, he took care of the horse and mule and shushed one of the dogs that was raising a cane. The bunkhouse was dark. Feeling with his hands, walking through the length of the dining room, he opened the door to the line of beds greeted by snores and tired cowboys sleeping in every position possible on the narrow beds. Eating and showering were impossible; it was late. He ran his fingers across his chin feeling a stubble, but it was too late to shave. He'd just wash his face in the morning and be done with it. No one around cared. They all smelled as bad as him.

Without a sound, he discarded his clothes and lay down on the mattress, being mindful not to wake the men. They'd be on his tail tomorrow if he cost them a wink of sleep. Somehow, he had to make it through tomorrow without sleeping at all.

CHAPTER THIRTY-ONE

Hide and seek can be a dangerous game.

Billy

Billy bid goodnight to Levi and walked to his shack. All the way, he thought about the outlaws and how close he came to being added to the ones they wanted to kill.

He didn't bother locking the door, as there was nothing of value anyone would want. But his corn-shuck mattress, an old wood-burning stove, and a roof over his head meant everything to him. Old Weasley repeatedly told Billy that his name came from respected English ancestors who had a family crest. Billy took that as another grand story taken from a fairy tale that his daddy had told before.

He decided it was best to talk to Mr. Randy first. He'd never forgive himself if Miss Grace attempted to handle the outlaws alone and got injured. Or killed. But without a horse or mule, he'd have a hard time finding Mr. Randy. He washed underneath the water pump outside, shook the water from his hands, and inside, he lit a candle to remove his clothes. After smoothing the old quilt beneath him, he fluffed his pillow and lay naked on it, worrying how he'd get word to the threatened couple in time to stop the murderer.

Searching the rafters, he prayed for a solution. A thought grew, clear as crystal, and he smiled before turning over to sleep.

At six-thirty the next morning, Billy knocked on Dr. Woodcock's door. Surprised when the door opened a minute later, he was more surprised to see the doc fully dressed down to his spectacles and day clothes.

"Billy! What are you doing so early in the morning at my door?"

Fifteen year old Billy jerked his hat from his head. "Sorry to bother you so early, Dr. Woodcock, but I have an urgent message."

The doctor stepped back and opened the door wider for Billy who rushed in like a mad dog was chasing him. He motioned Billy to sit when they entered the parlor, and Woodcock sat across from him. The boy's eyes were bloodshot as though he hadn't slept.

Billy studied the carved wood molding etching the edge of the ceiling and the wooden mantel piece held up by carved angels on each end.

"What is it, Billy, that's so important?"

He jerked his head around. "Oh, sorry. It's about your assistant and her friend, Mr. Jackson."

"Miss Grace? Go on."

Billy bobbed his head up and down. "Mr. Levi told me to clean up the spittoons that were worse than a pig's belly filled with slop. While going from one to the next and taking 'em out back to wash, I had to crawl on my knees to pick up two from under a table where these two was sitting playing cards. They're bad men, doc. I have been thinking hard about who to tell what I overheard 'em saying."

"Go on, Billy. I'm listening."

"One of those men was the same as accosted Miss Grace at Trails End."

"The saloon?"

"Yes, sir. He's laid all over the table talking low to the other fella. He told him he wanted Mr. Jackson dead. Said something else about Mr. Jackson and some Mexican killing all his men. Don't know nothin' 'bout that, but it don't sound good for Mr. Jackson. And he mentioned the outlaw should scare Miss Grace, too. Maybe steal any money she's keeping 'round the house. I don't have a horse to look for Mr. Jackson to tell him to be on the lookout for that fella. He's liable to be almost anywhere smithin'. But I thought at least, maybe Miss Grace could stay here at your place for a few days until Mr. Jackson takes care of those two outlaws."

Dr. Woodcock knocked the ashes from his cigar. "Is that all you know, Billy? Those murdering thieves had nothing else to say?"

"No, sir. That's all I recollect. I'd been too noticeable if I'd lingered any longer rounding up those spittoons under their table. I'm praying they had no idea I'd wanna listen in." Billy swallowed as he regained his breath.

"Young man, you did a swell job." The doctor stood up to walk Billy to the front door. "Now, I want you to keep your ears open at the saloon. When Miss Grace arrives here this morning, I'll relay these men's plans and have her remain here for the rest of the day. I'm going to drive out now to Red River and see if I can catch Mr. Jackson before he heads out to who knows where. Seems he's needed everywhere to fix something. You keep your ears open at the saloon, but mostly, keep your mouth shut. We don't want anyone to suspect we're on to them, especially those two men."

"Yes, sir. I'll sure tell you if I hear more."

The doctor stuck out his hand. Billy looked at it for a second, then smiled and took the doctor's palm. Billy's chest swelled, and he walked away standing taller than when he arrived.

Woodcock raced to the back door to find Johnny. The boy was playing with a baseball and bat that the doc had given him. "Johnny!"

The ten year old wearing knickers and barefooted, immediately dropped the bat to the ground. The doc had never looked so disturbed.

"Yes, sir?"

"See how fast you can harness Toby to the gig."

"Yes, sir!" The ball ended up with the bat on the ground. He stood on his toes to pull a bridle over Toby's ears, but the tall black horse wasn't cooperating. The Percheron was more cooperative, but Toby was faster. Johnny stood on a corral pole and cursed the ornery horse with words he heard cowboys use in the saloon. He threw a lead rope over Toby's neck, jumped down, and quickly had the harness equipment in place. The horse backed slowly between the shafts, and Johnny swore appreciation that Toby stood still while being hitched to the gig. He walked the animal to the front of the house and held him while the doctor stepped on the iron and pulled himself to the seat.

"Johnny."

Again the terseness in his voice caught Johnny's attention. "Sir!"

"Miss Grace is coming here today instead of my office. When Miss Grace arrives, relay this exact message to her. Only her. Our secret is between just us." He pointed a finger at the boy.

Johnny's eyes widened. "Yes, sir!"

"You must tell her that it is urgent that she stay within the confines of the house. She should avoid looking out from a window. I pray I'll be back soon and explain everything. If you fail to do as I ask, terrible things are going to happen. Do you understand?"

Frightened now with big eyes, the boy whispered, "Yes, sir."

"I suggest afterward, you get home and stay there. I'll summon you when things calm down a bit. Understood? You'll understand things later."

Johnny shook his head.

"Now, go inside and wait on Miss Grace. I'm depending on you, boy! Don't say a word, even to your own mama!"

Johnny's heart was racing causing him to answer loudly. "Yes, sir, I won't fail you."

"Good boy!" Woodcock flipped the boy a nickel. He could only hope Johnny would follow his orders. Though it was early morning, the sun was climbing higher by the minute. He prayed he and Randy Jackson crossed each other's paths. He'd only traveled a short way down the road when he saw a rider in the distance. He slowed Toby to a walk as the man shortened the distance between them. It wasn't

Randy by the rider's height. As the stranger rode past the gig, he nodded his head and moved on. A froth of sweat covered his horse. The doc thought, *Coming up from Shawnee?* The only other thing Doc noticed as being different from any other cowhand was the bullet hole in his hat.

A minute later, his jaw dropped as things became clearer. He was the drunk at the saloon who tried to draw on Randy. He slapped the horse with the reins and galloped through Red River's gate.

The gig bounced and rose up on one wheel around a sharp curve. He jerked the horse to a hard stop and searched the compound for Randy. Unsure what to do next, he sat on the seat to calm his nerves. A door slammed with a bang from a cabin porch a few yards away.

"Howdy. Do you need some help, mister?" Rupert narrowed his eyes as he questioned the stranger. The stout man remained seated, appearing disoriented.

"Yes, I do." The man before him looked like an Indian with thick, plaited braids hanging over his shoulders. He wore two Colt 45s, one on each hip. "I am looking for Randy Jackson. I'm told he is employed here at Red River."

"You kind'a got a scared look, mister. If'n you don't mind tellin' me what's so important that you slide in here like a locomotive without any brakes, I'll help you find 'em."

"I'm Dr. Warren Woodcock. I've been in Annona for about two years." He held out his hand and gave Rupert a dainty handshake. A while back, Randy was involved in a shooting—he didn't do the shooting—"

"We all herd that story an' I don't think he'd take kindly to you saying he's involved in it."

"Oh! No, no, I didn't mean that a'tall."

Rupert spat on the ground. "Well, doc, I'm Rupert Rawlinson, ranch manager. Now that we understand each other, I'll help you round that boy up. Let me grab my hat."

268

Woodcock ran the conversation through his head trying to understand where it went wrong. The cowboy, thin as a wafer, had the most bodacious mustache he'd never seen, so thick that it covered his top lip and extended beyond his cheeks on each side. He returned with his dust covered hat resting on the crown of his head and a rifle in his hand. "Rattlers," he said. Without another word, Rupert pointed beyond the series of corrals, the barns, and the bunkhouse.

Dr. Woodcock let Toby trot over the rough ground going through woods, then across a cleared pasture. About eight men either stood on the ground or sat on their horses. One rope was around a steer's neck, a horse and cowboy stretching it enough to keep it from struggling.

Another man had its back legs caught up in his loop, stretching the bovine out at its tail end. Two other men brandished a hot iron on its hip, while another applied bands to its testicles for castrating the bawling animal.

Rupert jumped from the gig and a cowhand left the others to ride over. After a minute both men were both standing on the ground.

"Randy, this feller is Doc Woodcock. Says he has somethin' real impor'nt to tell ya." He turned to walk over to join the others working on a different calf on the ground.

"Hi-do, Doc Woodcock. Glad we're here under better circumstances. Rupert says you was anxious to tell me some news."

"You can let me know whether it's better or not, Randy, after I get through. You know Billy Thompson who works at the saloon?"

"Yeah."

"He heard two drifters planning to do some folks some harm. Billy was pretty upset and didn't know who to tell. As Miss Grace works for me, he thought I might be the one to tell."

Randy stiffened waiting to hear the whole story after hearing Grace was in the conversation.

269

"Do you remember the fellow at the saloon who got shot?"

Randy nodded.

"And the fellow that tried to draw his gun on you?"

Randy's lips thinned. "I do."

"Billy was working near his table. Levi had him cleaning those disgusting spittoons. Anyway, he had to reach under the table where these two were sitting to fetch one. He dawdled a minute because they mentioned you and Grace. Oh, and a Mexican. The one you had a run-in with was John Callahan and he was giving the orders. He told the other fellow to get into Miss Grace's house and take whatever he could. And that if you showed up, to kill you. He said you and the Mexican killed most of his men down at Red Oak. Then after that, you had him arrested over a woman."

"When did Billy hear this?"

"Yesterday."

"Was Grace working today?"

"I left before her arrival. I told my errand boy that when she arrived she was not to go back outside or open a door for anyone. And to tell her I will explain all later."

Randy turned and put his foot in a stirrup. "I'm going to town to check on Grace and let her know she could be in danger. Then I'm going to her place and hang out for a while and see who shows up."

He dug his spurs into his horse and disappeared in a cloud of dust. Before the doctor could say *I'm coming with you*, Randy was out of earshot.

* * *

Grace rode Coyote to the horse shed behind Dr. Woodcock's house to leave with him later to make rounds through the county. She removed the saddle, blanket, and bridle from the horse. After stalling it with hay and water, she knocked on the back door and waited for someone to open it. When the door swung open, Johnny

270

standing there surprised her. He stepped back to allow Grace's room to enter.

"Miss Grace!" He took her hand and led her to the parlor. She sat on a sofa while Johnny shifted his weight from one foot to the other. "Doc ain't here. Billy showed up early this morning. He told the doc some things that were urgent, and the doc said for me to tell you as soon as you got here. And he said turrible things could happen if I didn't tell you right."

Grace stood baffled and stooped down to Johnny's height. "I'm listening, Johnny."

"The doc says something's going on but didn't explain what. He said *you* tell Miss Grace she can't even look out a winder. It's turrible, Miss Grace. And I'll be in trouble if I don't tell you right and you look out a winder. I don't want 'em mad at me, Miss Grace. Just sit here nice and quiet like til he gets back"

More bewildered, Grace inhaled deeply and asked, "Wha—where is he, Johnny?"

"I don't know. He had me to hook up the gig, and he took off headed that way. He pointed a finger toward the road going to Red River."

"Come here and sit, Johnny. I guess we better do what the doctor said." The boy was wild-eyed. Grace patted his back. "Would you like some toast and jam?"

"Yes'm. That'd be awful good."

Grace checked the front door to be sure it was locked. The kitchen was in the back of the house and not viewable from the road. After Johnny ate his toast, they went to the library where he picked out a book for Grace to read to him. It served both her and Johnny. She had no idea what Dr. Woodcock meant about terrible things. Only waiting remained.

CHAPTER THIRTY-TWO

"Fast is fine, but accuracy is everything." *–Wyatt Earp*

Surprise

Randy rode hard from Red River Ranch to Grace's house outside Annona. He saw the pasture was empty of horses. He climbed the stairs two at a time and pounded on the locked door. When no one answered, he assumed she had ridden to the doc's place.

In a hurry, he leaped down from the top step and ran to his horse and jumped into the saddle as the horse took off. With Billy's limited information, he had no idea how or when these threats would be implemented. It could be anytime.

Inside the doctor's sitting room, Johnny had fallen asleep on the settee. Grace was searching the shelves for something to read other than the medical books that lined walls. She jumped when a loud pounding from the back of the house began. Johnny slept, despite the noise. She picked up a heavy poker from the fireplace hearth. Pressed against the wall, she headed to the kitchen, peeking through the entrance door. A loose horse, reins dragging along the ground, grazed in the yard. She recognized Randy's mare and jerked the door open before his fist came down on it again.

Momentum pushed him past her, and he grabbed her by the arm and hugged her close to him as if he were about the die.

The sight of him, unexpected, brought a wave of relief, yet a knot of anxiety tightened in her chest that pushed her to the brink. "What is it? Tell me! Dr. Woodcock told Johnny I wasn't even to look out of a window." Her face had gone ashen, while Randy's color was returning to normal seeing that she was safe. She looked toward the parlor. "Johnny's in the other room asleep. Let's sit here at the table. You sit. I'll get you something to drink."

Randy waited for her to return to the table with a pitcher of water. His first sip was cool and eased his dry throat. He watched the bubbles in the water rise to the top until he caught his breath, then gulped the rest down. "Grace, three days ago, when the man died in the saloon, and that stranger wanted you to join him for a drink… you remember? And after that, he went to jail?"

Why is he even mentioning that? Her voice was shrill with impatience. "Yes."

"Yesterday, Billy saw that man. He'd gotten outta jail and was sitting with another fella that Billy didn't recognize. There were four of 'em gambling at a table. When two left, Billy said the drunk who tried to shoot me was leaning over the table talking real low.

"Levi told Billy to gather the spittoons and clean 'em out. Seems Billy crawled under their table to get a spittoon that somehow had landed in that spot. He said the fella mentioned your name and wanted the stranger to break into your house to steal whatever he could, and God knows what else." Randy lowered his voice. "And kill me."

Grace didn't know what to say, but her eyes were wide with fear. "Kill you! Why? Just because you protected yourself? What will we do?" she whispered.

She'd dug her nails into his palms. "You're not gonna do a thing. You stay here as Dr. Woodcock said. They won't think to look here. I'll take care of it. I'm leaving now to go to your place. If he's not there now, I'll be able to find a good place to hide." He prayed for once that Grace listened to him.

Do I have to get on my knees? "Randy, please don't! Can't we find another way? And I thought you'd be going to Red Oak today!" Grace raised his hand to her lips. "I don't want you to get hurt."

He stood and hitched his gun belt. "I'm not the one who'll get hurt. Before this morning, I knew nothing 'bout this man, Callahan. I won't let an outlaw bulldoze us into ignoring what he's doing. Especially, when it involves you! You can believe, Grace, this ends the way *I want.*"

The last statement ended their discussion. Despite her pleading, he was determined to go. She followed him to the door, seeing the

273

resolute expression on his face. He pulled her to him, held her tight, then gave her a passionate kiss. He left before she said another word. Furious at his lack of self-regard, she watched him ride away.

* * *

His horse was used up, but Randy pushed his sweating mare as hard as he dared without winding her. Again at Grace's house, he jerked the animal to a standstill. If Doc Woodcock's assessment was accurate, they faced a criminal who was nothing like Clyde Twizzle, the town drunk, or an occasional pickpocket.

He scanned the grounds and trees for any unnatural signs, but there were no signs of anyone beating him there. After unsaddling his horse, he poured water from the yard pump over her back to cool her off. He gave the mare a tad of water to drink and tied her in a stall out of sight. The breeze rattling the trees would help the heated horse cool down faster. Grace kept another door key in the barn that he fetched from the bottom of a bucket.

Now at the house, he studied the windows and doors. There weren't any forced entry signs. He tried the knob first, then used the key, making as little noise as possible. Randy wrapped his fingers around the butt of his gun. If anyone was hiding, he needed the advantage of jumping them first. He opened the door, listened, and then placed a foot inside. A voice made him freeze.

"Don't turn around. Lower your gun."

He flinched, and with careful deliberation, lowered the Colt to his hip.

"Throw it on the ground. Do it now."

Randy's eyes darted, and he cocked his head, struggling to recognize the speaker's voice. Then he said, "Doc Woodcock? It's me, Randy." He turned around.

The physician lowered his derringer, snatching a handkerchief from his pocket to mop up his face. "I didn't hear you ride up or understand that you would be coming to Grace's place, Randy." He held up his derringer. "Sorry about this."

Randy stepped aside to let the stressed man enter the house first. Locked windows made the room hotter than a lit match. Dr. Woodcock found the settee and lowered himself to the cushions."

Randy took a deep breath to calm his nerves after being bested by a derringer. "What are you doing here, Doc?"

"I'm intent on safeguarding my assistant. She's the best I ever hired." He removed his bowler and ran his already damp handkerchief over his hatband.

"Well, that ain't no reason to get yourself killed. I planned to handle this myself."

"Handle what? Getting killed?"

Randy started laughing, and the doctor joined in. But the joke didn't begin to lower the thorniness of the situation.

* * *

Throughout the vast plains of Texas, and known as a shootist, Mal Wesson was a recommended gunman who could carry out John Murphy Callahan's worst nightmare for a fee. They struck a deal in the Annona saloon.

Mal hid out for a couple of days, planning his strategy for carrying out Callahan's hopes of bringing a cowboy to his knees. And there'd be no problem scaring his girlfriend by ransacking her house. But Mal had his own ideas.

Callahan was bad to the core, wanted by lawmen in different places from Oklahoma to Texas. Mal checked around and found out Randy Jackson and Andelacio Slade were friends. The Jacksons owned a good sized ranch below Red Oak. Word got around that the Jacksons, with Slade's help, wiped out Callahan's crew when they raided the Jackson ranch. Callahan's gang intended to murder everyone there and rustle all the cattle. He realized those two men managed quite a feat when they wiped out an entire gang of rustlers.

Asking around town, he picked up information regarding the woman he sought. People loved to talk about others who they either liked or hated. The girl worked as the doctor's assistant, and the townspeople respected her and usually mentioned that she and that cowboy, Jackson, were courting.

He charted and analyzed the layout of any place he contracted to rob or shoot up. He crept through the copse, using the trees as cover, until he was just yards away from the house. Still daylight, he needn't worry about a lamp inside. To his right, he saw no activity or sound in the small barn, either.

Mal followed a worn path to the back steps and looking through a glass pane, saw that it opened to a kitchen. Nothing special jumped at him outside of a blackened wood cooking stove and a single sink with a curtain over the shelves beneath it. But the unlocked door seemed suspicious. He thought about it a minute, then slipped inside and stopped, listening intently. His next step caused a board to creak stopping him in his tracks.

He whispered a cuss word. When nothing happened, he started toward the next room where he saw a sofa.

Randy, hiding behind a closed door, heard a noise. He held his breath and waited a minute after hearing footsteps in another room. *Shit.* Hiding and waiting on the outlaw sent by somebody named Callahan was more aggravating than running straight forward into him. He eased the bedroom door open and walked out. After canvassing the hall, he moved with the caution of a cougar. He halted after a faint sound caught his ear. With his gun in his hand, he stepped into the parlor.

"Hands up, stay put!" The stranger did as he was told, and Randy walked to where he stood.

"Can I turn around?" Mal was smart, but not too smart, as he let himself get caught in the house. He'd berate himself later. Right now, there was a bigger problem. He knew steady was the best way to stay alive. He'd killed nine men in his career and lived by the motto, *"Get the job done,"* however, this assignment was going haywire fast.

"Sure," Randy said. "Just don't lower your arms or I'll shoot your ass." Darkness filled the hall. But, the setting sun caught the stocky intruder standing in the parlor window's light. If this was Callahan's hired killer, the stranger dressed more like a gambler than an outlaw. His brocade vest and striped trousers looked new, as did his Brick hat.

"I believe you, mister."

The hired killer faced two men. The younger man dressed like a cowpuncher held a Colt SSA. And, the older man pointed a derringer his way that resembled a child's toy. But it could still kill. He wore a suit and a fancy hat; Mal figured he was the town doctor. For the sake of his own survival, he investigated the lives and habits of his targets. Now, he had to think quickly. Harder to do with two guns pointed at him.

Randy locked eyes with the hired murderer. If he twitched, he would shoot him. He moved forward and removed the gun from his holster, and stepped back. He thought the grinning drifter was a bit touched.

"Randy Jackson, ain't ya?" Revealing his knowledge had worked before, so Mal thought he better get to talking.

Mal nodded at the doctor. "And you're Dr. Woodcock, who Miss Grace works for."

Randy cocked his head, his brows drawn down. "Who are you? And why are you breaking into her house? Are you a common thief or a murderer? Maybe both?"

A smirk played on Mal's lips as he looked from one man to the other. "Say, ain't you the fella who shot those outlaws down at Red Bank? A bunch of cattle thieves, weren't they?

With a tucked chin, Woodcock eyed Randy. No one in town had heard that story. It seemed Mr. Jackson didn't need any aid in a fight. The clever outlaw sidestepped their questions by exposing he somehow learned everything about them.

"Where'd you get your information?" Randy watched the man standing in front of him, wary of his every move.

"How'd you find out I'd be coming here? Ohhh. I know what happened. That kid working there was climbing under our table. He was eavesdropping, wouldn't he?"

Randy grimaced at Woodcock who shrugged. "You're a curly wolf with a bit of loco mixed in, ain't ya?"

Another smile spread across Mal's face and disappeared just as fast. "Don't know about *loco*, but, say, we quit playing games. Let me reach easily into my pocket. It'll explain a lot." Having no more bullshit to fall back on, he either had to bring these two locals into his trap or trust them to stay quiet and out of his way.

Randy gritted his teeth as he searched for a reason to not do as he asked. He was pointing a gun at a would-be murderer and had no reason to trust him. "What say I do it for you? Who knows? If you pull out a knife, I'd hate to shoot 'fore I know what's going on here." He glanced at Woodcock to be sure he was covering him should the grinning coon make any bad move. Woodcock nodded at Randy to go-ahead.

"Help yourself. This pocket over here."

Randy reached in his vest pocket and touched metal. He pulled it out and stared a long minute at it. He backed up and handed the silver star within a circle that resembled the Texas flag, to Woodcock.

Motioning his arm toward the kitchen, Randy said, "Go sit at that table there with your hands on top, palms down. If you move one hand, I guess we'll be guessing the rest of our lives what the hell is going on."

"Fine with me."

The three men took chairs and then sat. Randy's gun was resting in his palm. He was twitching with curiosity all over.

Mal puckered his lips, then showed his pearly white teeth.

"Fellas, I'm a Texas Ranger. Been with 'em 'bout six years. My name is Mal Wesson. I have been investigatin' this feller, John Murphy Callahan, for a year and a half. It was his gang that banged up you boys at Red Oak. Then you, Mr. Jackson," he pointed a finger at Randy, "and your hired hand shot two more of the gang on the train. Seems Mr. Callahan doesn't much like his men getting killed.

"What cattle his hired men don't outright steal, they round up strays and sell 'em at auction like they owned 'em. That's breaking the law when you don't report stray cattle to the law so as to find the owner. He's got men, other than those you disposed of at the Bar J, who do his bidding. He pays well, too, to keep 'em in line. Callahan thought it'd be easy to kill your family and take the ranch. You were unknown to Callahan. He learned that after you got 'em locked up. Now, you are hindering his progress. I reckon hurting Miss Madden is his way of getting back at you.

"And I know, too, you have a woman you're trying to protect. I can't hold that against you. And you say, Doc, you got a downright excellent assistant, but I'd feel a lot better if you'd put that toy away. I was just startin' setting up the story Murph Callahan will want to hear when I let him know I was here. Now, I need to giddyap from here and find Mr. Callahan to tell him I did my job. That means you and Miss Madden should go someplace else temporarily. Then, all hell's gonna break loose when I put the shackles on 'em. He's the type who's gonna fight, not run. If I get 'em in jail, his last hour will be attending a hemp party."

Randy glanced at the doc as they lay their guns on the table and returned Mal's badge and gun. A smile remained on the ranger's face as he put the items in their original places. "It was a pleasure talking to you." Mal shook hands with Jackson and Woodcock appreciating they had nothing to do with Callahan. "I think it'd be wise if you and your lady go somewhere else for a while, 'cause if this ain't done right, and he goes free, Callahan will hunt you down."

Hunt me down? He worried not for himself but for Grace. "I appreciate the tip, Mal."

The temperature in the house wasn't going down. A trickle of sweat slid from Mal's hair down his nose. He nodded. "Oh, forgot one thing. Tell your friend, Mr. Slade, he might wanna watch his own self, too. Callahan has so-called friends everywhere when he needs 'em. He'll go to prison if he survives. Even locked up, these fellers can access outside sources to handle things. And I recommend that you not look for me again and take my advice, Mr. Jackson. Get outta town. Fellas, it's time for me to ride to where I'm staying for a while. I want to avoid being seen with you if a nosy someone bothers us."

Mal's advice sounded like an order that Randy intended to follow. One thing was clear. This stakeout exceeded his wildest expectations. He welcomed it, as shootouts held no appeal. "Thanks, again."

The three shook hands and they walked Mal to his horse. The cocky Ranger swung onto his horse, the leather creaking under his weight, and rode off in the opposite direction from Randy and Dr. Woodcock. They listened till they no longer heard hoofbeats.

As Mal rode away, Randy returned to the dark house to ensure everything was just as they had found it. He locked the door and took his horse's reins from the doc who was already astride his horse. To Randy's surprise, Dr. Woodcock could ride. He'd never seen him except in a horse-drawn vehicle of some type.

They couldn't see their hands beneath a new moon's sky. The doctor replayed the past hour in his head. Now, more shaken than when they apprehended the outlaw, he had to convince himself the ordeal was past. He swiped his face with a handkerchief and purposely slowed his breathing. "That was quite the surprise. I'm still disturbed *we thought* we had caught a killer, yet glad he was not. It was a good thing Mal's shrewdness prevented his being shot.

"I pray not to experience such adventure ever again." Woodcock spoke over the swishing of the brush and trees in a steady breeze. "I agree with Mal's advice and think you and Grace should leave Annona to prevent any more risks. But, if you choose to leave, we will sorely miss you here."

Randy noticed the doctor sat a horse like a sack of potatoes, but he was a brave man. "Yeah, leaving makes sense to me. It's a good idea to lie low. I can't let my place go to hell or me get shot to hell here if Mal Wesson doesn't do away with Callahan."

"That's so. What about Miss Grace?"

Randy looked at Woodcock with a *damn if I know* face. "You know as much as I do, Doc," he said, and the doctor had no further questions. He wondered himself about being able to talk her into leaving Annona.

Only a few dim, flickering lights spilled out from the windows along Main Street in Annona, casting long shadows on the deserted road. A dog barked, then, silence enveloped the empty street. They didn't talk again until they approached the doctor's home.

After meeting Mal, Randy aimed to sidestep being fooled again by anyone. He didn't worry about Grace now that they were back in Annona. But his mouth became too dry to spit thinking of her reaction to Mal's suggestion they skip Annona until the Ranger completed his operation.

As they rounded the corner of Woodcock's home, the light of a flickering lantern preceded the click of Johnny's boots on the wooden porch. He greeted them at the horse shed. Randy ruffled his hair as the boy took the horses. "You're out late tonight, bucko, and your momma's going be worried 'bout you."

"No, she ain't, Mr. Randy. I sleep over at Doctor Woodcock's sometimes."

On the short walk to Woodcock's house, it didn't escape Randy's mind that Mal might take the heat off him and Grace for a while. However, if he goes to the Bar J alone, he'll worry himself to death if Grace refuses to listen to reason. What did she want? His patience was growing old, always uncertain of Grace's intentions. He lacked money or luck to charm her into coming with him. He only had his hands, a clever mind, and loved her. If that weren't enough, he thought to blazes with it, though he'd never quit worrying.

CHAPTER THIRTY-THREE

Facts are stubborn, but statistics are more pliable. — Mark Twain

Randy & Grace

"Grace, Ranger Wesson said it was best for us to leave town as Callahan's likely to sic another shooter on us. Just for a while till a judge has time to send him away permanently." Grace's face was blank, without a trace of emotion. He'd seen the look before. He may as well be talking to her cat who was wrapping her body around his boot.

"I don't understand exactly what you are telling me, Randy."

She wasn't smiling. Her voice broke, flat with discontent. Chagrined that she doubted the seriousness of the situation, he said, "Two days ago I wanted you to come with me and get married. Now, I'm saying," he rolled his eyes, "because Callahan might kill us, that you *need* to go with me to the Bar J. I'd be worried sick all the time if you stay in Annona with no one to protect you from a deadly outlaw."

Randy watched her survey the room. She refrained from meeting his eyes. "I ain't asking for nothing, Grace, except for you to stay away from this part of the country. It's only till Wesson locks up a cold-blooded murderer or shoots 'em. You can come back here when it's safe. Seeing you want to keep your independence and all. Helping others is an honorable thing. But, it's not worth risking your life. Your choice to stay, despite I'm trying to protect you, is yours."

His hands rested on his belt. She hadn't meant to hurt or anger him. Grace gently placed her hand on his face. "I can't move to a cattle operation when that's what I ran away from.

"Randy Jackson, you know I love you. When we met, we hit it off perfectly. We had our problems, but we cared enough about each other to resolve them."

"A ranch ain't like that, Grace. Lots of unemployed cowboys are out there looking for a place to bunk down. So, no need to think you'd have to work cattle. Anyway, herding beeves ain't nothing like a dairy." He took a breath feeling he was wasting it. She ran away alright because she mistook an innocent act. And this time, she was running from him because of what he lived for, to run his ranch.

Hurt, angry, and nowhere to release his feelings without making things worse, he said, "Okay. I've got to go since I can't convince you. I have no idea what's on your mind. You can send a telegram if you change your mind." He glanced back at her as he opened the door, then walked straight to his horse, and trotted away.

Grace hurried down the steps but changed her mind three times about running after him. She returned to the kitchen table and ran her fingers through her hair. Afraid she had gone too far, she convinced herself he would come back. He always did. *Damn cows. They ruin everything.*

At length, his annoyance flickered out and his heartbeat returned to normal. Wistful the conversation had been different, there was nothing else he could do. Though their rift left their futures swinging in the wind, his instinct said he must put that aside. It wasn't a simple decision for Grace. She would be giving up much more than him. For now, he had something else to wrap up before he left town.

* * *

Randy and Billy

Tossing and turning during the night, he reconciled his relationship with Grace to his liking. He believed she'd change her mind. He just didn't know when that would be. Stubborn to the bone, that woman.

The next morning in Annona, Randy telegraphed Lasso that he was coming the next day. He would have left for Red Oak right then, but he had unfinished business in town.

Still early, on his way to do some blacksmithing, he stopped at the saloon hoping Billy was there. Billy Thompson's bravery and quick thinking was impressive. Daring to eavesdrop on a murderer, saving more than one life, showed the boy's character.

The saloon wasn't busy at six in the morning, and Levi sometimes kept a hot pot of coffee in the back room. "Here you go, Randy. Just made this fresh. And here comes Billy," Levi checked his pocket watch, "and right on time." He slapped the cup on the counter with a *thunk*. "That Texas Ranger pursuing Callahan? You heard he took off, right? Don't know if the Ranger caught 'em, but neither one's been around here this week."

Randy nodded, glad to hear he'd left town. There was no protection by the law in Annona, too small to afford a sheriff, and Callahan was still free and just as dangerous.

"Morning, Billy. Join me for a cup of coffee?"

"If Mr. Levi doesn't mind."

Levi flipped his hand toward a table to say it was okay. He brought a cup of coffee to the table for Billy.

Randy took a sip of steaming caffeine. "You like it here, Billy?" Randy eyed the bar.

"It's alright, Mr. Randy. It keeps me from starving." He turned his hot mug into a small circle.

"You ever thought about working cattle or other chores on a ranch?"

"Naw, I don't know of anyone who'd hire someone like me. I've lived here in town all my life," he shrugged his shoulders, "but I wouldn't mind trying it." Billy took a sip of coffee. He couldn't loiter too long without making Levi mad as a hornet, but it made him feel like a man drinking coffee with Randy Jackson.

"I've got a little spread at Red Oak. I've been looking around for some good hands, and I think you'd make a grand cowhand. I'd be proud if you came to work for me, Billy. You've got courage, smarts, and from what I see, you work 'bout as hard as anyone I know."

Billy winced at a loss for words. No one had ever uttered that kind of praise in his direction. "I don't know, Mr. Randy. I don't ride too good or know much about cattle."

"I don't expect instant skills from you that you've never experienced. I just expect you to try your best. I'm leaving tomorrow morning if you see your way to accept my offer. I'll pay your expenses for the train ride to Red Oak. Then, I'll pay you a dollar-fifty a day, and provide a bed and meals."

"I don't even have a horse, Mr. Randy."

"I do. You'll use one of the ranch's."

Billy didn't reply, not sure he'd heard correctly. Sorting it all out for a minute, he stood and stuck out his hand. "When do I start?"

"Tomorrow morning. The train comes through around eleven-thirty. I'll pick you up in front of the saloon at ten-thirty. I don't think you're going to be sorry, Billy. I need to get to work now. See you here tomorrow."

Billy's head nodded, his face still wearing a wide grin.

* * *

Early Wednesday, Randy packed his smithing and equipment tools in a wooden box and loaded it on a wagon. Next came a carpet bag filled with his shaving mug, brush, razor, and a bar of lye soap. He heaved his saddle, blanket, and bridle into another crate in the wagon bed, then added his spare pair of boots to the pile. He put his folded clothes into a clean croker sack.

He shook hands with the men who gathered to see him off.

"Hate to see ya' leave, Randy, even if you never could throw a rope straighter than a sidewinder could crawl!"

The others guffawed and slapped Randy on the back, and wished him well. He drove off slowly and stopped down the long road, turning in the bench seat to stare at the barns, corrals, the big house, and the big water tank. At sixteen, Mr. Sullivant had given him a home when he asked for a cowhand's job, and he planned to do the same for Billy.

As planned, Billy was waiting there at ten thirty. He'd tied his few belongings in a sack, too, holding it in his lap where he sat on the bench in front of the saloon.

"You ready to do this, Billy?" asked Randy as the gangly boy settled on the wagon.

"Yes, sir! I don't know what lays ahead, but I'm up for almost anything."

Randy smiled liking Billy's attitude. He guided the horse to the right side of the road, but his mind took him where he didn't want to go. Plain as day, he saw Grace in her robe, her wet hair cascading over her shoulders. If not for Billy beside him, he might have broken down and turned around. There was nothing else for him to do except leave Annona. He loved her so much that he'd traipsed over Texas like a mad dog to bring her home. Only she didn't want to come home. Least not with him. Now, he'd endured everything he could handle and still come out being a man. His ranch marked the start of a new life. He liked the sound of that. Still.

CHAPTER THIRTY-FOUR

"The secret of getting ahead is getting started." — Mark Twain

Makings of a Cowboy

Randy stole a glance at the boy beside him as he gazed out the window. His brown wool Fedora hat had a few moth holes and a faded silk band. Sandy hair fringed his ears and the back of his neck. It appeared he was in a trance, brought on by the sway of the car and clickety-clack of the wheels against the track. He imagined the kid had never been on a train or been anywhere except Annona his whole life.

"Get some rest, Billy. The ranch extends further than one can see. Do you want to be worn out?"

"No, sir. I'll try, but I can't promise."

Randy smiled, put his hat on his knee, and settled back. Sleep didn't happen right away. A beautiful woman in a robe stole it. She rejected him, for lack of a better word, but he knew in his heart this wasn't the end of his love for her. And impossible to stop seeing the image of his hands touching every part of her. An unexplainable look of peace came across his face. They'd meet again. He just had to be patient.

As the train pulled into Red Oak, Andelacio was waiting at the station with a buckboard. Randy introduced Billy as a new hire. "About time my partner found a promising cowhand to help. I was thinking we two were going to handle the entire ranch. Glad to have you, son." Lasso didn't tell Billy he'd sleep in the barn until they got a proper bunkhouse erected.

They settled on the wagon seat after loading the horse tack and all of Randy's tools that he needed to work on machinery. Lasso leaned forward to look around Billy at Randy. "Hope you don't mind, but Phoebe is doing the bookkeeping. She demanded to do her part."

"Demanded? I more than mind. I couldn't be more grateful my sister wants a part in this operation. There's more to do now than we can get done. Almost." He grinned and thumbed toward Billy. "Now, with our new hire, I reckon we'll do well for the time being. First, though, we got to teach this young'un how to ride and rope!"

"Be easier if we don't teach 'em. Just turn 'em loose and let the cow pony do the training. He can practice his roping standing on his own two feet until he has the hang of it. Don't need his horse taking off for Oklahoma 'cause his rider accidentally slapped 'em in the head with a lariat."

The others laughed. Billy was eager, but anxious, too. He didn't want to seem a greenhorn by making too many mistakes but was game to learn everything about ranching from the two cowboys whom he admired. From the stories circulating Annona, they were braver than anyone who frequented the saloon, sober most days and didn't answer to an irritable barkeeper. They were free to make their own decisions concerning the ranch, and he planned one day to have their level of success. He looked across the landscape of open land, forests, hills, and gullies, till within the hour, they drove through the wide gates of the Bar J.

Billy's eyes swiveled from two large barns, lots of corrals, a large two-story house, and a chicken coop. He made out a large mass of forms in a far, large pasture. It had to be cattle. He wondered fleetingly what his father would think of him now that he could make his own way with a job and an honest living as a cowboy. He smiled. From cleaning spittoons in a saloon to becoming a cowhand, was a notch up in his life.

When they pulled into the wide barn aisle, Phoebe and her mother greeted them. Randy began to unhitch the horses, and as he pulled the collar over one of the horses' heads, he introduced the women to Billy.

"Billy Thompson, this is my mother, Miz Jackson, and sister, Miz Slade."

"Don't be silly, Randy. Call me Phoebe, Billy. We're not at all formal here. Randy said in his telegram that he'd hired a nice youngster who's going to be a great cowpuncher. I reckon he's pretty hungry, don't you, Momma?"

"After that train ride, he must be. Randy, y'all come on in when you're done out here. Dinner'll be ready."

"Thanks, Momma."

After turning toward the house, Rachael looked back. "By the way, Billy, we fixed you a place to bunk in." She looked at Randy and Lasso. "Of course, you won't have to stay here once the bunkhouse is complete."

"Thank you, ma'am." Billy nodded his head.

Through with unharnessing the horses, Randy turned them out to pasture and returned to the barn hallway. He joined Lasso and Billy at the far end in the space the women had created for their new hand.

Billy was speechless. The barn lodgings were far grander than the shack he lived in. Smooth swept stone lined the floor. He passed his fingers across a wood stove in the corner that smelled of last winter's burning wood. He stopped in front of a stack of wood piled high close by and took a seat on an iron bed neatly made with clean sheets over the goose-down mattress that stretched along the opposite wall. Piles of blankets lay on top of a small bureau with an oil lamp, and a bowl and pitcher on top. A fragrance of sweet hay, feed, and horses pervaded the entire building. He stood, thinking it was the finest room imaginable. Most amazing was Mr. Jackson who had given him a home and a chance to be something other than a saloon boy emptying slop jars.

"Well, come on, boy! We got dinner waiting."

Billy sat another minute to admire his bunk room. But when the older men headed out the door, he jumped up to follow them. They used a rear entrance, entering a room having a hat rack, basin, and water pitcher. Towels lay on the table. They took turns washing their hands with lye soap and splashing their faces with the water. Billy waited his turn, repeating their moves. Then they walked through a well-equipped kitchen with a cast-iron stove, cabinets, and shelves. His mouth went slack when looking through a doorway to the dining room filled with fine furniture. A long table was set with more food than he could eat in a week. An older gentleman occupied a chair at the table's head. Billy noted he was pale with not much meat on his bones.

"Well, Billy. I hope you like it here."

"I'm sure I will, Miz Phoebe." He watched the men pull the chairs for the ladies before they seated themselves. A keen observer, he took it as his cue to sit, too. A trait that kept him out of trouble many times. He was ashamed of his dusty, worn clothes. He also needed a haircut. He'll address those issues once he's paid. Red Oak was larger than Annona, so he was eager to visit the town to get acquainted with the territory. Everyone bowed their heads. Billy peeked through one eye and closed it quickly at "Amen."

Later, Randy walked Billy to his bunk to see him settled in for the night. "How 'bout we get you a decent horse tomorrow and let you get a little riding practice in. When you learn how to gee and haw, you can work cattle with us. 'Course, you've gotta swing a rope, too, then land it on a steer's horns or around his neck. Then, there's learning how to rope two hind legs. In between, I'm sure Miz Phoebe or Miz Jackson'll have something for you to do." Randy turned to go. "Oh, yeah, breakfast is at five a.m. We'll go over your schedule for the next few days in the morning. Sleep well." He pointed two fingers in Billy's direction and left him to explore his room.

Lasso sat on the porch step smoking, and Randy guessed his father had gone to bed. Randy rolled himself a cigarette after sitting down beside Lasso.

"You know your sister is a very smart woman?"

"Why wouldn't she be? I'm her brother!"

"Phssss," Lasso hissed.

"Okay. Tell me why she's so smart."

291

"She figured out your father's books, all the expenses for past years, and profits. Now, she is managing the new books. Whatever supplies we need to run the Bar J, we just tell her. Then, she will take care of it. And your madre takes care of Dah-nyehl when Phoebe is working on the numbers."

"Got me there. Phoebe sure didn't learn all that from me. Guess that takes a load off us and keeps us from spending too much on things we don't need. I'm trying to make that loan stretch as far as I can 'til we sell some cattle."

"Si." Lasso ground his cigarette into the ground with his boot heel. "So, how will we teach the boy how to do a man's job."

"He can figure that out for himself for a while. We can show him the details of throwing a rope and turning a horse around. Then, let him show how much he knows in a few days. He'll be doing things till he gets it right. Might take a while, but we can't babysit him."

The screen door opened and slapped the frame when it was released.

"Si." Lasso stood up and stretched his arms. "Now, me and my cherished wife are off to bed. See you at five." He slapped Randy on the shoulder and took Phoebe's hand before they disappeared through the door. Little Daniel's dark eyes stared straight at him over Lasso's shoulder.

Would he ever start a family? Or sleep solidly again all night? "Damn," he muttered. He'd been angry when he left Grace. All he could think of as no matter what the number of cows dotting the pastures, or that his family had reunited, and all the chores ranching demanded, it was nothing if he felt empty in his soul. He missed her blue eyes and her beautiful grin. But what mattered most was the warm comfort he felt holding her, knowing all was well. He might benefit from a short trip for a change of pace.

Dallas was a big city. He needed a reason to go, a way to lose himself in the city's offerings and to finally forget her. He scoffed at the big lie he just told himself. *But who knew? She might come a-*

292

searchin' for him. With a shrug of his shoulder, however, she had given the impression that she didn't care about his thoughts or his concerns. He blew out the last draw of cigarette smoke and ground it into the dirt.

CHAPTER THIRTY-FIVE

The cake's better eaten than to let it get stale.

Grace

The baby protested her abrupt entrance into the world with a loud wail. Grace finished cleaning her, secured a diaper, and wrapped the tiny infant in a soft blanket. She returned the baby to her mother's outstretched arms.

Mr. Watts was called in and rushed to his wife. He bent over her with tears in his eyes. A wide smile covered his face. She had lived through the birth, and the child was healthy. He called her *his darling wife* and kissed her and the baby.

As she watched the love shared between husband and wife, she yearned to have a man to care for her as blatantly as Robert Watts had just displayed for his wife. She didn't even have a man's shoulder to cry on. Nor did she have a worthwhile reason for going home to an empty house. The only friend she had was Alice Ann, but Grace didn't relish crying on her shoulder. As Randy said, it was her choice that caused the regrets that haunted her.

She listlessly started collecting Dr. Woodcock's medical instruments and pill bottles, packing them into his case. The mothers-in-law ousted Mr. Watts from the room to clean the bed and make it comfortable for Mrs. Watts.

Mr. Watts walked the doctor and Grace out the door, asked a few questions, and shook their hands with gratitude. Once seated in the doctor's buggy and headed toward his office, he looked at Grace. "Miss Grace, I detect a bout of melancholy around you. Are you feeling well?"

"Yes, I'm fine." She knew he saw that she was lying. She wanted to burst into tears. Then, she debated telling everything to him about the differences she had with Randall Jackson and the bad choices she seemed to have made her entire life.

"There is a small thing."

"What is it? I don't enjoy seeing you this way, Miss Grace. Honestly, my dear, I think of you as a daughter I never had. I pray it's alright to verbalize my affection for you."

Grace stared at Dr. Woodcock. He was always the perfect gentleman who treated his patients with immense care. Despite his words of fondness, she wondered if she should burden him with her problems.

"Dr. Woodcock," she began as she fought back tears she was too embarrassed to shed. What on earth was the man going to think of her? "I have never been happier in an occupation than the one shared with you." She pulled a handkerchief from her sleeve and dabbed at her eyes. "I have a lover." There she said it.

Dr. Woodcock acknowledged her presence with a head turn. "Has he been cruel to you or hurt you?"

"No, not at all. He's sweet and kind. A very hard worker. And a cowboy."

"I see." He knew of Grace's and Randy Jackson's fondness of each other and assumed she knew of the meeting they'd had with Mal Wesson in her house. *But maybe not.*

"The problem is, he wants to marry me. And I chose my career over…"

"Over accepting his proposal? Yes, Grace, that is a perplexing problem. I am sure this bothers a great number of young people today, especially women. You are a very independent young lady who is self-reliant. Marriage is not a necessity for you, unlike others. So, how are you planning on spending the rest of your life? I'm an old man retiring one day in the distance. What other means of support do you plan on having?"

Grace gave a shake of her head. "I haven't planned that far ahead. Your retirement never entered my thoughts."

"I'm seriously considering the idea. I wasn't ready to discuss it, but I think we should. However, it's not retirement I wish to discuss.

We should discuss your future. Those females who don't want to work outside the home and are content caring for family or pursuing other interests sometimes must marry or live with their parents. Marriage isn't essential for you, unlike some.

"Grace, we all traverse this life with expectations. However, my dear, reality doesn't follow our dreams. We don't matter at all. It seems each day passes on its own accord, not caring what we plan or do. Every day that slips away leaves less chance to force time to bend to our will, and the feeling of time slipping away serves as a reminder of our limited control over the passage of time. Think, Grace. Surely you can balance your affection for this man with your commitment to helping others. It doesn't have to be 'or,' my dear. It can be both."

Embarrassed, her cheeks were hot. Near tears, she said, "I have considered that a possibility, Dr. Woodcock. You are much wiser than me. I—I will give your advice much thought," she stammered, "and I appreciate your concern for me."

He gave her a slight smile as she patted more tears on the sodden handkerchief.

Three weeks had passed since Randy left her. A deep relief replaced the tension of holding in the pain she'd shared with the doctor. Lately, she found it hard to concentrate. At times, she listened, expecting to hear Randy ride up her drive. Still, she clung to her decision to stay in Annona. Familiar with the Bar J, she knew his role played a tremendous part in bringing it back on its feet. She wondered what role she would have played had she gone with him. It became clear, either she'd stay a spinster or give up all to have him. After all, Randy said *'It was her choice.'*

Back at the Bar J

Billy

Happier than a fat puppy, three weeks had passed since Billy joined the Bar J as a bona fide cowboy. At this time, he lay on his back, propped up on his elbows. The horse that just threw him stood over him with a sneer on its face. Billy stuck his tongue out at the pigeon-toed, mule-headed, sway-back bag of bones that he swore was laughing. He stayed in that position a few more moments catching his breath, then smacked its muzzle to make the cussed horse back away a few steps.

When he sat up, he wrapped his arms around his knees and surveyed the surrounding fences, the big barn, and corrals, and listened to the chickens squawk and the bleating of the goats. Every direction offered him peace, and the adults showered him with unwasted love. He thrived on it.

The money he had earned bought him a haircut and a few clothes. He saved any change left over in a glass jar and hid it under a bale of hay. He had not met anyone in Red Oak he cared to know better, and made do with Randy and Lasso's constant bantering and Mrs. Slade's rubbing his head and giving him a hug now and then.

He jumped up and brushed off his pants before anyone noticed the horse threw him again. He caught old Mule Face determined to get the best of the ornery old horse. He prepared this time for any of the tricks the old nag might try on him. Then, with a kick in the ribs, he turned toward the far fence line.

Without warning, came an unfamiliar sound, somewhere between thunder and a roar. A cloud of dust darkened the sky over a far hill, and a moving mass appeared over the hilltop. "I swear, Muley! That looks like a stampede! Get your sorry butt moving!" Billy slapped the horse's behind with his lariat, sidled up to the gate, and unlatched it, then kicked the old gelding into a fast gallop towards the herd. The cattle had to be stopped before they reached the fence line, destroying it and cutting themselves to pieces. Jerking on Mule Face's bit, he maneuvered him to stand beside the gate latch and fumbled to open it and shut it back from the other side.

A quick look at the approaching crazed cattle, Billy saw that Randy and Lasso were riding hard to get to the front of the cattle to turn them back into a circle. Billy learned that in lesson number one. He used his quirt to urge the old horse into a hard gallop, heading him straight toward the herd. He waved his arm holding his lariat and yelled at the cattle to get their attention.

Mule Face was an old ranch horse that had worked cattle his entire life. As Billy urged him on, he responded to Billy's shouts and charged straight into the oncoming beeves at the front of the herd.

Seeing Billy's intent, Randy fell back. Lasso, on the opposite side, slowed his horse to encourage the herd to take a left turn. It took a lifetime for them to change course and turn to the left. Near the herd's rear, Randy and Lasso remained on the perimeter, preventing strays from escaping. As the cattle formed a circle, they slowed little by little and milled around until they became calmer and slowed to a walk.

"What spooked 'em?" shouted Billy.

"It was lightning out of the blue! Scared us as bad as the cattle. You did a hell of a job out there, Billy. You're learning might fast!"

Billy grinned from ear to ear and nodded his head in appreciation. They turned the cattle toward the back pastures and herded them from the fences and buildings which could maim them and do a lot of property damage.

Satisfied the cattle were calm and grazing or laying down for the night, the three riders rode back to the large barn to feed other livestock and put their horses away with feed and hay. As they approached the gate Billy had opened earlier, Mule Face sucked backward and wheeled around. The movement was fast. Billy pitched to the side, but could not recover his place in the saddle seat. He hit the ground with a loud *oaf*. "Come back here, you wall-eyed jackass!" Billy shouted as he picked himself and his dignity up from the dirt.

Randy turned to chase Mule Face, and Lasso patted Billy on the back. "I believe you've earned a better horse today. Pick anyone you want in the morning." He winked. "The blue-eyed piebald is the best."

"Mighty glad to hear that, Mr. Lasso!" Billy grinned.

298

Billy swatted the dust from his pants and put his hat back on. Later, after completing the evening chores, he splashed water on his face, put on a clean pair of pants, and combed his hair. He flayed his hat against a barn post to remove the film of dirt that covered it when Mule Face threw him for the fourth time, and right in front of Randy and his immediate boss, Lasso. He entered the kitchen door for supper. After they said the blessing, Mrs. Slade passed him the potatoes. "I heard about your heroism today, Billy. I have to say you're a quick thinker."

Billy turned red. He'd never heard such praise. He hardly knew what to reply. "I guess it's what any cowboy would do, Miz Slade."

Phoebe smiled. Billy was full of surprises, his modesty was beyond his years. She loved the young cowboy as much as Daniel. If he wasn't working, she sat in his room in the barn and, so far, he had learned his ABCs.

As the days passed, they set up a pattern of work, accomplishment, and responsibilities, bringing with it Randy's jealousy of Phoebe and Lasso. They had what he could not because *she* was selfish, hurting him so badly that he held it against his sister and husband that they were happy and in love.

No, you ain't. You're just taking your anger out on the nearest and closest of your friends and family.

Some days, he didn't notice the little things that were important. A limping steer, a pregnant cow past her due time, and where he put his favorite, broke-in rope. If anyone noticed his lack of focus, they didn't mention it to him. He thought again about taking a few days in Dallas to clear his mind. There were lots of women there. He might get lucky. *Huh. Like hell, you will. Lucky enough to catch syphilis was more like it.* Anyway, touching another woman other than Grace wouldn't cure what ailed him. Only Grace could make him whole again.

The best thing for him would be to go to Dallas to attend a U.S. Stock Growers Association meeting. It was a fairly new organization formed to stand for cattlemen only. He felt sure, he'd learn a lot mingling with other ranchers, and escape the worry he suffered daily over his break with the only woman he'd ever loved.

That night, he asked Phoebe to contact the association, get the details, and reserve him a spot at the meeting. "And Phoebe, will you please see where a room might be available near the convention hall? Since the telephone lines between Dallas and Red Oak aren't up yet, maybe there's time to write the association. The convention's three weeks off."

They received the reply a week and a half later. The cattle association was using The Oriental Hotel for all the attendees. Randy stopped breathing for seven seconds when he read that. Instead of relishing the trip, he hated The Oriental Hotel had been chosen as the host for the association. The name brought back too many memories that he had no desire to relive. He closed his eyes, shaking his head a few times in disbelief.

CHAPTER THIRTY-SIX

Where the senses fail us, reason must step in. — Galileo Galilei

Grace & the Doc

Five thirty was Grace Madden's wake-up time every morning. This morning, she woke up at three a.m. and found she had no one other than an elderly doctor to whom to pour out her heart. She sat in the kitchen for two hours sipping coffee thinking about his counsel. The doctor laid barren the future for her if she stayed in Annona.

The sun was rising in a painted sky as she dressed for the barn and fed her family waiting for breakfast. *Family?* What was she thinking? She had no family other than the four-legged ones. Astounded by her own stupidity, that she turned down a man's proposal who loved her more than himself, she had to do something at once. Her heart pounded as she raced from barn to pen, and then the chicken coop. In the house, she went from room to room. She stood in the doorway and studied their contents from years of gathering bits and pieces of things that held meaning for her. Whether it did or not, none of it brought the warmth of a man's hand on her cheek. A warm sheen of sweat pooled beneath her arms. What if it was too late?

* * *

"And that's why, my dearest friend, I'm giving notice today. The way Mr. Watts expressed his love for his wife and child revealed what I was missing." Grace gave a small shake of her head, looking out a window. "His devotion made me realize no matter how much I care about being your assistant and helping you do so much good for others, I must pave the way for a life of my own. As you suggested, perhaps there is a need for someone with the skills you have taught me in Red Oak." I've long needed to reconcile with Randy. I know he loves me. I have never stopped loving him."

Dr. Woodcock stood up and took Grace's hand. He placed an arm around her shoulder. "Of course, go to him. You have my blessing, dear Grace. I will miss having your sharpness of mind here to help me through, but I understand your need to set up a life of your own with your family. I pray you will find love and peace. But I think I would have a difficult time replacing you and will choose retirement instead. Still, you must go. You are going to make one lucky man overjoyed."

"Thank you for all you've taught me!" She cried on his shoulder, then laughed at herself for wetting his jacket. Dr. Woodcock dabbed at his eyes with a handkerchief, chuckling along with her. He'd thought long about Grace and that she might leave Annona. What would he do? Then, he wondered what Mrs. Goss might be doing.

Three days later, Grace packed her cherished items. Her mother's favorite apron and hand mirror, a framed portrait of her mother and father when they married, her mother's gold wedding band, and the only thing she had of Corrine's. Her mother had saved her baby shoes. She rented a post office box to store important papers. She would deal with a change of address later if she were lucky.

Dr. Woodcock said he will handle the sale of her house, the other horse, the goat, and the chickens. Grace decided to ship Coyote to Red Oak on the same day she planned to leave. She planned to surprise everyone at the Bar J with an unannounced arrival, unsure of their reaction. They couldn't stop her from coming if they weren't aware.

At the train station, she supervised Coyote's careful loading onto the boxcar. All her belongings were checked in by Dr Woodcock who insisted on helping her to the train station where they waited for its arrival. For better or worse, she prayed Randy would forgive her for her shortcomings, excited to see the surprise on his face. A melancholy swamped her when she looked at the doctor who was studying the floor. He saw her pointed study of his face and wrapped an arm around her shoulder.

"Don't worry about this old man, Grace. I might go traveling abroad soon. Or see a certain lady I have in mind. There's no need to feel sad about following your dreams."

She drew back and looked at his smiling face. *Oh, my.*

At the sound of the train arriving, he patted her shoulder and escorted her to the boarding platform, and hugged her goodbye.

"Grace, I wish you well and all the happiness you deserve. You have been a loyal friend and employee and one of the best assistants I've ever had. Be safe in your travel, my dear. Please send me a letter from time to time."

"I will miss you, too, Dr. Woodcock. The town of Annona is so fortunate to have a fine man like you as their physician. I've learned so much under your tutelage. I will write, I promise."

She kissed him on the cheek and turned to board the steps to the car. It wasn't until she sat down that Bea, her cat, yowled to be let out of the tapestried bag Grace had used the last time to transport the aging pet. She let the feline poke its head through the opening and petted it back into complacency without further complaint. She rested her head against the seat, closing her eyes letting different images flit through her mind of the outcome of her pursuit of the man she had turned away. Would he still be angry? Would he be happy she had regained her senses? Would he remember all the details of when their bodies and lips met? A faint smile lifted her lips as she remembered the heat, her heart racing, and loving every advancement he made on her willing body. But not the last time. She'd hurt him.

When at last in Red Oak, the small town had one livery having two horses and a buckboard or a cart. There were too many bags to carry on Coyote's back or she would ride him to the Bar J. She shivered when memories flooded her thoughts of the outlaw who chased her down the road terrifying her, and being one of the reasons she left the Bar J. She prayed the elder Jacksons were doing well. She thought her heart might burst to be seeing Phoebe, little Daniel who was crawling now, and Lasso. And most of all, Randy.

At the ranch gate, she stepped from the wagon and led the horse through, shutting the gate behind them. It was no longer made of wire, but a fine gate of oak. Once more on the seat, she saw the drive was free of weeds. New lumber replaced the missing boards in the big barn wall. They painted the intact structure a dark red and topped it with a shiny tin roof. Further down the graded drive, the house came into view. Flowers grew in the yard and under a new planted tree. The drive continued into a circular route heading back out past the biggest barn and corrals and onto the gate. She tethered the horse to a twenty-pound hitch stone. Backing up a few yards, she studied the house. They had miraculously restored its early Victorian style; its gingerbread trim was replaced and painted, its scrolled brackets gleaming white in the sunlight.

A large house was being raised half an acre away. The smaller buildings and pens for the chickens, goats, and a milk cow looked sturdier with new fencing. As she held the new banister, the door flew open.

Phoebe heard the horse and the squeaking cart as it neared the house. She hurried to the bedroom and placed Daniel in his crib, as he had finally drifted off to sleep. She peeked out a window and saw Grace ascending the stairs. She ran through the door and, as her friend set foot on the porch, she threw her arms around her.

"Oh, I'm so happy you're here!" she cried out with joy. She stepped back. "What! You didn't mention to anyone you were coming?"

"I intended this as a surprise."

"Well it is! Let me help bring your things into the house. I want to hear all about your trip and to what do we owe this visit!"

No one was home except Phoebe, the baby, and the elder Jacksons. Randy's mother joined Phoebe and Grace in the parlor after Grace had a brief visit with Mr. Jackson who was bedridden.

Grace asked Mrs. Jackson if she could look in on him as she had some nursing experience to which she agreed.

Later, she and Phoebe sat in the parlor talking about the past and the present, how fortunate she and Lasso were to have a place to work and live.

"I saw the new structure going up. Is that your new home?"

Phoebe nodded excitedly. "Yes. I hope you stay long enough to help me make some purchases to furnish it." She took Grace's hand in hers. "We've talked about nothing but the family. Tell me. Are you and Randy . . . ," she searched for words that wouldn't single her out as a nosy friend, "still courting?"

"Randy and I had a serious discussion before he came back here permanently. I truly love your brother, but I hurt him, Phoebe." Grace's eyes were tearing up. "I also love nursing and helping the sick. When he wanted me to come with him, I didn't know how to talk to him and explain properly how, while I love him with all my heart, I could not adjust to the idea. Overwhelmed, he became agitated, angrier than I've ever known him to be. He's changed, Phoebe."

"He's a stronger man in ways, but cast down, Grace. When he went to Dallas and then here, looking for you, there were outlaws in this area threatening and stealing cattle from our parents."

Grace shivered remembering the man who chased her to the Bar J. More goosebumps appeared when the leader of the outlaws assaulted her in the saloon while she helped Dr. Woodcock aid a man who'd been shot. It was like it had happened yesterday. Randy saved her from the man who wouldn't take no for an answer. That's when she realized Randy was a changed man from their first meeting. However, she didn't know him as well then, either. The easy-going man she had fallen in love with was no longer a biddable person or as likely to turn away from hostilities. One day he might tell her why, but she would never ask.

"He never mentioned such an event to me. I understand him more than I did. Thank you, Phoebe, for telling me."

Phoebe looked at her clasped hands resting on the tabletop. "There's something I haven't told you, Grace."

"Oh?"

"Randy and Andelacio have worked so hard to bring this ranch back to where it was. I understand you were here for a while. I know you'll notice a vast difference. I believe that my father turning the place over to Randy was a huge turning point for him. He takes it seriously using everything he knows to bring it back to its beginning. When he returned, I believed a rift had formed between you, and I understand that now." Phoebe had no choice but to tell Grace she'd come too late.

"Randy's not here, Grace." A tiny shake of Grace's head and the wrinkle between her eyebrows made it obvious she was confused. "He may not return for a week or so. There's a cattleman's convention in Dallas. Randy left two days ago to attend."

"Oh," Grace expelled a deep breath now that she understood. "What should I do, Phoebe? I came to tell him he doesn't have to wait any longer. If he asks me, I will marry him. I'll be heartbroken if he's turned against me. I guess I can't blame him."

Phoebe stood to wrap her arm over Grace's shoulder. "No. He loves you, Grace. He searched for you. Maybe you should search for him."

Grace's mouth formed an 'o.' "I should go to Dallas?"

"Why not?"

"It never occurred to me until you mentioned it. Where would I look?"

"I made the reservations for him at The Oriental."

"Wha—"

"Yes. It's a delightful hotel. I remember his room number is 143."

Nice indeed. Then all her doubts ambushed her common sense. "Phoebe, perhaps he won't want to see me?"

"He wants to see you, Grace. I should know. He walks around here with a frown, he's no fun anymore. All he does is work cattle or hang around with Billy Thompson."

"Billy Thompson is here?"

"Randy hired him and brought him down here. He's made a good cowboy, and the men depend on him more each day. He's very attached to the boy. And," she drawled, "I'm a hand, too. In a way." She giggled. "I keep the ranch's books, order all the supplies, and the best part—I'm on the payroll, too!"

"I don't know what to say." Nothing was as she thought.

"Grace, the family wants you and Randy to marry, to join us, but most of all to be happy." Pleading, Phoebe's voice broke. "You and Randy love each other. Please . . . find him, Grace."

Phoebe's appeal stirred her. Yes, she had the confidence to travel to Dallas and achieve her goal. Finding him. A crooked smile lifted her face. "I will, and we'll return together. I don't know what may happen then, but—"

"He loves you, Grace. You will marry. The family loves you, too. You'll see."

They stood and hugged each other. "I think I should unpack. I'll catch the train tomorrow. Thank you for loving me, too, sister-of-mine!"

A tear tracked down Phoebe's cheek, which she wiped away. She grabbed Grace's hand, and they walked toward the bedroom where Grace's things lay scattered across the floor.

CHAPTER THIRTY-SEVEN

Does playing hard have any good endings?

Randy Jackson & William Sullivant

The train ride from Red Oak to Dallas wasn't a long one. Randy stepped from the car with changes of clothes in two heavy bags. He wore a new Stetson, and a silk bandana with his best trousers that Phoebe had ordered, along with a sack suit that he planned to wear when he attended the convention. He hailed an electric streetcar that had a stop close to the hotel where he walked two blocks to the Oriental.

Near the entrance, another man wearing a cowboy hat, with luggage, almost collided with him. "Excuse me, sir." The man turned around surprising Randy.

"Mr. Sullivant? So good to see you again! I'd shake your hand if we both weren't carrying all this cargo."

William Sullivant could identify his favorite cowhand from anywhere. "Randy Jackson! How are you doing, son?"

"Me and the family's doing fine. You and the Mizzis?"

"The same. I assume you're here for the convention."

"Looks like both of us are."

"I'd like us to talk awhile, curious to know how you're getting along with your ranch. Let's meet and catch up with a drink later."

"Yes, sir. I'd like that."

They entered the grand lobby, still talking. The front desk appeared the same as his last visit searching for Grace. William Sullivant and he shook hands after obtaining their room keys, agreeing to meet the next day.

Randy turned toward the stairs. "I swear!" he whispered. He'd never seen a live animal in a hotel before. A Hereford bull was in the lobby, tied in a stall bedded with straw. Ranchers gathered around it, discussing its merits and flaws. An enormous banner above the stall announced the beginning and ending dates of the U.S. Stock Growers Association Convention welcoming sign. It held his attention for a moment, then he remembered the day he stood in the lobby in his search for Grace.

His jaw knotted. He needed to release her from his thoughts—in mind and body. As a man with responsibilities, he had to pick himself up and continue with his life. Hell. The weight of her absence settled like a heavy fog in his mind. It'd be rough going to chase Grace from his mind.

The next morning, Randy took a bath and gave himself a shave. He donned his new clothes and looked himself over in the oval full-length mirror and straightened the knotted silk scarf under his collar where the two points hung evenly. William Sullivant and he sat next to each other during the updates of the meatpacking industry and the Meat Inspection Act. After the government and industry speakers addressed the beef industry, the event provided drinks and food.

Later, they walked back to the hotel and shared a few drinks at the bar. They agreed to meet each other the next morning and tour Dallas before the convention opened. After parting, Randy headed to his room to unlock the door.

* * *

Grace

"I understand your hotel has rules and regulations, and I assure you that my husband, Senator Jackson, will be furious with you when he learns you questioned giving his wife a room key so I can join him at the convention tomorrow." Grace scowled at the desk agent.

"I understand, Mrs. Jackson. But I am not allowed—"

"Ridiculous," Grace said with indignation when she slid a five dollar Liberty gold half eagle coin in his direction.

"Oh, yes. Of course, *Mrs. Jackson*. Here is your key, and this gentleman will carry your luggage to your room. The elevator is to your left."

With the key in hand, Grace headed for the elevator where it all started: the man with the fancy boots. The Bar J.

The porter took the key, opened the door for her, and sat her bags at the foot of the bed. He returned the key and left counting the coins she left in his outstretched palm. The room, similar to her previous one, appeared smaller. Perhaps the massive wardrobe armoire took up all the space. Her stomach was queasy. Unsure if it was hunger or nerves, she decided not to eat a full meal. She asked the porter to have room service bring her a plate of scrambled eggs and coffee.

She removed her shoes and jacket without unpacking, unsure how the rest of the night would end. Excitement and dread turned her hot and cold. *How would he react when he saw her in his room? Was this how it felt when he searched for her?*

A door knock made her jump. She stood on her toes to see through the peephole. It was food service. She opened the door and a woman in a black top and skirt carried the tray to the lamp table and sat it down. Grace handed her a tip and settled in the chair to eat. When the clock struck nine, she lay on the bed to rest for a few minutes, tired from the day's travel and telling those pesky white lies at the hotel that depleted her of energy. Didn't conventions have entertainment, speeches, drinking, and more speeches? The clock struck nine-thirty, and she closed her eyes, expecting Randy's certain return. She tossed on the bed, unable to settle as she imagined the first time she saw him. He'd stripped down to his long underwear shirt, clinging to his muscular body. Sweaty... she fell asleep and dreamed the rest of her thoughts.

* * *

Randy and William parted at midnight after a last drink and a long handshake. They both planned on leaving Dallas the next day.

Not quite drunk, Randy took the stairs, hoping to tap down the hangover coming on. He fumbled his key from his pocket but stopped short of opening the door. A light was showing beneath the closed door. He was positive he'd turned them off before he left. He stepped back and drew his gun from under his coat, then turned the knob. He rushed through the door scanning the room, but no one was in sight.

He checked the bath and looked in the extensive wardrobe. As he turned toward the bed to put his gun away, he stopped, stunned. A mop of hair poked from beneath the quilt. *It can't be.* He removed his boots as quietly as possible and set them down without making a sound, then shrugged off his jacket and draped it across the chair back.

Down to his long johns, he pulled down the covers on his side of the bed and settled in. He eased over to lie on his side.

He drank in the scene. She was as beautiful as ever. Dark, arching eyebrows framed her eyes above her pink cheeks. It looked like she had lost weight, but still alluring as she slept.

Not fully incapacitated, he became aroused and looked at the ceiling. She might not like that he climbed into bed with her, but *it was his bed.* And her objections were feeble, the last time he slept in hers. While she had made some noise about it, her sleepy sighs revealed her true feelings about lying beside him.

Still inebriated, it was a good thing she didn't wake up. He figured he'd make a better impression in the morning rather than now, leering at her in a stupor. Whatever brought her there and whatever happened in the morning, he prayed he didn't mess it up. She was a stickler for propriety between men and women. He understood that if a woman didn't trust a man, she would never entrust her body and soul to him. Yes, he wanted more. Just with her. He loved her.

The next morning, Randy awoke with an annoying stream of light in his eyes. His head throbbed and there was too much warmth beneath the coverlet. He felt pinned to the bed, moved his arm, and hit warm flesh across his ribcage. He breathed deeply, then let the air out silently as he remembered every inch of the female pressed against his back. Her warm breath fluttered against his shoulder blade, making him go hard. Had he died and gone to heaven? Or would all hell break loose when she realized her breasts were pressed against him and one of her legs between his?

Heaven, it was for now, so he didn't move. He watched tiny particles of dust float through the light. Suddenly, he remembered he had a train to catch and by the amount of light in the window, it had left by now without him. But, he didn't give a damn. Grace moved, hitching her hips forward to a more comfortable position. Randy didn't know how much more he could take of soft skin against his tough hide.

His headache had become bearable, but other parts of him were suffering with longing and desire. Soon he would have to move for a trip to the bathroom, but too afraid it would ruin the dream he was having. If he removed her arm and her leg entwined with his, she would wake up.

When the situation was no longer possible, he eased his leg onto the mattress. Then her arm. When he stood up, her eyes were wide open, watching him.

"I'll be back in a minute," he whispered. The hotel had modernized the bathrooms years ago, and Randy wasted no time relieving himself and returning to the bed.

Grace was lying on her back, propped against the headboard, the cover pulled over her chest. While her heart thumped wildly, he gazed at the thin fabric of her nightgown covering her shoulders. Scooting backward to sit up, she looked at him with a questioning look on her face. Randy sat on the side of the bed and twisted his body, leaning toward her on one arm.

"Grace? How'd you get into this room? Why are you here?"

Even though she slept through the night, her senses were still aware of his presence. His deep voice was calm. She felt embarrassed revealing her duplicity. But what else was she to do? "I couldn't do it anymore."

He raised a hand gesturing *do what?*

"Live without you. I—I told the clerk you were a senator, and I was your wife. Then, I gave him a gold Half Eagle. He gave me the key." She pushed against the headboard. Not accustomed to a man seeing her wearing so little, she pulled the sheet over her breasts.

Randy watched her with a tiny twist to the corner of his mouth. The gesture wasn't because she was cold. Also, her willingness to do such a thing to sleep with him was risky. He held back a laugh but was glad her ruse worked.

"What about the Bar J? You told me cattle and a move to the Bar J was not to your liking."

The tenseness had left his face, encouraging her to continue. "I had no other reason than to voice silly objections, a weakness in my character." A weak smile crossed her face. "Remember, I once was an employee of *your* ranch."

"Our ranch."

Grace leaned forward gripping his hand, all thoughts of impropriety gone.

"Let me tell you a story. I don't know why, but the last patient I attended with Dr. Woodcock weighed heavily with me." She looked away, gathering her words. "A woman from Annona was giving birth. Of course, Dr. Woodcock delivered the baby, a precious little girl. I aided, but mostly I watched the miracle before me." She pushed a lock of hair that fell across her face. *I must look like a crazed coyote!*

"Her husband hovered over her and cried with relief and love, so happy his wife had survived the ordeal. The baby, too. I've never seen such fear, then relief and love on a man's face as he showed for his wife.

313

"It made me think of you—how you suffered and the lengths you went to... I think we share that love, Randy. You searched high and low for me at the lowest time in my life." Her sight blurred from tears. "Then, you waited for me to come to terms with what I need in life. I need you, Randy."

Randy's constraint of emotion shattered. It was all he ever wanted to hear. He settled beside her, his arm a gentle curve behind her head against the worn wooden backboard. "C'mere." She yielded and rested her head against his shoulder. Her hand rested on his chest. "I'm yours until death do us part." He tipped her face up and kissed her, then rolled over to kiss her neck.

"Is this our wedding night?"

He looked at her, searching every inch of her face, but all he saw was sorrow and hope. "If you want it to be."

"Yes, to everything. I love you so much." She wrapped her arms around his neck and pulled him close to her.

There'd be no stopping him. And making her feel safe was his primary concern. Safe to share herself with a man, safe knowing it was a lifelong love, and that he would never hurt her. He kissed her, taking his hand from her hair, and trailing slowly to her breast.

* * *

Four days later, they rented a cart to drive to the ranch. The cow dogs made a hullabaloo alerting the family that they were home. Happy and tired, Randy lifted his wife from the cart and unloaded their baggage.

It had taken a few hours to get a wedding license, then another hour to round up an available chaplain. When Grace went with Randy to the cattlemen's convention in her new dress wearing a gold wedding ring, Mr. Sullivant congratulated the couple, and the three enjoyed a wonderful dinner.

After Phoebe read the telegram she received from Randy, when they arrived that evening back at the ranch, Phoebe and Rachael threw a private wedding party with cake and ice cream for the newlyweds. Billy threw in a few tales of his episodes with Lasso and the cattle. Daniel was happy as his father fed him cake.

Later, Randy shut the door to the newlyweds' bedroom that had been decorated with streamers and wildflowers.

"When do you want to visit Annona again, Grace? While we're there, we'll see how Dr. Woodcock is doing about the sale of your house. It will take a few days to pack the rest of your belongings to ship."

She came from behind the dressing screen in the new gown she bought in Dallas. "Whenever you want to, dearest." A one sided grin said she was baiting him. "You're my wheel-horse. Always."

Randy knew what he wanted to do. They could discuss the trip later.

A month later, they didn't forget to visit Miz Goss. They caught up with the town gossip while at her boarding house for two nights.

They relaxed on the train the entire trip back to Red Oak, holding hands with Grace's head resting on Randy's shoulder.

www.ingramcontent.com/pod-product-compliance
Lightning Source LLC
Chambersburg PA
CBHW070216260626
47160CB00002B/570